Praise for Don Gutteridge's
Marc Edwards series

"Don Gutteridge has taken up his quill and written a riveting yarn of 1830s Upper Canada, steeped in conspiracy and political intrigue. Gutteridge is not only a master of this historical period, he writes like a veritable visitor from it. Canadian history has never been more gripping and enlightening. The story burns, the pages turn, and the reader learns. Fans of Bernard Cornwall and Patrick O'Brian will love Don Gutteridge and his Marc Edwards mysteries."

—Terry Fallis, author of *The Best Laid Plans*

"Canadian history brought to muddy, cold, vicious, and sometimes heroic life."

—*The London Free Press*

"Gutteridge weaves his tale perfectly, with believable characters and perfect scene-setting."

—*The Globe and Mail*

"Don Gutteridge has created a fascinating cast of historically accurate characters as he follows a trail of murder and political intrigue with a bit of romance thrown in. Great mystery, great history, and a terrific read."

—David Cruise and Alison Griffiths, authors of *Vancouver*

"A well-written, graphic, and moving history."

—Saskatoon *Star-Phoenix*

DEATH
OF A
PATRIOT

A MARC EDWARDS MYSTERY

DON GUTTERIDGE

A TOUCHSTONE BOOK
Published by Simon & Schuster
New York   London   Toronto   Sydney   New Delhi

Touchstone
A Division of Simon & Schuster, Inc.
1230 Avenue of the Americas
New York, NY 10020

This Touchstone export edition January 2014

TOUCHSTONE and colophon are registered trademarks of Simon & Schuster, Inc.

For information about special discounts for bulk purchases, please contact Simon & Schuster Special Sales at 1-800-268-3216 or CustomerService@simonandschuster.ca.

Designed by Akasha Archer

Manufactured in the United States of America

1   3   5   7   9   10   8   6   4   2

ISBN 978-1-4516-9052-1
ISBN 978-1-4516-9053-8 (ebook)

For Tom, Tim, James, and Kevin,
my new generation of readers

ACKNOWLEDGEMENTS

I would like to thank Jan Walter, my editor, for her insights and helpful suggestions. Thanks also to my longtime agent, Beverley Slopen, who has been with this series from the outset, and to Alison Clarke and Kevin Hanson of Simon & Schuster for their constant support of Marc Edwards and his mysteries.

AUTHOR'S NOTE

Death of a Patriot is wholly a work of fiction, but the border raids of 1838 did take place much as they are described herein. I have added my own cast of military characters and created the minor skirmishes central to the novel's plot. Many of the captured invaders, or "Patriots" as they dubbed themselves, were indeed hanged, while others suffered the more humane fate of being transported to Van Dieman's Land (now Tasmania). However, particular actions and characterizations attributed to actual historical personages like Sir George Arthur, John Beverley Robinson, and William Warren Baldwin are fictitious. In fact, Robinson was in England in 1838, campaigning against the union of the Canadas, but I have kept him in Toronto to oversee the trial in the novel. While the Hunters' Lodges played a major role in the so-called Patriot Wars, my depiction of individual members is purely imaginary. Finally any resemblance between invented characters and actual persons is coincidental and unintended.

I am indebted to the following works, which provided helpful background information: George B. Catlin, *The Story of Detroit*; Frank Angelo, *Yesterday's Detroit*; Mary Beacock Fryer, *Volunteers & Redcoats, Rebels & Raiders: A Military History of the Rebellions in Upper Canada*; David H. Flaherty, ed., *Essays in the History of Canadian Law*, Vol. II; and R. D. Gidney and W. P. J. Millar, *Professional Gentlemen: The Professions in Nineteenth-Century Ontario*.

ONE

Briar Cottage
Toronto, Upper Canada
November 5, 1838

Dear Uncle Frederick:

Your October letter is happily received, and while you insist that I
address the unpardonable omission of details political and military
from recent correspondence, I must once again beg your indulgence
and begin this report by bringing you up to date on matters much
more compelling and germane to Clan Edwards.

The doctor has now confirmed what my darling Beth and I
had already deduced: a new addition to the family is expected
to make his or her debut sometime about the middle of April.
Our joy at this prospect is tempered only by the regret that Uncle
Jabez did not live long enough to celebrate the arrival with us,
and that you are thousands of miles away in a foreign land. I
trust that you have come to accept the irrefutable fact that I have
become—with no malice aforethought—a permanent resident
of this provincial dominion of the Crown. But you of all people
will understand such a decision, having married your French

*sweetheart and settled with her in a far country. Certainly I was
pleased to learn that you have been able to complete the probate
of Uncle Jabez's estate and return to Normandy and the bosom of
your family. Josh Henchard is a good and honest man who will
manage the property well in your absence. Also, your suggestion
that Jean-Marie take up the "squiredom" when he comes of age
seems a wise one: we don't want the Edwards name to disappear
entirely from Queen Victoria's domain, do we?*

*I should tell you too that Beth has reopened her shop in the
commercial property she inherited from her late father-in-law.
The revived enterprise, proudly sporting the "Smallman's" name
over the window, provides dressmaking services to the town's
fashionable ladies and is unquestionably a going concern. At first
I remonstrated with her, as tactfully as possible, but had little
influence. What I have learned in my three and a half years
here is that women, particularly those born and raised in rural
settings, are independent and toughened by experience, both
physically and mentally. They often do a man's work in addition
to their feminine responsibilities and demand to be respected
for it. They even participate in political affairs, as you'll recall
my Beth has done. However, be assured that her role in the new
enterprise is administrative and managerial: she feels obliged to
use the premises on King Street to provide work for half a dozen
local women and to honour the memory of her dear father-in-
law. And I applaud both sentiments.*

*Finally, to round off this personal segment, I can say that
I am thoroughly enjoying my legal studies. There's much to be
said for choosing a profession on one's own. When not at home
getting in Beth's way or disrupting Charlene's household routine, I
divide my time between the reading room at Osgoode Hall and a
cubicle in the far reaches of Robert Baldwin's chambers on Front
Street, with occasional sojourns to the high court of Chief Justice
Robinson.*

Now to meatier matters. The political situation is more precarious than ever. Two days ago, our best hope for a mediated solution to our problems resigned his commission and embarked for Britain from Quebec City. The measure of Lord Durham's significance to these troubled provinces could not be better illustrated than by reference to the send-off he was given—in the capital city of the ancien régime and site of Montcalm's defeat. Thousands of citizens, French and English, cheered his procession from the castle to the quay. People came from hundreds of miles away and camped out on the Plains of Abraham so that they could wave a handkerchief or a capote of farewell and genuine lament. (We had these details given us by a captain of the 34th, whose regiment passed through Quebec en route from New Brunswick to Toronto as part of the general buildup of regular troops here.) Our fervent wish is that he will be able to frame a report and present it to Parliament in Westminster before things fall apart on this side of the Atlantic. At the moment an eerie calm pervades the Canadas, as if we were holding our collective breath. The principal action is the dull rumbling of the rumour mill and the sight of fresh redcoats arriving daily. Spies are everywhere, according to both camps, spreading lies and half-truths.

What we do know is this: the threats being made upon our sovereignty from the United States are real. Early last March a group of self-styled "Patriots"—four hundred strong, mostly American "liberators" with a scattering of exiled Canadian rebels—crossed on the ice from Sandusky, Ohio, and bivouacked on the south shore of Pelee Island, just off the main coast of Lake Erie and within striking distance of our own fort at Amherstburg on the Detroit River. News soon reached Lieutenant-Colonel Maitland, who marched to the area with three hundred regulars and a handful of militia from the nearby town of St. Thomas. In an elegant flanking manoeuvre (which you, as a veteran of

the Peninsular campaigns, will savour), Maitland took the main
body of his outnumbered force around the island (on sleighs!) to
the south side, where he expected to surprise the invaders and cut
off their retreat. On the northern tip of the island, in dense bush,
he stationed a force of seventy men under Captain Browne, whose
task it was to pick off any of the enemy fleeing north to escape
Maitland.

However, just before the latter reached his destination, a
preposterous contingent of sleighs arrived from the American
shore, full of excited Ohio gentlemen (and not a few "ladies"),
come to enjoy a bit of Sunday morning melodrama. Espying
the British regulars advancing through the mist, they elected to
abandon their front-row seats and hightail it back to the land of
liberty, taking a number of soldierly fainthearts with them. The
invaders, alas, had already detected the presence of Maitland's
force and determined to plunge northward across the island.
When Maitland arrived, the Yankee encampment was deserted.
He set off in hot pursuit, but the invaders had already reached
the north shore of Pelee, and a fierce encounter took place with
Browne's picket, hunkered down in the brush. Outnumbered three
to one, Browne spaced his men a yard apart to give the illusion
of a greater force and directed a steady fire at the attackers, who
returned it in kind. Fearful of losing too many men in such a
sustained series of volleys, Browne ordered them to fix bayonets
and charge. As you know, nothing turns a man's bowels to liquid
quicker than the sight of a line of ululating redcoats advancing
upon him. The invaders broke ranks and scampered off in several
directions. Dozens were killed and eleven captured.

There was a local angle to this military victory. The St.
Thomas militia, who fought with Browne at Pelee, were led by a
Toronto man, Gideon Stanhope, even though his only connection
with that area is a brother who farms nearby. Stanhope happened
to be visiting when the call went out to the recently embodied

militia unit. As he was a veteran of the 1812 hostilities (he'd been at Lundy's Lane, though did not see action) and keen to participate, he was invited to head the unit. No doubt his being a prominent member of the Family Compact and the possessor of a fine horse influenced the choice. In any event, "Captain" Stanhope fought valiantly alongside Browne, rallied his green troops, and took part in the pursuit until a wound in his thigh compelled him to halt. Even so, as he was being evacuated later in the day, he spotted two figures on the ice just offshore, ordered his driver to stop, and proceeded to hobble out towards them, his worried ambulance men two steps behind. Coming up to the startled intruders, he drew his pistol and took them prisoner before they could recover their wits. The taller of the two Americans was none other than Thomas Jefferson Sutherland, the commander of the invasion force who had arrived late for his own battle and was ignominiously brought to heel by a man with one good leg. The upshot of this deed was that Gideon Stanhope, dry-goods importer, was given a hero's welcome upon his return to Toronto in June, and thereafter dubbed the "Pelee Island Patriot"—in ironic salute to those misguided souls he helped defeat.

While Captain Stanhope was being fêted, another raiding party of Patriots, all Americans we believe, crossed the Niagara frontier and carried out several forays in the Short Hills below St. Catharines. Most of them were eventually rounded up and imprisoned. James Morrison, their leader, was hanged at Niagara, and a series of courts-martial have been staged over the spring and summer, all of which keep the pot boiling, so that the divisions in the community—the established administrators v. more recently arrived settlers, Orange Lodge loyalists v. republican sympathizers, Tories v. Reformers—are only made deeper.

Then in July, three more incursions occurred along the western border, one of them repulsed by local Chippewas. There are persistent rumours that the Hunters' Lodges in the United States have recruited ten thousand men, all eager to liberate the enslaved populace of the province. In September, a convention of the lodges was held in Cleveland and a "Republic of Upper Canada" declared under the presidency of a U.S. citizen, Lucius V. Bierce. The Hunters are also reputed to be in league with rebels from Lower Canada, now living fugitive in Vermont and New York.

The only encouraging result of all this commotion and uncertainty, including the loss of Lord Durham's conciliatory leadership, is that most of the ordinary folk here have rallied to meet the external military threat, though no one is fooled by this apparent cohesion into believing that domestic political differences have been moved an inch closer to compromise. As I say, we are in the grip of a tension-filled lull, momentarily resigned to the reality that our immediate future is in the hands of a new lieutenant-governor, Sir George Arthur, and Her Majesty's army. Only when our physical safety has been assured can we turn our attention to the task of rebuilding the polity—with, I trust, the guidance of Lord Durham's report.

Have I not, you may ask, been tempted or shamed into taking up arms again, as so many with less experience have willingly done? I have not. I have been there and have the scars to prove it. I see my own role clearly, and it is to use my talents for the law to help with the necessary reconstruction. Of course I would defend my city and my home, as any man would, but the presence of three thousand regulars and nearly twenty thousand militia suggests to me that we have little to fear other than these nuisance border raids, and these too are nearing their climax.

We are informed, for example, that Mackenzie and other rebel leaders have withdrawn from active involvement with the Patriots, and that President Van Buren is at last about to move against these vigilante soldiers disrupting life on both sides of the border. We are bracing for a "final push" to be made sometime this month by the Chasseurs in Vermont and the Hunters in Michigan. In this regard, our own Pelee Island Patriot has taken up Governor Arthur's request for the embodiment of eight new militia regiments (with "regular" army uniforms promised). Stanhope has formed one of two Toronto units, has been promoted to lieutenant-colonel as its commander, and has been observed marching his recruits up and down Front Street, with his battle limp poorly disguised. Indeed, he has been so impressive that he and six of his NCOs have been dispatched to Fort Malden at Amherstburg to help train the latest volunteers from the Essex region and provide an inspiring example to all and sundry. I'm sure we'll hear more from that quarter before the "war" is finally won.

I realize that all this may sound picayune to one seasoned at the side of the Iron Duke and tempered in the hellfire of Waterloo, but as you also know, any battle however modest is, to each individual in its midst, both an ordeal and a testing ground for personal courage. A bullet is a bullet, particularly if it be aimed at you!

On such a pleasant note, I sign off for now. Write soon, and tell me only of vintage harvests and hearth stories in ancient Normandy.

Your loving nephew,
Marc

TWO

December 4, 1838

Billy McNair was sweating and shivering at the same time. He could see his breath, like a visible exhalation of fear, floating before him on the icy, predawn air. Yet this morning was what he had wished for every day since he'd cheered the triumphant return of the York militia, marching to fife and drum up Yonge Street from their successful excursion in the Short Hills: he was going into battle. When the formation of new militia units was approved in July, he had been the first to enlist and the first corporal to be promoted to sergeant. Dolly had done her best to dissuade him, but even she had come around in the end. Her farewell kiss lingered still on his lips. And he had promised her that he would proudly don his "regular" uniform on their wedding day, should that glorious tunic of scarlet and green ever arrive.

He and his companions were marching north along the well-travelled road towards the village of Windsor, all of them members of the raw and untried Windsor militia whom Lieutenant-Colonel Stanhope and his elite corps had been doing their damnedest to whip into shape before the anticipated invasion. An hour earlier, Sergeant Walsh and a dozen of his regular troops had stumbled into their makeshift barracks at Sandwich, bloodied, scorched, and exhausted. Theirs was a hair-raising tale. The American Patriots, it seemed, had come across the river from Detroit, three hundred strong, and landed under cover of darkness just above Windsor. There they set fire to a ship in the harbour, routed the small picket on duty, and moved against the village. Before the alarm could be raised, Sergeant Walsh and thirty of the 2nd Essex were surrounded and trapped in their own barracks. They held out as long as their ammunition lasted and surrendered only when the Patriots set the compound afire. In the ensuing mêlée many of them escaped, leaving their dead and wounded behind. As Walsh was scuttling into the bush, he saw General Lucius V. Bierce climb onto a beer barrel and begin reading a proclamation which informed the local citizenry that they had been liberated and would be welcome recruits in the inalienable struggle for freedom and democracy.

Lieutenant-Colonel Stanhope had neither flinched nor hesitated to act at this news. Now the interim leader of the new Windsor regiment—thanks to the titular commander having been felled by the gout, again—he had integrated the NCOs he'd brought with him from Toronto into the fledgling units to stiffen them. With the presence of mind and steadiness of purpose that had prompted Governor Arthur to dispatch him to the battle zone along the Detroit River, he directed some two hundred men, a six-pounder, and a dozen pack animals towards Windsor, three miles upriver.

The colonel, as Billy and others invariably referred to Gideon Stanhope, led the way, tall and lordly upon Pegasus, his alabaster Arabian gelding. He was fully accoutered in scarlet and green, and the sabre in his gilded scabbard tinkled like a sleigh bell. Slightly behind him rode the company captains, Charles Onslow and Jonathan Muttlebury, each of whom had seen action at Pelee Island in March, and who welcomed the fortuitous arrival of their comrades in arms from Toronto.

"Are you scared, Billy?"

The urgent whisper came from Corporal Melvin Curry, who was striding alongside his friend Billy on the snow-packed trail. The young men had been comrades in every adventure since they had first met in the schoolyard, fist-fought to a draw, shook hands, and pledged themselves to mutual protection and eternal friendship.

Anxious not to break the colonel's interdiction against conversation, Billy mouthed his response: *We all are.*

Mel grinned his relief, took the Brown Bess off his shoulder, pointed it at the bush, and mimicked an explosion and recoil. And grinned again.

Billy smiled his approval, then swung his head smartly back into its proper position, facing the soldier immediately ahead of him and quick-stepping to the common beat. There was no drum, of course, only the rhythmic tramp of these soldier-citizens, all of whom had, mere days ago, been tending a farm, wielding an axe, or minding a country store.

Billy and Mel had kept to their boyhood pact, entering the carpentry trade together in Toronto as apprentices to Billy's uncle and, just this past summer, going into business for themselves. But when the word went out that eight new militia regiments were being formed—one of them to be led by the Pelee Island Patriot himself—the young men had only to glance into each other's eyes before heading up to Gideon Stanhope's estate at the western edge of the city and signing on.

Of course, they trained and paraded only three times a week and had to be content, for the nonce, with green hunting jackets, gray trousers, and their own boots. The remainder of their time had been spent productively if mundanely in hammering and sawing at Mrs. Edwards's rejuvenated establishment on King Street, where, by an act of divine providence, Billy had caught the eye of one of the seamstresses employed there and had fallen madly, giddily in love. Dolly had feigned indifference, for a day, then capitulated. Mel, who had been engaged for a year, pretended such romance was a routine business, but Billy knew better. So here they were, each twenty-two years old, employed, in love, and marching out to defend the country they had been born into and had subsequently decided was worthy enough to preserve for their own future.

Billy wanted to whistle his contentment but settled for a muted hum.

Back in November, it had seemed that they would see no action. Lieutenant-Colonel Stanhope, his laurels already won and displayed with daily dignity, had brought his handpicked crew of NCOs, among them Billy and Mel, to the district at the beginning of the month. They had been thence involved in intensive training sessions with the freshly embodied local regiment, intensive because their spies had informed Governor Arthur that a sizeable incursion was expected across the Detroit River on November 21, to be coordinated with a second attack somewhere along the St. Lawrence. The latter had indeed occurred, in the middle of the month, and though they had received only sporadic and incomplete reports, the raid had been repulsed and the enemy routed. "We've been sent to the wrong end of the province!" Mel had complained. November 21 came and went, without incident.

The tedium of the daily training sessions was soon broken, however, by a diverting exercise carried out by Colonel Stanhope, Captain Muttlebury, and the twenty-man troop of which Billy McNair was now acting sergeant. It turned out that, back in July, following the Yankee raids across the St. Clair River, the generals had decided to sequester a number of arms caches in strategic spots along the western frontier for emergency use against any large-scale invasion. One of these was a long-abandoned earthen fort beside a creek in the bush about halfway between Windsor and Sandwich. It had last seen service in the War of 1812. Sixty rifles and ten boxes of powder and shot had been secreted beneath the crumbling forward wall. However, fearing that one or more local republican sympathizers might have learned about the location, Major Sharpe, commanding officer of the 34th in the region, ordered the arms removed and brought to Fort Malden at Amherstburg. Billy had noted, from a distance, an animated discussion of the order among the officers, including several exasperated gestures from Colonel Stanhope. As a reward for his commentary, the colonel was assigned to effect the removal of the ordnance.

So it was that they found themselves sweating and grumbling on a warm Indian summer afternoon as they dug away the sod used to camouflage the crates of rifles and ammo and loaded them onto two wagons. The colonel disdained any direct involvement in the ongoing indignities after he had completed the routine task of indicating where the crates were located, referring to a sketch provided him by the major. Thereafter he sat rigidly upright and aloof on his Arabian, staring down the little creek while the breeze rippled his epaulettes. Billy had felt fiercely proud to be serving under such a man.

"You got them all?" the colonel inquired of Captain Muttlebury, casting a cursory glance at the wagons and then riding up to the earthworks for a quick inspection of the hastily repaired devastation there.

"Yes, sir," Muttlebury replied. While he had taken no part in the actual labour except to point with his sabre to those spots along the thirty-foot embankment where the crates had been stashed, he was sweating and alarmingly pale.

"Are you well, Captain?" the colonel asked. The steel-blue eyes suggested that his concern was military, not personal.

"I've had the shakes since this mornin', sir," Muttlebury said. He was a corpulent man, bluff and friendly to a fault. And more at home behind the counter of his hardware store in Sandwich than in the saddle of a warhorse. But no one questioned his dedication to the cause or to the tasks at hand.

"Then you should have reported yourself unfit for duty," the colonel said. "You may ride up on one of the wagons if you need to.

We've got twelve miles or more to go before we get these rifles safely tucked inside Fort Malden."

Billy and Mel had taken turns riding Muttlebury's abandoned bay.

The private in front of Billy stumbled to a halt, and Billy nearly crashed into him. Behind them the column came to a staggering stop. Everyone peered anxiously ahead. The sun had risen and now sat amid a brooding mist above the forest rim to their right. No one had yet spoken. On his stout bay, once again Captain Muttlebury came plodding softly towards them along the double line of men.

"The enemy have been spotted in François Baby's orchard two hundred yards ahead," he said to Billy and his troop. "They're fixing for a fight. The colonel is going to organize four squads and attack them head-on. Our company will form up on the far right. Then, after the first volley or two, we'll veer off through the bush and out-flank them. Check your powder and fix bayonets."

Muttlebury then wheeled and galloped back to the head of the column, which had already begun to come apart as the five companies moved wordlessly forward behind their subalterns. Billy led his troop towards the right-hand side of the clearing that lay before them, with Mel at his heels. Several of the men were taking deep, rasping breaths and squinting ahead through the dissipating mist in search of the enemy. The invaders made themselves heard before they could be seen, however. A nervous, boastful shouting rose up from the leafless trees at the far side of what must have been one of Baby's pastures. Then the first rifle shots, crackling and ineffectual. Billy tried not to look at the puffs of snow being kicked up a few yards in front of him.

The officers had dismounted. Colonel Stanhope began issuing orders in a calm, almost offhand tone. Billy knew the drill by heart. He and Mel set up their troop in three ranks, chivvying several men into position when they simply froze. At Muttlebury's signal, the troop advanced in concert with the companies on their left. The snow underfoot was not deep, but it was heavy, thanks to alternating days of freezing and thaw.

Billy strode manfully forward, letting his fear drive him to his duty rather than stall it, and all the while conscious of his responsibility to the inadequately trained men relying on him. As they reached the halfway point across the clearing, random fire from the orchard spattered snow all about them, and ahead they could see more than a hundred blue-tunicked soldiers, the invading Yankees, dashing about the barren orchard in apparent disorder and discharging their muskets and rifles in capricious bursts. Nearby, someone gave a brief cry of startlement, then a groan, and Billy turned to see a fellow named Carter pitch forward into the snow, then roll over and clutch his belly as if his bowels were about to escape.

"Positions!" Muttlebury cried, his voice suddenly falsetto with fear.

Billy, in the first rank with his Brown Bess already primed and loaded, waited for the order to fire. The man behind him swore and dropped against him.

"Fire!" Muttlebury squeaked.

Up and down the front rank of the five companies the initial volley rang, splitting the air with its calamitous impact. Billy's rank dropped to one knee and, seconds later, the second rank let loose, dropped to one knee, and shuddered as the third rank followed suit. Billy's ears had stopped hearing anything, and he could see nothing but the thick roil of exploded gunpowder. When it was lifted gently upward by the morning breeze, he was able to appraise the effect of this classic military gambit. Enemy bodies lay prone upon the ground or draped in ghastly silhouette against the apple trees, while others writhed and spun madly in the snow, flailing their arms as if beating off enraged bees. Their whooping bravado had been displaced by moans and curses.

One of their officers, however, had already begun rallying his remaining troops, and the air once again shook with a ragged but deadly counterfire. It took twenty seconds for crack British troops to reload, but these fresh militia recruits were months away from that level of proficiency. It was during such an interval that real danger lay. Reloading infantrymen in close rank were certain prey for the American marksmen. Half a dozen toppled before Billy's rank was able to repeat its initial volley. Seasoned British regulars would just keep up the sequence of volleys until they died where they stood, but there was a good chance that these raw volunteers would simply break and run.

Billy could not stay long enough to find out, for he was already following Captain Muttlebury on the flanking manoeuvre ordered by the colonel and frantically calling on A-Troop to do the same. Mel, he was pleased to see, brought up the rear, and was hollering words of encouragement to the fellows they had worked beside for almost a month, whom they knew by name, and whose lives they valued as much as their own. Colonel Stanhope had trained the trainers well.

The going through the scrub brush to the east of Baby's fields was much less comfortable than travelling the road had been. The slush among the evergreens and rotting stumps had frozen overnight, and the men hobbled over it as if over a rocky beach, with the added risk of pratfalling on a hidden ice patch. To their left they could hear the singular blast of their comrades' volleys interspersed with the motley, sputtering snap of Yankee sharpshooters. Just ahead of Billy, Muttlebury was huffing like a spent draft horse as his big-bellied figure slipped and skidded.

Five minutes later they again emerged into the clearing, but this time they were fully east of the orchard. The firing between the opposing forces had not ceased, the air was blue and acrid with smoke, and there were more bodies on the ground, on both sides. All Billy could see for certain was that the panic and confusion seemed to be limited to the Patriots, not because of the helter-skelter dashing about of individuals—that was the trademark of these freebooters—but because of the desperate cries and peremptory discipline of their officers. He saw one of them grab a fellow about to turn tail and fling him back into line with one powerful thrust of his right arm. The left was dangling helplessly at his side. The regular, timed fusillade from the companies across the clearing was indication enough that the incomparable colonel had succeeded in molding his apprentice soldiers into an effective fighting unit.

Captain Muttlebury now ordered his men to form a single rank at the edge of the bush. They had not yet been seen. Less than a minute later, they loosed a killing volley of enfilading fire upon the surprised and hapless occupants of the orchard. The effect was immediate. All those capable of doing so broke and scampered towards several outbuildings to the north of them. Many had no legs to flee with.

"After them!" boomed the stentorian voice of Colonel Stanhope, and the four companies at his side charged across the clearing with bayonets fixed and a local variant of the redcoat's ululation.

Muttlebury was about to follow suit, particularly because his unit was already closer to the routed men than the colonel's, but the order never came. Billy was tugging at his left sleeve and pointing towards the northeast corner of the orchard, where it was almost contiguous with the spruce and cedar woods they themselves were sheltering in.

"Who's that?" Muttlebury wondered, spotting a Yankee through a screen of boughs waving an arm and hissing out some kind of command.

"I think it's one of their generals, sir," Billy said. "I been watchin' him. He seems to have been hit in the left arm."

"Why don't he skedaddle with the others?"

"I think he's organizin' a retreat through the bush somewhere."

"Then we better get after him. If he's the CO, he may be carrying papers we'll want to have a gander at before he burns 'em."

"Yessir. Shall I send Corporal Cox to inform the colonel of our intention?"

"Yes, yes, we oughta do that."

Cox was clearly unhappy about being left out of the chase but was soon on his way over to the advancing body of militia, and Billy's unit was trotting, with bayonets at the ready, along the edge of the bush towards that point where they had spotted the Yankee officer in action. When they approached the place—cautiously, for an ambush was a distinct possibility—they saw its attraction for those fleeing soldiers with enough presence of mind not to dash blindly for the dubious cover of Baby's flammable barns. Just inside a line of cedars, a small creek meandered and then curved away into thick forest. The creek was iced over, and the dozen or so sets of bootprints upon its crusty surface suggested it was firm enough to hold a pack of frightened fugitives.

"They've scuttled up the crick!" Muttlebury declared. "They'll leave us a trail a sick cat could follow."

"It seems to twist and bend a bit, sir. Don't you think we better be extra careful as we go?" Billy said.

"Yes, yes. We oughta be careful."

"Whenever we come to a bend," Billy said, "Mel an' me'll scout on ahead to make sure the coast is clear."

"Good idea!" Mel cried, then realized he should have waited for his captain to speak first. But merchant Muttlebury had not noticed.

"The corporal and me useta go huntin' together," Billy explained. "We can tell what a creature is thinkin' just from the tracks it leaves."

"Good idea, good idea," Muttlebury said, and so the unit proceeded, twenty strong with two outriders, in pursuit of the routed enemy and possibly a bigger prize.

●   ●   ●

Another hour found the pursuing troop somewhat less enthusiastic than they had been at the outset. The fourteen men they were trailing had stuck to the interminable winding of the creek and, so Sergeant McNair informed his charges, were retreating southwards in a steady, organized fashion. Each time they approached a sharp bend, Billy and Mel slipped into the woods on the inner curve and moved stealthily forward until they came to the next straightaway in the streambed, where they made sure all fourteen sets of boot-prints were safely visible in the middle of the creek before stepping out into the open and signalling the all clear.

"Just like old times!" Mel exulted.

"Yeah, ain't it, though?" Billy said, as they waited for the captain and the others to trudge up to them. "But this fella leadin' the retreat is no fool. He knows he'll haveta leave this easy path sooner or later if he's goin' to make a break for the river and home."

"But this crick's runnin' *away* from the river, ain't it?"

"Right. We're goin' upstream, which is puzzlin' to me."

The arrival of Muttlebury stopped further discussion of the matter, and the troop tramped forward once again.

The next bend lay a hundred yards ahead of them, and as they approached it, Billy could see plainly that the tracks had veered away to the right—to the west and towards the river. The Yankees had apparently decided to make a break for the shoreline. No doubt a ship or several boats had been placed along the Detroit at strategic intervals, just in case the liberators should encounter the unthinkable: opposition from the ordinary serfs of Queen Victoria's fiefdom.

"They've headed west into the bush!" Billy shouted back to his captain against the rapidly building northwest wind.

"We've gotta pick up our pace, then," Muttlebury puffed, struggling to maintain his dignity while clutching his rebellious belly.

"They could've left a picket just inside the bush over there to slow us down," Corporal Curry suggested, remembering the lectures on withdrawal tactics that the colonel had delivered with such passion back in Toronto and repeated after their arrival here.

Muttlebury tried to take this in, blinking into the slanting sun-light with watery eyes. "What's best to do?" he said at last, uncon-cerned that a commissioned officer was asking the advice of a junior not yet permitted in his mess.

"The safest way, sir, is to send a volley at that spot where the tracks disappear," Billy said.

"Yes, the safest way," Muttlebury said, and nodded at his sergeant.

A half-minute later the squad was positioned in rank and Muttlebury was poised to bring his sword down to ignite the volley, when they saw the cedar boughs at the point of target waver. Mut-tlebury swung his sword, the forest was rocked by the thunderous discharge of twenty muskets, and the cedar boughs shattered before them. Several agonizing cries assured Billy's troop that a suicide picket had indeed been set up to ambush and stall the pursuit. Ap-parently they had made the fatal error of choosing to wait until the enemy had come within easy killing range before firing upon them.

Billy didn't bother waiting for the obvious order, and it did not come. He sprinted across the creek ice with bayonet bristling, and Mel and the others simply followed suit.

Two shots suddenly erupted from the bush ahead. Billy heard a bullet whiz past his left ear. Someone behind him yelped, but Billy kept on going. The time to attack, the colonel insisted, was during the moment of greatest confusion among the enemy, before they could regroup and inflict serious damage. Casualties could be expected, of course, but they would be within the "perimeter of tolerance." Billy did not have time to think that he could be one of them. The adrenaline pumping through him had either anaesthe-tized fear or been its manifestation. With a war cry that would have impressed Tecumseh, Sergeant Billy McNair leapt up onto the low bank and plunged into the evergreens.

There would be no more shots. Three men lay dead, sprawled grotesquely in various postures of flight as the volley had roared in upon them. A fourth lay moaning on his back, his Kentucky rifle still clutched in one hand and smoking.

"It's all right, lads," Billy called back to his advancing troop. "We've wiped them out."

Mel was already busy examining the bloody corpses. "Only one of these muskets has been fired," he said to Billy.

Billy nodded and then knelt beside the dying soldier. His eyes were blinking furiously and his lips trembled in a parody of speech. Billy leaned down farther, and the whispered words rose up to greet him.

"Tell my daddy I got shot in the gut, will ya?"

"You were the bravest of this lot," Billy said, feeling suddenly sick. The soldier was no older than he was. "But why didn't ya shoot at us sooner?"

Through a bubble of blood between his lips, the soldier said in what Billy afterward remembered as a kind of laugh, "We ain't got no bullets. None of us. That's why we run."

Captain Muttlebury had come up to survey the scene. "We need to get this man back to the village," he said. "We can make a stretcher outta them cedar boughs, eh, Sergeant? Chalmers has got a busted arm, but he can walk okay."

"Too late, sir. This fella's a goner."

The trail of the remaining fugitives through the bush—treacherous with sudden swamps, breakaway ice, and waterlogged deadfalls—was not hard to follow. At least one of the Yankees had been wounded and was conveniently depositing droplets of blood as vivid as Hansel's bread crumbs. But the pursuit was arduous and demoralizingly slow. They were about half an hour into the bush, heading due west and probably no more than a mile from the river, when Billy whispered to Mel beside him, "Don't this terrain seem awfully familiar to you?"

Mel paused, glanced around, and said with a chuckle, "Every tree's been lookin' the same to me fer the last hour—mean and ugly."

But before Billy could respond, he, Mel and the captain had stepped out into a broad clearing, a beaver meadow, in the middle of which stood an impediment that was neither tree nor swamp. And suddenly they knew precisely where they were.

"My God," Mel breathed, "it's the old sod fort."

It was indeed the abandoned earthwork redoubt that they had visited less than two weeks before, on the last day of Indian summer, to remove the stashed powder, rifles, and ammo. They had, of course, then approached it from the main road that lay due west.

"It's a good thing we got that ammo out of there when we did," Mel said, but Billy, who had assumed the role of scout without being assigned it, was already crouched behind a small cedar with his hand raised for silence.

A minute later he came back to his captain and said, "I don't see no movement of any kind from behind the walls, but their tracks are pointin' towards the fort as far as I can tell. There's too much sunlight on the snow fer me to be sure. But the bastards've put up a Stars and Stripes to let us know they been there."

"They wouldn't sit in there with no powder or shot, would they?" Mel asked.

Jonathan Muttlebury, hardware merchant–cum–militia captain, did not, as might have been expected in the circumstances, seriously entertain the question. Billy's reference to the impertinence of running up a Yankee flag on their own fortification—however devalued—had the effect of a red hanky flung across the bull's nose. "Lads, I'm sick and tired of this goddamn cat-and-mouse game," he cried, and brandished his sabre like a paladin of old. "Follow me!"

Billy knew he should have grabbed his commander by the arm and pulled him back towards common sense, and he would regret his indecision for the rest of his life. Instead, he waved the men behind him forward. With bayonets glittering in the mid-morning sun, Company C of the Windsor Regiment sped across the clearing towards the crumbling redoubt. While Billy was braced for a sudden assault from the still-silent ruin ahead of him (he was not ready to believe utterly that the Yankees had *no* bullets left), neither he nor any of the others was prepared for the abrupt and devastating ambuscade that roared out at them from the woods on the right.

Billy felt bullets zinging past him, one of them grazing his right thigh. He dropped to his knees, his head spinning and his ears deafened. A second later he was almost blinded by a wave of gun smoke that rolled over him on the northwest breeze.

Relying entirely upon instinct, he twisted around to discover the source of the ambush, fully expecting a second and more lethal volley. In the woods thirty yards away he could see men shuffling about and branches swaying. Somewhere in the numbness of his terror, his brain was telling him that a bayonet assault was imminent, that he had to get back onto his feet and prepare for hand-to-hand combat, as he had been trained to do. But as the smoke cleared, he could detect no one moving out of the woods or in it. Groans, curses, and sobs sullied the air behind him.

Abruptly, Billy's terror was transmuted into a consuming rage. They had been taken for suckers! Those Yankee pickets had been deliberately left behind to sacrifice themselves for their fellows and to perpetrate the ruse that the fugitives were without ammunition. That officer with the dangling arm was both brave and diabolical! And he was about to escape scot-free. Billy found himself galloping towards the ambushers with his coattails flying and his Brown Bess clutched carelessly in one hand, with no thought but to run down this mad adversary who had crossed the border to inflict unjustified mayhem upon his peaceful neighbours. Breathless and spent, Billy staggered into the bush and prepared to fight to the death.

But there was no one to take up the challenge. Paper cartridges littered the ground, grim evidence of the murderous volley just unleashed, but not one of the enemy had remained to deliver a final, fatal blow or pick off the wounded as they struggled to their feet in the clearing. Nor had any of Billy's troop followed him on his foolish, suicidal sprint. He was alone, and his rage was soon deflated.

Just as he turned to face the horrors that he knew must lie on that bloodied meadow, he heard a low sigh. And spied a boot sticking out from behind a rotting stump a few feet away. Cautiously he eased over to it, gave it a gentle kick, assured himself that the body attached to it was unconscious or dead, and stepped around the stump, bayonet poised.

It was the officer he had first seen in the orchard. Of what rank he could not tell because the blue and yellow tunic, though ostentatiously draped with insignia of several kinds, was homemade. His old-fashioned tricornered hat had fallen off his head and lay beside him where he had apparently attempted to rest against the stump and then tipped sideways into a thick tussock of desiccated grass. The head seemed too large for the body, though the shaggy mane of yellow hair, a high forehead, rugged goatee, and aquiline features may have given the illusion of size and grandeur. With his dirt-spattered uniform and wind-blown hair, his sharply hooked nose and thin, near-invisible lips, he resembled nothing so much as an American eagle shot out of the sky in the fullness of flight.

A tiny cough tremored through the thin lips. The man was alive. Billy could now see that the left arm was indeed useless: it hung at an eccentric angle and a dark stain oozed out at the elbow. The fellow had organized the retreat of his men and effected their escape with one arm and a suppurating wound. And from the evidence here, it appeared that his last command had been an order for them to leave him to his fate. Without thinking, Billy pulled out the kerchief that Dolly had given him as a good-luck talisman, knelt beside the enemy, and after slitting open the sleeve of his tunic with a jackknife, fashioned a tourniquet above the wound. The fellow moaned weakly but did not open his eyes.

It was at this moment that Billy realized the significance of capturing such an officer and, in all probability, having saved him from bleeding to death. Taken back to Colonel Stanhope, he could be interrogated and vital information elicited. If he were in fact a major or a colonel, he might even be carrying sensitive papers. Billy leant down, opened the fellow's leather kit, and drew out four sheets of heavy rag paper.

On the first sheet he saw what were obviously military orders, from Brigadier-General Lucius V. Bierce to Major Caleb Coltrane. Billy was unable to decipher much of the tactical lingo, but he was certain that the colonel would have no trouble doing so. The second sheet contained a sketch of some sort, composed of arrows, lines, and strategic *X*s—a plan of attack, no doubt, and probably linked to the orders on the previous page. The third sheet was a printed "Proclamation to be read aloud to the enslaved peoples of British Canada"—likely the one already declaimed by Bierce in the village square at Windsor. The fourth was quite another matter. It was written in a hand entirely different from the others, on a fine vellum paper. Billy skimmed through its contents:

November 1, 1838

> *My dearest C:*
>
> *Come soon or I'll be driven to find my own route
> to your heart, with all the risks and fretful dangers to
> our secret. And when you do, tucked in your strong arms
> and safe in your embrace, I promise faithfully to supply
> you with enough kisses to keep you forever attached
> to me and our mutual goal. And should our reward
> be in Heaven only, I'll treasure those blessings received
> already. But I must go—he's had me watched since Saturday!*
>
> *Ever yours,*
D

A love letter from the fellow's mistress. Well, whatever assignation they had hoped for would not happen. "Major" Coltrane was destined for jail and a rope necklace. Billy put the other three items safely into his own pouch, but something compelled him to fold the billet-doux, unfasten the top buttons of Coltrane's tunic, and slip the letter under his blouse, next to his heart.

The first thing Billy saw when he stepped out of the woods was a lone soldier running across the killing ground towards him. There were no bodies prone and lifeless on the icy turf and no moaning from the wounded and maimed. For a moment he thought he must be in the middle of a cruel and improbable dream. But the soldier's voice and the look of shock and horror on his unlined face were all too real. It was Lévesque, a farm boy from Belle River.

"Where is everyone?" Billy said.

"We're all in the fort, sir. We've moved the injured men inside."

"That's good. The Yankees have skedaddled, but we've got their ringleader."

"Sir, you must come and see what we've found in the fort. Right away." Lévesque's eyes were as round as the buttons on his overcoat.

"What do you mean?"

"We know where they got the powder and bullets from."

"From the fort? But—"

"We found two crates busted open and looted. They must've dug 'em outta the wall somewheres."

"That can't be," Billy said, as they raced back towards the crumbling redoubt. "Captain Muttlebury removed them all last month."

"He must've missed out two boxes."

Bill stopped. "Jesus, Lévesque, they'll court-martial him!"

"I don't think so, sir. The captain's dead."

They had propped Muttlebury up against one of the walls, where he had died. Someone had had the courtesy to close his eyes.

Sitting there with his hands folded in his lap and his chin resting peacefully on his chest, the captain looked as if he were taking an afternoon snooze at the back of his shop—with a blood-red carnation in the left lapel of his suit coat. And next to him, similarly propped, was another soldier: an avenging bullet had ripped the perpetual grin from his boy's face.

Billy's knees gave way. He sank to the ground. His stomach heaved. He put both hands flat upon the earth to stop it from spinning. But it didn't.

THREE

Marc Edwards, Esquire, closed the cow gate and stared back fondly over the spacious grounds of Osgoode Hall, still pastoral despite the wind-chiselled drifts of snow covering them and the leaf-shorn maples standing sentry here and there around them. A mere two months ago, the lads from up-country had been kicking a pig's bladder across the greensward and in their animal exuberance, uttering very unbarrister-like whoops of joy. As the training centre for the province's attorneys, Osgoode could not have been more removed from the urban hurly-burly of London's Inns of Court had it been bivouacked on the moon. Summer or winter, the handsome three-storey brick edifice, not yet nine years old, was lapped in silence, save for birdsong in one season and the whine of arctic wind around its cornices in another. The grand colonnaded library on the second floor was as quiet and serious as the thousand tomes that sat in mute expectancy on its shelves.

It was here that Marc had spent much of his time during the thrice-weekly visits he made to the home of the Law Society of Upper Canada, ever since Robert Baldwin, MLA and son of the famous Dr. William Warren Baldwin of Spadina, had agreed to serve as his principal and convinced his fellow Law Society benchers that his newest apprentice needed no entrance examination to test his mettle or determine his suitability for the most learned of professions. The benchers themselves provided the periodic lectures held in Lawyers' Hall but otherwise left the students to their own devices. And a motley lot they were, though Marc no longer found himself shocked or even surprised to find himself elbow to elbow with the sons of farmers, physicians, greengrocers, bankers, surveyors, mill owners—a polyglot mix that would have made any self-regarding squire dyspeptic. But in this strange new world, anyone who could find thirty-seven pounds for a year's room and board and pass the qualifying entrance exam was free to try his hand at lawyering. And if you happened to live in Toronto, as eight thousand people now did, or have a maiden aunt with a spare room on Peter Street, then so much the better.

When he was not studying or attending lectures at Osgoode, Marc would go down to the law offices of Baldwin and Sullivan on the northeast corner of Front and Bay. This splendid brick building, designed by the multigifted Dr. Baldwin, with its Doric columns and elaborate portico, served the Baldwin family as town residence and place of business. Here, in the four rooms to the right of the entrance hall, Marc had spent dozens of pleasant hours observing the work of Robert, Clement Peachey—a junior barrister and solicitor—their clerk, and three copyists. One of Marc's more frequent tasks was to look up references in the Osgoode library pertaining to ongoing briefs, laboriously transcribing salient points and disentangling granny knots of legalese. A welcome change occurred whenever Robert or Clement Peachey was scheduled to plead a serious case in the Court of Queen's Bench at the fall assizes.

Alas, such cases, outside of civil suits in the newly formed Court of Chancery, had been few and far between this past autumn, not because there were no murders, assaults, or treasons to prosecute—the aftermath of the rebellion had provided more than enough of these—but rather because Governor George Arthur had ordered the trials of the several dozen captured invaders and border raiders to be courts-martial, with most of them taking place in London, Niagara, or Kingston. Hence, the opportunity to see such cases play out in criminal court had been lost, not to speak of the healthy fees associated with same. It appeared that the actual military threat, however ineffectual or farcical, was now over. But the trials had been constant, with consequent public hangings, incarceration, transportation to Van Diemen's Land, and the occasional acquittal. In some quarters, independent extralegal reprisals were still being carried out with stealth and undiminished venom.

Just three days ago in London, the first captives of the Battle of Windsor to be tried and found guilty had been hanged in the town square. And even though the majority of citizens, whatever their political stripe or country of origin, longed for peace and stability, such violent public events invariably stirred up emotions. Yesterday there had been a noisy demonstration and march to Government House, organized by Boynton Tierney, Toronto alderman and newly appointed leader of the Loyal Orange Lodge in York County. With penny whistles asquealing, thunderous drums and raggedy swagger, the Orangemen demanded the expulsion of all United States immigrants, severe restrictions on naturalized Americans, and a declaration of war upon the apostate nation to the south of God's chosen country. Governor Arthur had listened politely before retreating to the sanctuary of his official residence.

This would not be the last of such disruptive and potentially ruinous demonstrations. There were a dozen trials still scheduled or under way in London. And closer to home, one case loomed large and portentous. While Lucius Bierce, commander of the incursion force at Windsor in December, had escaped, Major Caleb Coltrane had been captured by a unit under the direction of a staunch Tory, Lieutenant-Colonel Gideon Stanhope. The latter, while not immediately present at the capture, had adroitly taken credit for the coup. With his local reputation as the Pelee Island Patriot already established and a fresh (flesh) wound sustained at Windsor during hand-to-hand combat with bowie knife and bayonet, who was to deny him the pleasure of being lionized by his civilian neighbours and grateful townsfolk? A parade in his honour had already taken place on Yonge Street the week before Christmas, and the squirearchy of the capital was all abuzz about next week's Twelfth Night Charity Ball at Somerset House, where the colonel would receive official civic and military recognition.

Marc and Beth would have found all this amusing if they had not, in a way, been personally connected to the events. Billy Mc-Nair and Melvin Curry had been hired by Beth to carry out the renovations at Smallman's, transforming two adjoining shops on King Street near Bay into a single commercial space. One half of the establishment was now a large work area where the dress designs of Mrs. Rose Halpenny were executed by three young seamstresses chosen for their skill, enthusiasm, and neediness. The other half, connected by a door and with a rebuilt interior, contained the showroom, several fitting cubicles, and the millinery display. The workroom had been furnished with tables, shelves, and storage bins constructed to Beth's exacting specifications. While Marc fussed and secretly fumed over the state of their unborn child, Beth worried about the state of the economy and the growth of her enterprise. One of the happier results of its founding had been the engagement of Billy McNair to Dolly Putnam, the most vivacious and accomplished of the seamstresses.

Billy and Mel, excited by the prospect of adventure, had been among the first to sign on with Stanhope's Toronto regiment. The passage of four months saw them doing much more than strutting and preening in marches along Front Street. The war they had dreamed about had become suddenly real, and as Marc himself knew, there was no way to prepare oneself for its terror-inducing contingencies. Mel had not suffered these long. An hour after his first contact with the enemy, he was dead, his face blown away and unrecognizable. Billy had distinguished himself under fire and had brought

Major Coltrane bound and bowed to his commander. But he had come home a bitter and disturbed young man. He refused to take part in the victory parade at the colonel's side. He spurned the governor's offer of a military medal and declined to be interviewed by the press. Worse, he became so moody and irritable that, in an uncharacteristic fit of pique, he had quarrelled with Dolly Putnam and broken off their engagement. Dolly's unhappiness had become the principal subject of dinner conversation in the Edwards household.

Meanwhile, both Stanhope and Coltrane seemed, for better or worse, to have a gift for keeping themselves in the public eye. The colonel had stunned his admirers by offering to imprison the major at Chepstow, his grandiose estate at the far western end of Hospital Street. This gesture had followed upon two earlier decisions by the governor: first, the removal of some of the military prisoners ("war criminals" to the Tory press) to Toronto and Kingston because of dangerous overcrowding in the jails and the logjam of the dockets in the county courts; and second, an audacious proposal to have ringleader Coltrane tried as a common felon in a regular criminal proceeding here in the capital city. It was the kind of trial, Marc thought, calculated to unite the populace against the "real" enemy—American republicanism and its agents provocateurs— though more likely to incite than to appease. And even though the courts-martial had thus far proved to be efficient (at the expense of justice) and draconian, the governor apparently felt that the military courts were giving the miscreants more honour than their perfidy deserved. A message needed to be sent across the border to other so-called idealists bent on liberating the Canadian natives: armed incursions were acts of thuggery in the guise of military manoeuvres and would be treated as such.

The trial was scheduled for the middle of January, less than two weeks away. That the felon was immured in the cellar of Chepstow House under the watch of his captor merely added relish to an already tasty affair. It seemed that the colonel could do no wrong, that nothing could tarnish the sheen on his armour. Immediately after the massacre at the Windsor redoubt, Gideon Stanhope had accepted full responsibility for his captain's ineptness in clearing out the buried crates of ordnance from the earthen walls. That meant taking the blame for the bushwhackers' attack on that fateful December morning, a dastardly ambush rigged by the cunning and unrepentant Major Coltrane that had seen five men die (including the hapless and silenced Muttlebury) and eight others seriously wounded, two losing limbs and another blinded. But the regular staff would not hear of such a selfless gesture on the part of the colonel, however nobly intended. Instead of a court-martial, they recommended a citation, particularly in light of the colonel's courage under fire in Baby's orchard and his subsequent pursuit of the routed enemy, and of course the bayonet scrape on his thigh. From the narrow perspective of field tactics, the brass were inclined to fault Captain Muttlebury for his precipitate action in assaulting the Stars and Stripes fluttering above the redoubt before a proper reconnoitering and for his being naive enough to believe his opponents were out of bullets and powder, merely because one of them had claimed it was so with his dying breath.

When it was learned that every cell in every jail in the province was now full (the diseases of overcrowding had provided only temporary relief), the colonel graciously offered to incarcerate Coltrane, also recovering from wounds suffered at the Battle of Windsor, and to personally guarantee both his safety and his appearance in court. Indeed, if rumour were even marginally true, Colonel Stanhope was insisting on accepting his adversary as a military officer worthy of humane and dignified treatment. Several crates of the felon's effects—an extra uniform, vintage pipes, numerous books that no loyal citizen would peruse, and a collection of rare silver snuff boxes—had been shipped from his home in Detroit. And despite a gentle remonstrance from the governor (who knew when to leave a popular hero alone) and in the face of the periodic picketing of Chepstow by Orangemen and Tory youth groups, Colonel Stanhope persisted in "doing the honourable thing." Although no disinterested lover of justice had stepped forward, he even made a gentlemanly attempt to secure defense counsel for his prisoner.

The good colonel's reward for such magnanimity was to have Coltrane give interviews to three newspapers, one of them a right-wing organ that was not about to let politics interfere with circulation. In these front-page pieces, Major Coltrane adumbrated his outrageous views and partisan opinions. The virtues of American-style republicanism were retailed ad nauseam and the corresponding failures of the Canadian provinces maddeningly set out in xeno-phobic chapter and verse, all the more irritating because many of them were true. The upshot was an even more strenuous picketing of Chepstow, not as a criticism of the colonel (his forbearance in the face of such ingratitude nudged his star even more steeply into the firmament) but as umbrage and outrage at the arrogant ingrate in his cellar. So unruly were the protests and so credible the threats to seize and lynch the Yankee murderer that a phalanx of the 85th Highlanders had to be placed in front of Chepstow's iron gates day and night. It seemed likely that two phalanxes would be needed to escort him to the Court House at King and Toronto Streets.

Only yesterday afternoon Marc had been privy to a fascinating discussion between the Baldwins, *père et fils,* as to whether they ought to offer their services as defense attorneys for Caleb Coltrane, despite the obvious risks. Both men realized, as many in the town did not, that any hint of a kangaroo court being held for Coltrane—charged inter alia with murder, attempted murder, conspiracy to commit murder, armed robbery, and forcible deten-tion—or the least intimation of Star Chamber proceedings had the potential to ignite the still-smouldering passions of the thousands of Hunters and libertarians across the border. And just as tempers were beginning to cool and the U.S. government was getting a grip on its own renegades!

On the other hand, young Robert Baldwin had himself narrowly escaped being branded a rebel and seditionist and was still under a cloud of suspicion for his ambiguous behaviour during the rebellion. So much so that he had refrained from attending the Legislative Assembly except on rare occasions and did not speak on any matters pertinent to the current crisis. Sir George Arthur had a steady hand on the tiller of the executive and the legislatures, and Robert was content to let him guide the ship until Lord Durham's report was published sometime in the next month or so. But Coltrane had to have legal representation, and some Tory hack would probably be appointed at the last moment to provide token counsel, if that.

"Perhaps we could have him defended by one of his own kind," Dr. Baldwin had suggested, looking both pensive and mischievous.

"That would require special dispensation from the chief justice and the tacit approval of our fellow benchers," Robert had responded, puzzled but ever aware that his father rarely spoke without some point in mind, however oblique.

"Not if said barrister were a well-known and experienced criminal lawyer from New York and one who has been residing here for the past two years."

"You can't mean Richard Dougherty! Doubtful Dick?"

"He lives just a block and a half away." William smiled wryly.

"But he's a known sybarite and, in all likelihood, something worse."

"You mean he's no gentleman?"

"Precisely. The Law Society would sooner see him in jail than a courtroom."

William smiled even more wryly. "Expediency makes for strange bedfellows, eh?"

Robert, diffident and possessing less humour than his illustrious and ebullient father but his equal in perspicacity and political astuteness, said after a moment's reflection, "I see what you mean. A corrupt, licentious, and debased Yankee lawyer from New York City defending an odious miscreant and arrogant pretender in a hopeless case—what could be more palpitating to the Tory heart?"

"If he has one."

"I don't have the slightest idea whether Dougherty would accept the challenge—he's been well retired for two years now—but the chance to be admitted to our bar would surely be irresistible for a man who was once at the pinnacle of his profession and an American legend at law."

"You leave the benchers to me," William said. "I'll have him installed within the week if you'll agree to approach him about representing Coltrane."

And before Marc could take Robert aside to learn more about the intriguing Mr. Dougherty, an important client had arrived, ending the conversation. After lunch tomorrow, though, he intended to get all the unsavoury details.

A light snow was falling as Marc left the Osgoode grounds and walked south along York Street. "Christmas breath" the children here called it, a hushed exhalation of flakes and a fitting prelude to the Feast of the Epiphany on the morrow. Marc thought of *Twelfth Night,* Shakespeare, and his friend Horatio Cobb. He thought of Beth and the child to be. And felt blessed. At King Street he turned east, making his way quietly through the shoppers who, lulled perhaps by the perfect peacefulness of the snowfall, lingered in doorways or spoke in muted tones to friendly passersby, reluctant to enter a shop and break the spell. It was near closing time, but Marc was nonetheless surprised to see that Smallman's was shut up tight, with curtains drawn across the bow-window display. There were lights in the adjoining workroom and in Mrs. Halpenny's apartment over the shop. Puzzled but not worried, Marc continued along King towards Briar Cottage, several long blocks away on Sherbourne Street. In fact, he began to feel pleased because it occurred to him that Beth, now well into her fifth month, seemed prepared to take his advice and spend only a few hours in the shop each day until the time when she would let Rose Halpenny fully supervise the workroom and Bertha Bethune, her assistant in the millinery section, greet the customers.

Whistling tunelessly, Marc came up to his house, now settled in the snowy dark as if it had arrived here with the glaciers and decided to stay. He opened the front door, the aroma of roasting fowl struck his nostrils, and his stomach rumbled pleasantly. Then he was stopped where he stood by the sight of the three women in his front room. Beth was seated beside Dolly Putnam, trying with minimal success to ease the girl's wracking sobs. Charlene Huggan was hovering at Beth's elbow with a steaming teapot in one hand and a cup and saucer in the other, though the two items seemed not to be in the least associated with one another. On the tea trolley before them sat a plate of hot biscuits, cooling. (Charlene, under the impetus of necessity, was actually learning how to cook food that was edible.)

"Dolly, dear, you must try to get a hold of yourself. Tell us exactly what happened. We can't help you if you can't tell us *why* Billy's been put in jail."

"In jail?" Marc questioned, and two of the women looked up, startled to see him in the doorway.

"Oh, yes, Mr. Edwards, Billy's been tossed into a dungeon and they're gonna hang him!"

"Charlene," Beth said firmly, "pour us all some tea and then go see that your roast isn't burning."

"Everythin'll be all right now that Mr. Edwards is back, won't it, ma'am?"

Beth gave the girl—for she was all of seventeen—a look that said, Oh, don't be daft, though I know you can't help it.

"Everything'll be fine," she said aloud.

At this soothing remark, Dolly burst into fresh tears and dropped her head into her hands. Charlene set out three cups of tea with trembling fingers and quivering lip.

Marc came across the room, dripping melted snow onto the carpet. "*Is* Billy in jail, dear?"

Beth nodded grimly. "It looks like it. All I can get out of Dolly is something about Billy trying to kill someone. She can't get any further without garbling her words to death."

The reference to death induced even harder sobbing.

"How did she find this out?" Marc pulled off his boots and then tossed his hat and coat over a chair. He sat down next to Dolly, her raven curls matted with sweat and her sloe eyes blurred and reddened with weeping. He gave her his handkerchief, then took her right hand into both of his.

"Dolly wasn't feeling well, so Rose sent her home at three o'clock. It was her mum who'd been downtown shopping who heard the news about Billy being arrested. So, as far as I can tell, the two of them went straight to the police to find out what was going on."

"Cobb'll know all the details, then," Marc said. He lifted Dolly's chin with his hand and peered into her beleaguered face. "Billy wouldn't deliberately hurt anyone, Dolly, you know that. There must be some sort of mistake here. I'm a very good friend of Chief Sturges and Constable Cobb. I'll go down to the police quarters and sort this all out. Just tell me what you know so far. Please."

Dolly bobbed her head up and down, then took two sips of tea. She swallowed hard and began at last to speak. "Mr. Sturges told us that Billy was caught doin' a duel this mornin'."

"A duel?"

"Uh-huh. I told him only rich gentlemen did such things, but he said Billy was found with a smokin' pistol in his hand, and under the law he had to be charged."

"Is duelling against the law?" Beth said to Marc.

"Not as such, though it'll get you dismissed from the army quick enough. However, if someone is hurt, then attempted murder charges may be brought against the one who inflicted the wound. Usually, though, neither party nor the seconds report on the episode. There's a sort of code of secrecy."

"But some boy was peekin' through the fence and come runnin' to the police. And they got caught!" Dolly sobbed at the injustice of it all.

"Whose fence? Who is Billy supposed to have shot?"

Dolly looked up, and through her tears said with a sort of puzzled pride, "It was that awful Yankee!"

"Good God," Beth said.

"Not Caleb Coltrane?" Marc said.

"That's the one," Dolly confirmed.

Exhausted, Dolly fell asleep on the chesterfield. Beth and Marc decided to have supper—it was the first complete meal Charlene had prepared from scratch and they were loath to disappoint her—and then, afterwards, mull over some sensible course of action. How Billy McNair had managed to get himself into a duel with an imprisoned felon at the far end of the city was certainly a mystery Marc wanted to have cleared up before he went to bed.

"Chief Sturges will have the whole story," Beth said, as they returned to the front room and saw Dolly sitting up and rubbing her eyes.

"I'm sure they will," Marc said.

"But what about Billy, Mr. Edwards? Will he haveta stay in jail?"

"I doubt it, Dolly, especially if he hasn't actually killed Mr. Coltrane."

"If we post bond," Beth said to Dolly, "he can go free till his trial in the spring assizes."

"But we ain't got the money!" Dolly cried with a wail only the young can achieve in their despair. "He'll die in there! He will! And I love him still!"

"We know you do," Beth soothed. "And when he comes to his senses, he'll see how foolish he was to break off your engagement."

"I can't imagine the bond being more than a hundred dollars," Marc said.

"I'll pay it," Beth said.

"We'll pay it," Marc said, and was rewarded with Dolly's Billy-winning smile.

"And if the charges stick," Beth added, "Billy'll need a good lawyer."

"But—"

"We'll pay for the lawyer, too," Beth said.

Dolly looked at her like a grateful pup who has just been picked from a litter of contenders. "Do you know a good lawyer?"

Beth turned to her husband. "I believe I do," she said.

FOUR

It was Constable Horatio Cobb who had been unlucky enough to interrupt the duel early that Monday morning. The sun was just a scarlet disk on the frigid horizon behind him as he reached his temporary patrol on Hospital Street at Bay.

Following the first of several demonstrations by the Orange Dislodgers, as Cobb called them, and impromptu protests by a gang of Tory toughs (in raccoon coats and beaver hats) outside of Chepstow, Chief Constable Wilfrid Sturges had placed three supernumerary constables and Ewan (Able-but-Unwilling) Wilkie in charge of the eastern sector of the city, and set himself and his three most experienced constables the task of patrolling the western sector, where Chepstow was located. Sir George Arthur's orders had been clear: the blackguard Coltrane was to be kept alive as fodder for the gibbet at any cost. And so Cobb had left the billowing warmth of his wife's body, forced down a cold breakfast in the dark, pulled his greatcoat over his food-stained paunch, jammed his helmet down over his stocking cap, and headed west up Front Street towards the seat of trouble.

But trouble there had been none for the past two days. Perhaps the fanatics were having difficulty ratcheting up their venom day after frigid day. After all, Coltrane would surely dance to their cheers from the gallows in the Court House yard. They could pursue his tumbrel from Chepstow to the courtroom with spit and spleen every morning for as long as the trial lasted. Why harass the colonel and frighten his servants when it was the newspapers who insisted on publishing the Yankee's gibberish and the protesters themselves who scooped up every available copy so they could curse it? The queer ways of his fellow man had ever remained a mystery to Cobb, and he had long ago decided that trying to solve it was not worth the effort. If people ran afoul of the law, then they ran afoul of him. What could be more straightforward than that?

It was a surprise when, as he crossed Peter Street and was almost within view of the front gates of Chepstow, one of the many street urchins who acted as scout and runner for him when they needed a penny (perpetually, that is) sprinted out from the brush beside the road and almost bowled him over.

"Hold on there, Samkins! You'll bust yer head on my belly!" Cobb cried as he reached out and hauled the boy up with one hand.

Sammy was wide-eyed and pasty white. His lips moved but only his frosted breath hit the air.

"You seen a ghost, have ya?" Cobb said, not unkindly.

"G-guns!" Sammy stammered.

"Whaddaya mean, *guns*?"

"Pistols, sir," the boy gasped. "With handles as big as . . . as big as . . . yer nose."

Cobb decided to bypass the insult in the interests of communication. "And just where did you see these big pistols?" he demanded. The mere mention of weapons in the neighbourhood of Chepstow made him jittery.

"F-follow me, sir, and I'll show ya."

Before Cobb could reply, Sammy wheeled and leapt back into the scrub brush and woodlot that encircled Colonel Stanhope's estate, all of four acres on the northeast corner of Hospital and Brock. Cobb trotted behind, happy to feel the slap of his truncheon against his left thigh. Stumbling through the frozen undergrowth, they emerged about half a minute later onto a broad meadow behind the estate. Here in other seasons the colonel would graze his horses, but now it was a snow-covered expanse whipped by a northwest January wind and ringed by an iron fence that kept intruders at bay.

Sammy bolted straight ahead towards an iron gate and, in the distance behind it, a wooden-walled enclosure at the back of the sprawling mansion, which, Cobb had always supposed, was a sort of kitchen garden off the old servants quarters. The infamous inmate was said to be housed there in unwarranted comfort. Cobb's heart skipped several beats. Had someone got past the guards at the back gate and broken into the garden? With an assassin's pistol in hand?

When Cobb and Sammy reached the gate, they found it wide open with sentries at both posts asleep on their feet, like a pair of exhausted hogs. They appeared to be ordinary militiamen and members of the colonel's regiment. So much for security.

"Hurry, this way!" Sammy yelled, and pointed at the Dutch door in the garden wall ahead. His cry brought the sentries awake. Cobb barked at them to follow him.

Cobb and Sammy were four or five paces from the little half door when they were stopped in their tracks by the sharp snap of pistols discharging, two of them in such quick succession they might have been one shot and its instant echo. Cobb sprang into action. He pushed Sammy aside and charged at the door, which, being unlatched, facilitated his rapid entrance into the minor drama being enacted behind it. The protagonists, three of them, froze in their places.

Directly before Cobb, in front of an unbarred door that must have led to the "prison" behind it, stood a large, red-faced man attired in the same green militia uniform as the two laggard sentries. He stared at Cobb in speechless disbelief, uncertain as to whether he ought to be fearful or outraged. At his feet a limp silk handkerchief lay like a jettisoned heirloom. Cobb directed his eyes left and right, and now it was his turn to be astonished. A few feet in front of one wall stood a tall, imposing figure in yet another military costume, a blue and yellow confection Cobb had not seen before. From his right hand, a smoking pistol dangled, its menace spent. At the wall opposite stood a young man Cobb had met several times while loitering about Beth Edwards's shop: Billy McNair. And he too clutched a smouldering pistol, glowering at it as if it had inexplicably betrayed him.

The man with the hanky at his feet found his voice first. "What is the meaning of this intrusion!" he bellowed with more gustiness than conviction. "This is private property."

"I am a policeman and you, sir, have just broken the law," Cobb snapped. "You stay put and tell yer pals to bring their weapons over here. Now!"

"I will do no such thing, you have no juris—"

But Cobb was already on his way to Billy. The two sentries had come up to the Dutch door and were standing there with mouths agape.

"Get him out of here!" the big man yelled at them. "That's an order!"

The sentries didn't budge. They had spotted the man whom some were calling the Antichrist—with a pistol in his paw.

"Give me the pistol, Billy," Cobb said quietly. "Fer yer mother's sake." As the Widow McNair was a longtime friend of his wife, Cobb felt justified in invoking her name here.

Billy obliged but said nothing. His face was a blank. Shock, Cobb thought. By some miracle the lad had just survived a duel with the notorious Caleb Coltrane, a fellow reputed to be fearless, treacherous, and deadly. For that surely was he, still standing erect at the far wall with a kind of indulgent smirk on his craggy face. The blue and yellow tunic was Yankee, through and through.

"I'm going to have to arrest these men," Cobb said to the big fellow, who had obviously been acting as umpire and second for both duellists. He was respectful but in control. "What is your name, sir?"

"Lardner Bostwick," the fellow said, his bravado dissipating rapidly. His rheumy eyes, the cross-hatching of veins on his bloated cheeks, and his blue bulb of a nose bespoke much of drink and inadequate restraint. He blinked and added, "Lieutenant Bostwick, adjutant to Colonel Stanhope of the 2nd Regiment, Toronto militia."

"And are you in charge here, Lieutenant?"

"I am Major Coltrane's jailer."

"And is conductin' duels part of yer duties, sir?"

"That is none of your—"

"Men shootin' at each other are attemptin' murder, even if they can't shoot straight," Cobb barked, and was pleased to see Bostwick wince and blink.

From the far wall came a hearty guffaw. "You're going to charge me with attempted murder, are you, constable?" It was Coltrane. His voice was deep, with a basso's vigour and masculine authority. "You can add it to the seven capital crimes they've already trumped up against me!" And he roared with laughter. Even the bumbling sentries seemed to find this amusing.

"If I'd've wanted the little weasel dead, he'd be stone cold by now." He tossed the spent pistol at his feet with a dismissive gesture.

Cobb returned to Billy, who had not moved. "I haveta take you in, son. You've gone and done a very foolish thing here."

Billy seemed to snap out of his daze, but it was not Cobb he was paying attention to. He was glaring at his adversary with a look of raw hatred that sent a chill down Cobb's spine.

"Arrest who?"

Cobb turned in time to see a man emerge from the house through the prison door.

"What the hell is going on here?"

It was Colonel Stanhope, bristling with umbrage. Cobb

recognized him from the parade in December. He was whippet-thin, and the rigidity of his posture would have embarrassed a ramrod. He was in full dress uniform—scarlet, green, and white—with his feathered shako perfectly square on his head. Here it was not yet eight o'clock in the morning and the fellow was turned out for church parade. Did he sleep in his tunic?

It was Bostwick who fielded the colonel's question. "The duel, sir," he sputtered. "I thought you—"

"I did no such thing! My God, man, what was to prevent Major Coltrane here from turning the pistols on you and galloping through that door to the United States?"

"He gave me his word, sir. Didn't you, Major?"

Coltrane had taken several steps towards the group near the prison door but remained happily aloof from the clamour. "I merely defended my honour, Colonel. You of all people will understand that." He gave Stanhope a cryptic smile that seemed both conspiratorial and contemptuous. "And as you see, the duel has taken place—with both participants unmarked."

The colonel seemed suddenly to realize that it took two men to fight a duel. He swivelled about and aimed his gaze at Billy McNair, his sometime sergeant. "Is that you, Billy?" he said, his tone softening. "I can't believe this. I can't."

Billy stared at the ground, abashed. And began to tremble.

"Don't you realize you might have killed Major Coltrane?" the colonel said, anger creeping back into his voice. "And if you had, my sworn word to Sir George to deliver the major to his trial unharmed would have been broken! And everything you and I stood for down there in Baby's orchard and after would have been dishonoured."

"He's a murderer," Billy mumbled to his feet.

"He's a soldier! And an officer!"

Who was going to be dragged into criminal court and hanged for his crimes, Cobb thought, but said nothing. Somehow he had to take charge of the situation again.

"And you, Lieutenant. I'll have you drummed out of the regiment for this. Your behaviour is inexcusable."

Bostwick looked stunned, bewildered—though why he should be surprised by the reprimand when he had recklessly endangered two lives and given the prisoner access to loaded pistols was difficult for Cobb to understand.

The moment of awkward silence gave Cobb a chance to reassert his authority. "I'm goin' to haveta take Billy to the magistrate," he said to the colonel, "and he's likely to be charged with attempted murder."

Stanhope took this in. In fact he seemed to acknowledge Cobb's presence for the first time. He smiled thinly, exposing a ridge of tiny, pointed teeth. "And did you yourself, Constable . . . ah—"

"Cobb."

"Did you actually witness these men fire upon one another with intent to kill?"

Cobb was taken aback but managed to reply, "I was just outside the garden here when I heard both pistols go off."

"Indeed." He broadened his sawtooth grin. "And how can you be sure they were not shooting at pigeons or a bit of ivy on the wall?"

"Well, now, I can't, but I found Lieutenant Bostwick here with an umpire's hanky at his feet and the two men facin' each other with smokin' pistols in their hands."

"Then, as the lawyers say, your evidence is merely circumstantial, and I'd like you to apologize for invading my home and then leave me to take care of the business I have pledged this community to execute with—"

"We were duellin'," Billy said suddenly. "I tried my best to kill the bastard, but I missed." Some steel had come back into his voice, and the look that must have carried him through the rigours and horrors of the Battle of Windsor now returned. For a fleeting moment he was again Sergeant McNair.

The colonel stared at him, sighed exaggeratedly, and said, "So be it. Do your duty, then, Constable." He turned to Bostwick. "Lieutenant, escort the prisoner back into his quarters. Patricia will be down with his breakfast in ten minutes. Then report to me in my study."

"I oughta charge yer man with aidin' and abettin'," Cobb said stubbornly.

The colonel looked daggers at him. "Don't press your luck, sir."

Coltrane had come over to stand beside his jailer. "Don't be too hard on ol' Bossy here," he said to Stanhope. "McNair and I duelled over a point of honour, something I know you appreciate to a fault. Besides, you know I can be very persuasive when I've a mind to."

The colonel appeared to ignore the comment, but his eyes narrowed nonetheless. Then he spun and literally marched back into the house, almost stepping on a servant hovering nervously in the doorway. He was followed by Coltrane and his keeper. Cobb was left in the yard with Billy, the sentries, Sammy, and two weapons to be taken in as evidence.

"Come along, Billy," he said. "I got no choice."

"He ain't seen the last of me!" Billy cried.

"Now, then, son, you don't need to go makin' things worse. We got witnesses here—"

"I'm gonna kill the fucker! I swear it! Hangin's too good fer him!"

Cobb failed to see the logic of these remarks, but he was more concerned with their implications for Billy than for this unrepentant republican who had had the impertinence to tell the editor of the *Examiner* that he too had fought at Pelee last March and was himself known throughout Michigan and Ohio as the Pelee Island Patriot.

As he took Billy by the arm and flipped a penny to a goggle-eyed Sammy, Cobb noticed that the colonel had come back into the prison doorway. He had heard Billy's threat, and on his face there was an odd expression—a grimace of concern or, perhaps, a curious smile.

While Marc assured Dolly Putnam that he would help Billy in any way he could, he was not hopeful of doing much before the evening was over. Nevertheless, he gave her mittened hand an extra pat at her doorstep, flashed her an avuncular smile, promised to return in the morning with good news, then walked quickly through the softly falling snow down to the Court House on King Street. At seven-thirty on a Monday he was not surprised to see there were no lights in the windows of the court offices. However, when he followed the familiar path around to the back of the building, he noted with some relief a faint glow coming from the police quarters there.

Wilfrid Sturges was often in his office these days, now that tensions in the city were escalating in anticipation of the Coltrane trial. (A special court date had been set for the week following, mandated by the lieutenant-governor outside the usual assizes.) Charges of petty trespass and property damage, in addition to increased brawling in the taverns, had kept his four constables and many supernumeraries busy on the streets and the chief and his clerk busy in the office completing the necessary paperwork for the magistrate.

Marc eased open the door, knocked the snow off his boots, and called out, "You in there, Wilf?"

"Where the hell else would I be, eh?" Sturges's round, red Cockney face popped into the doorway of his cubicle, and he grinned broadly. "Ain't you glad you caught me in a good mood?"

"I've never known you to be otherwise."

"You're just in time fer a cup o' tea, Marc. Sit down and take a load off." He rubbed his hands together over the pot-bellied stove, upon which a kettle was about to whistle its greeting. "I've a pretty fair idea why you're 'ere."

* * *

The news was not good. Gussie French had just finished writing out—in his obsessively neat hand—the various reports that had been dictated to him regarding the morning's incident. The damning affidavits of the militia sentries lay before them on Gussie's table. While Sturges sipped his tea and tried not to yawn too conspicuously, Marc read them through. Cobb's detailed account was clear, compelling, and—for Billy—less than hopeful. The testimony of the sentries as to Billy's own statements certainly established motive and intent. But the fact that no one had been injured would surely mitigate the severity of any sentence, should he be convicted. Still, there were other, more worrisome aspects of the affair.

"Did Billy say how on earth he managed to be involved in a duel with the most carefully guarded and notorious felon in the entire province?" Marc said to Sturges, who was pouring himself a second cup of tea.

"Magistrate Thorpe asked him that this mornin'. Seems like the lad was crazy enough to go and visit Coltrane yesterday, and they got—"

"Coltrane is allowed visitors? On a Sunday?" Marc was surprised.

Sturges chortled. "Regular caravan of 'em out there at Chepstow. Two or three a day. It's made our life hell up there on Hospital Street, and most everywhere else."

"But that's ridiculous. Coltrane is a dangerous man. There's constant talk of his escaping and rumours of his agents poking about and stirring up mischief—"

"You don't need to tell me that, ol' chum. But the colonel insists the blackguard is a military prisoner and oughta be treated honourably," Sturges said with a fierce aspiration of the *h*. "He's had the bugger's duds and doodads brung up from Detroit, he's given 'im a bloody suite to reside in, and he lets 'im see whoever he pleases."

"But who, besides alien republicans, would want to see him?"

Sturges spat, missed the spittoon, and said with undisguised contempt, "The editors of every paper in town and two in the nearby counties, to start. And a couple of Tory gentlemen and that Orange alderman to boot. Seems they all wanta take a gander at 'im. I been told he gets a kick outta arguin' with 'em. Some stay in there an hour or more. We know 'cause we gotta control the crowds out on the road hootin' and hollerin' and all riled up 'cause they don't know whether they're ragin' at Coltrane or the idiots goin' in to gawk at 'im."

"After which our loyal editors print his seditious prevarications and give a credence to them they don't deserve," Marc said, glaring at his cold tea. "The man is clever, isn't he? He knows he's going to swing, so he's decided to use the governor's trial for his own political ends. He'll end up a martyr, and the whole affair will have blown up in Sir George's face."

Sturges muttered agreement. "You c'n always count on a politician undoin' himself," he said with philosophical satisfaction.

"So Billy got in there legitimately, then? Did he say what they quarrelled about?"

"Point of honour," Sturges said, hitting the spittoon. "That's all he'd say."

"And he's in the cells, I assume."

"And likely to stay there awhile."

"What do you mean, Wilf? The lad's not really dangerous to the public at large. In fact, as far as the local populace is concerned, Sergeant McNair is a war hero. They know full well it was he, not that puffed-up brevet colonel, who distinguished himself at Windsor and captured Coltrane. There's not a man or woman among them who won't, when they hear of the duel, wish that Billy had finished the job then and there."

"Christ, Marc, take it easy. I gotta sleep nights, ya know."

"Oh, I am sorry, Wilf. I should've realized that having to arrest

Billy and hold him here has put you and Cobb in a very ticklish situation."

Sturges sighed. "It won't be the first one we been in, but I sure ain't lookin' forward to a bunch o' frothin' Orangemen struttin' up and down in front of this place fer days on end."

"So you'll want Billy released as soon as possible?"

A deeper sigh. "I wish. But Magistrate Thorpe won't 'ear of it."

"But that makes no sense—"

"It does to him. He says he's got two affidaveys there swearin' to the fact that Billy vowed to kill Coltrane before he could be hanged. He knows Billy wouldn't stand a chance of doin' so, and will probably regret what he said when he's cooled off after a chilly night in the cells, but Thorpe's terrified of the governor. He knows Sir George wants this trial and a public hangin' more'n anythin' else, and so he can't take a chance on lettin' Billy loose. He's denied bail, at least until Coltrane gets turned off. After which I figure the charges against Billy'll just fade away."

"But it's freezing in the cells. If Billy's kept in there for three or four weeks, he could catch a fever and die!"

"Some do. Though the mob is more likely to bust 'im out before that happens."

The two men let these grim possibilities settle between them for several minutes.

"I'm going to enlist the services of Robert Baldwin to defend Billy," Marc said quietly. "He may have more luck with posting surety. At any rate, we'll need to see the prisoner as soon as possible tomorrow."

"You seem to 'ave a personal stake in all this."

"I do. Beth's friend and employee, Dolly Putnam, was engaged to Billy and is still in love with him. Billy's been a troubled young man ever since the business in Windsor, and his troubles look to be a long way from over."

At the door, Sturges said, "I'll find a nice warm room upstairs fer you and Baldwin to interview Billy. Just send me a message about the time."

"Thanks, Wilf. You're a good man."

"Upholdin' the law can be a bitch, can't it?" Sturges replied.

FIVE

Jasper Hogg, the young man next door who did odd jobs for Beth around the house and garden while conspiring to effect as many side glances as possible at Charlene Huggan, came over to Briar Cottage at eight o'clock and hitched Dobbin to Beth's sleigh. Marc had insisted that if she were foolhardy enough to work at the shop in her delicate condition, the least she could do was drive there in comfort and safety. And as Beth had already determined on this course of action, she was pleased to assent to it. Marc decided to walk to Baldwin's this day so that Beth could pick up Dolly, take her to work, and break the disquieting news in a tactful, womanly way. Robert was still at breakfast in the domestic section of the grand house on Front Street but came over to the offices of Baldwin and Sullivan shortly after receiving Marc's note from a servant.

"I heard about this duel business late yesterday," he said with uncharacteristic enthusiasm, and Marc realized that keeping a low profile and abstaining from the rough-and-tumble of political debate had left the committed young man restless and bored. "What can we do to help?"

Physically, Robert was a younger version of his handsome and multitalented father. They were both of medium height with heart-shaped faces, weak chins, slicked-back brown hair (the elder's now graying elegantly), and dark, darting eyes that observed much and understood more.

"I would like you to represent Billy McNair."

Baldwin smiled. "With able assistance from my apprentice, I presume?"

"I would be pleased to help."

Robert went over to his desk, brushed aside some papers there, and sat down. "Well, then, put your feet up on the fender and tell me everything you think I should know." He reached over and nibbled at a macaroon.

Marc gave him chapter and verse about the incident and its aftermath. When he had finished, Robert said, "It'll be a pleasure defending a local hero from the wrath of the law, won't it? It's been a while since I've been on the right side."

Billy McNair was brought through the tunnel that connected the jail with the Court House about eleven o'clock that Tuesday morning and taken up to a commodious, carpeted room warmed by a sizzling coal fire. The winter sunlight backlit the padded armchairs and glazed the tea tables. Seated and awaiting him were Magistrate James Thorpe and two wool-suited gentlemen, one of whom Billy recognized instantly. Calvin Strangway, the jailer, pushed him into the room, then—realizing where he was—steadied his prisoner and stepped on the shackles to keep them from rattling.

"Good God!" Marc gasped. Billy was dishevelled, hollow-eyed, shivering, and bound hand and foot. "Get those chains off the boy!"

Strangway blushed. "Rules is rules, sir. I ain't allowed."

Magistrate Thorpe intervened to say, "It's all right, Calvin. Take them off and wait downstairs." Thorpe had offered Baldwin the use of his own study as interview room, in part, Marc thought, to compensate for his refusal to grant bail. A communiqué had arrived from Government House instructing Thorpe not to release the prisoner under any circumstances.

The jailer unlocked the various shackles and scuttled away. Billy, apparently shamed by his experience in the cells or perhaps just exhausted by it, rubbed absently at his wrists and stared at the carpet. Thorpe quietly left the room by the other door. Marc wasted no time.

"Billy, this is Mr. Baldwin. He's an attorney and has agreed to act for you. Please, sit down. There. I'll pour you a mug of coffee while you tell us what happened and how you think we can best help you."

Billy nodded glumly but took the mug eagerly in both hands.

Robert smiled at him and began. "We need you, first of all, to tell us precisely how this unfortunate incident came about. We need to understand what provocation may have been proffered and what sort of collusion took place to allow the duel to proceed."

Billy stared at the lawyer. "What difference does all that make?" he asked. "I aimed a pistol at the bastard and missed. End of story."

Marc was not displeased to see some fire come into Billy's eyes. Defiance, even surliness, was better than silence and despair. If they were to argue extenuating circumstances and possible criminal collusion on the part of the organizers of the fiasco, then they would need Billy's spirited cooperation.

"Humour me, then," Robert said, unfazed by his outburst. "We're told that you requested an audience with Major Coltrane and that, apparently, he agreed to it. What was the purpose of your visit?"

Billy finished his coffee and fingered the abrasions on his wrists. "I wanted to look the murderer in the eye and tell him what I thought of him."

"But you were the one who captured him at Windsor and brought him to your camp some miles away," Robert said, remembering the newspaper accounts provided by everybody concerned except Billy himself.

Billy's reply was delivered without emotion, as if the details were self-evident and unimportant to boot. "He was unconscious. He never opened his eyes all the way back. The colonel's eyes just about popped out of his head when he saw it was Coltrane and I gave him the papers he was carryin'. Then we took him away to the hospital at brigade headquarters in Fort Malden. I waited for a bit while the surgeon worked on his wound, then left. I never saw him again till last Sunday." He smiled grimly. "And I never got to look the bastard in the face till then, did I?"

"I think I can understand your motive for going to Chepstow," Robert said, "but you must have known that Coltrane was certain to be condemned by a public criminal proceeding, after which he would hang in the yard outside this very building."

"I guess I just wanted to tell him that it was me that saved his miserable life," Billy said evenly, "the one who allowed him to be brought here and strung up like a Christmas goose."

"You saved his life?" Marc interrupted, incredulous.

"He was bleedin' to death. He'd just rigged up a trap fer my unit and killed my best friend. And fool that I was, I put a tourniquet on his left arm, an orange silk kerchief of Dolly's that she give me before I left Toronto." Tears of anger or regret blurred his vision, and he looked away. "I never did get it back."

"So, tell us what happened when you got in there to see him on Sunday."

Billy held out his mug for more coffee, then stared at the sunlight on the carpet as if he might not see its like again. When he spoke, his voice was subdued, almost solemn. "It didn't go the way I thought it would. He's a big braggart of a man. He didn't seem the least afraid of dyin'. When I told him I was the one who captured him, he laughed and said, 'You wouldn't've got me if I'd had even half an eye open!' I wanted him to know that a lowly militia sergeant had trailed him through the bush and got the better of him, but I never got to it. Instead, I started yellin' at him, callin' him a killer and a connivin' ambusher, but he just laughed louder and started lecturin' me on the 'realities' of battle, as he called them. Then he boasted how his mates were comin' to rescue him and how he'd never see the inside of a tyrant's courtroom."

"So he doesn't know you actually saved his life?" Marc asked.

Billy shook his head. "All I could see was Mel's ruined face and his killer was sittin' across from me snortin' snuff and tellin' me it was all part of war and fightin' fer a cause you believed in. So I stood up and said I was gonna go to the papers and give 'em the story they'd been tryin' to get outta me fer a month."

"Why would that bother him," Robert wondered, "when nothing else seems to have?"

Billy smiled, and this time there was a glint of satisfaction in it. "I got to him with that, I did. I told him I'd tell the papers that he ran away like a coward from the fight in the orchard, that he wasted his troops' ammunition, and they had to scuttle away like whipped hounds. Only a lucky find at the old fort allowed any of his men to escape."

"But isn't that what happened?"

"No. I was the one that saw the bastard organizin' a proper orderly retreat, just like our own colonel taught us. He was already wounded, and only left the battle when it was lost and he had to regroup."

Something occurred to Marc that had been puzzling him ever since reading the varying accounts of the Battle of Windsor in December. "Just how did Major Coltrane find the crates that were left in the redoubt? It's obvious that the fortification was beside the creek they were using as an escape route, so they could hardly miss that. But I'm told that Colonel Stanhope indicated in his official report that, although overlooked by Captain Muttlebury during the removal detail, the crates were still buried. If not, then even poor Muttlebury would have noticed them."

"Coltrane told me about that, before we both lost our tempers," Billy explained. "He said his men wanted to surrender. Four of them'd died at our hands already. They begged their commander to let them hunker down in the old fort when they spotted it. There they could run a white hanky up the flagpole and surrender peacefully."

"But it didn't unfold that way."

"No. Coltrane said he'd heard we had hidden caches of arms all around the county, and he suspected the sod wall there would be a logical place. He claimed our fellows had left two or three spilled cartridges in plain sight nearby."

"So they dug around and came up with a crate or two of bullets, powder, and some muskets?"

"Yeah. I figure it must've been them cartridges the captain left that gave the show away, 'cause we weren't more'n ten or twelve minutes behind them. Then that bastard, instead of usin' the fort to fight a proper battle, comes up with the idea of runnin' up the Yankee flag and hidin' in the bush to cut us down from the side."

"Couldn't you see their tracks leading there?" Marc said, recalling his own winter battleground in Quebec.

"The sun was in our eyes, and they sneaked out the back and circled around."

"He seems to have counted upon the inexperience of your officers," Marc commented. He knew all too well the occasional carelessness of officers whose vast experience had not been sufficient to temper their arrogance.

Billy just shook his head.

"Take us back, then, to the point where you threatened Coltrane on Sunday," Robert said.

"Well, like I said, I finally got to him," Billy replied, perking up.

"He said I didn't have the guts to lie about somethin' as sacred as courage in battle, he blustered on about codes of honour and a lot of other horseshit, but I kept the picture of Mel's smashed face in front of me and told him flat out that I'd say he ran from the fight. It's true enough that he was a cowardly assassin and I was going to let the whole world know about it. His name'd be so blackened, no one would lift a finger to rescue him."

In the retelling, Billy's eyes lit up and Marc could see the grit and self-confidence that had carried the lad through slaughter and its random terrors. War had darkened Billy's view of humankind, as it had done for Marc, who had also seen his best friend cruelly cut down. But in doing so, it had also made him a man. Which could prove more difficult than helpful in the present situation.

"You were very foolhardy to do that," Robert said gently.

"I started to think so this mornin'," Billy said more soberly. "But two days ago I didn't care, I just wanted to puncture that bloated vanity of his, and I did. He huffed up like a rooster and said I'd insulted him, and if I thought he really was wicked and cowardly, he'd give me a chance to settle scores—man to man."

"He suggested a duel?" Robert said, knowing it was so but still finding the fact incredible.

"He caught me off guard," Billy said, reddening slightly.

"Sounds as if he's rather skilled at that," Marc said. "But how can a constantly guarded prisoner arrange for a duel outside his cell?"

"He said he could persuade his jailer, Lieutenant Bostwick, to set it up for the next mornin'. I had enough breath still in me to ask about weapons and seconds, and he said Bostwick would supply pistols and act as umpire and second fer both of us. Bostwick is the colonel's adjutant and an old crony, so I figured I didn't haveta worry about him bein' unfair or dishonest."

"No wonder Bostwick was chagrined to see Cobb arrive," Marc said.

"And the colonel," Robert added. "So you agreed?" he said to Billy.

"Yes. I was to come to the little garden he used to exercise in at seven o'clock the next mornin'. When I asked about the guards on the back gate, he said they were usually asleep, but he could arrange fer Bostwick to take care of them." Billy looked at Marc, then Robert. "I couldn't say no, could I?"

Marc said nothing but had to agree.

Billy did indeed arrive at the back gate of Chepstow shortly after seven, while it was still dark, and the sentries were, as predicted, fast asleep. Lieutenant Bostwick was waiting in the enclosed garden with two pistols on a tray. Major Coltrane then came out of the back door of his quarters (always barred on the outside by the jailer but not so that morning) in his tunic with no overcoat. Bostwick explained the rules and then held the tray out to Coltrane, who chose a pistol with no great care or seeming concern. The adversaries exchanged no words. At twenty paces apart the two men were to turn around, wait till the umpire's hanky hit the ground, then fire at will.

Billy had never before fired a pistol, even though he was an experienced hunter of small game with a rifle and musket. But as he took his ten paces, all his anger and outrage at Coltrane—which had mellowed somewhat during a sleepless night—flared up as he thought about his life without Mel at his side and the failure of his engagement to Dolly, and the last thing he saw before he wheeled and prepared to blow this demon creature to the far reaches of hell was his friend's inexhaustible grin. He heard his own pistol explode, then Coltrane's. Something thudded into the wall behind him. (In his report, Cobb had noted that he and Constable Brown had returned to Chepstow and examined the garden wall behind each of the shooters. They dug out a ball four feet to the right of where Billy had stood and two feet above his head. No bullet was found in the wall opposite. Cobb's conclusion: Coltrane, a crack shot, had deliberately missed his opponent; Billy, with malice aforethought, hadn't even hit the garden.) Billy readily admitted making the death threats before witnesses but confessed now that he genuinely regretted doing so.

"You mean to say that you wouldn't carry them out now even if some miracle were to occur and you would be given a second chance?" Robert asked carefully.

"I had my chance to do it honourably," Billy said with conviction. "If I was to do it now, I'd be no better than an assassin. Like him."

"At the moment, as I'm sure Jailer Strangway has informed you, those threats are going to keep you in that miserable cell for at least two or three weeks," Marc said, "by order of the governor."

Billy's face fell. "I'll freeze to death in there," he moaned.

"Our only hope is to somehow persuade the governor and magistrate to drop the charges," Robert said, and before Billy could get his hopes raised, he added quickly, "but at the moment I can't see how we'll go about that."

"I do," Marc said.

Billy and his attorney listened with increasing optimism as Marc outlined his plan. First, there was the fact that not only was no one injured, but even the police had concluded that Coltrane had consciously chosen to miss his target, an honourable tactic often used in duels where honour alone was to be satisfied. No bullet having been found in the wall behind the major, Cobb had assumed that Billy's errancy had been due to his inexperience and understandable nervousness and not to any conscious decision to aim elsewhere. This inference was made plausible only after the fact, when Cobb had been witness to Billy's tantrum. But could the latter not be attributed to the young man's embarrassment by the arrival of outsiders who had observed his ineptness? Young and impulsive, he had shouted threats and uttered boasts to cover his shame and maintain his manhood before strangers.

"My God, man, you're almost ready for the bar," Robert said, smiling.

"I won't lie," Billy said. "I did mean to shoot him, but yes, those stupid threats were made 'cause I was angry and frustrated."

"You don't have to lie," Marc said. "Under British law, the Crown must prove intent. You have the right to remain silent. In a court of law, the Crown is obliged to demonstrate on its own and without your help that you wished Coltrane's death before the incident and at the moment when you pulled the trigger. Your shooting four feet over his head may speak louder than any words could."

"But we can't wait for a trial or for bail a month from now," Robert reminded his apprentice.

"Exactly. Before we take our plea for bail or an outright discharge to the magistrate, we'll need to do two things. First, we'll need to convince Mr. Thorpe, and Sir George, that the duel was a pro forma affair between two army officers who, by deliberately shooting wild, inflicted no harm while preserving their honour. Second, to give credence to our claim that Billy's spate of after-the-fact threats was a momentary and uncharacteristic outburst, we'll need assurance from the other participant that he himself did not take Billy's words seriously and, indeed, has no present concern for his safety in that regard."

The latter part of this proposal was greeted with awkward silence.

"You aren't suggesting that we get Coltrane to swear that the duel was more or less staged and that Billy's intemperance was entirely benign?" Robert said at last.

"I'm sure he's quite delighted I'm rottin' in a cell somewhere," Billy said bitterly.

"Perhaps," Marc said. "But then he doesn't yet know you saved his life, does he?"

Ten minutes later, a course of action had been sketched out. Billy would refrain from making any statements about the incident to anybody—not even to Dolly, should she be magnanimous enough to visit him. (She would, bringing warm clothes and extra food.) Robert would draw up a sworn statement stipulating conditions for Billy's release on his parole; to wit, he would remain within the confines of his mother's home until such time as the court disposed of the charges against him, on pain of forfeiture of a hundred-dollar bond and his freedom. At the same time Robert would work out the particulars of the defense that Marc had earlier suggested, in anticipation of presenting it to Mr. Thorpe and, if necessary, to the attorney general. None of these tactics would actually be deployed, however (save Billy's silence), until the third part of the plan had been successfully completed: convincing Coltrane to go along with the defense's version of events.

"I want you to see Coltrane this afternoon," Robert said.

Marc looked surprised but not displeased.

"Well, you were a commissioned officer yourself," Robert explained, "and you too, if I recall, know the glory that can attend battle. If anyone can get through to this Yankee yahoo, it's you."

"I'm not sure whether I'm supposed to be flattered by that comment or not."

"But you will go, won't you, sir?" Billy said. "Fer Dolly's sake?"

"I'll go," Marc said, "but on one condition. It's entirely possible that Coltrane, given his eccentric behaviour so far, may want to see you in person before he accepts my version of events and your sincerity."

"He could go there under guard," Robert said. "I'm sure I can get Thorpe to agree."

Marc looked at Billy McNair. "Do you think you could face him again?"

"Yes," Billy said, but not very convincingly.

Cobb had snapped at Fabian over breakfast for no particular reason except that he was uncharacteristically irritated with the state of the universe. The events of the past few days had conspired to subvert his bountiful good nature. Then, when eleven-year-old Delia interceded in defense of her younger brother, he had snapped again, bringing *her* close to tears and her mother charging in from the next room to adjudicate matters in her evenhanded way. Which is to say that he received a pincering glare and the kids a soothing, "There, there, Mister Cobb's just grumpy 'cause he woke up grumpy, so you run along to school whilst I go about ungrumpin' him." His ears were still ringing from Dora's efforts on his behalf when he reached Jarvis Street and began to think about what lay ahead.

The arrest of Billy McNair had been a dispiriting affair all around. Although Billy had come willingly enough, they had no sooner stepped onto Hospital Street than they had run smack into a gaggle of protesters on the way to picket outside the front gate of Chepstow. Within seconds he and Billy were surrounded, and the ringleader—a rail-thin fellow with pop-eyes—had demanded to know where a city constable might be escorting a war hero. Cobb had ignored them, pushing through their flimsy encirclement and telling them to mind their own business. But they had trailed him to the station, and an hour later the news of the arrest and the outrageous charge was out and abroad. By the time he and Constable Brown returned to the scene to check for physical evidence (as Marc Edwards had taught him), a full-blown mob of Orangemen, self-proclaimed Loyalists, and assorted troublemakers were waiting for them with cries of "Free the hero! Free the hero!"

Luckily, the constables were able to slip into the woodlot and enter Chepstow's grounds through the rear gate. Finding the bullet would not help Billy's case, Cobb realized, nor would the testimony of the malingering sentries who, when they woke up to the facts of the incident, had proved reluctant but truthful in their affidavits. But the bald truth was that he, Cobb, had taken into custody a much-admired young soldier for attempting to shoot a man detested and despised by nearly every citizen in the capital. And to top it all off, the sarge (as he called his superior, Chief Constable Sturges) had informed his men before they left for the pleasures of hearth and home that Billy would be kept in custody by order of King Arthur, the lieutenant-governor himself.

Crossing Jarvis, he could see the open space before the Court House and the jail next to it. His heart sank. Dora's sausages sat up in his stomach and complained. Not yet eight o'clock and the defenders of everybody's virtue but their own were already on the march. And what was worse, he could see as he drew closer that they were women! Instinctively he veered north up Church Street and made his way past the rear of the Court House and west along Newgate. At Yonge he decided to go into the British-American Coffee House for something hot and consoling.

He had just settled down in comfort with his coffee and a copy of the *Constitution* when he was accosted by a wretched creature, skinny as a starved greyhound, with rheumy eyes and greasy locks that would have given Medusa a fright. With a resigned sigh, Cobb waved at the waiter, who brought a steaming mug and set it as close to the newcomer as the length of his arm and the twitching of his nostrils would permit.

"Good mornin', Nestor," Cobb said to Nestor Peck, his most reliable, and bothersome, snitch. "Why don't ya sit down and have a cup of coffee?"

Nestor ignored the sarcasm or else was too busy warming his chapped fingers against his mug while the steam melted the stalactites from his whiskers.

"You got somethin' helpful that might pay fer that coffee? And perhaps a hot biscuit?"

"With butter?" Nestor pleaded hopefully. His teeth would have chattered if he'd had enough teeth to knock together.

"Whaddaya got?" Cobb demanded, still grumpy and resigned to staying that way.

Nestor gave his coffee a long, slurping gulp and spoke low. "That Yankee fella up at Chepstow." He glanced over at the counter where a platter of fresh biscuits had just been set down.

"What about him?"

"There's a plan to spring him," Nestor said, with evident delight that he should be father to such a revelation.

"There's been humpteen plans to rescue Coltrane ever since he come here, three or four a day. And the bugger's still in his cell, ain't he?" Cobb turned to his newspaper.

Nestor looked crushed, at Cobb's rebuff or the potential loss of a warm breakfast. He recovered adroitly. "A strange character's been seen skulkin' around the colonel's place. One of them Hunter fellas, they say, from Michigan."

"Is that so? And just how do *they* know all this? Spotted a tattoo on his arse, did they?"

"No need to get nasty," Nestor said, attempting a pout but finding his cheeks were not yet sufficiently thawed to effect one.

"I ain't begun to get nasty. Now gimme whatever ya got, straight out!"

Nestor put down his empty mug. "Fella's been seen twice outside Chepstow. Easy to spot, too. He's got yella curls, stringy and long as a girl's, and a scar down his cheek big as an eel. And he walks with a limp."

"The perfect disguise fer a secret agent."

"There's more."

"There better be if ya expect breakfast."

"I seen him myself in the Cock and Bull yesterday. And I heard the fellas he was talkin' with—Americans livin' here, I'm sure. I heard them use his name."

Cobb's ears pricked up.

"Sounded like Rung-gee."

Cobb smiled, feeling a portion of his grumpiness fade slightly. It was enough to take to Sarge, who would pass it along to the governor. On the other hand, maybe they'd all be better off if somebody did liberate Coltrane and take him back to the land of the free.

He sighed, and beckoned the waiter.

SIX

The messenger that Robert Baldwin had dispatched to Chepstow to seek an immediate interview for Marc with Caleb Coltrane returned an hour later with disquieting news. The major was fully booked for the day, with extensive afternoon interviews scheduled with the editors of the Hamilton *Free Press* and the Cobourg *Star*. In the evenings, it appeared, the captive commander reserved his time for reading and reflection. Moreover, at least two days' notice was normally required. However, in light of the fact that the request was being made in the name of a former military officer, an exception would be made and a Wednesday morning meeting would be entertained. Mr. Edwards might call on Major Coltrane at ten o'clock.

"Who does he think he is?" Robert fumed, as they stood open-mouthed, listening to the clerk read aloud Coltrane's written response, "some petty panjandrum offering an audience to a grovelling serf?"

"More to the point," said Marc, "is the eccentric behaviour of the man nominally in charge of the panjandrum's imprisonment."

Robert nodded. "You're right. Do you suppose that the victory parade before Christmas and all the public adulation since has softened Gideon Stanhope's brain?"

"Well, I intend to find out when I go there tomorrow, that's for sure."

"I'm sorry it couldn't happen today. It's not healthy to have Sergeant McNair locked up in our jail—not for him and not, I'm afraid, for the well-being of the citizenry."

"The natives are getting increasingly restless, aren't they?" Marc said.

A few minutes later he excused himself and headed straight up to Smallman's to bring Dolly the latest word and suggest that a timely visit to the prison, with food and fresh clothing, might go some way to preserving the sanity of her beau, and a long way towards reestablishing a broken engagement.

When Marc returned to Baldwin House, he encountered Dr. Baldwin on his way out.

"Marc," Baldwin greeted him, pausing on the porch, "you've done a good thing in getting Robert involved in this case. I haven't seen him this excited since Augusta died. Thank you."

Before Marc could respond, the elder Baldwin strode away down the walk with that much-admired air of confidence and purpose.

Robert was waiting for Marc in the vestibule with his coat and hat in hand. "I want you to come along with me," he said with some of the enthusiasm his father had just alluded to.

"Where are we going?"

"Up the street two and a half blocks, to call on a retired barrister."

As they headed north on Bay in the crisp, clear air of January, Robert explained the nature of their errand. Dr. Baldwin had gone to see Chief Justice Robinson the previous evening and proposed putting Coltrane's defense in the hands of the American émigré attorney, Richard Dougherty. In his quiet but forceful way he had presented the self-evident advantages of having the renegade major defended in the high court by a fellow Yankee, who was himself considered a renegade and a pariah by the New York legal bench. They had not actually disbarred Dougherty, but his moral turpitude had apparently been flagrant enough to see him squeezed quietly out of the profession and, as it happened, out of the country as well. If he agreed to accept the brief, then all that was required was that the chief justice should hold his nose and recommend Dougherty's admission to the Upper Canadian bar. His current flouting of decorum and decency would permit the benchers to promptly disbar him when he was no longer needed.

Robinson, a staunch Tory and astute jurist, immediately grasped the ingenuity of the proposal: Coltrane would be defended by a lawyer with an international (if debased) reputation and acknowledged skill. Thus the trial would be fair and legitimized. Coltrane would hang, of course, but he would be no martyr condemned out of hand. Robinson gave Baldwin his assurance that the moment Dougherty agreed to serve, he would be made a licensed lawyer in his adopted land. The two men, among the most powerful in the province, then shook hands.

"So all we have to do," Marc said with as little irony as he could manage, "is talk this scandalous creature, who hasn't done a lick of law for the two years since he came here and apparently doesn't need to, into taking on a hopeless case, whose political fallout he will readily discern?"

"You've got it all in a single sentence," Robert said, and nearly laughed.

Robert Baldwin was not a spendthrift with his laughter. At thirty-four and only six years older than Marc, he had the air and posture of a man who had decided to take the world seriously at the age of eighteen and only occasionally regretted it. Unfortunately, his natural solemnness had turned to melancholia after his wife's untimely death. For his part, Marc was happy enough to have such a person act as his legal principal as well as advisor in matters political and public. He knew he could not find a better tutor anywhere. As for Robert, he soon acknowledged and appreciated Marc's native wit and quick insights into human motive and behaviour. After all, Marc had lived on both sides of the political and class divide, had been a man of decisive action under fire, and was now a committed adherent of the Baldwins' obsession with responsible government. They had thus spent many evenings in the Baldwin family parlour, smoking their pipes and ruminating on the future the province might have when Lord Durham's report was completed. And sometimes they even discussed the finer points of the law.

As they crossed King Street, Marc said, "What sins is this chap supposed to have committed in New York that got him drummed out of town?"

"Well now, there are several tales to choose from. One story has it that he was an opium addict who fell asleep once too often during an address to the jury. Another insists that alcohol was his downfall, causing him to be belligerent with clients and outrageous to their ladies. A third has it on unimpeachable authority that he was a womanizer and frequenter of low-life brothels."

"I know a few gentlemen here who would qualify on all three grounds," Marc said dryly.

"Alas. But whatever his vices, it seems that the public flaunting of them became too much even for the New York bar and their claims to being egalitarian."

"'License they mean when they cry liberty!'" Marc intoned, quoting Milton.

"Exactly."

"Well then, I am looking forward to meeting such a paragon of unvirtue."

"You needn't wait long. We're here."

The house was set back from the street and shrouded in the

shadow of a dozen capacious evergreens, drooped with snow. The walkway was unshovelled and bereft of human footprint. Ahead of him Marc noticed a sturdy, utilitarian brick cottage of one storey, ungabled. The windows were frosted and seemed to cringe inward in self-defense. There was no knocker or bell pull.

"Not much of a residence for a blasphemous sinner, is it?" Robert said, as he raised a gloved fist and rapped on the door.

"Why advertise?" Marc replied, and when no sound was heard from within, added his fist to the rapping.

A further minute passed.

"No one's home," Robert said, disappointed.

"I'm sure I saw a shadow in that front window."

Sure enough, a few seconds later the heavy oak door was eased inward an inch, squealing on its hinges.

"Mr. Dougherty?" Robert queried anxiously.

"No," came the reply, tiny and feminine.

"Are you the maid?"

After a pause, "No."

"We'd like to see Mr. Dougherty, the attorney," Marc said. "Does he live here?"

"Yes." The door inched back yet again, exposing a swatch of blond hair and a single blue eye.

"We're here on urgent government business, miss," Robert said. "We must see Mr. Dougherty right away. Would you kindly convey that message to him, and inform him that we represent Baldwin and Sullivan, attorneys-at-law."

"We don't have visitors," the voice said, with enough volume for its youth and vulnerability to register. Then came a second voice from the depths of the house.

"For Christ's sake, Celia, open the goddamn door and let Mr. Baldwin and his lackey in!"

There was no hallway or vestibule. Marc and Robert stepped immediately into the parlour with their dripping overcoats and slush-covered boots. The frosted windows, curtained thickly, let in little light, but a smoky blaze in the hearth offered an uncertain glow in which they were able to make out the figure of the young woman pointing them towards a ponderous, horsehair, wingback chair beside the fender, and a pair of bare feet with wriggling toes resting upon a footstool next to it. A penumbra of cigar smoke rippled above the chair back like an agitated feather boa.

The young woman—she could not have been more than eighteen—had the blondest hair Marc had ever seen, and her skin was so white as to be almost transparent. But when she turned to face the visitors and present them to the profane voice in the chair, her eyes, blue as cornflower steeped in sunlight, indicated that she was not albino. Her dress was little more than a cotton shift and clung to her woman's silhouette like wet silk. She wore no stays or corsets. And her beauty left Marc momentarily stunned and unaccountably distressed.

"I apologize for shouting, my dear. Now would you be kind enough to rustle up some coffee and edibles for our guests?" Even when it was not shouting, the voice—its progenitor still hidden behind the wing of the chair and its angled back—literally boomed, delivering its message with a tragedian's trajectory.

"Yes, Uncle," the girl said, and fled.

"Come in, gentlemen. We mustn't keep the government from doing its business, eh?"

Robert was glancing about in search of a place for his hat and coat.

"Jesus, throw the goddamn thing on that stool over there and park your arse on that chair. I haven't got all day to waste on William Baldwin's best boy. I've got a nap to take!"

Doubtful Dick Dougherty was holding forth on the woeful inadequacies of the courts, the justices, and the Upper Canadian legal system in general, as if Marc and Robert were a two-man jury unsympathetic to the prosecution's case. It is doubtful, however, whether either was much affected by his grandiloquence. They were still in shock and staring. Richard Dougherty had been born large and imposing, with a lumberjack's bones and a wrestler's physique, and had apparently set about, as one of his life's tasks, to enlarge it. His black bottle-brush brows leapt straight out, their impertinence exaggerated by the contrast of his bald and gleaming pate. His ears, tufted and crenellated, flapped like a rooster's wings in unsuccessful flight. His nose was gargantuan, fleshy and sagging, except for a pugnacious upturn at its very tip. His lips were protuberant and sensuous, made more so by their being set below a pair of bloated, rubicund cheeks and above an endless ripple of pale, pink chins. The latter did not so much hang as ooze over his collar, inundating it and the cravat beneath it.

A plaid, food-stained waistcoat had attempted to contain the mountainous chest and belly and given up. Its extruded buttons lay dangling on errant thread, and hairy yolks of flesh pressed up and through, as if seeking air. The trousers, agape where they shouldn't be, were supported not by his suspenders (one of which, cast adrift, dribbled forlornly down a leg) but by a kimono sash knotted at the left hip. In fact, the only thing diminutive about Counsellor Dougherty were his eyes, just visible deep in their pouches of flesh: tiny, green, piggish, and as tough as a pair of withered black-eyed peas.

"Contrary to the views of the hoi polloi, the American experiment was not launched over the tawdry business of tea and import duties and rep by pop. No, gentlemen, our magnificent Constitution was a direct and necessary response to the inescapable corruptions that follow upon the executive appointment of judges to posts they can only be persuaded to vacate upon death and, even then, reluctantly." At this witticism, he paused to flick the ashes of his cigar upon the only unblemished spot on his waistcoat and laughed—something between a chuckle and a whinny.

Neither Marc nor Robert seized the opportunity to stem the monologue's tide, for they were still trying to take in the fascinating anomalies of the émigré's household. On three sides of Dougherty's chair, as far as his reach or whim would permit, was the same dissolute disorder that characterized his person and clothing. Scattered about within this self-imposed perimeter were dozens of books, tossed on their backs, pages aflutter, ripped apart where they had struck stone or iron, scorched by the adjacent fire, thumbed, and bookmarked. Helter-skelter among them were cigar butts, coils of pipe ash, mouldy bread crusts, rotting apple cores, a broken wine goblet, and several discarded (and overused) handkerchiefs. However, beyond this personally supervised hemisphere of chaos, the room was as neat as a royal chamber. The chairs on which the guests sat opposite their host were clean and comfortable. Oriental throw rugs and polished tables, a sideboard with gleaming crystal decanters, framed portraits and certificates on the walls, and dust-free china figurines on the mantel—all suggested a tidy and industrious hand at work. Celia's, most likely.

As if privy to Marc's thoughts, the young woman appeared with a tray. While Dougherty followed her every move with a darting eye, Celia—unaccustomed, it seemed, to the protocol of distinguished callers—managed to pour their coffee with a minimum of spillage and only a single, prolonged blush. She did not offer her uncle any; he flicked a finger and sent her scurrying to stir the fire, which had begun to flag. As she bent over to do so, the flimsy shift rode up upon her calves, and just before Marc succeeded in averting his eyes, he was certain he caught Dougherty leering at her. When he looked back, Celia had taken a white cloth out of the pocket of her dress and was wiping the sweat from her uncle's forehead and hairless dome with slow, tender strokes.

"Be sure and tell Brodie to say good-bye before he goes off, will you?" Dougherty said to her.

"Yes, Uncle. You know he always does," she said, and left.

"Miss Langford and her brother are not my niece and nephew," he said to his guests. "They're the children of my late, lamented law partner. As they had no one else, I brought them with me."

Robert cleared his throat. "I'm sure you suspect that we have not come here today to pay you a belated social call or exchange views on constitutional practice, as edifying as that would no doubt prove."

Dougherty may have smiled, but it was hard to be sure because his lips were continuously in motion, as if they were forever about to formulate a phrase or were just finishing one, while his eyes were correspondingly still, sequestered in flesh, and watchful. "I would say the question has already moved beyond suspicion," he said. "My bones tell me not only that it is close to nap time, but that you gentlemen are here to discuss the sham legal proceedings concocted by Sir George and shamelessly agreed to by your 'independent' judiciary."

Robert blinked but did not falter. "My father and I are concerned that Caleb Coltrane get a fair trial."

Marc was wondering how Dougherty, who had not been espied in the open air since his arrival two years before, knew so much about the local scene, particularly as he saw no sign of discarded newspapers among the detritus.

"That's noble of you, Mr. Baldwin, but a fair trial implies an impartially empanelled jury, a disinterested judge, and appropriate legal counsel."

"I am here, sir, to guarantee the first two."

This time Dougherty was genuinely amused. He gave out with his horse laugh, initiating a rippling of chins and a spray of spittle. "And you'd like me to guarantee the third?"

"Can you think of anyone more qualified?" Robert said. "And partial to the accused and his cause?"

"The latter point is, as you ought to know, irrelevant. As

barristers, we are sworn to pursue the law, not causes or clients with causes, however laudable."

"But you must see, sir," Marc said, "that a court-appointed and, shall we say, less than enthusiastic local attorney would not only be detrimental to Coltrane's defense but would be perceived as—"

"—a typical British ploy to guarantee the wretch's conviction?"

"Something like that."

"Perceived by whom? By my compatriots in the United States, eh? With the risk of more border raids and discomfort for Sir George and his merry men."

Robert looked down. "I must confess that that motive is the one animating the governor and the chief justice." Then he looked up and said with passion, "But it is not my motive, sir, nor my father's. You must realize that not every citizen of this province is a Tory, nor is every man loyal to the Crown a fawning Jacobite. I belong to a party that has promoted responsible government for this colony for more than a dozen years. We have high hopes that, if the madness of these border raids can be curtailed, Lord Durham's recommendations will be instituted, reforms that will give us a substantial measure of autonomy and personal liberty."

"Lord Durham is no Tallyrand," Dougherty said, "but he has some acceptable notions that a more thorough reading of the *Federalist Papers* would sharpen and improve."

"What I'm saying, sir, is that a genuinely fair trial for Coltrane would best serve everybody's interests. An end to these suicidal raids would enhance the Reform group's efforts to introduce responsible government. Coltrane would get a first-class defense. Neither Sir George nor Justice Robinson could, or could be seen to, manipulate the process or predict the outcome."

"And me?" Dougherty suppressed a yawn, but his attention was fierce.

It was Marc who replied. "You win admittance to the Upper Canadian bar and an opportunity to show the world, here and back home, that you still have what it takes."

"You're telling me that John Beverley Robinson, who was born with a poker up his arse, is going to bend down and buss my big toe after I waddle into Lawyers' Hall?" The green eyes ignited, and suddenly those were the only features of his outrageous face worthy of notice.

Robert held that gaze in his own. "I am. In fact, the way has already been cleared." (That the man would likely be disbarred the day after Coltrane hanged need not be mentioned.)

Unfortunately, Broderick Langford chose this moment to enter the room from the kitchen, taking two tentative steps and pausing to stare at the interlopers. They stared back.

Noting their amazement, Dougherty laughed again. "Come on in, Brodie, and meet these gentlemen of the law."

Dougherty's "nephew" was a near copy of his sister. He too was alabaster blond, with curls only slightly shorter than Celia's, startling blue eyes, and almost bleached skin. He was of slight build and impeccably dressed. A youthful intelligence shone in his eyes. He shook hands with the visitors, touched Dougherty fondly on the shoulder, and went back to the inner door. "I'll be at the bank until about eight."

They heard a far door open and close.

"Brodie labours at the Commercial Bank. He's doing well."

The room fell silent. The pouches above Dougherty's eyes met those below them. He was sweating. The littered expanse of his waistcoat rose and sighed.

"Have you read *The Republic,* Mr. Baldwin?"

"I have. Some time ago."

"In the original Greek?"

"I'm afraid my school Greek didn't take me that far."

"No one remotely interested in political constitutions can ignore that great treatise. And there aren't enough words in our paltry lexicon to capture its logical niceties. The Athenians were born to articulate law. We eschew them at our peril."

"And what about the *Euthyphro*?" Marc said quietly.

The slit in the eye pouches widened slightly. "You are referring, of course, to Euthyphro's boast to Socrates that one must prosecute a murder, even if the accused be one's own father."

Marc smiled. "I am. And would not the same ethic apply, obversely, to the need of the accused, however heinous he may be, for a proper defense?"

Dougherty was now looking directly at them—first one, then the other—as he might scrutinize and appraise witnesses on the stand. Seemingly satisfied with whatever he discerned, he spoke.

"I have decided to be Mr. Coltrane's defense attorney," he said without emphasis. "I am fully aware of the risks and unpredictable consequences. If I lose, I may be seen in the country to the south of us as a turncoat and dupe of a detested monarchy. I care not about that. I have burned all those bridges—or, rather, they have been burned for me and the water under them poisoned. Nor do I give a fig for the petty and intractable political squabbling you've all got yourselves into. I disdained it in New York, which no doubt contributed to my squalid downfall. But I was nonetheless devoted to the spirit and letter of Jefferson's liberative words, and to the law itself."

A sudden and unexpected animation seized his wayward features, sending askew earlobe, jowl, nostril, eyebrow, cheek pouch, and dewlap. "Only the law with its crisp, incorruptible language is worthy of our passion and our humility. All else is 'writ in water,' as the poet said."

"You won't regret this, sir," Robert said.

"Indeed, I may, Mr. Baldwin. That is the whole point of risk.

But be forewarned. I am taking this brief with a single objective in mind."

"You're not serious," Marc said, before he could help himself.

"I am. I fully intend to see that the wicked Mr. Coltrane is acquitted."

Outside on the snowy walk, Robert sucked in the cleansing, wintry air and said to Marc, "It looks as if any or all of the stories about the man's demise could be true."

"I was not impressed by the way he had that young woman dressed or the manner in which he ogled her. I hope that's all he does."

"I don't think I've ever encountered such a distasteful mien. But, oh, the *mind* inside that repellent body!"

"Whatever happened in New York was a tragedy of sorts, don't you think?"

"What I'm thinking is that we may have crossed some moral or ethical divide here. Are we being merely expedient? And does the end justify the means?"

"Well, he may do his damnedest to keep the major from the noose, but it'll take more than a New York lawyer to get Coltrane off. The Crown has a dozen witnesses to his atrocities. And his claim to military status will hold no water in the Court of Queen's Bench."

"True. And the more vigorously Dougherty argues, the more he serves Sir George's purpose to have both a proper trial and an outcome favourable to Her Majesty."

As they turned into the British-American Coffee House for tea and scones, Marc asked, "By the way, how did Dougherty get the nickname of Doubtful Dick? Was it a question of reliability as his vices began to affect his performance?"

Robert stopped. "Lord, no. He got that moniker in mid-career, an ironic and somewhat barbed tribute from his peers, but a tribute nonetheless."

"What do you mean?"

"Well, whenever he went to trial in New York, the result was, in fact, never in doubt. Dougherty has yet to lose a capital case."

SEVEN

The next morning found Marc strolling in leisurely fashion westward along Front Street. It was out of his way, but he had plenty of time to get to his ten o'clock appointment at Chepstow, and besides, he never missed an opportunity to view the bay in wintertime. Lake Ontario was iced over as far as the eye could travel, and only a fringe of evergreens and other skeletal trees suggested the presence of the peninsula and nearby islands between him and the distant shore. The snowdrifts that rippled the near distance, the island woods, and the white plain beyond created the comfortable illusion of a unified groundswell upon a solid, unbroken foundation. A few yards offshore near the Queen's Wharf, Marc could see a gang of youths on skates, playing some age-old game of tag on a rectangular area they had cleared of snow. He even imagined a son of his own doing the same someday.

By now the memory of this morning's brief exchange of views over Beth's going in to work a full day had begun to fade. (She had merely pointed out that with the gala coming up on the weekend and Dolly nearly useless in the shop, she had no choice in the matter.) However, passing by Somerset House, where the Twelfth Night extravaganza was to take place, brought their argument back to him. When Marc had suggested that the baby's intermittent kicking during the night was an obvious protest against rough treatment received at Smallman's, he knew he had gone too far. He had conceded defeat but less than graciously, he regretted. As he turned north up Peter Street, he was thankful to direct all his thoughts towards the difficult task ahead.

None of the habitual protesters had chosen Chepstow as their target that morning, and Marc was able to approach the front door unimpeded. He passed a pair of uniformed sentries and pulled the bell rope. As he waited, he quickly reviewed the salient points in his planned approach to Caleb Coltrane. As Marc saw it, he had two trump cards to play. First, he could claim justifiably that he had helped secure for the major the services of a skilled New York lawyer. Second, he would reveal to him the sobering truth that the young man he had challenged to a duel and landed in jail was the enemy soldier who had saved him from bleeding to death four weeks earlier. The rest would have to be improvised, and Marc trusted his own ability to read character and manage personalities in shifting circumstances. It had not let him down thus far—well, not very often anyway.

The door was opened by a man in full morning dress, the coat and trousers each a size and a half too large. His hair was greased and parted down the middle, and an ill-trimmed moustache did little to distract attention from a broken and indifferently set nose. His brown eyes watered perpetually, causing him to blink like a hound who's been skunked. Marc almost laughed, for he seemed a parody of the English stage butler.

"Good mornin', sir. Who shall I say has come to call?"

Marc caught the Yankee twang under the British phraseology. "Would you inform Mr. Stanhope that Mr. Edwards has come to keep his appointment with the prisoner."

"Major Coltrane?"

"The same."

"You bin approved, then?"

Marc smiled. "I believe I have."

"I'll inform the colonel. He insists on screenin' all the major's callers."

And Marc felt himself being thoroughly screened by the colonel's man, before the latter turned and slow-trotted down a hallway. Marc stepped inside and knocked the snow off his boots. He was glad that Gideon Stanhope was here to greet and preapprove him. He was as curious about Coltrane's solicitous jailer as he was about his prisoner.

They met in Stanhope's study, a pleasant if overfurnished room.

"You'll have to pardon my butler," Stanhope began the moment the fellow had left them. "He tries hard to please, but he hasn't quite got on to our ways."

"He's American?"

"He is. My wife brought Absalom here several years ago upon the recommendation of her sister in Port Huron."

"As you know, sir, I have come to see the notorious Mr. Coltrane."

Colonel Stanhope's regimental moustache twitched. The fellow was in full regalia, including his sabre in its ornamented scabbard. His shako cap and greatcoat lay on a nearby chair—at the ready for what, Marc could not imagine. The overall impression was of a rigid self-discipline. His soldier's back was as straight and taut as a yeoman's bow. It was difficult to believe that less than a year ago Stanhope had been a prosperous importer of English goods whose main claim to public attention had been his manor house and his bank account. But Marc knew from personal experience never to underestimate the allure of a uniform and its capacity to alter a man's priorities.

"We refer to him here as Major Coltrane, whatever Sir George may think or wish."

"So I've heard," Marc said evenly. "But you are aware, are you not, that many of the same citizens who cheered you heartily on Yonge Street in December are not pleased with the way you have been hosting your prisoner?"

Stanhope essayed a smile but succeeded only in making his moustache quiver and his chin flinch. "I have only to look out my front window every morning to see that, sir. But you of all people ought to understand the absolute necessity of adhering to military protocol."

It was Marc's turn to smile. "As an officer, I don't recall billeting captured rebels in my home and giving them the unfettered pleasure of a steady stream of visitors."

"Well, you must judge these conditions for yourself, sir, when you visit the major. My point, however, is that Coltrane is a fellow officer, and I fully intend to keep treating him as such until his trial has begun and he is taken out of my jurisdiction. And when you've had a chance to meet him, I believe you'll agree that he is not only a true soldier but a remarkable man."

"I'm told you and he were face-to-face at Pelee last March?"

"We were, though we did not know it at the time."

"At which battle you won your spurs, so to speak?"

"You're referring to this nonsense about my being dubbed the Pelee Island Patriot?"

"I've suffered the embarrassment of similar appellations."

"I know. And so you'll realize that it is one's actions—in battle and after—that really matter, not the trappings of fame."

Like parades down Yonge Street or places of honour at the Twelfth Night Charity Ball, Marc thought. "So you don't mind that Coltrane has claimed the same appellation for himself?"

Stanhope's gaze narrowed and his moustache did a nervous jig. "Major Coltrane is a Yankee, sir. Braggadocio is part of his charm."

"But he is still a soldier worthy of special treatment?"

"Most certainly. He distinguished himself at Windsor, and as second-in-command was compelled to lead the assault force when his own general, Lucius Bierce, remained a mile or more behind his troops. While gravely wounded, the major kept his head and organized an orderly withdrawal of his men, even as Bierce scrambled aboard his ship and took off for Detroit. The major engineered an ambush against our pursuers—devastating for us, but perfectly understandable from a tactical viewpoint. Then, convinced that he was dying, he gave orders that his troop were to abandon him and escape to the river, which they did, all of them returning safely home."

"Which is when Sergeant McNair found him and brought him and his papers to you?"

Stanhope's gaze tightened. "Yes. I recognized instantly that we had captured their de facto commander, and in his kit Sergeant McNair had found a set of strategic plans covering the next three months along the western border. They have since proved invaluable in dampening down the raids and even the threat of raids."

Marc hesitated a moment, as if absorbing this irrefutable truth, then said, "So you can't have been too pleased when the same heroic sergeant was found in your garden with a smoking pistol in his hand and your prisoner a mere twenty paces away."

Stanhope's response was unexpectedly mild. "I was not. Billy McNair was a fine NCO, a source of great pride to me as his mentor and commanding officer. I thought he understood the awful necessities of being a soldier. Indeed, throughout the entire month we spent in the western district and during the action at Windsor, he behaved in exemplary fashion. Even after the fiasco and slaughter at the fort, he was disciplined enough to bind up Major Coltrane's wound, search his person, secure those critical papers, and then bring him straight to me—all the while grieving the loss of his best friend."

"Those who know Billy McNair will not be surprised to hear that."

"I understand you too lost a friend down at St. Denis."

Marc nodded. "Like Billy, I could do nothing to save him."

"We all lose friends and acquaintances in battle, don't we? But we can't let that turn us into savages, wreaking vengeance on helpless prisoners or innocent civilians."

Marc had witnessed the horrific consequences of retaliation in Quebec the year before. "No, we can't," he agreed.

"And that is why I am treating Major Coltrane with all the respect and courtesy due a captured enemy commander, and why I am doing it publicly. If the governor wants to try the major as a common cutthroat, then let that be on his conscience, not mine."

"Nonetheless, sir, you are taking a great risk that Coltrane will be sprung loose by his compatriots, whose sympathizers are everywhere amongst us, or that he will be assassinated by one of the many visitors you allow him to entertain."

"There you are wrong, sir. As you will see, the chamber downstairs is barred and reinforced, I have my own militiamen at the back gates day and night, the regular army patrols the street at intervals and guards the front door, and Lieutenant Bostwick has been assigned as the major's full-time jailer. He sleeps in the anteroom next to the prison chamber."

"The same gentleman found umpiring the illegal duel?"

Stanhope sucked in several breaths in an effort to swallow his anger. "That sad business has been taken care of."

"Has it? With Billy McNair in prison without bail and Coltrane living like a pasha in your home?"

"The lad was unforgivably reckless. Had he succeeded in killing the major, he would have deprived the governor of his trial and stained my honour for all time. I have given my word to Sir George: the major will be delivered to the Court House next week healthy and whole. As far as I'm concerned, Billy McNair is on his own."

Marc said nothing to this callous remark. "What puzzles me most about the duel, sir, is how Caleb Coltrane contrived to get

Billy, Lieutenant Bostwick, and two loaded pistols into your garden at dawn."

Stanhope's face brightened into a practised congeniality, the kind he must have used to ingratiate himself with his customers in the mercantile life he seemed now to have abandoned as frivolous and unmanly. "Ah, Lieutenant Edwards, that is easy to explain. Major Coltrane is a most beguiling man—as you're about to learn."

He extended his hand to Marc, signalling the end of their conversation, and informed him that the butler would direct him down to the prisoner. But Absalom was not in the hall when Marc reentered it. Having spotted a stairwell near the front door when he had come in, Marc assumed that it led to the lower chambers and headed towards it. One of the hall doors was ajar, and as he passed by, he heard female voices behind it, raised in anger. He stopped to listen.

"Abe tells me you were down there this morning for more than an hour! What on earth are you thinking of? The man will be dead in three weeks!"

"It was only half an hour, and I won't be spied upon by that little toad!"

"In this house you'll do as you're told, and as your father wishes."

"And it's Papa, remember, who's given me orders to serve Caleb his breakfast and take the tray away when he's finished."

"It doesn't take an hour to eat sausages and eggs!"

"So he likes to talk. What's wrong with that? And is it a crime that a man—a real man—should find me pretty?"

"Lots of men find you pretty, my darling. You're going to be a sensation at the ball on Saturday."

There was a pause here, and Marc, somewhat embarrassed to be eavesdropping, was about to move on, when the dialogue started up again.

"What did you say?"

"I said I'm not going to the ball!"

"Don't talk such foolishness. Your father is counting on you."

"He just wants another pretty creature in a dress to decorate the podium and show the town what a fine and prosperous gentleman they have in their midst!"

"Where did you get such an idea?"

"Caleb says—"

"Caleb, Caleb, Caleb! Is that all you can talk about from morning till night?"

"You're just jealous—"

"Don't be stupid, girl. Caleb Coltrane is a cold-blooded killer and a user of women. I don't want you spending any more time down there than you absolutely have to, do you hear?"

"Caleb says I'm too beautiful to go to a ball in a hand-me-down dress."

"So that's it, is it? You're too proud to put on a magnificent gown worn on a single occasion months ago—just because it belongs to me."

"It's the wrong colour. Caleb says it clashes with the delicate tones of my skin."

"Well, you can tell Caleb when you take him his breakfast tomorrow morning that you've had a second fitting, despite your delicate skin colour. Your father will be driving you to the dressmaker's this afternoon."

At this, a far door slammed. Marc then heard a soft weeping and another door opening.

"Oh, Abe, what am I going to do?"

"It'll be all right, ma'am. You'll see."

At the end of the hall a large, florid face swam into view.

"You come to see the prisoner?" Lardner Bostwick called out to Marc.

•   •   •

Gideon Stanhope was right about one thing: the rooms designed to contain Coltrane were a substantial and well-fortified prison. Following the burly, uniformed Bostwick down the stairs, Marc came into a spacious, fully furnished anteroom with a good-sized window at one end. This was no cellar. As Chepstow was built into the slope of a hill, this section at the back was really a ground floor, one which had likely been intended as servants' quarters. A low wooden door near the bottom of the stairs no doubt led to a wine and root cellar. But straight ahead Marc was confronted by an iron-reinforced door, secured by thick hinges and a formidable padlock.

"We keep his majesty in there," Bostwick said, and Marc winced at the whiskey breeze that blew past him. "When he wants something, which is quite often, he raps three times." Bostwick gave out a congested chortle, coughed twice, and reached down for a key from among several chained to his belt. "The silly bugger likes codes."

"Is he expecting me?"

"If he wasn't, you wouldn't be here. Now, sir, please sign your name and the time in that big book over there. The colonel wants a strict record kept of everyone goin' in and outta here."

Marc signed in, noting the familiar names of a number of previous visitors. They represented a cross-section of political interests. One was surely meant as a joke: E. Mohican. Something unusual was drawing people who should know better to converse with a character who was, on the face of it, a foreign outlaw. Marc's curiosity intensified as he watched Bostwick fumble with the key in a vain attempt to control the shakes that gripped him. "I'm comin' in with yer guest, Coltrane, so I better find ya behind yer desk when I open this here door!"

Marc smiled at this, suspecting that if it were not for the constant presence of militia sentries and regular-army patrols, the prisoner would easily overpower his inebriated jailer, who would be lucky to find his sword, let alone draw it for deployment. Marc did wonder though whether, as the trial date approached, Coltrane would not attempt to take the colonel's wife or daughter hostage. The colonel's naive trust in soldierly conduct could prove to be tragically misguided. As an officer once in charge of security at Government House, Marc concluded that these security arrangements, whatever the structural adaptations of the chamber itself, were seriously flawed. He would speak to Wilfrid Sturges about it soon.

The heavy door swung open on well-oiled hinges.

The man who seemed to have mesmerized an entire community sat waiting for him in a padded chair behind an impressive oaken desk. He was taking snuff.

"You seem to forget, my good fellow, that it was a citizen army under the command of amateur generals who, inspired only by the power of an ideal, managed to defeat the most potent military force in the world. That same spirit, the democratic ethos, is sending thousands upon thousands of young men who love liberty to our recruiting centres. The United States Army conveniently leaves its armouries unguarded, so that we are even now building up a formidable ordnance and massing troops along your borders."

Caleb Coltrane, accoutered in his major's getup, sans pistol and sabre, was talking—something he liked to do almost as much as soldiering. Marc was quite content to have him do so, for his plan was to get Coltrane comfortable with him before presenting his proposal concerning Billy. That did not prove difficult. The major was accustomed to conquering his visitors with the force of his personality and his skill with words. Certainly his physical presence was imposing. While of medium build, he gave the impression of size with his ruffed hair, hawk's nose, menacing chin, and penetrating glance. While his irregular tunic was meant to impress, it was nevertheless worn carelessly, as if the man inside it were too important and preoccupied to be bothered with neatness or decorum.

"I'm quite familiar with the campaigns of Burgoyne and Washington, Mr. Coltrane. I trained at Sandhurst," Marc said.

"You don't have to have gone to West Point or Sandhurst to be an effective officer. My superiors at Pelee had been to military school, and none of them could organize a poke in a whorehouse. I was the only one who didn't lose his head in that fiasco. My men fought like tigers, like the minutemen at Concord, but they were betrayed by inept leadership. I vowed that would not happen the next time."

"Colonel Stanhope certainly seems to admire your battlefield prowess."

Coltrane's dark eyes glittered with contempt. "That pompous martinet! Don't even mention his name in the same breath as mine!"

Marc was taken aback. Had the prisoner shown his indulgent host this kind of dismissive scorn? Surely not. Still, the colonel's naiveté seemed bottomless.

"My impression is that he—though a brevet colonel in the militia—is nonetheless a man of military bearing who observes the strict protocol of his profession. Moreover, he has twice been wounded in battle. I thought you would be more sympathetic."

"What you fail to appreciate, Edwards, is that what you see here about you—a carpeted room with a cozy fire, a capacious desk for my work, a never-empty wine decanter on the sideboard, three shelves of books and mementoes—all this has been accorded me because of who *I* am, not who the colonel thinks *he* is. I am the commander of a citizen's army, ten thousand strong, chosen by Fate to liberate the enslaved peoples of Canada from the chains that bind them."

"But these same people seem to have chosen slavery, have they not?"

Coltrane chuckled. He reached over and opened an ornate, silver snuff box in front of him, one of two such, sitting beside a leather Bible. Marc was accustomed to seeing gentlemen take a pinch of snuff between thumb and forefinger, place it below a nostril, and decorously sniff it. But Coltrane set a thick wad on the back of his weakened left hand, leaned down to it, and gave a loud snort with a flared nostril. He blinked, sighed, and repeated the procedure with the other nostril. Marc politely declined to join him.

"Bierce was a worse fool than he was a coward. That proclamation he read at Windsor village was rhetorical drivel."

"The locals certainly thought so. It was, after all, a citizen's army that defeated you in Baby's orchard."

"That was precisely the problem for us. Our best hope of liberating this pathetic backwater is to do what George Washington and William Henry Harrison did: defeat the British regulars, who are the armed agents of the Crown and the prima facie oppressors of the people. Reading proclamations and conducting monthly border raids will not put backbone into the serf who has been so long enslaved he knows no better. What we require, and are preparing to effect, is a showdown battle with the redcoats, like Waterloo or Saratoga." Here he glanced cryptically at the papers on his desk.

Marc suddenly recalled Bostwick's remarks that the man was fond of codes. Could he be orchestrating an invasion from this very chamber? Did those newspaper articles that the obliging editors had so enthusiastically printed actually contained hidden instructions? Was this braggart, self-styled major gleaning information from the very worthies who assumed they were picking *his* brain?

"But you won't be here to take part in any such battle," Marc said quietly.

Coltrane grinned. "We'll have to wait and see about that, won't we?" he said, and took another gargantuan snort of snuff. It brought tears to his eyes. "You should try this tonic, Edwards. I never indulge before ten in the morning, but when I do, I wake up to the world like a hibernating bear, hungry for the day!"

"I'm a pipe smoker myself."

"Dulls the mind, Edwards. Makes a man content and self-satisfied. And that's the state in which a citizen's liberty is most likely to be snatched from him."

"Milton spoke of the confusion of license with liberty, did he not, in his *Areopagitica*?"

"That petty sod! What about Voltaire and Paine and Rousseau? What about Franklin and Jefferson? You English are stuck with religious zealots like Milton and cynics like Hobbes and Bentham."

"You've found time to read all these gentlemen?"

Coltrane leaned back in his chair to the point where it approached tipping, and roared with laughter. "By the Christ, I like you, Edwards. You keep talking straight from the shoulder like that and we'll soon make a Yankee out of you!"

"I'll need to be convinced first." Marc was now certain that Coltrane was enjoying their conversation and that the moment was nearing when the delicate business of the duel could be broached.

"You presume, of course, that because I am a Yankee and not reluctant to enumerate the permanent advances that America has made in the evolution of the human species, I'm an unlettered boor. Such misconceptions do not bother us in the least. In fact they play directly into our plans for the future of the race." At this he rose and walked with great dignity over to the bookcase, which sat beside the curtained doorway to what must have been a sleeping chamber. Marc noticed that Coltrane's left arm swung awkwardly at his side.

"I have read all these books, many of them several times. Not in their original tongues, alas, because, unlike you, I was not born with a silver spoon between my gums. I had to go to work at age thirteen and abandon my formal schooling. But as America grows to become the greatest nation on earth, its language will soon be the lingua franca of the world. Nonetheless, it has already given me Caesar and Hannibal and Alexander and Pericles. That batch of newspapers there just arrived from Buffalo this morning. It includes the *Times* of London."

"I am impressed. You must be beholden to your host."

Coltrane ignored the barb. "And on this shelf, and there on the right side of my desk, you'll see part of my extensive collection of old-world snuff boxes. I had them shipped up here from Detroit." He picked one off the shelf with his good hand and fondled it as he might a lover's breast. "This one is from Bohemia, handcrafted in Prague about 1706. The filigree at the base is a continuous ring of succubi. Beautiful to behold and delightful to the touch."

He came over and sat down again. "Now, Edwards, it is clear you have not come here merely to gape at the circus grotesque. Tell me what you really want."

"You are correct in your assumption. I have come to ask a great favour of you. That you are evidently a man of refinement and learning ought to make my task that much easier."

So, while Coltrane sat and listened without interruption—except for periodic snorts of snuff—Marc explained the consequences of Billy's involvement in the duel. He stressed the obduracy of Sir George in regard to bail and Billy's assent to Robert Baldwin's proposal. Billy would sign a peace bond, pen a guarantee not to issue any false or libelous statements regarding Coltrane's behaviour at Windsor, and agree to stay in his house until charges were dropped or prosecuted.

"He genuinely regrets what happened," Marc finished up.

"I'll bet he does. The fellow is a hothead and a know-nothing. He got himself into this mess, didn't he? Why should I feel pity for him?"

"True, he did threaten to spread libels about you, but it was you who took umbrage and challenged him to a duel, an event which only you could somehow arrange in here."

"You know perfectly well I could have shot his brains out."

"I assumed that. Your bullet was dug out yards from its target.

Conversely, it is not inconceivable that Billy might have shot you, however feckless he might have been with a pistol."

Coltrane's gaze did not waver. "I know that. But I've survived two battles already, and I am not destined to die just yet."

"In a battle we have to think that, don't we?"

"True. Also, it seemed the only way to prevent the slanders, whatever the risk to my person. They were bound to be believed— here for certain and perhaps even by my enemies at home."

"Your reputation means that much to you, that you would let Billy take a free shot at you?"

"What else do we have, besides our life and our virginity, that can be lost only once?"

"And since you are now approaching your trial and possible—"

"Do I look like a man worried about the gallows?"

Marc had to agree that Coltrane showed no such signs. Perhaps as the day drew closer, though, that might change.

"Surely Sergeant McNair's promise to refrain from any slanders is exactly what you wanted out of this situation in the first place?"

"What good is his word, eh? I'll need more compelling reasons than that flimsy hope."

Marc played his first trump card. "Robert Baldwin has agreed to be Billy's defense counsel. As an earnest of his good faith, he has arranged for you to be represented next week by a renowned New York lawyer here in Toronto, a chap named Richard Dougherty."

Coltrane sneezed extravagantly, sending snuff across the papers on his desk. "Doubtful Dick!" He laughed.

"The same."

"Well, tell Mr. Baldwin thank you, but should I actually end up in court, an eventuality quite remote, then I intend to defend myself. And thoroughly enjoy doing so."

Bravura or bravado? It was impossible to say.

Marc had one card remaining. "I believe you ought to inform Sir George that you consider Billy McNair no threat to your safety and that the duel was merely a pro forma affair to salvage your honour. And I believe you should do so because it was Sergeant McNair who saved your life back there at the fort."

Coltrane was surprised at this assertion. He took several seconds to let its import register. For a moment a flicker of doubt, obviously a rare occurrence, showed itself. Then he grinned. "That's absurd. I collapsed in the woods after ordering my men safely away. I woke up in an army hospital, a captive. I was told that McNair dumped me on a travois and hauled me back to his master's tent like a trophy."

"Then how did the tourniquet that prevented your bleeding to death get onto that ruined arm of yours? Did you put it on yourself?"

"I assumed one of their medics did that."

"They had no surgeon out in the field. It was McNair who did it, minutes after your ambuscade took his best friend's life."

Coltrane sat back. Unconsciously he reached over and touched the upper portion of his crippled left arm. "How do I know it was he? He's already threatened to spread lies about me. Besides, it could have been any one of a dozen men there that day."

"He used a silk kerchief that his fiancée had given him as a good-luck token."

Coltrane took this in slowly, perhaps thinking back to what he could recall of that fateful morning near Windsor. Then the smile reappeared, and this time it was edged with the kind of cunning confidence he had shown throughout the interview. "Well, he'll be pleased to know I've hung on to it. I figured it had helped me survive, so I put it away among my souvenirs. It's in one of those kit bags over there."

"Then you'll know Billy's telling the truth."

"Why don't you describe it for me."

Marc flinched but managed to say, "He told me it was silk, orange with some figures or pattern on it."

"I've seen a lot of ladies' kerchiefs like that."

"I'll get a detailed description of it for you," Marc said quickly, upbraiding himself for not doing so earlier.

"Better still, why don't you bring the boy back here tomorrow, so I can look him in the eye and he can tell me all about his girl-friend's tourniquet? Can you arrange that?"

"I'm sure I can," Marc said, not at all sure, considering Sir George's intransigence. "First thing in the morning."

"Make it the afternoon, say, one o'clock."

"All right. Then what?"

"Then, if I'm satisfied, I'll do what I can to help the little weasel out of his predicament. If I give Sir George a further case of the jitters, then that'll be a bonus, won't it?" He laughed, then added, "And tell Doubtful Dick that I'll think about letting him join my legal team—as a junior."

Marc duly signed out while Lardner Bostwick, half a bottle of sherry further into inebriation, lurched and grunted to get the cell door closed and secured. Whatever punishment the colonel had doled out for his jailer's earlier transgressions, it had not included outright dismissal. Marc found his hat and coat on the hall tree by the front door, put them on, and stepped out into the cold sun-shine. As he was pulling the door closed, he caught a glimpse of a slim female figure darting down the stairs leading to the prison chamber. Uh-oh.

He nodded to the sentries and, whistling with satisfaction, headed east on Hospital Street. On a whim, he decided to have a look at the garden and Coltrane's apartment from the rear, thinking he would be able to talk his way past any guard posted there. He cut through the woodlot, as Cobb had done, and was about to step into the clearing behind the house when he saw a movement in the bush nearby. He called out "Stop!" but this only sent the figure fleeing.

It darted in and out of the sparse scrub bush, making itself momentarily visible, then vanishing. Marc had no doubt that he—the figure was definitely male—had been spying on the rear entrance to Chepstow, for he had been positioned directly opposite the gate and the sentries. Moreover, he was not likely one of the protesters: they did their dance in full view of the public on the street. But a minute later, he could no longer hear the crash of footfalls, and he was compelled to slow down and try to track the fugitive across the crusted snow. Eventually the tracks led him back up onto Hospital Street. He had lost the chase.

However, he had seen enough to assemble a mental picture of a man of medium height and build with flowing yellow locks who ran—like himself—with a limp.

EIGHT

The rest of the day was consumed with negotiations aimed at winning Governor Arthur's consent for Billy to visit Caleb Coltrane at Chepstow the following afternoon. Shoppers along fashionable King Street, many of them carrying out last-minute expeditions to the tailor or jeweller in preparation for the Twelfth Night Charity Ball, were startled to see the same sleigh hurtling westward from the Court House towards Government House and then, minutes later, pounding eastward for home—only to have the procedure repeated several more times before the supper hour. Magistrate Thorpe, convinced of the wisdom of settling the unfortunate "McNair affair" quickly, had agreed to act as go-between in the official negotiations. When exchanged notes failed (Sir George: "I don't want that young hothead anywhere near Coltrane—he damn near killed him the last time!"), Thorpe himself was driven up to Government House and then back to the police station to report his lack of progress to the lawyers and a not-uninterested chief constable.

At Robert's suggestion, Thorpe finally played up the incidents of civil unrest caused by Billy's incarceration, which, combined with the protests outside Chepstow over the coddling of Coltrane, were beginning to pose a threat to public order. What if these mounting protests turned violent, with the governor compelled to call out troops to fire upon citizens whose principal sin was loyalty to the province and the Crown? And further, was this the atmosphere in which Sir George wished to stage Coltrane's trial next week, a trial designed to demonstrate the cohesion, probity, and determination of a beleaguered colony? The clincher was Marc's offer not only to post bail and a peace bond for McNair, but also to personally supervise the accused during his "house arrest."

Ultimately, the governor caved in, but not all the way. He told Thorpe (shouted it actually) that if Coltrane signed an affidavit exonerating McNair, then the charges would be dropped, though a peace bond and confinement to residence would remain in effect until Coltrane swung from a rope in the Court House square. Moreover, Arthur had had enough of Stanhope's mollycoddling an enemy of the Crown. He'd give the colonel his evening of glory at the ball on Saturday, but on Sunday morning a platoon of regulars would descend upon Chepstow, clap Coltrane in irons, and haul him off to a dungeon in Fort York where he would be kept "on ice" until his trial.

There remained the question of the protesters, who were now alternating their attention between Government House and the jail. If Billy were to be driven up King Street or any other thoroughfare tomorrow, was there not the risk of a rescue attempt or some unseemly demonstration? To avoid this, Marc suggested that Billy be smuggled out of the rear doors of the Court House after being brought there through the connecting tunnel, and put in disguise for the trip to Chepstow. Robert offered his third-best wool coat, an unfashionable top hat, and a pair of his brother-in-law's suede boots. Calfskin gloves and a silk scarf would complete the ensemble. Meanwhile, Magistrate Thorpe himself would go up to Chepstow to apprise Colonel Stanhope of these arrangements, with no mention of the Sunday-morning prisoner transfer.

Stanhope was furious enough at the notion of another visit by McNair. He had apparently been told of Coltrane's desire to meet

Billy on the morrow and had not objected because he assumed Sir George would put the kibosh on it. But when Thorpe explained patiently that Sir George now wished the visit to take place "in the best interests of the province," the colonel had no choice but to agree. But he did not do so gracefully. Instead, he fired off a note to Sir George in which he asserted that he would take no personal responsibility for anything that might happen as a result of "this unwarranted interference in my sworn duty to protect the prisoner and deliver him holus-bolus to the court." The consequences, he declaimed, would be on the governor's head.

Next morning, Beth and Marc rode in their cutter to Smallman's, just two blocks above Baldwin House. The weather remained clear and cold. To Marc's annoyance, Beth insisted that she drive ("I'm pullin' on the reins, not the baby!") while he gave an account (slightly censored) of the day's hopes for Billy McNair. Just as they reached Yonge and swung south to enter the service lane behind the shops on King Street, Beth remarked, "That's a coincidence, then."

"In what way?"

"Almeda Stanhope and her daughter Patricia came into the shop Monday afternoon and again yesterday."

"To have a dress refitted, I presume."

"Now how did you know about that?"

Marc laughed, pleased to have their daily disagreement about Beth's working forgotten for the moment. "I heard the two women discussing it at Chepstow yesterday."

"I don't think they get on all that well."

"That was my impression. The daughter didn't want to wear Momma's hand-me-down."

Beth whistled, either at Marc's comment or at Dobbin, who had decided not to stop outside the rear entrance to Smallman's. "Some hand-me-down! They brought in a fifty-dollar gown that Almeda wore to Lord Durham's gala last June."

"I think their disagreement was more likely about Miss Stanhope not wishing to be trotted out as a trophy in her papa's collection."

Beth smiled, then—to Marc's horror—hopped to the ground. She gave the bulge in her coat a proprietorial pat, waved good-bye, and skipped up the steps to her place of business.

Marc spent the morning at Baldwin and Sullivan, trying to be useful in order to keep his mind off what was to come. He realized that he had been adamant in his assurance to all concerned that Billy McNair would behave and carry out every one of the necessary commitments. He did know Billy, had watched as he and Mel Curry worked at Smallman's, had admired his respectful courting of Dolly Putnam, and had been impressed with his efforts during the training period with the colonel's regiment last summer. However, combat and its inevitable calamities could, and usually did, change a man.

Just before noon, Dr. Baldwin came into chambers to inform them that the chief justice had agreed to let Doubtful Dick Dougherty serve as Coltrane's counsel. Smiling broadly, he waved an official-looking paper at them. It was a letter from Justice Robinson authorizing Dougherty to practise as a barrister in Upper Canada on a temporary license until such time as the benchers of the Law Society could convene to review his application and grant him permanent status. Dr. Baldwin then went off to deliver the license and the good news in person.

"Do you think Dick will invite him to lunch?" Robert grinned at the thought.

Billy, of course, had been informed of their success with the magistrate and the governor on the previous evening, along with the gist of Marc's encounter with Coltrane. He seemed, Robert told Marc, genuinely contrite and eager to resolve the situation as soon as possible. When the jailer brought him through to the police quarters at twelve-thirty to meet his escort, Marc quickly learned why: Dolly had visited late Wednesday afternoon. Jailer Strangway, who sympathized with the marchers out front, had been extremely indulgent and the lovers' tryst had lasted more than an hour. During those intimate minutes, the couple had not only reconciled but had agreed to a date for their wedding.

"May the first, sir," Billy said to Marc and the walls behind him. "She doesn't know about this meetin', of course, but she said she'd marry me even if she had to drag the preacher into prison!"

"That's wonderful news," Marc said, helping Strangway remove the shackles. "But the most important thing you can do for both of you is to make a positive impression on Caleb Coltrane. He was truly affected by the revelation that you put the tourniquet on his arm and saved his life."

"And I can tell him every detail that's on that kerchief. I spent many a lonely night down there in Essex with it in my hands." He blushed in saying this, but Marc, who well knew the pangs and abashments of romantic love, recognized the emotions here as genuine and heartfelt and was encouraged. Billy would cooperate, even humble himself, despite the anger he must still harbour against Coltrane, because he now had a reason: Dolly and a shared future. Like Marc's friend Rick Hilliard, Mel would become a gradually receding tableau of fixed memories, painful and pleasant in equal measure.

"What are those?" Billy asked, pointing to the clothes Robert had brought along.

"Your disguise," Marc explained, offering the topcoat.

It was decided that Marc and Billy would ride together in one sleigh, as two gentlemen out for an airing, to be followed by another within hailing distance, carrying Chief Sturges and Constable Cobb. Marc's view was that the less conspicuous the entourage, the better. (Sir George had wanted a regimental escort.) The "gentlemen" slipped out the rear door of the Court House, climbed aboard, and made their way to Newgate Street, which they followed westward towards Brock Street at the edge of town. However, near John Street, Billy begged Marc to let him stop at his house for one minute to reassure his mother, whom Dolly had reported as sick with worry. Marc could see no reason not to. He waited in the front room of the cottage while Billy talked quietly to his mother in the kitchen. Billy then went into the bedroom briefly, "to fetch a rabbit's foot Mel gave me in grade three." Chief Sturges was visibly relieved to see Marc and Billy emerge intact a minute later. The rest of the journey to Chepstow was uneventful.

Colonel Stanhope was not on hand to prescreen the visitors. It was a maid who answered the bell, looking decidedly nervous.

"Please, wait here, sir, while I fetch Mr. Shad," she said, but instead of going down the hall to the butler's room, she went to the head of the stairs and called down, "They're here, Mr. Shad!"

Moments later, Absalom Shad came padding up from the anteroom below. "Ah, right on time, gentlemen," he said without making eye contact. Then, as if out of long habit, he reached for their hats and coats and moved to arrange them on the hall tree. "I'll follow you down," he said.

As Marc and Billy started down the stairs, Cobb and Sturges came in and were likewise relieved of their coats. Cobb was stationed at the top of the stairwell, while the chief thought he ought to make contact with Stanhope and utter helpful noises of reassurance.

"He's in his study," the maid directed.

On stepping down into the anteroom, Marc was surprised to discover that Lardner Bostwick was not there to greet them. "What happened to the lieutenant?" Marc said.

Shad muttered, "Gone off somewheres." And good riddance was the clear implication. "I been made the zookeeper," he grumbled, rubbing his lopsided nose self-consciously.

"Do you propose to beat back the escaping prisoner with your clothes brush?" Marc said, with a wink at Billy, who had grown strangely quiet and tense.

Shad found no humour in this quip. "When the visitors come this mornin', I called one of them Highlanders down here to help me open and close the door."

Marc showed Billy where to sign in. As he scrawled his own signature, Marc noticed the two morning visitors: Boynton Tierney, the Orange alderman, and a Mrs. Jones.

"I see Mr. Tierney has been here again," Marc said to Shad, who was peering up the stairs. "It's all right, that's a police constable up there, and his chief is in your master's study. You may open the door."

Shad actually smiled, weakly. "Mr. Tierney's been here four times that I know of," he said, extracting a large key from his pocket. "He's fond of arguin', he is."

"He and Mr. Coltrane have heated discussions, do they?"

"Go on fer an hour or more, they do."

"Who was this Mrs. Jones who came in after eleven?"

Shad looked confused for a moment, then said with elaborate casualness, "Oh, her. Some lady from Streetsville, I think, who brung him a book or somethin'. She didn't stay long." He essayed a smile as he added, "And I didn't feel the need to call in one of them Highlanders on the porch."

"A young lady?"

"Why're you so interested?" Shad said with sudden alertness.

"I'm trying to get to understand Mr. Coltrane, that's all."

"Why bother? He'll be stone cold in a month."

Billy was to go in alone. Marc would sit in the anteroom and wait, in case there should be any trouble. Shad reluctantly agreed to leave the chamber door slightly ajar. Even more reluctantly he was persuaded to go upstairs and tend to his butlering until needed again.

"You're sure you're all right with this?" Marc said to Billy when they were alone.

Billy was pale, but there was a willed determination in his eye, the kind the sergeant had no doubt called upon more than once down in Essex. "I've got to do this," he said. "For Dolly."

Billy then vanished behind the big, iron-reinforced door. Marc heard Coltrane's hearty "Hello!" and little else. The two men, so recently adversaries in war and a life-threatening duel, were apparently sitting across from each other and having a civil conversation. Billy carried with him an affidavit drawn up by Robert and Magistrate Thorpe, the document Coltrane would sign if all went as planned. The murmur of their voices was a satisfying music in Marc's ears. He felt justifiably proud of what had been achieved in the past twenty-four hours. He was happy for Billy and, for himself, was now more certain than ever that he had at last chosen the right profession.

Suddenly Coltrane's voice rose in anger, then Billy's in heated response. Marc moved towards the door, but just as he was about to throw it open, the voices died down. Seconds later came a roaring chortle from Coltrane. Marc sat again. Ten minutes passed. Marc yawned.

A strangled cry from the cell brought Marc upright in an instant. It was a sustained, gurgling half scream, as if a man were being inexpertly throttled. Before Marc could reach the door, it was flung open and Billy, whey-faced, shouted at him, "For God's sake, get a doctor!"

Marc grabbed Billy by the shoulders. "What's going on?"

"Coltrane's havin' a fit!"

Marc let Billy go and dashed into the prisoner's room. Coltrane had staggered up and away from his desk and was now crouched on the floor, teetering upon one knee. Both hands tore at his throat and face as if trying to rip them off his body. His hawk's features were contorted in pain, his eyes bulged grotesquely, blood gushed from both nostrils, and a snarling gargle shot out of his twisted lips. By the time Marc reached him, he had toppled onto the carpet. A final breath, like a sigh of surrender, eased into the waiting air.

Caleb Coltrane was dead.

Much of what happened next remained a blur for Marc until he was compelled later on to recall and sort out the precise coherence of events. When he raced back into the anteroom—there was nothing he could do for Coltrane—it was empty. He could hear Billy's voice, strident and terrified, shouting and pleading above him. Footsteps came pounding down the hall. Women's voices mingled with men's, none of the words distinguishable. The front door was opened and slammed shut. Finally Wilfrid Sturges appeared on the stairs, meeting Marc on his way up.

"What's happened?" he said to Marc.

"Coltrane's dead."

"Jesus, did the kid shoot 'im?"

"No. He's had some kind of seizure, apoplexy, I'd guess. I don't see how Billy had anything to do with it."

"Christ, man, I hope not. All hell's going to break loose when Sir George gets wind of this."

"Well, you'd better come and have a look."

"Right. I've got Cobb up there holdin' off the colonel and his women. Billy's given 'em quite a fright."

The two men reentered the cell. Sturges knelt beside the rapidly cooling body. He whistled through his teeth. "This wasn't no conniption fit," he said.

"Shouldn't we get Doc Withers to tell us that?"

"Oh, we'll do that all right. But it's pretty obvious. I seen two or three of these back in London when I was on the force there."

"Two or three of what?"

"Poisonings. Strychnine, by the look of it. It boils a man's throat out. The ghastliest way to die I can think of. You wouldn't wish it on a rat."

While his heart beat wildly, Marc forced himself to remain calm enough to think. If it was strychnine, then Coltrane had been murdered. Moreover, he had been murdered in the sole presence of a man who had engaged him in a duel and subsequently threatened his life before witnesses. But how could it have been done?

"We've gotta keep everybody outta here," Sturges said, "till the doctor can be fetched. You stay with the body, Marc, while I go up to tell the Stanhopes."

"I won't touch anything," Marc said. "But we have to find out how the man was induced to pour strychnine down his own throat."

"Well, there are easier ways to kill yerself."

Sturges went back into the anteroom, and Marc heard him call up the stairwell, "Constable Cobb's just doin' his job. Now get back, all of ya!"

Next came a woman's piercing shriek. Patricia's, no doubt, on her hearing the news.

Marc cast about in search of the source of the poison. It didn't take him long to find it. Evident upon Coltrane's shrunken left hand, now seized about his throat, was a dusting of snuff. Marc recalled that Coltrane snorted it like a horse with the heaves. He went over to the desk. Two snuff boxes of ornate silver and some pedigree sat next to the leather-bound Bible where they had been yesterday. One of them was wide open. Marc leaned over and very cautiously gave its contents a sniff. No odour beyond that of the ground tobacco registered. He held the box up so that the window light illuminated its contents. He couldn't be sure, of course, but the snuff there seemed to be mixed with a number of paler, more sinister-looking grains, like pollen. If Coltrane had been paying close attention, he would have noticed, or even felt, the alien presence. But he was a man of supreme confidence and histrionic gesture. It was during this thought that Marc spotted Dolly's kerchief on the desk. Beside it lay the magistrate's document. It was signed. The major had done one good deed before taking a snort of snuff to celebrate his magnanimity.

It took Doc Withers less than half an hour to arrive, accompanied by Constable Ewan Wilkie, and to confirm Marc's findings.

"I've seen many a fox and wretched coyote looking like this, but never a fellow human being. It's strychnine all right."

The question now was straightforward: who had put powdered strychnine in the snuff box, Coltrane himself (unlikely) or one of his enemies?

"If this had happened the day before the trial or the night before his hanging, then I might believe it was suicide," Marc said to Sturges in the anteroom. Cobb and Wilkie were still struggling manfully upstairs to keep the commotion down, but the colonel's shouts and threats still mingled with the wailing of one or more women.

"I agree," Withers said, coming out of the prison chamber. "He could've hanged himself in there easily enough. Less painful and equally dramatic."

"So we're lookin' at murder here," Sturges said, with the deep sigh of a man who knows there is trouble ahead.

"Definitely," Withers said, "unless we find a suicide note."

"What sort of mood was the man in?" Sturges asked Marc.

"I wasn't in there with Billy, but the door was ajar. For most of the time they seemed to be having a friendly conversation. As you will see, the result of it was Coltrane agreeing to sign the affidavit Billy needed to have the charges against him dropped. I even heard Coltrane laugh out loud."

"Hardly the behaviour of a man about to swallow hellfire," Withers said.

"Just so," Sturges said. Then he looked nervously at Marc. "You said 'most' of the time. What else happened?"

"Well, I have to admit that at one point the two men exchanged angry words. I almost intervened. But it lasted only a few seconds, and it was after that that Coltrane laughed. And later on signed the affidavit."

"I see. But what are we gonna tell the governor when he finds out that Billy was in there alone with Coltrane . . . and that his prize bull's been butchered?"

"But surely it's just a terrible coincidence," Marc said. "We brought Billy straight here from jail. What's more, one of the two visitors who came this morning could have diverted Coltrane's attention long enough to plant the powder just before leaving, knowing that sooner or later he would make use of the poisoned snuff box."

"He used more than one?" Sturges said.

"They were his toys, Wilf. There were two of them on his desk when I was here yesterday. I checked both of them in there today, and only one of them appeared to have been seeded with strychnine."

"That's how it looks to me as well," Withers said. "So, in theory, you're suggesting that almost anyone with access to the prisoner within, say, the last twenty-four hours, could have seeded one of the two containers on the desk?"

"I am. And in addition to any visitors, that would have to include the colonel and his family, as well as Bostwick the jailer and Shad, who replaced Bostwick this morning."

"Good Lord," Withers said, "we may never find out who did it!"

"That's a long list," Marc agreed.

"Where is this Bostwick fella?" Sturges said. "Wasn't he the knave who was part of the whole duel business between McNair and Coltrane?"

"He's disappeared," Marc said. "According to Shad, he went off somewhere last night, leaving the butler to do his job. And, it has just occurred to me, he may have taken the ring of master keys with him. I saw Shad use a single key to open the cell door when we arrived."

"Then he's the most likely suspect," Sturges said with obvious relish. "Still, we better get Billy down here to find out if he saw anythin' in there we oughta know about."

Constable Wilkie came down from the hallway above with Billy in tow. Billy looked bewildered and apprehensive. He glanced pleadingly at Marc, who gave him a reassuring smile.

"Coltrane's been poisoned," Sturges said to Billy. "So we need to know everythin' that happened in there."

In a slow but deliberate manner, Billy went over the details of his half-hour in Coltrane's chamber. They more or less corroborated Marc's account. Billy concluded his version with these words: "The major signed the document. He congratulated me on my engagement. He handed me Dolly's kerchief. He offered me snuff to celebrate. I refused, politely. He took two great gaspin' puffs himself and then . . . It was horrible!" He couldn't contain a shudder.

Sturges said quietly, "I hear you two did have some sorta disagreement."

Billy looked at Marc. "Mr. Coltrane got angry when we was discussin' the glories of democracy, as he called it. I asked him why, if all men were created equal, republicans still kept slaves."

"That would have ruffled his feathers," Marc added.

"But when we started to talk about the war and what happened at Windsor, there was no shoutin' and no anger. I was surprised that he felt as sad as I did. He reminded me that we had shot and killed four of his men near the creek, and one of them was a cousin of his. And he did sign the paper to help get me outta jail."

"As I suggested earlier, Wilf," Marc said, "Billy had no cause to murder Coltrane."

"I haven't been thinkin' he did," Sturges said curtly. "But I gotta do my job." Then he smiled to convey his general satisfaction that Billy's story had jibed with Marc's.

"Perhaps you can get Cobb to put the word out on the whereabouts of Bostwick," Marc prompted the chief.

At this point, there was a clatter on the stairs. They all turned to see Cobb coming down, as if on cue. Draped over one arm he had the coat that Robert had supplied for Billy's disguise.

"What is it, Cobb?" Sturges said, noting the strange look on the constable's face.

"This is Billy's coat, ain't it?" Cobb said.

"It's the one he wore, yes," Marc said.

"Well, sir, I was scrummagin' in the pockets and I come up with this." In his free hand he was holding out a paper packet, the kind that druggists use for medicinal powders.

"Let me see that," Withers said. While the others watched in stunned silence, the doctor took the packet over to the window, held it up to the sunlight, and said, "There's a few grains of something still in here." He moistened a finger and stuck it into the packet. "And I think we'll find these are bits of strychnine powder."

"But that's not mine!" Billy shouted, dismayed.

"It's true," Marc said. "There was nothing in those pockets when I brought the coat into the station from Baldwin's place."

"And you brought Billy straight here?" Withers said.

"Not quite," Sturges said, looking to Marc.

"We did stop for five minutes at your house, Billy."

"But I was with you or my mum the whole time! You can check with my mother: we just talked. Tell them, Mr. Edwards."

"Was he ever alone in there?" Sturges asked, his face suddenly grave. "For even a minute?"

Marc hated himself for what he was obliged to say next. "I'm afraid he was. He went into his bedroom to fetch his lucky rabbit's foot."

Cobb held up the talisman, as if to confirm Marc's reluctant assertion.

"But I didn't go in there to get poison!"

Sturges walked right up to Billy. "I ain't happy about this, son, but I gotta put you under arrest for the murder of Caleb Coltrane."

NINE

It was early evening, and Marc and Robert were in the latter's office going over the calamitous events of the past few hours. Billy McNair had been formally charged with murder and returned to his cold cell. Doc Withers had confirmed strychnine in one of the two snuff boxes and in the druggist's packet. It fell to Magistrate Thorpe to bring these tidings to Sir George Arthur. The consequent reaction—heard, it was claimed, by the officers a mile away at Fort York—was an apoplectic explosion on a par with Coltrane's death throes. The creature who had been the centerpiece of Sir George's scheme to bind his people to him and to the monarch he embodied had been squalidly assassinated. What was worse, he knew but could not admit that it was he who had indulged Stanhope and his quixotic notions of chivalry, hoping to keep the fool's status as Pelee Island Patriot alive and politically useful. And it was he who had, over the mad colonel's objections (put in writing, alas), sanctioned the disastrous visit of Billy McNair. Being lieutenant-governor, however, encouraged him to vent his initial wrath upon the hapless magistrate and any of his own staff within scolding range of his tongue. "This business is not over!" he vowed to all and sundry, hoping to divert attention away from his culpabilities and towards the guilt of others.

Marc sipped at his brandy and stared into the blazing hearth. "If I hadn't let the lad go in to see his mother, he would be a free man now."

"You can't blame yourself, Marc," Robert said, then added delicately, "You're absolutely certain Billy didn't do it?"

"Absolutely. I was there. I heard the tenor of that conversation. And you saw Billy before we left the station. He had just set his wedding date. He was heading off to play it humble and safe so that he could be released to his sweetheart's arms. In order for us to accept him as a conniving killer with a packet of poison hidden in his bedroom at home, we'd have to believe him capable of an incredible deception, of a level of dissembling quite beyond his abilities. Nor was Coltrane any fool. The chances of Billy slipping strychnine powder into one of those snuff boxes, which sat on Coltrane's side of the desk, are nil and none."

Robert held up his hand. "You don't need to convince me, Marc. I just wanted to be sure you felt as I did."

"What really angers me, though, is the cavalier way in which Wilf Sturges cuffed Billy and hauled him away to be charged."

"Well, you must admit that all the obvious evidence points to his guilt. He did have a powerful motive, however much we ourselves feel it may have evaporated. He did threaten to kill Coltrane after failing to do so in a duel. He did have the chance to obtain and secure the poison. And the near-empty packet was found in the borrowed coat."

"But that skein is full of holes. Anyone in the day leading up to the incident could have salted the snuff. We do know who came there officially and who might have slipped in for a casual visit. Bostwick has run off with the estate keys in his pocket. I wager we'll find that Stanhope has demoted him or drummed him out of the regiment for the fiasco over the duel. So he may well have a motive: revenge against the Yankee who duped or suborned him. Moreover, why would Billy keep strychnine cached away in his bedroom when he fully intended to shoot Coltrane on Monday morning?"

"Right. And Cobb took him straight to jail after the duel. Unfortunately, Billy won't get a chance to testify to these matters because under our laws the accused cannot take the stand on his own behalf."

"I'd forgotten that. Still, there are other suspects here besides Billy, aren't there?"

"Like the Orangeman, Tierney," Robert said. "He hated Coltrane enough to go there more than once."

"Nor can we discount the Stanhopes. The daughter was enamoured of Coltrane, I'm sure. She and her mother were feuding over it. If Stanhope found out, he may have taken matters into his own hands."

"Though I really doubt he would kill the man he had sworn, on his soldier's sword, to protect—at least not until after his coronation at the ball on Saturday."

"The point is that Sturges has gone ahead with the charge and let Sir George know about it. Getting it reversed will be almost impossible."

"I agree," Robert said, reaching for a macaroon and then resisting its temptation.

"I begged Wilf to interrogate everybody immediately—a necessity in any attempt to investigate a murder. He refused. I pointed out that the only substantial incriminating evidence he had was the packet in the greatcoat. He saw that. Then I asked him how he thought Billy poured the strychnine out of it into the snuff box and subsequently managed to sequester it in a coat hanging upstairs on a hall tree. He reminded me that Billy had rushed out and past me, then raced up the stairs crying havoc. Cobb says there was so much hollering and confusion that Billy could easily have slipped the empty paper into the pocket, though he himself didn't see him do so. When I asked Sturges why Billy would do so, he said to keep us from finding it."

"That makes rough sense, I suppose."

"By the same token, in the confusion up there, anyone could have done it. Cobb was at the door, he swears, all during the interview, but after that it was instant mayhem. Anyway, that alone should have warranted more investigation before charging Billy."

"If the killer did plant it to cast blame on Billy, then that would seem to eliminate any of the earlier outside visitors from suspicion."

"True, but I never rule out conspiracy or collusion."

"I see: one person to set the poison in place and another to secure the frame-up."

"I even asked Wilf, and then Cobb, if I could just speak briefly to the Stanhopes, to give them some details they might find helpful, but I was forbidden to do so. I really just wanted to get a look at the colonel and the women, to study their faces in the immediate aftermath. But they refused."

"You must understand why the police, despite your helpfulness to them in the past, had to behave as they did."

Marc looked puzzled.

"Well, you are one of the accused's advocates, aren't you?"

Marc instantly understood. "Of course! We're on different sides now, aren't we? I mustn't be too hard on Cobb, especially. He's a good man, and I consider him a friend."

"Don't worry, that's allowed in the colonies," Robert responded, then asked, "Is there any possibility that an outsider could have come in through the garden in the night?"

"I thought of that. I took a good look around in the prison chamber, even poked into the curtained-off sleeping area and the water closet. Then I checked the back door and the bars on the window. I found nothing suspicious." Marc paused, recalling something from his first visit to Chepstow. "Come to think of it, I did spy a suspicious person skulking about the rear gate yesterday morning. I spooked him and he ran off. Still, even though the sentries back there are unreliable, when that back door is locked, the prison chamber itself is like a fortress."

Robert drained his brandy. "Well, it looks as if we began as defense counsel for a man accused of attempted murder and inherited one charged with the real thing."

"You'll stay on the case, then?"

"If Billy is innocent, and I believe he is, he'll need all the help he can get."

"Beth and I will foot the bill. She's devoted to Dolly. They'll both be devastated by the news." Marc waved off the brandy decanter. "I've got to go. Beth will be worried. But tell me quickly what I can do to assist you."

"I've already thought of that. It occurred to me that you are an apprentice barrister but a seasoned and successful investigator of homicides."

Marc was half expecting this turn of events and tried not to reveal his disappointment. "You want me to find the real murderer, then?"

"I do. In the circumstances, I think it is our best hope. You just said yourself that the police believe they have their man and enough evidence to convict him. They will look no further. And remember, this case won't go to trial until the spring assizes begin in April. That gives you almost three months."

"I trust I won't need that long."

"We should be able to get Billy released on bail shortly. But he may have to put his wedding on hold."

The door opened and Dr. William Baldwin took two steps into the room. He waved a sheet of paper at his son.

"News, sir?"

"Could be. It's a note just received from James Thorpe."

"Then it can't be good news."

Baldwin senior began perusing the letter, while Marc and Robert waited impatiently.

"It looks as if Sir George has decided upon the means of saving his face," William said.

Robert got up and stood beside Marc.

"Since he's been robbed of his trial and its star performer, then by God he's going to show the world—meaning, of course, the skeptical Yankees—that British justice is fair and evenhanded and not the product of tyranny. Or something like that."

"He's going after Billy?" Robert asked.

"I'm afraid so. He's ordered the chief justice to conduct McNair's trial here in the Court of Queen's Bench a week from tomorrow."

"But that's madness," Marc said. "Billy is not only innocent, he's a local hero. We'll have riots in the streets."

"I believe the governor has concluded that that risk is the lesser of two evils. The cold-blooded assassination of an American 'liberator' is bound to ignite the anger of the Hunters' Lodges, just when things were beginning to quiet down there. A quick public trial of the culprit is Sir George's response. In the least it will make it easier for President Van Buren to clamp down on the renegades' border activities."

"But that gives us only eight days to find the real assassin and prepare a defense for Billy," Marc said.

Robert, however, did not look overly concerned. In fact, he was smiling. "Well, if Sir George wants a fancy trial, then I propose we give him one. Let's invite onto our defense team a lawyer who has never lost a capital case."

Dr. Baldwin laughed out loud, invigorating the laugh lines around his lips and eyes. "By God, Robbie, won't that give the old Tory the dry heaves!"

"Richard Dougherty?" Marc said.

"He's got a license to practise here until the benchers convene next month, doesn't he?" Robert said.

"We'll wait until Sir George has made his tactics public," Dr. Baldwin said with a mischievous grin, "then we'll announce our own. By then, it'll be too late for the old bugger to renege on Dougherty."

"In the meantime, Marc here is going to catch the real villain, aren't you?"

Marc nodded with what he hoped was convincing confidence.

Beth was waiting anxiously for Marc when he arrived home about nine o'clock. Robert had suggested that the legal aspects of Billy's case be left entirely in his hands (and Doubtful Dick's, if he chose to join him). Marc would be the investigator, working on his own and reporting in only when he had important information to relay. As was his custom, Marc filled Beth in on the salient developments of the day, a process that allowed him to sift and sort matters as he narrated them to his wife. Beth, as was her custom, listened carefully and said little.

"How can I help?" she asked, when he had finished.

"By not working so hard."

Beth yawned. "You'll want to get started right after breakfast to-morrow. You drop me at the shop and I'll tell Dolly what she needs to know about Billy's situation."

Marc pinched out the candle and leaned over to kiss her. She was asleep.

Marc did begin first thing Friday morning, driving the cutter from Smallman's to Chepstow. Unlike in his previous investigations, he would be carrying out this inquiry with neither executive authority or the police. And given the kind of people involved, all prominent in the community, he would be hard-pressed to find a killer among them in seven days. "You'll just have to use your charm," Robert had declared.

The news of Billy's rearrest had begun to spread. Driving by the Court House, Marc encountered three or four grim-faced marchers wielding placards: "Free the Hero of Windsor!" and "Who's the Tyrant Now?" Some faint hope arose in him that perhaps Sir George would call off his misguided scheme before it was too late.

Absalom Shad opened the door at Chepstow. If he was surprised to see Marc, he did not show it. "You'll wanta see the colonel," he said.

"If he'll be gracious enough to see me so early in the morning," Marc said.

"He's always gracious, ain't he?"

Marc was shown into the colonel's study at the far end of the central hall. The doors along the way were firmly shut.

"Good morning, Lieutenant." Stanhope turned from the fire to greet his guest. The buttons on his tunic glittered. "What brings you here again so soon?"

Marc summoned all the geniality he could muster so soon after breakfast. "First of all, I wanted to offer you my personal apology for what happened here yesterday."

Stanhope pursed his lips and raised his brow. "Oh? But it wasn't you who slaughtered an unarmed officer under my protection, it was that ungrateful wretch of a sergeant." Marc expected venom to spurt from the colonel's eyes. "It was I who turned him from a lowly carpenter into a soldier. And look how he chose to repay me."

"But it was I, sir, who negotiated his meeting with the major. I had hoped for an amicable resolution to the duelling matter."

"That's big of you to admit it," Stanhope said. "But it's young Billy who will have to pay for his sins."

"I am told that you objected to the visit in writing."

Stanhope grinned like a ferret that's caught the rabbit out of his hole. "I did indeed. And that is my only solace in regard to this sorry business. It is Sir George who must accept ultimate responsibility for what happened. And I shall enjoy watching him squirm at the charity ball tomorrow night."

Marc feigned surprise. "You're still planning to attend?"

"Of course. My wife, my daughter, and I are the guests of honour at the governor's table. He is to present me with a medal."

"For your heroic action at Windsor?"

"And Pelee last March."

"It is unfortunate, is it not, that Major Coltrane's death has, through no fault of your own, compromised your honour?"

Stanhope frowned, but it was forced and brief. "It has, sir. But that is not the source of my anger at Billy McNair. It is his betrayal, his perfidy, his disservice to me who treated him like a son. Of course, I will suffer some embarrassment tomorrow night. But I will hold my head high, like a true British officer."

"And it won't hurt, will it, that ninety out of a hundred citizens are secretly or overtly pleased that someone did away with a man who was going to be hanged anyway?"

Stanhope's grin was closer to a smirk, suggesting that he too had had such a thought. "Well, sir, you'll be happy to know that I accept your apology. Your reputation as an officer and a gentleman precedes you, and you do not disappoint."

The man's vanity was unquenchable, Marc thought, and he pressed his advantage. "I must now tell you, sir, that I have been engaged by Baldwin and Sullivan to discover whether Billy McNair really did poison Major Coltrane."

For the first time Stanhope looked flustered. "But there can be no doubt, can there? I spoke at length with Chief Sturges last night. They caught him red-handed."

"Not quite. I sat in the anteroom down there with the cell door ajar and listened to the entire conversation between Billy and the major. It was not only amicable but, by the end of it, the major had signed an affidavit exonerating Billy for his role in the duel. I believe I was about to be called in to sign as witness when the major took the pinch of snuff that poisoned him."

"But surely all that was a charade by Billy to cover his tracks?"

Marc paused. "Sir, no one besides his mother knows Billy as well as you do. Lacking a father of his own, he looked to you for guidance and moral authority. I realize that you are angry about the duel and the murder, but do you think that Billy—tempestuous as he is, being a man of spirit—do you really believe he is capable of arranging and executing such a subtle scheme?"

Stanhope said nothing for some time. Marc could see emotions contending in his face. "The lad never wavered under fire. I'm sure he's capable of sudden and decisive action—the farcical duel didn't surprise me in the least—and I suppose it's more likely he'd've leapt across the desk and throttled Major Coltrane than he'd've slipped poison into his snuff like a sneak thief."

"That's my reading of his character, sir."

"But the empty packet of poison was found in his coat."

"I know. And what I need to do to help Billy is to determine whether or not someone else put strychnine in the snuff box and then planted the empty packet to incriminate him."

The colonel took this in. "You mean one of the persons who visited the major?"

"That seems most likely."

"Or someone in this household?"

Marc hesitated, knowing matters were getting close to the bone. "I wouldn't rule that out, I'm afraid."

"You're thinking of Bostwick?"

"Exactly. He seems to have vanished."

"I sent him packing a day ago. The bugger ran off with my keys and two bottles of my best whiskey."

"When did he actually depart the premises?"

"After supper on Wednesday evening."

"It is conceivable, then, that he, out of spite, might have put the poison in the major's snuff box before he left. As jailer he'd have plenty of opportunity. But he couldn't have put the packet in Billy's coat."

"Yes, I see."

"What would be helpful, sir, is for me to know exactly where everybody was when the murder took place. Would you mind casting your mind back over the events of yesterday afternoon and telling me what you recall of them?"

"You really think Billy might be innocent?" From the look of concern and confusion on the colonel's face, Marc was now convinced that Stanhope had indeed been very fond of his protégé and correspondingly hurt and angry at what he perceived to be a filial betrayal.

"I do. And anything you can tell me may help free him." Stanhope looked uncertain, but Marc pressed on. "I'd like to know exactly what you saw and heard yesterday afternoon, but first, it would be useful for me to know as much about the, ah, arrangements made for the major's incarceration."

Stanhope went over to the fire and gave it a couple of ineffectual pokes. "What do you wish to know, specifically?"

"Well, sir, Bostwick showed me the prison rooms themselves, the reinforced doors and so on. I've seen the sentry system front and back for myself. I've examined the sign-in book. But who took the major his meals, for example?"

"Our maid did that, and tidied up the chamber just after luncheon each day. He had his own water closet; the area was used as servants' quarters by the previous owner."

"I understood from Bostwick," Marc lied, "that your daughter served him breakfast."

Stanhope frowned, more likely at Bostwick's indiscretion than at Marc's impertinence. "That's correct. The maid, Stella, took him breakfast the first morning he was here. But she was ill the following day, so Patricia, who likes to be helpful, took the tray down for her. She and Major Coltrane got to talking. I'm sure you know firsthand how impressionable girls of nineteen react to a handsome tunic and stirring tales of war."

"They enjoyed each other's company, then?" Marc said with a man-of-the-world glance at the colonel.

"I believe so. But when he asked that she be allowed to repeat the procedure each day, I attached the strictest conditions to my consent."

"As any conscientious father would."

"She was to stay there only while he ate his meal and no longer than fifteen minutes. Bostwick was in the anteroom from seven in the morning till six at night and often slept there. He kept an eye on the situation."

Some eye, Marc thought. The fifteen-minute breakfast was an hour long and spiced with periodic, clandestine visits during the day. But Marc had no desire to complicate family relations here needlessly. He made no comment on Bostwick's probable collusion in Patricia's flouting of her father's will. Instead he said, "You negotiated these terms yourself, I take it?"

"I did, sir."

"You saw the major often?"

"Only for the first two or three days. I felt it an officerly courtesy to get to know the man who was my worthy adversary at Baby's orchard."

"And what did you find?"

Stanhope coloured. "A brilliant, vain, garrulous man of middle years who was obsessed with American republicanism and all its clichéd claptrap."

"Who wouldn't cease telling you about its glories?"

Stanhope smiled thinly. "I forgot that you spent an hour with him the other day. Well, then, you know why I quit going down there. But I'd given my word that he would be treated like a captured general, and I kept it. I allowed him to see anyone he liked, within reason. He had good food and drink. I even had his books and trinkets shipped here from his sister's place in Detroit. And to show the cynical world out there that I am still a man of my word, I sent Shad down to the major's room an hour ago to begin packing those personal effects in the wooden crates they arrived in. They will be on their way back to Detroit by special coach before noon."

"You have gone well beyond the call of duty," Marc said, unsure what ironies were entailed by the comment, if any.

"Thank you. Now, you were asking about yesterday."

"Yes. You'll recall that Sergeant McNair and I arrived in concert with Chief Sturges and Constable Cobb. The chief came down to this room, did he not, while Cobb was stationed at the head of the stairwell near the front door?"

"That is so. I heard you arrive and stepped out to greet Wilfrid. We came in here and we smoked a pleasant pipe together. By then I had reconciled myself to Billy's visit, having said my piece in a communication to Sir George. It was out of my hands."

"And when did you realize that something was amiss?"

"That's easy. Billy came hurtling up the stairs hollering at the top of his lungs, 'Get a doctor! Get a doctor! He's dying!'"

"So you dashed out into the hall—"

"Wilfrid was ahead of me, but yes, we both ran out, just in time to see Billy try to skip past the constable, still hollering his head off."

"But Cobb stopped him?"

"He did. Billy was white as a sheet, I'd even say hysterical if he were a woman. We knew right off that something terrible had happened downstairs."

"What then?"

"Wilfrid reached the stairs and called out to Cobb to hold on to Billy and to stop anybody else from coming down the stairs after him. Then he disappeared."

"Surely you were anxious to get down there yourself?"

"You're damn right I was. But Mr. Cobb is a powerful man for all the fat he carries around his middle. He gave Billy a push into the arms of the two Highlander guards who'd come charging in at that moment, and then plunked himself in the cellar doorway. I'm embarrassed to report that we exchanged angry words."

"I was, of course, in the anteroom by then and I heard women screaming as well."

"Almeda and Patricia were in their sewing room next to the vestibule. They came out to the fright of their lives. Their home was suddenly full of police and soldiers and an hysterical man and a great deal of shouting. They were terrified and distraught. Then Stella came down from upstairs, equally upset. I had to turn my attention to them, regardless."

"Who went for the doctor?"

"Absalom Shad. He had been in his butler's carrel across from this study and was the last of the household to arrive on the scene. Following my orders, he managed to fetch Angus Withers and incidentally recruit another constable on the street."

"That would be Wilkie." Marc paused to emphasize the importance of his next point. "The police are claiming that Billy slipped the incriminating poison packet into the pocket of one of those coats on the hall tree during the mêlée—with a view, they will claim, to disposing of it at the first opportunity or, if it landed in someone's coat other than his own, of shifting the blame."

"Sounds far-fetched to me," was Stanhope's response.

"I agree, but I suppose they will claim Billy's hysteria was a calculated act. He may have thought he could push past Cobb and reach the porch, where he could toss the paper into the snow before being stopped."

"Preposterous!" Stanhope declared. Then his face darkened. "I just remembered something."

"About the coats?"

"Yes. When Billy got pushed by Cobb, he stumbled into the hall tree and fell against the coats. The Highlanders caught him up. But he was sprawled there for several seconds among the spilled coats and hats."

Marc was appalled. His clever interrogation had elicited the most damning piece of evidence yet, a point that Stanhope might otherwise have overlooked. In straightening the coats a little later, Cobb must have thought to search the pockets and thus found the packet. Even the famous Richard Dougherty would be flummoxed by testimony of this ilk.

"You realize, Lieutenant, that if I am put on the stand and asked about these events, I am honour bound to tell the truth and the whole truth. I cannot let any personal feelings I may have for Billy or his possible innocence compromise my duty."

What could Marc say to that but amen?

"I appreciate that, Colonel, as I do your forthrightness and honesty."

"Is there anything else?"

"Yes. I'd like to speak to your wife and daughter, if I might."

"Surely you do not suspect the ladies of murder, sir?" The moustache flipped to rigid attention.

"No, no, no. You mistake my purpose entirely. It has occurred to me that their timely arrival might have allowed them to have observed Billy's actions from another angle than your own. If they were witnesses to his tumble into the coats, they might provide me with invaluable, exculpatory information."

"They were in a state of terror and bewilderment, sir. Indeed, they are still extremely upset. Having a man poisoned in a most ghastly manner in one's home is hardly an everyday occurrence. We are one day away from the Twelfth Night Ball, and I am having enormous difficulty in pointing their attention towards that end. Your interviewing them will only stir everything up again. I cannot permit it."

"As you wish, Colonel. But perhaps after the ball, say on Monday, I could approach them?"

Stanhope considered this while his moustache relaxed to the stand-easy position. "Only if they themselves agree. Come here then, and I'll have an answer for you."

"Does your interdiction include Stella?"

"Our maid fainted on the lower landing. She saw nothing."

"That leaves Mr. Shad, then."

"You may speak with him before you leave. He is downstairs packing the major's effects, all save the snuff box the police have confiscated."

So much for securing and preserving the crime scene, Marc thought.

He thanked Stanhope and headed once again down to the site of the murder.

Absalom Shad was forthcoming enough. He had just finished tapping the lid onto a big wooden box, and sweat had stained his white shirt. He was of no help in regard to Billy and the coats in the hall. By the time he had come up behind his master, he said, the Highlanders had Billy pinned against the outside door. Then he, Shad, was ordered to fetch Dr. Withers, which he did, bringing the doctor and Ewan Wilkie back with him.

"Is there a side or tradesman's entrance to Chepstow?" Marc asked.

"Yes, sir. At the end of the hall where my den is, the door there leads down to the summer kitchen, just a storeroom now, but you can get out to the side yard there."

So it was possible, if unlikely, that an outsider could have slipped in and down the hall to the coats. But only if Cobb were distracted, and there was little chance of that. Marc realized he was now clutching at straws. With motive, means, opportunity, and physical evidence in hand, the Crown had all it needed to put a noose around Billy McNair's neck. His last hope here was the women, and he might or might not be given access to them. They could be subpoenaed, of course, but it was never wise to question hostile or resistant witnesses who might surprise you with their answers.

Marc tried another tack. "You greeted and let in two visitors yesterday morning."

"I did. I was up and down all mornin' doin' two jobs because of that drunkard Bostwick."

"Did you perchance overhear the conversation between Coltrane and Alderman Tierney?"

"A bit. Ya couldn't help hear it, 'cause one shouted as loud as t'other."

"They were arguing?"

"Carried on like that every time they met, accordin' to Bostwick. I reckon they loved it, the both of 'em."

"You don't think Tierney got angry enough to kill Coltrane, do you?"

"Why bother? The man was as good as dead already."

Shad had a point, and one which was going to make it nigh impossible for them to posit a perpetrator other than Billy, whose motive was personal and who had already made one attempt.

"What can you tell me about this Mrs. Jones from Streetsville?"

Shad seemed startled by the question. "Well, she just come here, on her own, like. Just after eleven, I think."

"I thought all visitors had to be preapproved by the colonel."

"That they do. But the colonel was out at his tailor's. Mrs. Jones give me a note to take into Coltrane, and he said he knew who she was, a friend of one of his pals or a distant cousin, somethin' like that. She had a book fer him. I didn't take much notice. She looked harmless enough. Had a big bonnet on. Motherly sort, I should think. So I let her in."

"Did she stay long?"

"I don't think so. I had some chores to do upstairs, and when I come back down here, she'd gone."

"She didn't sign out?"

"I don't really know. Reckon she did. Ya see, sir, I'm a butler and a val-ay, not a jailer. It was Bostwick shoulda been doin' all this."

"When did Bostwick leave?"

"Wednesday night, before the murder. He and the colonel had a set-to in the study. I heard Bostwick stomp down the hall and come down to the anteroom here to pick up his things. I come out into the hall just in time to see him almost bowl over Mr. MacPherson at the front door."

"You don't mean Farquar MacPherson? From the Commercial Bank?"

"I do. He had an appointment with the colonel."

"And Bostwick has vanished?"

"To the nearest blind pig, if ya want my opinion."

For all the good he had done here, Marc felt he might have better spent the morning in a blind pig himself.

Shad trailed Marc up to the entrance hall. Marc waved off his assistance in donning his overcoat and hat, and Shad scuttled away. Just as he was opening the front door, Marc heard Amelia Stanhope's voice calling out from her sewing room, "Is that you, Abe?"

"I'll be right there, Duchess."

Somehow, Marc realized, he would have to find a way of talking to the Stanhope women. There was still a great deal he needed to know about what really had been going on between the notorious Yankee and his accommodating hosts.

TEN

Marc went around to Boynton Tierney's tack shop on John Street. The big, bluff Irishman greeted him heartily, and even when he discerned the purpose of Marc's visit, he showed no indignation at being quizzed about his five meetings with a man he despised in his Loyal Orange bones. He cheerfully admitted to the blazing arguments that he had no doubt were audible throughout Chepstow. But he concluded his defense with the irrefutable point that a man due to be strung up within a month was not likely to attract assassins opposed to his politics.

As Marc was about to depart, he noticed a stack of wooden and cardboard signs in a far corner of the shop. Nothing appeared to be written on them yet. "Getting ready for the Glorious Twelfth a bit early, aren't you?" Marc asked good-naturedly.

Tierney grinned. "If Sir George thinks he's going to get away with hanging Billy McNair, he's got another think coming. It's no secret—in fact we don't want it to be—that we're planning a series of street marches, with signs and fife and drum and all the trimmings. That boy is a true loyalist. We're going to force the governor to choose between the lad and President Van Buren, whose ruffled feathers he hopes to settle by going after Billy. He can't have it both ways. And there's more of us than him."

"You're not about to resort to violence, I trust?"

Again the grin. "Ah, now, you know we don't condone violence. In fact, it's because we're worried about the unorganized protesters lurking about Government House and the jail that we're going ahead with our own peaceful march. By tomorrow, they'll be redundant."

Marc thanked him for his time and his candour and headed for the door.

"Say, you don't happen to need any tackle for that new pony of yours, do you?"

Before reporting in at Baldwin House, Marc drove up to Smallman's to have lunch with Beth. Rose Halpenny always had a pot of stew on her stove upstairs and shared it with Beth and the hired help in the workroom. Everyone was being inordinately cheerful today in an effort to keep Dolly's spirits from flagging, but eventually Marc was able to draw Beth aside and, in the adjoining shop, give her a synopsis of his morning at Chepstow. There was nothing upbeat in his account.

"So it doesn't look too good, I take it." Beth said.

"The only hope I have at the moment is to get to the Stanhope women. If someone in that household poisoned Coltrane, I've got to discover their motive, one so compelling that they couldn't wait for the victim to be hanged. There's faint chance I'll be allowed to see them soon, but I've got to try."

"Not necessarily," Beth said with a twinkle.

"What do you mean?"

"I mean that I could talk to the Stanhope women for you."

Marc blinked.

"Mrs. Halpenny and I are due up at Chepstow at two o'clock. We've got Patricia's dress finished, and Rose is taking a box of hats for Almeda to choose from."

"But don't they usually come here?"

"The colonel's forbidden them to leave the house."

"I see," Marc said, mulling over this opportunity. "Do you think you can get one or both of them to open up?"

"It's more likely they'd tell me about their troubles than a man. We spend a lot of time in the fitting room here listening to the heartaches of half the women in town. And they don't need much prompting."

"I believe you can do it," Marc said with real enthusiasm. Then he made the mistake of glancing anxiously at the bulge in Beth's dress.

She smiled indulgently. "Don't worry, love. I'm plannin' to take the baby with me."

Robert was waiting for Marc in the hall of Baldwin House with welcome news. Richard Dougherty had agreed to take the case.

"I must confess I'm surprised," Marc said, as they turned into the suite of rooms reserved for the legal side of the Baldwin enterprise and headed for Robert's chamber. "Why do you think he'd take on the task of defending a local man accused of killing one of his own countrymen?"

"He didn't say. I had several cogent pleas rehearsed, but he said yes before I could deploy them."

They entered the cozy confines of the office-cum-library and its heartening fire.

"Personally, I think he just decided he was getting bored with trying to eat himself to death."

"Will he be coming here for conferences?"

Robert gave the half smile that was characteristic of a man who remained, through thick and thin, the cautious optimist. "I doubt it. He's asked that all relevant documents, including any written reports from you, be couriered to his home—which means his chair. I shall be summoned occasionally for oral debriefings."

Marc sat down opposite Robert and proceeded to recount in some detail the results of his morning's efforts. When he had finished, Robert said nothing for some time; then, "I'd say our best bet is the mysterious Mrs. Jones." It was typical of him not to dwell on the negatives, of which there were many.

"They do say that poison is a woman's weapon," Marc mused. "And it's conceivable that she and Lardner Bostwick, the former jailer, are somehow in league."

"Why do you say that?"

"Well, Shad implied he hadn't seen her before, but the ease with which she seems to have gained entry suggests she may have been there previously—without having to sign in or be vetted by the colonel. That is, Bostwick may have been letting her in without telling Shad or Stanhope."

"Well," said Robert, ever pragmatic, "there's no sense in speculating about the woman until we know whether there really is a Mrs. Jones from Streetsville."

"What are the odds of finding out?"

"Quite fair. My father's man Cummings has a brother in Streetsville who serves as the local postmaster. I'll have Cummings drive out there right away. If any Joneses do reside in the township, he'll know."

"Excellent. Now tell me, have you seen Billy?"

"I have. He's been pathetically forthcoming, but nothing he has to say is in any way helpful. He did admit tumbling about in the hallway, but since he won't be allowed to testify in his own behalf, we'll let the prosecution try to prove that."

"In that regard, it is the Stanhope women who may have been closest to Billy when he tumbled, and who could be critical to our defense."

"But the colonel is keeping both women locked up?"

"Not for long. While I'm busy here writing up notes for Doubtful Dick, Beth and Rose Halpenny will be delivering hats and a dress to Chepstow. Beth is hoping to wheedle some useful information from Patricia and her mother."

Robert frowned. "Do you think that's wise?"

"I never underestimate my wife."

Beth was shown into the sewing room by Absalom Shad. Mrs. Halpenny was then led farther down the hall to the parlour, where she would display the bonnets and cloches she had brought for Almeda Stanhope's inspection. This arrangement suited Beth fine. Shad had stared at her extended abdomen as if an opossum or kangaroo might pop out at any second, and Beth was still smiling when the door closed behind her and she came face-to-face with the young debutante.

"I've brought your ball gown, Patricia," she said. "Mrs. Halpenny's done a splendid job on it."

"Then she's wasted her efforts," Patricia declared. She was standing in the middle of the room with a fierce frown creasing her brow and her arms akimbo. Her feet were planted some distance apart, as if she were bracing for an onslaught she was doubtful of being able to resist. Her lower lip trembled. "I am sorry you had to come all the way out here, Mrs. Edwards, but I won't be needing that dress."

"You're not going to the gala?"

Her collapse was sudden and spectacular. Her hands flew to her face; all the rigidity went out of her body like air out of a balloon. Her legs shook and seemed about to fold under her. Beth dropped the dress box, stepped across the room, and grasped the girl, who promptly fell into her arms and commenced sobbing. Beth made soothing noises and led Patricia to a padded settee. They both sat down.

"What on earth has happened?" Beth said softly. "I knew you were not keen to go tomorrow night when you came into the shop for your fittings, but surely it can't be the dance that's upset you like this."

When Patricia's sobbing had subsided enough to permit speech, she blurted, "No. It's much worse than that. Much worse."

"But of course, you and your mother have had a terrible thing happen right here in your own house. How could I have forgotten that?"

Patricia gave out a single sob of acknowledgement but no further response.

"Mr. Coltrane was, I'm told, a wicked man, but still, to have him—"

The ravaged young face swung up, eyes ablaze through tears. "Caleb was *not* wicked! He was the most beautiful, the most honest, the gentlest man I've ever known!"

Beth realized that she had struck home with her first probe. She took Patricia's hand and waited for the weeping to work itself out. The burst of umbrage had sapped the last of the girl's strength. She wept quietly, and Beth could see, beyond the redness of her eyes and puffed cheeks, the purple streaks that signalled a sleepless night.

"You loved him?" Beth asked, the question very close to an assertion.

Patricia nodded.

"Then I know how you feel, having lost him."

"No one can," Patricia replied, staring at the rug. "Mother, especially. My life is over."

"No, it isn't," Beth said. "My first husband, Jesse, was killed, and it was I who found him in the barn. I thought my life was over too. But it wasn't. I met a wonderful man. And look, I have his baby here inside me." She took Patricia's limp hand and laid it upon the fabric of her dress.

Patricia looked down, amazed, then up. "But there'll never be another man like Caleb."

"That's so. And I'll never know another man like my Jesse."

Patricia accepted a hanky from Beth and blew her nose. After a minute she said, "The worst part of all this has been not having anybody to tell or talk to. My mother thinks it was puppy love and I shall be over it by the weekend."

"Did she know about you and Caleb all along?"

"She figured it out soon enough. Caleb talked Papa into letting me take him his breakfast—he was the greatest persuader in the world—and I did so every morning for three weeks. Even on Christmas Day."

"And you and Caleb got to talking."

"Yes. Old Bostwick, who fawned about Papa like a lapdog, grumbled when I started staying in there alone with Caleb for an hour every morning. But Caleb somehow swore him to silence."

"So your father never found out?"

"I don't think so. If he had, he would've been furious."

"He's not a man to hold his temper, then."

Patricia smiled wanly and nodded.

"But your mother guessed and confronted you?"

"Yes. Mothers are like that, aren't they?"

"I'm afraid so."

"She and I argued a lot, but I knew she would never tell Papa."

"Because of his temper."

"That, and the fact he would blame her. You see how mean and unreasonable he can be, keeping us locked in this house like criminals."

"For your own protection, I assume, with so much unrest in the streets and all."

"That's what he says."

"Why do you think, if he was so strict with you, that he let you go down there every morning and expose yourself to a man he took for a villain?"

"I don't know. But I think he may have been getting a bit suspicious near the end, because the night before it . . . the night before, just after Mr. MacPherson left, I saw Papa go down to the cellar."

Beth tried not to telegraph her surprise. Marc had told her that

Stanhope was adamant that he had not visited Coltrane after the first few days of his incarceration. "To warn him away from you?" she wondered.

Patricia's lip trembled again. "I think so."

"Why didn't your mother confront him?"

"I heard Papa forbidding her to go anywhere near him."

Very gently, Beth said, "When did you last see Caleb?"

"I gave him his breakfast that morning."

"You did?" Well, Papa's visit the evening before had not borne fruit. Or had it?

"Yes. We had a wonderful hour together. He was in good spirits. He was looking forward to his morning visitor. He told me every day that his friends in Michigan were going to rescue him—and that he would send for me. Then he kissed me." She tried to weep, but there were no tears left in her. "Now I've got to put this stupid hand-me-down dress on and go to the gala tomorrow night, where Papa will parade me up and down like a prize heifer!"

"My advice, Patricia, is for you to go ahead and do as your father wishes. Then on Monday, you can sit down and think about the life that lies ahead of you and what you might be able to make of it. And if it will help, please come into the shop and have tea with me anytime you like. I think you need to talk with someone who can understand your loss."

Just then the door flew open, and Almeda Stanhope breezed into the room, newly hatted, with Rose Halpenny and her half-dozen bonnets in tow. There would be no more intimate conversation at Chepstow today.

Beth dropped Rose Halpenny off at the shop and took the cutter down to Baldwin House. Robert hid his astonishment at a conspicuously pregnant woman making her way adroitly through the startled clerks in the outer office to the latter's chamber. There, over a cup of tea and a scone, Beth recounted her conversation with Patricia Stanhope as accurately as she could, while Marc and Robert listened with increasing fascination.

When she had finished, Robert whistled softly and said, "Well, Mrs. Edwards, you have triumphed where no man, however clever he may deem himself, could have. You have produced new facts that put quite a different complexion on Chepstow and its troublesome guest."

"First of all," Marc said, taking Robert's cue, "my suspicion that Patricia and Caleb were more than friends has been confirmed. Mama was objecting but was seemingly helpless. A volatile mixture of emotions, wouldn't you say?"

"And everyone afraid of the colonel's temper and prickly pride," Robert added. "But if he suspected that his daughter was having an improper relationship with Coltrane, he not only hid it very well, he seems to have inadvertently promoted it by allowing her to see him every morning."

"But he does finally go down there," Marc said, "the evening before the murder, a fact he deliberately withheld from me."

"Though the visit had no apparent effect on his daughter's access to the prisoner," Robert said, puzzled. "She's there bright and early the next morning."

"Maybe he didn't need to have a showdown with Mr. Coltrane," Beth said.

Marc smiled. "And I thought I was the detective in the family."

"You think he took the opportunity to slip the strychnine into one of the snuff boxes?" Robert said, arching a brow.

Marc thought about that. "It's possible, but consider the disadvantage of that manoeuvre. He knew, I'm sure, that Coltrane never or rarely took snuff until an hour or so after breakfast and in all likelihood saved his first snort for ostentatious display in front of his initial visitor each morning. Stanhope also knew that Boynton Tierney was due at ten o'clock and that Billy and I were scheduled for one o'clock. There were always two or more snuff boxes on that desk. Sooner or later Coltrane would take a puff from the poisoned one, perhaps throwing suspicion on whoever happened to be there at the time."

"But very risky, eh?" Robert said, taking up the theme. "His own daughter would be there at breakfast. What if Coltrane broke his routine and died a ghastly death right before her eyes? It's hard to believe he would take such a chance, remote as it might have been, especially when the prisoner was going to be moved to Fort York in three or four days, pending the start of the trial."

"After which he would be hanged and out of his daughter's life forever."

"But if he didn't go down there to poison Coltrane, and his daughter continued her daily assignation the next morning, why *did* he go there?" Robert said.

"I intend to ask him, if he'll see me again."

"But all he has to do is deny it or invent some plausible and innocent explanation, like taking the fellow some reading material," Robert said, playing the barrister.

"You're right. Certainly, if he is involved in some way, it's proof we need, not speculation."

"It might be wiser if we let Doubtful Dick loose on him when he cross-examines."

"I'm looking forward to that."

"And what about Almeda Stanhope?" Beth said.

"Yes, there's something we don't know about her yet," Marc said. "Is she so much under the colonel's spell or so afraid of him that she'd let her daughter's honour be compromised rather than tell him about Patricia's visits to Coltrane?"

"You're hinting they did more than kiss?" Beth asked.

Robert blushed and looked out the window.

"You've read my mind, love."

"Sometimes it isn't that hard," she said, and they both smiled.

Robert, his normal colour returning, coughed and said, "Don't you think we might be speculating a bit far here?"

"Maybe," Marc said. "But it's Beth who saw how devastated the girl is. And it was I who peeked into the cozy, curtained-off bedroom where Coltrane slept. The door to the anteroom is thick and was closed during my hour-long interview with him. A very private sort of arrangement, I'd say."

"Then you're suggesting that Almeda may have figured out a way to put a quick and permanent end to the affair? In her mind, even three or four more days might've proved disastrous for her daughter." Without intending to, he glanced at the pregnant woman in the room.

Marc sighed. "We've got to find Bostwick at all costs. He was the jailer there except for the day of the murder. If anyone knew what might be happening day to day and who could've been sneaking in, it's him. Perhaps Cobb will play truant long enough to set his snitches on the adjutant's trail."

"Good idea. Will you approach him?"

"As soon as I can manage it."

Beth got up. "I must return to the shop," she said. "We still have a ton of work to do before the ball tomorrow."

Robert was about to advise her to take it easy but thought better of it.

It was about four o'clock that afternoon when Horatio Cobb, his fingers and toes numb and his snout two shades of red darker, came ambling along King Street towards the Court House to report to the sarge that, miraculously, no marchers had yet appeared either at Government House or Chepstow. Now he knew why: they had all moved back for another go at the jail. This time, though, there were no women among the dozen or so placard carriers milling about in the courtyard like army ants without a hill. In fact he recognized no one. The usual Orange-a-tans were absent, gearing up, he'd been informed by Nestor Peck, for a massive protest tomorrow. These people here appeared to be ruffians from the township, bored or mischievous or both. Their signs were predictably banal: "Free Prince Billy Now!" and "McNair for Mayor!"

He strode through them with the disdain they deserved. Even though he himself was sympathetic to Billy and suspected that he might be innocent, Cobb disapproved of these bully tactics. Besides, he knew Marc Edwards (the major, as he called him affectionately), and if he were given time, the man would get to the truth. Deep down, he wished he could join him in the effort. Investigating sure beat freezing your toes off while traipsing up and down the same street like some donkey on a mill wheel.

Cobb was surprised to be met at the door by the chief, flanked by Constables Brown, Rossiter, and Wilkie.

"What's up?" he said.

"The governor's dander," Sturges said angrily.

"When ain't it?"

"Thorpe's just come over to tell us we're under orders to chase these hooligans away from the area," Sturges said, indicating the protesters.

"But they'll go away as soon as the sun goes down and their balls start conjellin'," Cobb said. "Don't Saint George know that?"

"He's decided he's had enough of protests." Sturges sighed. "He's got wind of the big march planned fer tomorrow. He's called all the militia officers in fer a meetin' first thing in the mornin'. Meantime, he wants the streets cleared of all riffraff."

"Get yer stick primed," Wilkie said helpfully, with a nod at Sturges.

Following their chief's lead, the four constables took out their truncheons and, moving slowly towards the crowd a dozen yards ahead, began tapping them on their gloved left palms.

"You are commanded by the governor to disperse yerselves

immediately!" Sturges shouted, trying to recapture the sergeant's intimidating boom from his salad days on the Spanish peninsula.

The youths looked more puzzled than intimidated. The handles of their placards were as thick as cricket bats and longer than the constables' truncheons.

"This looks like trouble," Sturges said. "Let me try to talk them down." He dropped his truncheon to his side, and his men followed suit. He walked towards a burly, pug-nosed fellow who appeared to be their ringleader. Sturges affected a smile. "We don't want nobody hurt here, and there's no reason why there need be. You've had all day to make yer point with nobody botherin' ya. The governor's in the process of callin' out the militia, so there's no call to provoke him any further, is there?"

Three of the toughs swaggered brazenly up to Sturges and the constables flanking him. One had a menacing grin on his face. "The army, eh?" he said, with much bravado before his chums, as if relishing the superior challenge.

"I'm afraid so, lads."

It was at this point that Ewan Wilkie, never nimble at the best of times and downright clubfooted when he was cold and sleepy, stumbled and pitched forward. Thinking to break his fall with the prop in hand, he instead broke the latter resoundingly over the left knee of the ugliest tough. Assuming an ambush triggered by treachery, the mob behind him flew into action. Placard sticks were brandished and swung viciously in concert with primal cries of outrage.

Cobb barely had time to get his truncheon up to parry a lethal blow aimed at his head. The force of it stunned him momentarily, just long enough for a second stout placard handle to crack against the seam where his helmet met his forehead. He felt himself falling backwards into unoccupied space. Desperately he flung his left arm out to cushion his fall. A spasm of excruciating pain dazzled its way up to his elbow. Then the daylight vanished, and everything else with it.

• • •

Robert and Marc worked for another hour or so, writing up detailed notes on the facts of the case uncovered thus far, along with their current interpretation of them. Robert would take these up to Dougherty after supper, where the great barrister's gloss would be added.

"Let's take a step back, Robert, and get a grasp of the larger picture, shall we? There are several things that don't add up in regard to the relationship between the colonel and Coltrane."

"For example?"

"My sense of Stanhope is that he is a vain, pompous martinet, but I feel that his obsession with military protocol and honour are genuine."

"So he'd need a powerful motive to murder the man he swore to protect?"

"True, but what's puzzling me is the extent to which he seems to have gone in coddling the prisoner. It's one thing to feed and clothe him properly, and even permit him nonhazardous reading material. But why grant visiting rights to journalists who then print inflammatory articles that disturb the very constituency who have placed the colonel on a pedestal and dubbed him patriot?"

"I see where you're going here. And we'd have to include the lengthy visits with his own daughter."

"There's also the duel, remember, where all this started. To get that to happen, Coltrane must have procured Bostwick's whole-hearted cooperation. How? Bostwick owed his position and status to the colonel, not Coltrane. Did Coltrane have some kind of hold over Bostwick?"

"Or over the colonel. Remember, he might have known about the duel and merely looked the other way."

"Exactly. I'm now convinced that it was the prisoner who was calling all the shots at Chepstow."

"But what threat could he bring to bear on the colonel and Bostwick?"

"That is something that we will have to find out," Marc said. "I'll get to Cobb before morning. He can alert his snitches to look for Bostwick without compromising his duty, I'm sure. And when I get to that drunken lieutenant, I intend to grill him within an inch of his life."

"That's the spirit!"

Cobb came to in the outer room of the police station. He was lying on his back on Gussie French's writing table. Around him, with faces so concerned that he became alarmed himself, were Chief Sturges, a white-cheeked Wilkie, Magistrate Thorpe, Doc Withers, and Gussie himself, peering anxiously at his toppled ink bottle.

"Jesus, my noggin hurts!" Cobb declared to the assembly.

"It ought to," Withers said, looking much relieved. "You got a bump on it bigger than your nose!"

"Did ya catch the bugger?" Cobb said.

"We didn't," Sturges said, with a scowl at Thorpe. "The magistrate come out and shot at the church steeple with his musket, and everybody scarpered—except you, of course."

Cobb tried to sit up and gave a yelp that startled the onlookers.

"I was just about to tell you not to try that," Withers said. "I've examined your arm. It's not broken, but you've got a very badly sprained wrist. You'll need to have it in a sling for at least two weeks, I'd guess."

Cobb was still wincing at the pain everywhere in his arm, but he managed to say, "But I can't work with one hand."

"Of course, you can't, Cobb," the chief said kindly. "I'm orderin' you to stay at home fer the duration. I don't want you in uniform anywheres near this place till you're fit again."

"But—"

"Put yer feet up and relax. Let Dora play nursemaid, eh?"

"But we'll starve—ow!" Cobb rolled over on his right side away from the throbbing.

"We've already started takin' up a collection. Gussie here's been put in charge."

Gussie tried to smile at this accolade but couldn't do it. "Watch that ink bottle, will ya?" he snapped at the patient.

Marc was surprised when he arrived home at five to find Beth already there. "Oh," he said happily, "I'm glad you called it a day. You've had a full plate of it."

"I just got in ten minutes ago," Beth said. "I thought you'd be here or I'd've driven the cutter down to Baldwin's."

"What's wrong?"

"Nothing. In fact there may be something right."

Marc tossed his coat over a chair. Beth was holding a paper in one hand.

"A short while ago, Annie Brush came over from the workroom to see me. She said that yesterday she'd been ripping stitches out of a side seam in Mrs. Stanhope's gown so we could make it fit Patricia, when she felt this piece of paper. It was sewn in between the gown and the lining. She gave it to Rose, who took it out and set it aside, and forgot about it till this afternoon. I think you'd better read it. It's a letter."

October 1

Dearest D.

I am appalled to learn that the tempestuous affair we shared in our youth—and oh so briefly renewed last spring in Detroit—has been discovered by the old ogre. But rest assured I shall make him pay for it and then rescue you from that humdrum and corrupt

*life under the tyranny of the British Crown. I know you secretly
share my cause and will not flinch at the actions that must be
taken. Your husband is both pompous and venal, a pretentious
bankrupt. I have already written to him outlining my proposal.
He may or may not wish to involve you, but he will accede to
my "suggestion." And when the province has been liberated and
securely attached to the only free republic in the world, you and I
shall be reunited—safe in one another's arms.*

Your demon lover,

L.

P.S. Please destroy this letter.

"My God, Beth, I could kiss you!"
"Don't make promises you can't carry out," Beth said, laughing.

ELEVEN

"What does it mean?" Beth asked eagerly.

"Well," Marc said, rereading the letter and thinking hard, "it was deliberately secreted in Almeda Stanhope's gown. We have to assume that she hid it there herself. Any other assumption is untenable."

"And the writer is 'C,' which could stand for Caleb, Caleb Coltrane."

"That would be my first guess, certainly."

"But then who is the 'D' it's addressed to?"

"That would be Almeda Stanhope."

"But she's not a 'D,'" Beth protested.

"To some she is. I overheard the butler, Absalom Shad, whom she brought to Toronto from Michigan, refer to her as 'Duchess,' a nickname from childhood, I'd wager."

Beth's eyes lit up. "I remember now, when she and Patricia came in the other day, I was sure I picked out an American accent. And she mentioned, when we got to talking, how much she'd enjoyed a trip to St. Thomas last spring to visit her brother-in-law—the colonel's family lives there—because it was so close to home."

"I'll bet she's from Detroit or thereabouts, then. And Butler

Shad as well. He was recommended to her by a sister in Port Huron, but I suspect they've all known one another for some time."

"Then this is a love letter, from Coltrane to Almeda?" Beth said, somewhat shocked.

"And a lot more than that. He warns her that the 'old ogre,' her husband, has learned of the renewal of their youthful affair 'last spring.'"

"You figure she slipped over to Detroit for a rendezvous?"

"I do. And the two became lovers again. But if the colonel knows," Marc went on, "then he certainly is not behaving like a cuckolded husband."

"It isn't something you'd go on parade with." Beth smiled, ever amused at the pockets of naiveté still present in her worldly beloved.

"I think I see what's going on here. You're right, in that public exposure of the relationship—a decorated colonel's wife consorting with an enemy 'general'—would be ruinous to Stanhope."

"Do you think he found some other love letters like this one?"

Marc smiled, marvelling at his wife's innocence. "No, I don't. I think Caleb Coltrane informed him—despite his disingenuous denial here—giving him chapter and verse, and threatening to go public with the sordid affair."

"But why would he do that?"

"Look at the date: October first. We have to assume it's last fall."

"I see. Two months before the raid at Windsor."

"The 'proposal' mentioned here, whatever it is, is undoubtedly part of the blackmail scheme. Either the colonel does his bidding or he exposes him as a cuckold, with a love letter or two, I'll wager, from Almeda as damning proof."

"You figure it was due to the army business, then?"

"What else? And my intuition tells me that the colonel, as

Coltrane hints here, may not have told his wife about the threat. My reading of him is that he is so brittle and so proud that he has likely been carrying on as if nothing has happened."

"But Almeda does know, eh? And she even kept this dangerous letter, hiding it in the dress."

"And was either ordered to stay away from Coltrane or was wise enough not to risk visiting him in his cell, though she must have been sorely tempted after learning about her daughter's attraction to him."

"But how could the colonel be helpful to the Yankee raiders?"

"Stanhope is a wealthy merchant, isn't he? The odds are that this was an attempt to extract money, to buy arms and bribe government officials. Remember, love, that the Hunters' Lodges are technically illegal in the United States."

"So you think the colonel sent him money?"

"I do. Stanhope must have been worried sick, not only about Almeda's affair being revealed, but if he did give Coltrane money, and Coltrane somehow had evidence of this—perhaps another letter—then not only could that fact humiliate him, he could be tried for treason."

"But the letter calls the colonel 'a bankrupt,'" Beth pointed out.

"A figure of speech probably. Even if Stanhope was cash poor, what with raising his own regiment over the summer, he still has property, possessions, and a business to draw upon."

"If you're right, love, it's no wonder the colonel was coddling the prisoner."

"Yes. I've thought all along that there was more than military courtesy involved. If Coltrane concluded he was going to hang, he intended to spend his final weeks on this earth in style. And in addition, his speechifying in the local press permitted him to propagate his fanatical opinions."

"And it would be a lot easier for him to be rescued from Chepstow than the jail or the fort, wouldn't it?"

"Exactly. When I spoke with him, he did not in any way appear to be a doomed man, though I believe he was a consummate actor and dissembler."

"But if all this is so, the colonel was playing with fire every hour of every day."

Marc whistled slowly. "Perhaps he got tired of the game with his unpredictable guest and decided to make sure that any agreement they had tacitly made would be rendered null and void."

"You mean by poisoning him."

"Exactly. Though I doubt he would risk it by salting the snuff box the evening before the murder, because of the possibility of involving his daughter. I really must interrogate him again."

"Do you believe Almeda is a republican sympathizer, as the letter says?"

"I don't know, but I intend to ask her."

Beth raised both eyebrows.

"I'll find a way to get to her, even if I have to hide in the bushes and wait for the old martinet to leave the house."

"Don't forget, he's a soldier."

"As I was," Marc replied with a reassuring grin.

Marc now felt as if they were getting somewhere with the case. He realized, though, that a vaguely dated letter with only a pair of initials to identify its author and his paramour would be neither admissible nor useful in court. He had to get corroboration from Almeda Stanhope in advance of the trial, and although that would not be easy, he was confident that he could find a way. The handwriting was very distinctive, and it occurred to Marc that they might be able to match it with that of the notes and personal papers Coltrane had in his prison chamber. But as soon as he had mentioned this possibility to Beth, he recalled that Stanhope had already packed everything personal of Coltrane's and shipped the lot to Detroit. Was this the act of a gentleman carrying out the murdered man's likely wishes or one of enlightened self-interest? Either way, it was hard not to believe that the colonel had rifled through every item looking for the evidence used to blackmail him, whatever it was. And if he had found it, it would be burned or buried by now.

All this was explained to Robert Baldwin the first thing Saturday morning. Marc and Robert went over the letter again, phrase by phrase, but came up with nothing that had not already been thought of.

"There's every reason to be hopeful," Robert said. "We're beginning to stir up the kind of information that Dougherty asked for in our two-hour discussion last night. The man's limbs may move slower than an adder in January, but his tongue and his brain are lightning quick and almost as lethal. He feels that our best approach is to suggest other candidates with motive and opportunity. For example, he's sure that the colonel will be a key witness for the Crown and that he'll be able to make hash out of him on the stand. I'm sure he'll know precisely how to use this letter, even if it doesn't make it in as evidence."

"But if I can get Almeda Stanhope to verify it, then we'll get it in and be able to call her as our own witness, hostile or not."

"That's a tall order, Marc, even for you."

"There's another aspect of the letter that intrigues me. It's plain that the blackmail was initiated and continued entirely by letter, sometime in late September or early October. By November fourth or fifth, Stanhope was in Amherstburg training the Windsor militia, but there would be no safe time or place for the two men to meet down there. The money, I'm sure, would have been sent by mail or letter of credit."

"What are you saying?"

"That it's conceivable, even probable, that one or more pieces of incriminating correspondence were still in Coltrane's possession—somewhere in that prison chamber."

Robert gave that notion some thought. "That would explain Coltrane's iron grip on the colonel. He could have made a copy of one of the colonel's letters to spook him and kept the original stashed nearby."

"If so, then Stanhope would have scoured that chamber while Coltrane took his daily exercise in the yard outside, or even in the middle of the night. But wherever it was hidden, it seems to have stayed so. Coltrane was still getting his way on the day of his murder."

"Perhaps the cunning bugger had made arrangements with one of his many sympathizers here or in Michigan in regard to the letter or one like it, to be made public should he be mistreated or hanged."

"Then why would the colonel risk killing him?"

"Good question, Counsellor," Robert conceded. After a pause he said, "By the way, I spoke with Cummings a while ago. There's only one Jones within a mile of Streetsville, and he's a sixty-year-old bachelor."

"Putting him in a dress and bonnet wouldn't fool even Butler Shad," Marc said.

"So we're not likely ever to discover the identity of the mysterious Mrs. Jones who signed Coltrane's visitor's book."

Marc agreed, but added, "It's possible, though, that Mrs. Jones is connected to the fellow I saw skulking about the grounds on Wednesday."

"An American sympathizer, perhaps, looking to free Coltrane?"

"That's the best bet, I'd say. Jones could have been delivering information about a rescue attempt. Perhaps they saw Bostwick leave and decided to make their move before a proper replacement was installed."

Robert hesitated before saying, "You don't suppose that Jones was sent by the Hunters to poison Coltrane, do you?"

"We can't discount that, can we? Thieves do fall out."

"You're referring to some internal feud or power struggle among the Hunters."

"What I'm doing," Marc admitted ruefully, "is clutching at straws."

Marc declined the macaroon Robert offered him from a crystal dish on his desk. "But I've just thought of something important in regard to the blackmail theory. There are only two ways that Coltrane could have had possession of incriminating material in his cell."

Robert said without hesitation, "It was shipped to him in the goods from Detroit or—"

"Or he had it on his person at Windsor and wasn't searched properly."

"Maybe our chivalric colonel was too courteous to do it thoroughly."

"There is one person whom we can ask about that, isn't there?"

Robert nodded.

Billy McNair was not in good shape when Marc and Robert met him in Calvin Strangway's anteroom at the jail a half-hour later. Despite his accomplishments, he was still a young man and thus susceptible to the sudden ups and downs characteristic of youth. Dolly's visit the evening before had lifted his spirits enormously and her departure had depressed them correspondingly. Robert tried to cheer him by briefly outlining the new evidence and playing up the vaunted abilities of Doubtful Dick Dougherty.

"I do appreciate what you're doin' fer me," Billy said with glum resignation. "But Mr. Strangway says the governor's fixed on me as the culprit and I better prepare to make peace with my Maker. I told him I didn't want to see no preacher in here!"

"Fortunately, your jailer is not your attorney," Robert said soothingly. "Nor is Sir George the maharajah of Upper Canada.

You will get a proper trial. Mr. Dougherty and I—along with Chief Justice Robinson—will see to that."

Marc cleared his throat. "But right now, Billy, you are the one who can help us most."

Billy looked up expectantly. He was a young man, fatherless since three, who was always more comfortable helping himself than relying upon the aid of others. "Tell me how," he said.

"I'd like you to think back to the day you captured Coltrane, painful as that may be," Marc said.

"I think of it every day. What do you need to know?"

"You were the one to go through Coltrane's papers, and you delivered them to Colonel Stanhope."

"I was."

"Can you recall what those papers were?"

"I can. There was one with military orders on it fer Coltrane's unit and with it a kind of battle sketch or route march. Most of it was mumbo jumbo to me. Then there was a silly proclamation to be read aloud in village squares. I just folded the three sheets up and gave them to the colonel. He seemed very pleased."

"And nothing else?"

Billy hesitated, then said casually, "There was a personal letter, but I tucked it back into the major's blouse."

"Personal?" Robert said with restrained excitement. "How so?"

"Well, it was a love letter from some lady, his mistress, I think. It was written in a woman's style anyways."

"Can you recall any names in it, or what it said?"

Billy had to think about this. "It was addressed to 'my dear C' or somethin' like that—no name. I don't remember anything particular about the message, except it was gushy. It didn't have anything to do with Coltrane's unit and so I really didn't want to read every word. There was another initial signed at the bottom."

Marc and Robert waited, but Billy just shook his head regretfully.

"Could it have been a 'D'?" Marc prompted.

"Yeah, but I couldn't swear to it."

"I don't think you'll have to," Marc said, thinking hard about how he might use this new information in any interview with Almeda Stanhope. Then he turned his attention back to Billy. "Was Coltrane taken to the surgeon as soon as you reached headquarters?"

Again Billy did not hesitate. "He was. I took him there myself, and I watched the surgeon cut off his shirt and cauterize the wound."

"Where was the love letter you'd tucked in there?"

This time Billy did pause to reflect. "It fell out. And I said to the doctor and one of the majors, 'It's okay, it's just a letter from his girl.' So the surgeon tucked it into a leather Bible Coltrane kept in his kit."

Marc whistled.

"What is it?" Robert said.

"That same leather Bible sat on Coltrane's desk, between the two snuff boxes."

Robert and Marc walked through the tunnel to the Court House. Robert had suggested that they inquire of Magistrate Thorpe, who had been assigned to prosecute the case, whether the Crown's attorney had taken possession of the affidavit Coltrane signed just before his death. After which, they intended to return to the office and mull over the implications of what Billy had just revealed. However, they were forestalled by the unexpected appearance of Chief Sturges in the hallway outside Thorpe's chamber.

"What's the matter, Wilf?" Robert said. "You look as if you've been hit by a cricket bat."

Sturges grimaced. "Not me, lads, but poor ol' Cobb got it, flush on his bald spot."

"Is he all right?" Marc asked, instantly concerned.

"Who would do that?" Robert demanded at the same time.

"That gang of thugs picketin' outside the jail yesterday afternoon. We'd been just ignorin' them, but 'is majesty ordered us to clear them off the road, so we went out to persuade them, like, and the next thing you know, there's a stampede, and Cobb gets clobbered with a stick, and when he falls, he manages to sprain his wrist. His helmet took the sting outta the blow, but he's got a mighty sore arm. I told him not to show up here for two weeks. I've just been signin' up supernumeraries to cover for him."

"I'll go over and see how he's doing," Marc said to Sturges, "as soon as I can. He's only two blocks from my house."

"I'd advise that," Sturges said, forcing a chuckle, "'cause Dora'll need people to keep him outta her hair—else he's likely to get another whack on the noggin!"

"It's too bad it was Cobb," Robert said. "You could use him when the Orangemen go marching later today."

"You're right, there. Cobb's my best man. But we've been promised help from the two Toronto militia regiments."

"Oh?"

"Yeah, Sir George has called in all the officers fer a strategy meetin' this mornin'. They oughta be there fer the next hour anyways."

Marc didn't even say thank you or good-bye. He was heading for the door and Chepstow, twenty minutes' walk away. Colonel Stanhope would be the first officer to answer the governor's call to arms. Which meant he would be absent from home, for an hour or more.

Almeda Stanhope would be on her own.

Marc walked north up Brock Street and approached the house cautiously from the side. It was past ten o'clock, and the colonel was almost certainly at Government House preening and advising. It was the butler he had to be wary of. He realized that this might be his only chance to confront Almeda before the trial next Friday. He crossed his fingers, nodded to the sentries on the walk, stepped up onto the porch, and tugged the bell rope. Thirty agonizing seconds later, the door was opened by Shad.

"Whaddaya want?" he snapped in a very unbutler-like tone.

"Kindly tell Mrs. Stanhope that Mr. Edwards must see her. It is a matter of life and death."

"She ain't home."

"Sir, I know she is, by the colonel's command."

"Know an awful lot, don't ya?"

Marc merely waited the man out. Finally Absalom Shad turned and disappeared down the hall, but not before kicking the door shut in Marc's face. With one foot against the jamb, Marc easily stopped it from clicking closed. He heard voices from what he took to be the women's sitting room near the head of the hall. Shad shuffled back to Marc, still truculent. "This way, sir. The lady will see you."

Almeda Stanhope was seated on the very edge of a brocaded settee near a Venetian marble fireplace. She turned to face her visitor, and Marc saw a striking woman of forty-five with rich, dark curls, faded gray only at the temples, and very delicate, feminine features of a kind favoured by porcelain artists. She was fashionably attired, and except for the perilous perch she had on the settee's edge, one would have taken her for the chatelaine at ease in her own home and ready to welcome a gentleman to tea and polite conversation.

Marc bowed. Shad had taken his overcoat, hat, and gloves: he sensed this visit would be neither brief nor pro forma.

Almeda looked directly into Marc's eyes. Her own revealed a woman of some character and depth, no cringing wife to a martinet husband. In a low but controlled voice she said, "You've found the letter."

This was not the way he had envisaged the conversation opening, but he recovered enough to say quietly, "We did."

"It was stupid of me to keep it in the first place," she said without emotion, as if the fact were in evidence and irretrievable.

"May I sit down, ma'am?"

"Please, do. You must forgive my manners; I've been somewhat distracted of late."

Marc sat down opposite her on a Queen Anne chair. "You've had a man murdered in your own house . . ."

She nodded. "The gown was mine, of course—Mrs. Edwards knew that—and the question of Patricia's having to wear it only came up after the New Year. You see, my husband has been paying so much attention to his army career, he has neglected his business."

Along with sizeable chunks of cash paid out to a blackmailer, Marc thought. "So you were a trifle, ah, impecunious?"

"Yes. It turned out that we couldn't afford to buy Patricia the coming-out gown she deserved. I tried to make it up to her by letting her choose one of mine to be made over for her. I was certain she'd pick one of the two I bought in September, but she chose otherwise."

She made a small grimace of self-recrimination and continued. "To my consternation, she took the gown with the letter in it to her room. Next day it went straight to Smallman's. I thought it best just to wait and hope it wouldn't be found, and even if it was, I counted on Mrs. Halpenny's discretion. I assumed she would immediately tuck it into one of the pockets or give it to me personally. My only fear at that time was that my daughter would find it. I didn't know, of course, what was to happen here on Thursday."

"Before that, however, I believe you'd been distracted by more pressing, personal concerns," Marc prompted.

"My life has been full of pressing personal concerns," she said with a rueful smile. "Don't believe only what you see around you here."

"You were worried sick about Patricia and Caleb."

She flinched. "I was. But someone helped me out there, didn't they?"

"I don't believe it was Billy, ma'am; that's why I'm here. I have no desire to disrupt your household and domestic life arbitrarily or needlessly, but I know you can help me prove the lad's innocence."

Almeda smiled with her lips, but her whole countenance seemed to darken. "None of us is innocent, Mr. Edwards. At least not after we're weaned."

"You realize that I have grasped the implications of the letter you kept and hid from your husband."

"You're only guessing that it concerned me and my husband. How do you know it wasn't sent to one of my servants?"

Marc decided to ignore the evidentiary aspects of the matter for the moment. "It is a love letter to an older woman with whom the writer had had an affair in their youth. The ogre-husband is wealthy and thus ripe for blackmail. The love affair was renewed last spring, a time when you and Gideon were visiting relatives in St. Thomas, a half-day's journey from Detroit. The lovers share a political ideal: to 'liberate this province.' A blackmail threat has already been made, and the ogre apprised of the liaison. None of this sounds like a billet-doux penned to a servant."

Almeda stared at the fire and played absently with her fine, manicured fingers. "You are very perceptive. They told me you knew how to investigate."

"Have I interpreted the letter correctly?" Marc said very gently, almost in a whisper.

"No, not quite. Not at all in any way that really matters."

"But blackmail is a powerful motive for murder."

Almeda appeared not to have heard this probing remark. She continued to stare at the fire. "You see, Mr. Edwards, Caleb

Coltrane and I were cousins. His sister Gladys and I were not only related but the best of friends. We grew up together just outside of Detroit. Caleb and I had a brief but passionate romance when we were very young, children really, trying on adult roles. It was over in a single summer."

"But you did see him last spring?"

"I went from St. Thomas to see Mrs. Dobbs—Gladys—who now lives in Detroit. We hadn't seen each other for a few years, not since her husband died."

"And Caleb was there?"

"He came on the second last day."

"The letter suggests you renewed your relationship."

"I know what it says. But I also know what happened."

Marc saw where she was going. "The reinfatuation was entirely on his side?"

"It was. He was obsessed with the republican cause and his role in the Michigan chapter of the Hunters' Lodge. He was a man of many passions. But we did not 'renew our relationship,' as you so tactfully put it. And I have lived happily in this province and this city for twenty years. Both are my home. My husband and daughter are British subjects."

"Then you're suggesting that the letter is a fantasy on Caleb's part?"

"He was a fanatical democrat. In his zeal he may have misread my response to him in Detroit."

"But he speaks of using that affair to blackmail your husband, and of reuniting with you when the province has been liberated."

"I assumed that he needed money."

"Surely your husband would have confronted you about the attempted blackmail and the grounds for it, doubly so if he were pressed for cash."

Almeda stared hard at the flames, as if her glare could douse them. "Of course, he did. I told him the truth. We never spoke of it again."

"But he didn't exactly believe you, did he? He is a proud and vain man. He feared any breath of scandal would scupper his hopes for standing and success, so he succumbed to the blackmail. And he continued to do so throughout Caleb's incarceration in this house—not with dollars but rather with favours of every kind, including the exposure of his daughter to the blandishments of a villain."

"Gideon does not discuss such matters with me; I'm only his wife," she said, with no attempt to acknowledge the irony or moderate her bitterness.

"You must have wondered why Caleb was treated so well, why he was able to insist that Patricia visit him for lengthy breakfasts."

"Of course I did!" She had turned at last to face him. "But I got no answers from my husband, and I had no control over my daughter's romantic foolishness!"

Marc leaned forward. "Mrs. Stanhope, we have every reason to believe that Coltrane had in his possession, at Windsor and here at Chepstow, an incriminating letter that he had hidden somewhere and with which he was able to threaten your husband. My hunch is that it was a letter in your handwriting, either a love note or a letter with enough ambiguity, given the circumstances, to persuade your husband of its potential dangers if made public."

"I did write Caleb a letter after I got home. As his cousin and friend, I begged him to abandon the Hunters' Lodge and stay where he was, safe in Michigan. And naturally I expressed my joy at seeing him and Gladys, the three of us together again . . .'"

So there was such a letter! Billy's hazy description of it did not do it justice. The question was, where was it?

"But why do you need to know all this? Even if I had had an affair with Caleb in Detroit—and I didn't, as my cousin Gladys will tell you—what pertinence does it have to his murder? You may be right about my husband's pandering to Caleb; I don't have any idea of what they discussed or why. If Gideon didn't believe my denial, he has not raised the issue since. And Caleb was destined to be hanged by the end of the month."

"Blackmail and threats, based on tangible evidence, are both sound reasons why Caleb might be murdered. After all, he still held a trump card—your letter, however tenuous its implications—one he could play before he could be hanged."

Almeda went white. "Oh, I see. You're trying to give my husband a motive for murder!"

"Yes. But rest assured we could never prove he did it. However, we need to show the court only that there were other, plausible sus—"

"And rest assured I will not take the witness stand and give evidence that might implicate my husband. It would destroy him."

"I understand, ma'am."

"And surely you would not deliberately smear his good name on the basis of one letter from a self-serving fanatic?"

"I would not, unless we were to find the other letter, the one actually used for blackmail."

"If such a letter exists."

Marc nodded. The thought of a subpoenaed Almeda Stanhope being grilled by the ruthless Mr. Dougherty sent a chill up Marc's spine. But it might be necessary. He was convinced that somewhere among her frank admissions lay a lie or two. But where?

"Thank you for speaking so candidly with me. Nothing you said will leave this room unless it proves vital to saving an innocent youth from the gallows."

Marc rose and bowed. He paused halfway to the door and turned around. "May I ask one last question? Why did you keep Caleb's letter in the lining of your gown?"

Her eyes were filled with tears, the dignified tears of one who has suffered and survived. "You don't understand, do you? You're not a woman. What Caleb and I had that summer long ago was the best thing that has ever happened to me. I've only felt half-alive since. I love my husband and daughter, but I wanted to keep some warm reminder that I could touch from time to time, when I was out dancing and trying to be happy."

Marc had a sudden and palpable image of this intelligent and mature woman on the arm of the nouveau-riche merchant who thought he was Lord Wellington.

The front door banged shut. They both froze.

"The colonel!" Almeda gasped.

Marc put his finger to his lips.

They heard the sound of Stanhope stamping about as he removed his outer clothing. Then the voice of Absalom Shad as he came running down the hall towards his master: "I wouldn't go in there, sir, the Duchess is—"

But the door to the sitting room burst open, and Colonel Stanhope marched in. His gaze took in his wife, then the intruder. His moustache bristled like barbed wire strummed.

"I specifically told you to stay away from my wife, sir, and you have deliberately and callously disobeyed me! Now—"

"I apologize, Colonel, but you left me with little choice. The trial is next Friday."

"How dare you continue your impudence in my very presence! I want you to leave my home immediately, or I'll be forced to draw my sabre and give you a proper thrashing!"

Marc's instinct was to take two steps towards the seething man in the tunic and, sabre or no sabre, thrash him till his moustaches dropped off. But he caught sight of Almeda out of the corner of his eye.

"Please, Mr. Edwards . . ."

Marc bowed to her and walked briskly out of the room.

Behind him came the trumpeting umbrage of the upstaged colonel: "I don't want to see you in or near this house again! You are not to speak to my family or my servants, or I'll have the law on you!"

As Marc let himself out, he noticed the butler hovering anxiously near the sitting room door.

"And I hope they hang the young hothead!" the colonel roared.

TWELVE

Robert nibbled at the last of the macaroons. A tasty luncheon had been brought in from the other side of Baldwin House, and its remnants lay forlorn on the silver serving tray.

"All right, Marc, indulge me while I play defense counsel summing up what we know and what we think we know. Stop me when you think I've got it seriously wrong."

"That should help me write up a proper chronology for Dougherty," Marc agreed. "Go ahead: my pencil is poised." Over lunch Marc had reprised the drama at Chepstow, and they had mulled over the information Billy had provided.

Robert cleared his throat, focused his gaze on an imagined jury, and began: "This entire sequence of events, of cause and effect, started late last February when Gideon Stanhope, importer of dry goods, enlisted in the St. Thomas militia while on one of his periodic visits to his brother. To his surprise and delight, his unit is involved in the action at Pelee, where he is slightly wounded and comports himself well enough to be hailed, on his return to Toronto, as a hero, indeed as the Patriot of Pelee Island. He may not have been aware of it, but at the same battle his wife's cousin, Caleb Coltrane, is fighting on the other side and, according to his own testimony, distinguishes himself so conspicuously that it is he who is crowned the Pelee Island Patriot."

"Perhaps it was those two who should have had the duel," Marc observed.

Robert chuckled and continued. "Having gotten a taste for military conflict and its attendant honours, our Mr. Stanhope leaps at the opportunity to form one of two proposed new militia regiments here in Toronto. He is eminently successful, enlisting competent and committed officers and men. He spends the summer training them, during which time he gets to know and like Billy McNair, his most accomplished sergeant."

"Meanwhile," Marc said, "back in the spring . . ."

"Quite right. In April or May, the Stanhopes go together to St. Thomas to visit the in-laws. Almeda Stanhope seizes the opportunity to slip over to Detroit to call upon her cousin, Gladys—"

"Dobbs," Marc prompted.

"—whom she hasn't seen in some years. Gladys's brother, Caleb, a major in the liberation army and big man in the local Hunters' Lodge, happens to be there at the same time. Caleb had a passionate affair with Almeda when they were teenagers, and he attempts to rekindle the flame when he discovers her staying at his sister's house."

"A house that appears to have been used by Coltrane as a base of operations, since we know that his library and snuff box collection were sent to Chepstow from there and are on their way back there as of yesterday."

Robert nodded. "Precisely what form this renewed affair took is still an open question. What we do know is that Coltrane wrote to his Duchess, expressing his undying love and indicating that, since her husband had discovered their liaison—"

"Probably because he himself revealed it, or possibly but less likely, if there were other letters lying about to be discovered, the colonel stumbled on one."

"Either way, Coltrane initiates a scheme to extort money from her husband. She tells you that most of this is wishful thinking on Coltrane's part, but we can assume from Billy's story that at least one compromising love letter, however circumspect, was sent from Almeda to her admirer in Detroit. That letter, we can be fairly sure, was kept by Coltrane, either because he did care for Almeda or because it was critical to his blackmail scheme."

"For example, if the American Patriots were inexplicably to lose the battle of Windsor and he were to be captured," Marc filled in.

"A fine lover, eh? Anyway, we can now pick up the story at Windsor in December. Again, both 'patriots' distinguish themselves in the conflict, but as Coltrane organizes a strategic withdrawal of what remains of his squad, he is spotted by Captain Muttlebury of the Windsor militia and his sergeant, Billy McNair."

"Who has, along with Stanhope and four other NCOs, been attached to that regiment since early November to assist in their training."

"Right. Muttlebury, we learn later, was in charge of removing a number of crates of rifles and ammunition from a nearby abandoned fort or redoubt. But despite being shown by his colonel where they were buried, he managed to miss at least two crates. This occurred a week or so before the Windsor skirmish. Muttlebury's mistake results in Coltrane's being able to arrange an ambush with fresh rifles and ammunition, during which poor Muttlebury is killed, along with Corporal Melvin Curry, Billy's childhood friend and bosom pal. Billy finds the treacherous Coltrane bleeding to death nearby. He behaves admirably despite his outrage at the ambush—"

"A point I'm certain Dougherty will exploit," Marc added. "Perhaps we should subpoena the official battle reports for that day."

"I agree. I'll put Peachey onto it. Now, where was I?"

"You've got Billy kneeling beside a wounded Coltrane."

"Right. It is Billy, then, who uses his fiancée's gift, her silk kerchief, to apply a tourniquet to Coltrane's arm and save his life. Again, still acting with the utmost military discipline, Billy searches the commanding officer's kit and discovers important military papers, which he keeps to present later to Colonel Stanhope. He also spots a love letter of sorts, written by what appears to be the major's mistress. Believing it to be personal and private, he tucks it safely inside the unconscious man's blouse. Back at their camp, Billy watches as Coltrane's wound is cauterized, and he observes that the love letter is put between the leaves of the fellow's leather-bound Bible."

"The same Bible I observed on Coltrane's desk at Chepstow," Marc said.

"Time now for some critical interpretation. The letter from Coltrane to Almeda, which we possess, when set beside an equally compromising letter from Almeda to Coltrane, presents compelling circumstantial evidence that there was a de facto affair between the two. And a comparison of their respective handwriting would be almost as persuasive to a jury as signatures would."

"Could that be why the colonel was in such a hurry to ship Coltrane's effects back to Detroit?"

"Why not just destroy them?" Robert asked.

"Too risky, at least until Billy was safely convicted. Nor would Sir George be pleased at an act guaranteed to rouse the Hunters' indignation further. After all, the governor's recast trial is meant to calm the waters in the republic. No, I think the colonel had to take a chance that anything still hidden in those effects would stay there undisturbed in Gladys's house."

"More important though, Marc, is the galling fact that we have only one of the two letters. Even if we can find samples of Coltrane's writing here in Toronto—one of our newspaper editors should have a screed or two of his lying about—we have nothing but innuendo without corresponding epistolary proof from Almeda or an admission by her under oath."

"Of which there is almost no chance, since she can't be forced to testify against her husband."

"Nevertheless, the story does continue. Stanhope, having been bled for money by one of the enemy, decides to take personal charge of Coltrane so that he can keep an eye on him till he's hanged. If he did search Coltrane's kit and effects for evidence implicating him in what is tantamount to treason, he missed finding Almeda's letter in the Bible back there in Windsor. Perhaps Coltrane himself was surprised when it fell onto his desk during a quest for religious comfort. We can readily assume that, having it still in his possession, he found a secure place to hide it, among his books most likely. I surmise he made an exact copy of it and began to threaten the colonel again, who must have gone once more to his wife for corroboration. But this time he was being blackmailed not for cash but for favourable treatment at Chepstow. The kow-towing and coddling were obvious to anyone who went near the place."

"The colonel must have been frantic with worry," Marc said. "Not only was the grandest night of his life fast approaching—the Twelfth Night gala where he is to be decorated—but there was the constant threat of his being exposed as a cuckold or worse. Not to mention his only child is visiting the cozy chamber every day and spending an hour or more closeted with the villain. All the while he has to pretend that nothing is amiss, to grin and bear it. He forbids his wife to go near the cell, but it seems that Coltrane is enjoying the daughter more anyway."

"Do you think the wife may have been jealous?"

"I considered that, Robert, but her demeanour this morning and the scrap of dialogue I overheard on Wednesday strongly suggest that she was primarily concerned for Patricia's reputation and well-being."

"Moving on, then, we come to Billy's fateful decision to look the devil in the eye, right in his den. Billy visits Coltrane, they exchange views, argue, and Billy makes an ill-conceived threat to go public with a false account of the battle, in which Coltrane would appear as a coward and a cunning bastard. Coltrane bridles, challenges Billy to a duel, and the silly lad accepts."

"Which brings us to the issue of how an imprisoned soldier can arrange a duel with pistols in the yard outside his cell."

"One word will suffice." Robert smiled. "Bostwick. We know that Bostwick and Stanhope have been associates for some time, and that the former was made the colonel's adjutant, despite having a reputation as a heavy drinker. With or without Stanhope's approval, Bostwick secures two duelling pistols and then acts as umpire and second for both men the next day."

"It would help throw suspicion on the colonel," Marc suggested, "if we could prove that he sanctioned the duel himself. We can show that he considered Billy his protégé and therefore hoped that the lad might be lucky enough to kill his enemy."

"But Cobb will testify that the colonel arrived after the event, enraged at the proceedings."

"A good piece of acting?"

"By the next evening, however, Bostwick is dismissed in disgrace."

"So the colonel will claim. For all we know though, Bostwick might be holed up in some comfortable county inn sniffing French brandy. Cobb has his snitches out looking for the drunken lieutenant—thankfully, something he felt he was able to do for us without compromising his duty."

"Excellent. But to continue: Billy is arrested, makes a public death threat against Coltrane, and is jailed. The rest of the story you know at first hand."

Marc sighed. "I do, and we've been over the variables and possibilities several times."

"What about Stanhope's surprise visit the evening before the murder? Do you really think he planted the poison then?"

"It doesn't matter for our defense, does it? The strategy is to throw plausible suspicion elsewhere and dilute the circumstantial evidence."

"Well, I see you've been reading your Blackstone and Phillipps these past few months." Robert was pleased and amused in equal portions. "You are quite right. It appears as if we'll never be able to discover or prove who did it, and if Billy is acquitted, no one besides Sir George will care. Coltrane's life was nasty, brutish, and short, to quote Hobbes."

"Well, then, Bostwick is a prime candidate for suspicion, isn't he? Perhaps acting on his commander's orders, he pretends to leave in a huff, slips back in—he possesses a full ring of keys for Chepstow—and while Coltrane sleeps, puts strychnine into one of the two snuff boxes. Then he heads for cover. And the colonel plants the packet in Billy's coat during the mêlée in the hall."

"Very possible. But an even more likely candidate is the mysterious Mrs. Jones, the last visitor before you and Billy arrived. Shad, unfamiliar with the jailer's job he has just been assigned, lets the woman get by him with no particular quizzing of who she is or why she's there. And once in, she distracts Coltrane long enough to salt the snuff with coyote bait."

"She would have needed a plausible excuse to obtain Coltrane's permission and to lull him into a false sense of security. He was pompous but no fool."

Robert agreed. "Which suggests she was working for the Hunters, not Bostwick."

"Bearing a password or entry code of some sort."

"His own people wishing him dead, as a martyr to the cause, so to speak?"

"With the added attraction of said martyr appearing to have been assassinated by an agent of the Queen."

"You really must find a way to question Shad further—at the risk of being bayoneted by the colonel." Robert pressed the remaining crumbs of macaroon onto his index finger and licked it contemplatively.

"They might also see Coltrane's upcoming trial as a common murderer as a form of humiliation for the Lodges and a staged triumph for their arch-enemy, Sir George Arthur. Coltrane himself no doubt still expected to be rescued by his compatriots, so he would certainly agree to see one of his own."

"But didn't Shad tell you Mrs. Jones might have been there before?" Robert was flipping through the pages of notes that Marc had compiled so far.

"He seemed confused or flustered about the entire matter. Perhaps he was just trying to cover up for his own insecurity as jailer. Only he could clarify this for us or give us a more detailed description of exactly what happened. But my own ineptness earlier this morning seems to have foreclosed that option."

"We could subpoena him, though. Or, as he'll be a key witness for the Crown, Dougherty could get at this business on cross-examination. I'll make a note of it."

Marc took a deep breath. "I suppose, also, to be absolutely thorough, we have to consider Patricia."

"Motive?"

"None, alas. Beth's reading of Patricia is that she was besotted with Coltrane and devastated by his death."

"You've done excellent sleuthing, Marc. I'll finish writing up notes on our conversation here and take them over to Dougherty."

"But I'm still putting my money on the colonel," Marc said, not ready to leave this discussion just yet. "If he isn't the killer, he's mixed up in the murder in some way. And if anyone knows more about Stanhope's possible involvement, it's Bostwick. He may be crucial to our strategy of pointing the jury to alternative suspects."

"Plus, if we could somehow unearth one or more of Almeda's love letters to Coltrane, Dougherty would have a mother lode to mine in court."

Marc rose, suddenly excited. "Well, Robert, I know where to start looking for them."

"You do?"

"Detroit. The colonel no doubt rifled through Coltrane's possessions before he shipped them off yesterday. But Coltrane was exceedingly clever, and the letter he brought with him to Chepstow was his very lifeline. I'm sure he hid it well enough to fool the likes of Stanhope. Moreover, if the colonel had found it after the murder, would he have been in such a rush to have the books and claptrap boxed and sent packing to Michigan? I'm convinced that he didn't find it and wanted to make sure no one else in the province did." When Robert made to object, Marc added, "It's probable there are other love letters from Almeda in her cousin's house."

"I see. What you say makes sense, but Detroit's two and a half days away over land."

Marc didn't hear this well-meant demurral. "Remember, too," he said, "that the Michigan Hunters are congregated in Detroit, and if this Mrs. Jones or the lurking stranger with the limp was in fact one of their agents, we need to find out somehow whether there was a death warrant placed by the Hunters on one of their own."

"But you wouldn't dare venture into that wasp's nest over there! Not on your own!"

Marc smiled cryptically. "I don't intend to go alone," he said.

"Missus Cobb, I'm outta ice!"

No response from the kitchen, other than a banging of pots and pans in what Cobb considered a needlessly noisy manner. Cobb tossed the cold, soggy towel on the floor. "Missus Cobb! I'm sufferatin' in here!"

Dora Cobb ambled in a few minutes later carrying a fresh towel stuffed with ice chips. "The louder you declamour, Mr. Cobb, the slower I waltz. I figure even you could deduct that."

"Well, it ain't you whose noggin feels like an earthshake!"

Dora edged her ample bulk to her husband's side and examined the wounded man's brow. "You don't need no more ice, luv. That bump ain't no bigger than the wart on the peak of yer nose!"

"It ain't the bump that's thrombosin', it's my whole damn head!"

"Well, shoutin' and gripin' ain't likely to be of much help." She plopped the fresh ice pack onto the aforesaid bump.

"Why don't ya just hit me with a hammer!"

"I would if I had one handy." With that riposte, she wheeled about and trotted out of the sickroom.

Cobb had been home and disabled now for a mere twenty-four hours, and already his sweet temperament had begun to fray and snap. The children, bless them, had done their best to keep him amused. After school, they had tiptoed into the room and with his enthusiastic approval had performed one of their many dramatic duets just for him. Like their grandfather, they had taken to plays and play-acting from the moment they had discovered speech and the power of gesture. He requested their series of scenes from *The Taming of the Shrew*, those jousting duets between Petruchio and Kate, in which the dominant gender of the human species invariably prevailed. The facility with which eleven-year-old Delia and ten-year-old Fabian delivered the ancient Elizabethan verse and their prodigious memory never ceased to amaze their father. "You sure ya didn't find 'em under a cabbage patch?" Cobb had said more than once to Dora. Their prowess in school also justified, in Cobb's mind, his abandonment of his parents on their farm down past Woodstock. He couldn't picture these two fair-haired and fine-boned children and their precocious intelligence meting out their days behind a plough or hoe.

Dora came bustling back in with a thick wedge of mincemeat pie.

"Maybe this'll soothe the headache a little," she said.

"Thanks, luv."

She watched him eat. When he was halfway through the pie, she said quietly, "I got another letter today from yer mother. Yer dad ain't any worse, but he's still askin' fer you durin' his sane moments."

"The man's had a stroke, he don't know hay from Heaven."

"I wanta take the kids to see him next month. He has a right. And Delia's been writin' them long letters, fillin' them in on all yer doin's."

Cobb set the last bit of pie down. "The man told me if I left the farm, I was not to darken his door again. I said I wouldn't. And I'm a man of my word."

"You won't come with us, then?"

"I'll think about it."

"Fair enough. But remember, the dyin' have privileges we ain't allowed."

"Who'll deliver the babies in this end of town if you go leavin' it fer a week or two?"

"I'll tell 'em all to cross their legs."

Cobb laughed, then winced.

"How's yer arm?"

"It hurts, but the worst of it is, it's damn useless. I feel like a one-winged hawk tryin' to fly."

Just then Fabian popped into the doorway.

"What is it?" Cobb said, noting the excitement in his son's face.

"Mr. Edwards is here to see you."

Fifteen minutes later, Cobb and Marc were left alone to talk. Marc was a favourite with the children, applauding their recitations and skits and otherwise fussing over them. And Dora just loved to hear Mr. Edwards "accentuatin'" in his cadenced English.

"I hope you're not worrying about lost wages," Marc said to his friend when they were alone.

"Wilkie come 'round this aft and brought me some cash from the fellas at the Court House."

"And Dora does well delivering babies."

"Don't get much cash, though. Mostly chickens and eggs and the odd slab of ham."

"Food on the table, nonetheless."

"The worst part is just languorin' about the house gettin' more bored by the minute. Delia even accused me of bein' grumpy."

"Well, I have a proposition for you that will address the issue of income and that of boredom, too."

"Proposit away, then. I'm a desperate man."

"As part of my investigation into the murder of Caleb Coltrane, I must go to Detroit and interview a Mrs. Gladys Dobbs, Coltrane's sister."

"And you want me to go with you?"

"I do. And I'll pay you your regular wage plus a bonus for the six days we would be away. It's a delicate operation for which I'll need a plausible cover story, one that entails my having a partner."

"Ya mean an English gentleman in fancy dress might not be too welcome in Yankeeville?"

Marc smiled. "Something like that. I'll explain the ruse I have in mind as we go, but right now I need to know whether you are both willing and able. You've taken a mighty blow to the head and that splint on your wrist looks serious."

"I ain't worried about my noggin or my useless left arm, Major. And I can sure use the money. But the chief's been told by Sir George the Dragon not to do any more pokin' about in the murder. I already bent the rules by siccin' Nestor Peck on Bostwick, so I could get into a pile of trouble helpin' you out any further."

"Thank you for that," Marc said, unsurprised but no less delighted that Cobb had seen the importance of finding the AWOL adjutant and had acted. "Could we come up with a credible excuse for your leaving Toronto for a week?"

Cobb hesitated. He considered the effects of another two weeks of crushing boredom and verbal fencing with Dora. "We can. I got a dyin' father near Woodstock."

"I'm sorry to hear that."

"Oh, we ain't spoke fer humpteen years," Cobb said without emotion. Then he grinned. "But the sarge don't know that, does he?"

Having had complicated relations with members of his own family, Marc was tactful enough not to probe further. Instead he said, "That should do nicely. It'll be a pleasure working with you again, old chum."

"Now don't go gettin' all drippy on me, Major," Cobb said, as the scarlet of his proboscis deepened. "Just tell me when ya wanta leave."

"First thing in the morning."

Marc was tired and hungry when he arrived home some time after six o'clock that evening. As he entered through the front door, he listened for the pleasant ripple of female voices, Beth and Charlene preparing to greet the great man of the house. He stepped fully into the front room and once again confronted a scene of lament. Beth rose to greet him.

"Oh, Marc, I'm so glad you're home. I come in fifteen minutes ago to find Patricia sitting here with Charlene."

Marc tossed his hat and coat aside. Patricia Stanhope it definitely was. She was a younger version of her mother, dark, beautiful, and tragic. Even her excessive weeping did little to diminish her intrinsic attractiveness. She turned her tear-stained, heart-shaped face up to Marc as he crossed the room and pulled up a chair opposite the women.

"What's happened?" he asked cautiously.

"I've been thrown out of the house, bag and baggage!" Patricia cried, indicating a pathetic bundle of clothes tied up with a man's belt.

"By your father?" Marc asked redundantly.

"He told me that unless I obeyed him and got myself ready for the ball tonight and behaved there like a perfect lady, I could go out into the street and fend for myself!"

"I'm sure he didn't mean it," Beth soothed.

"He's gone mad over that stupid dance!" Patricia sobbed, reaching for outrage but not quite getting there.

Marc sighed. "The man has certainly become obsessed about the honours due him at the governor's gala," he said to Beth. And while his heart went out to this wretched girl—her lover murdered and his adversary, captor, and jailer demanding her fealty—Marc's thought was that such an obsession was reason enough to do away with the one person who most threatened its fulfillment. Marc had to find the incriminating letter among Coltrane's effects or one like it in the hands of his sister. Everything now depended on it.

"What'll we do about this?" Beth wondered aloud, handing Patricia a dry hanky.

"I'm certain the colonel will relent once the gala is over and he's got his medal and citation. In the meantime, I suggest she bunk in with Charlene for the night, and if necessary you could arrange for her to stay with Mrs. Halpenny in her apartment above the shop. She'll be safe there and have lots of female company."

"I'll see to it," Beth said without ceremony, and Marc was once again grateful that his wife was a strong and highly capable woman.

Marc turned to Patricia. "Where was your mother when this happened?"

"She was there, and I could see she wanted to step in and stop it, but she didn't. She just stood there and watched." The thought of Almeda's timidity induced a further bout of sniffling. "She used to stand up to him, but lately she's just let him carry on and doesn't say a word."

"Well, I'll find a way to get news to your mother that you're all right. By Monday morning the storm will have blown itself out," Marc said in his most avuncular voice.

"I will be delivering some ribbon for the hat your mother chose for church tomorrow," Beth said. "I'll take it up in the morning and tell her what's happened to you."

"I'm pretty sure she knows where I was headed, 'cause I told Shad at the door. I didn't want her worrying all through the dance," Patricia said. "Oh, how can I ever thank you?"

By testifying to your father's obsession in court, Marc thought, but said nothing.

After supper, when Patricia and Charlene had been safely quartered in the latter's room, Marc told Beth about his day and his decision to go to Detroit. She took the news calmly.

"You're worried about me being alone here, aren't you?" she said.

"I am. The colonel is a volatile and unpredictable man."

"I'll get Jasper to come and sleep on the chesterfield. He's already over here most of the day; he might as well stay the night too. I'll take Charlene to work with me on Monday. We'll have a lot of tidying up to do after Twelfth Night. Jasper'll keep our stoves alive."

Jasper Hogg chopped their wood and did any heavy chores around the house that Marc was too busy or too clumsy to do himself. He was a carpenter's helper who worked whenever and wherever he could but had much idle time on his hands. He was also muscular, reliable, and pathologically shy around adults who were not of his own gender.

"And he'll be able to admire Charlene up close," Marc said. "I'll go next door and arrange it."

"I just hope you'll be careful in Detroit," Beth said.

"Don't worry, love. I'll have Cobb with me."

THIRTEEN

It was eight o'clock Sunday morning when the two-horse cutter carrying Marc and Cobb left the comfortable confines of the capital city and struck out through the bush along the snow-packed highway that would take them through Brantford to Woodstock and the forested districts beyond. This particular January morning was crisp and clear. Sunlight and new-fallen snow took turns dazzling the travellers. In the breezeless air, the drift-adroop boughs of cedar, fir, and tamarack preened like debutantes at the Twelfth Night Ball. As the runners on the sleigh sang against the grooved surface of the road and the horses nickered in delight of their task, Marc was once again enthralled by winter's breathtaking landscapes. So smooth was the thoroughfare and so swift the stalwart steeds that Marc was convinced they were flying, mocking gravity and the illusory grip of civilization. For a precious, distilled moment or two, tawdry tales of murder and intrigue, avarice and vanity seemed far away and insubstantial.

"I c'n drive a team one-handed, ya know," Cobb said quietly, but in the silence of the woods and empty skies, it sounded more like a shout.

"It's all right," Marc said, the reins relaxed in his hands, as the seasoned pair of gray geldings knew their own way and preferred to take it. "There'll be other days, and I'll let you know when it gets too much for an English gentleman to handle."

Cobb was supposed to find this reference amusing but didn't. As he and Marc had walked to Frank's livery stable near the market to pick up the cutter and team, Marc had explained the disguise he was planning to don in order to be able to move freely about the dangerous streets of Detroit. And just in case there were enemy agents lurking in or about the inns along their route, each was to take up his role and practise it twenty-four hours a day. The border raids of the past ten months had made everyone jumpy and suspicious. "Walls have ears" was their motto. The idea for the roles they would enact had come to Marc yesterday just as he was leaving Baldwin House and about to head for Cobb's. Marc himself would be an English gentleman, a journalist from London, and Cobb would be his "man." ("You took the easy part fer yerself," Cobb had complained.) Cobb would play not his customary valet but one he had scavenged along the way on his North American journey.

"I'll exaggerate my educated accent somewhat to impress the locals," Marc suggested, "and you can just be your winsome self." To further legitimate his own role, Marc decided to take on the name of an actual English journalist, Athol Briggs, whose byline appeared regularly in an underground, libertarian paper, *Egalité*, a publication known to be sympathetic to extremists among English Radicals and to American republicanism. Marc had a stack of back issues, from which he had selected half a dozen samples, each of which bore a front-page fulmination by Athol Briggs. Marc also decided to gild the lily a bit by awarding himself a life peerage.

"That mean I gotta call ya 'Yer Lordship'?" Cobb had spluttered.

"I'm afraid so, while I perforce must refer to you simply as 'Bartlett.'" The coincidence between this appellation and Cobb's silhouette was not remarked upon.

Cobb's aches and pains had kept him awake much of the night, and so he was content to pull the buffalo robe up to his chin, snuggle down, and snooze most of the way to Dundas. Meanwhile Marc tried to blank out as many details of the case as he could, partly because he had already mulled them over more times than was necessary. He wished to absorb and appreciate, with subliminal satisfaction, the scenery they were gliding through: rolling hills, snowbound lakes, the lowering edge of the escarpment, a spooked deer by the roadside. Their plan was to change horses two or three times a day, leaving the current team with the inn's ostler. These same teams would be picked up in reverse order when they came back by the same route. It would be costly, but then Lord Athol Briggs was a sponsored journalist of private means in search of sensational material for his famous weekly.

As they approached a two-storey clapboard inn near the village, Marc nudged Cobb awake and placed the reins in his good right hand. "A gentleman never drives his own team, Bartlett, unless he's trying to impress a lady."

"Yes, milord," Cobb said, giving the reins a brisk snap.

"If anyone wonders why his lordship is being served by a handicapped valet, I'll tell them that our sleigh overturned two days ago and you bumped your head and sprained your wrist."

"And I'll tug my tuque and look regrettable."

"Don't overdo it, Cobb. You're just a local chap I hired out of desperation when I reached Toronto a few days ago—after, ah, a week in Montreal."

"I'll try to curl-tail my uppitiness, Yer Earlship."

Marc's aristocratic credentials certainly had an immediate effect at the Queen's Hostelry. As no mention was made of *Egalité*, Marc was assumed to be representing the *Times*. The proprietor, a gushing chap with no teeth on the left side of his mouth, spittled a welcome at the distinguished arrival and rolled out the red carpet, actually a tarnished rug of indeterminate pedigree. Within the hour, a luncheon of venison pie and baked potatoes was prepared, and it was washed down with cold beer from a virgin cask. When Cobb hovered about, eyeing the food and especially the drink, Marc turned sharply to him and said, "Bartlett, please see to the horses. We shall require a fresh team. Make sure they're properly harnessed and ready to go by the time I've finished dining."

Bartlett came close to swallowing his Adam's apple.

"He can pick up a heel of bread and some cheese from the kitchen on his way," the innkeeper said graciously, not bothering to look at milord's man. "And my ostler will see that you have the best team."

Bartlett backed out of the room, seething and muttering under his breath.

"Now, milord, can I tell ya all about the day the rebels come prancin' through here last year?" said the loyal hotelier, rubbing both oily hands together.

When they were well away from Dundas and headed for Brantford, Marc pulled a handkerchief from his overcoat pocket and unwrapped a piece of cold venison pie. Cobb, whose resistance to his humiliating role took the form of feigning delight with the kitchen fare at the Queen's Hostelry and the companionable company of stableboys, ogled the proffered delicacy with unabashed desire.

"Go ahead and take it. It's your reward for egregious service."

Cobb acquiesced. When he had finished and licked the last crumb from his bottom lip, he said, "I sure hope we find somethin' useful in Detroit."

Marc just nodded. He had told Cobb very little about the puzzling intricacies of the case, mostly because Cobb would find Marc's logical peregrinations absurd, preferring to put his trust in what he could see rather than what he could imagine. It was for this reason that Marc valued him as a partner in any investigation. However,

Cobb did know that the object of this arduous and possibly dangerous journey was twofold: to interview Gladys Dobbs with a view to locating an incriminating letter among her brother's effects, and then to use the ruse of Lord Athol Briggs to attract the attention of any publicity-hungry Hunters' Lodgers in hopes of gleaning more information about the status of Caleb Coltrane within their organization. Just how these twin goals fitted into Marc's scheme for proving Billy McNair innocent was something that Cobb was happy to leave to his lordship.

There was only an hour or so of light left when they approached the village of Brantford. Marc had travelled this route three and a half years ago during his first summer in North America on a foraging expedition with Major Owen Jenkin, quartermaster of the regiment. A fine stone inn with an excellent livery stable awaited them a mile or so ahead, and none too soon. The sun had disappeared behind a phalanx of dark cloud in the west and, despite their furs and periodic stops at dingy wayside huts with fetid outhouses and limp fires, both men were chilled to the marrow.

Once arrived, Lord Briggs was wined, dined, and warmed all over at the Brantford Arms, while his man Bartlett chewed on bully beef and stamped his feet beside a woodstove that produced more smoke than heat. The inn served as a major stop for the Hamilton-to-London stagecoach, and thus had a large stable of fast horses. Marc had originally planned to push ahead through the early evening hours as far as a hamlet called Forks of the Grand, where a gypsum mine had drawn a few dozen hardy families and produced a single, ramshackle hotel. But the sixty some miles they had travelled so far, despite perfect weather and a smooth road, had left them fatigued beyond measure.

When he had finished his meal in the cozy dining area, Marc sat back like a pampered patrician and lit his pipe. The innkeeper hovered nearby with a flagon of brandy at half-staff, while his wife prodded the logs in the hearth into fresh flame.

"Is there anything more I can get you, milord?"

Marc paused long enough to effect an air of supreme detachment and aristocratic hauteur. "I trust you have a chamber appropriate to my needs and standing?"

"You are welcome to the suite that faces the road just above us," gushed the innkeeper, a Mr. Tolliver, who waved frantically at his wife. "It will take the chambermaid twenty minutes or so to prepare it, but we are honoured you have chosen to stay with us." The wife-cum-chambermaid was soon heard scuttling up the back stairs.

Marc was practising his lordship role not solely for the benefit of the feckless Mr. Tolliver. While Marc had been still on the soup course, a stranger had entered the room, signalled his desire for a meal, and sat down at one of the four other tables. He had dipped his chin slightly to acknowledge Marc's presence, then removed a newspaper from his coat pocket and begun reading. He ordered his supper in a barely audible drone and went straight back to his reading. But the angle of his head suggested that he was straining to hear whatever conversation the room might afford.

"Business is slight this evening," Marc said to Tolliver, who continued to hover.

"Well, it ain't quite evenin' yet, milord. And 'tis the Sabbath, of course, but we'll get a few lads in fer a belly warmer or two." Realizing his mistake, he added hastily, "But I'll see they don't disturb yer lordship."

"Don't worry, I'm a deep sleeper. By the way, I understand the mail coach makes regular stops here."

"Couldn't run without us."

"Were you here when it stopped by on Friday afternoon?"

"I'm always here, sir—milord."

"Did you happen to notice if it was carrying two large wooden crates?"

Tolliver pretended to think this over, relishing such intimate contact with greatness (and ready coin). "Yessir, there was a pair of big boxes up top. I remember askin' the driver if he was totin' pieces of eight—as a joke, you see—and he said they was just a bunch of stuff, books and such, some rich fella in Toronto was shippin' to Detroit. And I said, 'He must be mighty flush to waste his money mailin' readin' material.'"

"I trust you are excluding newspapers from your disdain." Marc smiled and, while poor Tolliver reddened at his gaffe, glanced at the stranger and his newspaper. Not a twitch. "I'll take another pipe by the fire, Mr. Tolliver, and while I'm doing that, would you fetch my man and have him take my bags up to the suite and lay out my nightclothes."

"Right away, milord," Tolliver said, still red and happy to be off.

A few minutes later, Cobb came in carrying two leather grips in his right hand. "You damn well took your time, Bartlett," Marc snapped at him across the room.

Bartlett winced, glowered at the rug on which he stood, and mumbled, "Yes, milord."

"So get on upstairs and tend to your duties."

"Yes, milord." Bartlett turned towards the stairs.

"And Bartlett, put your things in the adjoining room, will you? I want you nearby to heat up the bed warmer if it gets too cold in the night."

Bartlett swallowed a cough or snort of protest, then wheeled and stomped up the stairs. Ten minutes later, as Marc headed for the same stairs and the ascent to his suite (most likely the one customarily occupied by Mr. and Mrs. Tolliver), he could feel the black eyes of the stranger boring into his back.

Camped on his lordship's bed, Cobb was quietly seething. "You're exaggeratin' more'n yer accent, Major," he complained. "I damn near sprained my other arm."

"We've got to get immersed in these roles, Cobb. When we get onto foreign soil, we can't afford to let our masks slip an inch. Our lives may depend on it."

"If you say so."

"Anyway, I needed to make it clear to anybody watching exactly why I wanted a ruffian like yourself sleeping up here instead of in the stableboys' cabin out back."

Cobb managed a smile of gratitude. "I'll see to yer foot toaster," he said, "but I ain't emptyin' no chamber pot!"

As arranged with the compliant Mr. Tolliver, Marc and Cobb were wakened at five o'clock and, fortified only with a flask of brandied tea and stale rolls, they hit the highway with fresh horses before six. They hoped to be in Woodstock by ten, where a decent inn awaited and a hot breakfast. Then it would be straight on to London for supper and an evening dash through the Longwoods to a way station Marc knew near Moraviantown. From there they would make the remaining fifty miles to Windsor, arriving sometime past mid-day. That would give them less than a day to complete their business across the river, for if they were to get back to Toronto by Friday afternoon—when the trial was scheduled to begin—they would have to leave Windsor early Wednesday morning. Marc secretly hoped that Cobb's wrist would be strong enough to manage the reins so that they could take turns driving and resting. At least it now appeared as if the crates they were seeking would be waiting for them at Mrs. Dobbs's house. Whether they concealed the letter they needed or whether something similar existed among Coltrane's other effects was very much an open question.

At the Forks of the Grand they stopped at a log shanty for a shot of whiskey and a brief respite beside a pot-bellied stove. A mile or so beyond the hamlet, just after they had rounded a sharp curve in the road where the forest edged to within a few feet of its verges, Marc hauled back on the reins.

"What're we stoppin' here for?" Cobb said, coming out of his doze. "I thought ya went back there at the hovel."

"I want you to trot a little ways into the woods here," Marc said matter-of-factly, "and open your flies as if you were about to relieve yourself."

Cobb's response stalled between skeptical and amused. "What if I don't haveta go?"

"Just do it, please," Marc said, turning his head and cocking an ear. "And hurry."

Cobb did as he was told, seesawing his way through a knee-high drift to a protected spot among some spruce boughs, where he undid his flies, one-handed. Then he glanced over at Marc. "Ya want the whole show, Major?"

Before Marc could reply, the brittle silence was broken by the muffled pad of horse's hooves near the bend just behind them. Five seconds later, a lone rider cantered into view. His first instinct was to draw up at the sight of a sleigh parked where one would not expect to find one. But a quick look sideways, where Marc was staring, revealed the arched figure of a man going about one of nature's necessities. As the rider passed Marc, the two men exchanged glances. The rider's face was locked in an awkward smile, as if acknowledging something of significance. Then he was gone around the next bend. It was the man from the Brantford Arms, the one with a keen interest in newspapers.

"I seen that fella back in the inn," Cobb said, still fidgeting with his wayward flies. "I don't like the looks of 'im."

"Me neither, but somehow I don't think he'll be the last chap to be concerned with the progress of Lord Briggs and his faithful servant," Marc said.

After a full English breakfast and a change of horses at Woodstock, they drove out onto the Governor's Road and aimed the cutter due west towards London. Behind them a lone church bell pealed, reminding them that even though they seemed to be prisoners of a fathomless forest and the ribbon of rutted snow through it, there were human communities dotted throughout its vastness and, close by them, the hard-won acres of farmers and woodsmen, whose battle against the ancient trees was as steadfast and perpetual as the seasons themselves. A half-hour later, at a crossroads marked by the friendly presence of several cleared farms, Marc stopped the sleigh.

"I think this is it," Marc said. "Delia drew me a map before I left your house last night."

"What're you talkin' about?" Cobb said with an edge to his voice.

"Your father's farm, of course: the place where you were born and raised. Does this look familiar at all?"

"But we ain't goin' there. We just used it as an excuse in case Wilkie or the sarge come snoopin' about and quizzin' Dora or the kids."

"If we go there, just for an hour or so, you won't have to tell any lies when we get back."

Cobb was searching for the words he needed. "My dad told me if I struck out on my own and left him and my brother alone to run the farm, I wasn't ever to come back. That was fifteen years ago. I was only eighteen. But I knew what I didn't want."

"Your mother and Dora have been corresponding for years, and now she tells me that Delia has taken up the task. Dora says your girl's letters are like long stories, and your mother reads them aloud to your father."

"He can't understand a word," Cobb said, almost spitefully. "He's had a stroke and gone soft in the brain."

"Dora says he wants to see you before he dies."

Just then a one-horse cutter emerged from the side road to the north. A scarlet-cheeked farmer drew up beside them. "Mornin'," he said cheerfully. "You fellas lost?"

"Could you tell us whether the road you've just been on runs past the farm of James Cobb?" Marc said.

"That it does, about a half-mile up on your right. Ya can't miss it."

"Thank you," Marc said, and urged his team towards the side road.

As they glided past the farmer, he stared hard at them and called out, "You goin' ta see yer folks, are ya, Harry?"

Though it was difficult to tell for certain, with snow mantling field and fallow, the Cobb farm looked well tended and prosperous. Behind the neat split-log barn, half a dozen Ayrshire cows were exercising in the bright sunshine. From a distant coop the chatter of chickens reached Marc's ears. In a high, rolling field above the outbuildings where the wind had whipped the snow aside, the telltale stubble of a successful harvest pushed up towards the sky. Drawing up beside the quarry-stone cottage, Marc noticed a young man with a pail slip into the barn. Apparently he had not seen them. "Was that your brother?" Marc asked.

Cobb, who had resigned himself to what he considered a needless ordeal, said, "No, it wasn't. Laertes lives ten miles off on his own place."

"Your father was fond of Shakespeare, I gather."

"Nobody could stop him," Cobb said with a touch of quiet pride. "And now my kids've caught the affection!"

Marc, who had had more than one fatherly misadventure himself, felt for his friend, but he was convinced that this visit was a necessary one for the disaffected son. They had not touched ground before the front door of the cottage opened wide and an aproned woman with gray hair askew and a broad smile on her face trundled out to greet them.

"Oh, Harry, Harry, you've come at last!"

"I have, Mama. That I have."

Soon after, Marc and Martha Cobb sat at the table in the kitchen, sipping tea and nibbling at biscuits slathered with apple jelly. Cobb's mother was one of those farm women, so common out here, who in their late fifties put on a layer of plump flesh that in no way diminished their muscular strength and actually rendered them more sensually attractive. Martha Cobb had troubles enough for two, with a stricken husband and a farm to operate on her own, in addition to the estrangement of her firstborn and two miraculous grandchildren she had not yet laid eyes on. But every velvet wrinkle in her face could be traced to excessive laughter—at both the capricious joys of life and its sorrowful follies.

"I know I shouldn't giggle, Mr. Edwards, but some of the things poor James comes out with are comical, and even though he don't understand much most of the time, he loves to see me have a good belly laugh. You see, we've shared a lot of 'em in our life together."

"How is James today, ma'am? Is he likely to recognize Horatio?"

"He's havin' one of his better days, thank the Lord. Just an hour ago he was askin' after Harry."

"How are you managing the farm on your own?"

"Oh, bless me, sir, but the Lord has been more than kind to us, he has. A week or so after James went down, about the end of last February, a young man shows up at our gate beggin' fer work."

"There have been a lot of young men looking for employment since the unrest last year and so many farms being suddenly sold or abandoned."

"It was bad around here after the Mackenzie business, I can tell you. Anyways, I says to young Bradley, do you know anythin' about farmin'? 'No,' he says, 'but I c'n learn.' I told him we had little ready cash, but he said he'd work fer room and board and whatever else we could afford to give him."

"So he was the chap I saw going into the barn?"

"That would be Bradley. I reckon he spotted you, but he's

terribly shy, he is. Sometimes I have to stop him from workin' so hard, and I keep tellin' him he needs to go to town and mix with folks his own age. He keeps promisin' he will, but so far he sticks to his room in the barn and his Bible."

"Surely he goes to church?"

"I go every Sunday, but I go alone."

"Is he from this area?"

"Oh, no. He said he'd run away from home after his papa'd beaten him. He come here with the clothes on his back, that's all, and a bunch of nasty cuts and bruises on his head. I felt real sorry for him. We come to an agreement right away, and he's been with us ever since. Oh, Mr. Edwards, we've been so blessed, we have. First young Bradley arrives and now our dear, dear Harry. And Delia tells me Dora and her brother and her are plannin' a trip this way before Easter." Tears contended with her smile.

Marc suddenly heard a strange voice rise from the nearby bedroom, deep and sonorous.

"Oh, he's talkin' to Harry!" Martha cried. "Let's go and have a listen."

They edged up to the partly open door. Cobb was sitting on the bed beside his father, holding his hand. James Cobb was a big-boned yeoman of a man, now gaunt and almost fleshless, but the power and energy of that body were still intimated in its final, pitiable configuration. The stroke had taken some of the fire out of the bold, dark eyes and slackened one side of the angular face and the jut of the jaw. But the voice that emerged was only mildly slurred and the words uttered more candid in their skewed clarity.

"Master, young gentleman, I pray you, which way to Master Jew's?"

Then an answering voice: tender, antiphonal, impish. *"Talk you of young Master Launcelot?"*

"No master, sir, but a poor man's son."

"But I pray you, old man, talk you of young Master *Launcelot?"*

"Of Launcelot an't please your mastership."

"Talk not of Master *Launcelot, father, fer the young gentleman is indeed deceased, gone to Heaven."*

"Marry, God forbid, the boy was the very staff of my age, the very prop."

"Do you not know me, father?"

"Alack, sir, I am sand-blind, I know you not."

"Well, old man, I will tell you news of yer son. Give me yer blessing. Truth will come to light. Murder cannot be hid long. A man's son may, but in the end truth will out."

"I'll be sworn if thou art Launcelot, thou art my own flesh and blood."

Martha Cobb tittered behind Marc, and together they withdrew silently to the kitchen. Martha was grinning through her tears. "My word, Mr. Edwards, they were doin' the Gobbo recognizin' scene from *The Merchant of Venice*! James and Harry ain't done that since Harry was thirteen and decided he was too big to be indulgin' in such sissy behaviours."

"I know the scene well," Marc said, still amazed.

"It's a miracle, sir, that's what it is!"

"The mind often retains entire songs and whole swatches of verse even when ordinary speech deserts it," Marc intoned solemnly.

Martha gave him a surprised look. "Oh, sir, it's Harry I was talkin' about."

When he could, Marc slipped quietly away from the scene of reconciliation and made his way towards the barn. A curl of woodsmoke rose through a stovepipe near the rear of the building. Marc went back there, pushed open an outside door, and stepped into the alleyway between the cattle stalls. To his right a curtain had been crudely hung across an opening. He brushed it aside.

"Pardon me for intruding," Marc said to the startled young man, "but it is urgent that I speak with you."

•   •   •

Bradley Tompkins swept the blond forelock out of his eyes and, barely making eye contact, asked Marc, "How did you know?"

"It wasn't that difficult," Marc said. "The timing was too coincidental, and Mrs. Cobb's description of the circumstances of your arrival convinced me that you were a refugee from the Battle of Pelee Island."

"They hanged ten of us in London." The young man shuddered.

"I have absolutely no intention of seeing you hanged, Bradley. Cobb is my good friend, and you have been a godsend for his mother. Besides, I'm positive most of the locals already know or suspect and no longer give a damn."

Bradley looked astonished. "You really think so?"

"I do. Moreover, since you were not a soldier in a legitimate army, you are no deserter."

"But I daren't go back to Detroit. You don't know those men—"

"I've got an inkling. But you should be safe enough here. By the spring most of this fuss will have blown itself out. And it's not as if you were the sole American émigré in the county."

Bradley appeared considerably cheered by these assessments. Then he looked down and spoke in a sustained whisper. "I ran away from the battle. I realized as we were comin' across the ice from Sandusky that I'd made a terrible mistake. I'd let my disagreements with my father lead me to be duped by the promises of the Hunters. I thought we would be marchin' into Canadian villages with the local citizens cheerin' and clamourin' to join us. Half the fellas tried to skedaddle before we reached the enemy at the north end of the island. But I wasn't afraid for my skin. It was when I looked over the ice that morning and saw all them militia uniforms facin' us that I realized these were ordinary folks in homemade tunics. The people we'd come to liberate were prepared to leave hearth and haven and die resisitin' us. In the confusion of the first volleys, I took a bullet fragment off the forehead, then I just melted away and went on the run. I must've looked a right mess when Mrs. Cobb took me in."

"Were you perchance in Caleb Coltrane's brigade?"

Unsure of the intent of the question, Bradley Tompkins hesitated before answering. "I was. And I must admit, sir, that I admired him. He was a true believer and no coward. But I knew I could never be like him."

"I'm investigating his murder," Marc said, "and endeavouring to save a man who has been falsely accused of the crime."

At Bradley's startled reaction, Marc briefly outlined his purpose in Detroit and emphasized the short time they could spend there. "If there is any way your knowledge of the area might help Cobb and me, I'd be grateful. And so would Mrs. Cobb."

Bradley gave the matter some thought. "Well, sir, Major Coltrane had the loyalty and respect of all the men under him, but he wasn't liked very much by some of the other regional captains of Michigan Lodge."

"Political jealousy, perhaps?" Marc said, knowing much about such matters.

"I'm sure he was being put forward for president of the Michigan branch. But then he got captured, didn't he?"

"Is there any way I might be able to meet some of the executive members of the Lodge?"

"Oh, I can get you to the Hunters easily enough."

"You can? How?"

"The Michigan Hunters meet for three or four days in the middle of each month at the Wayfarers Inn, a tavern about ten miles south of Detroit on the main road to Toledo. They may have started yesterday or today, but most of 'em should still be in the area another day or two. They're pretty fussy about who they let near the place, though. The authorities know all about the meetings, but so far as I know, they look the other way."

"Is there a contact I could make in Detroit?"

"Yeah. Go to the Woodward Tavern and ask fer Phineas Quincy. I'll draw you a map of Detroit so you won't get lost. But you better have a good reason for approachin' him. He's a cunning, mean bastard."

Marc smiled. "Don't worry: Citizen Quincy will be delighted to see me."

FOURTEEN

It was early afternoon on Tuesday when Marc and Cobb found themselves crossing the icebound Detroit River, heading towards Wing's Wharf, a spot suggested by Bradley Tompkins as a safe and reasonably inconspicuous point of entry into the United States of America. An icy north wind chilled the sleigh's occupants and left them breathless, despite their furs, Cossack caps, and swaddling scarves, and caused the vehicle to lurch and yaw in random gambits. While the windswept ice looked from a distance as smooth and polished as silver plate, up close and on top, it was rough, bone-jarring, and unpredictable.

"I think my teeth might be chatterin'," Cobb shouted, "but I'm shakin' so hard all over I can't tell!"

"We're almost there!" Marc shouted in return, and jerked at the right rein to bring the skidding horses back to the straight and narrow.

Only the anticipation of the possibilities that lay a quarter mile ahead kept both men from being overwhelmed by exhaustion. So far, it had been a physically numbing expedition. After a change of horses and a quick, cold supper in London, they had raced through the snowy dark of the Longwoods road towards Moraviantown. Cobb insisted on driving with his one good hand so that Marc could doze fitfully beside him and, taking turns thus, they reached at ten o'clock the log hut near the hamlet that served as an emergency way station for desperate travellers. The place had been shut up and barred, but Marc pounded on the plank door with his frozen fist until the proprietor finally opened it a crack, just far enough to allow the barrel of his pistol to emerge at eye level. In his plummiest tones and with a flash of silver coin, Lord Briggs ingratiated himself to the point where the door was opened and the weapon lowered.

The inside of the place was even less appetizing than its exterior. "'Least there won't be no rats," Cobb had muttered. "They wouldn't be caught dead in this sty." There were only two other curtained-off rooms besides the main one, so the lord and his man curled up in the one not occupied by the proprietor and his woman, with only a smoky, fading fire in a wattle fireplace to provide an illusion of warmth and with much concern about that pistol and the distinguished guest's coin-filled purse. Neither proved an impediment to sleep, however, and with horses rested and fed enough to get them to Chatham the next morning, they were at last on the final leg of their arduous journey. As they were leaving Moraviantown, Marc thought he felt the cold shudder of ghosts, of the Shawnees and their charismatic leader Tecumseh, who had fought and died nearby for their own cause and, incidentally, helped preserve a less than grateful British colony.

"That must be the wharf over there," Marc said, and directed the horses towards a wooden pier to the left, now entirely encased in ice. It was deserted. On the steep riverbank above it stood several substantial brick buildings, warehouses most likely, with wind-tossed smoke roiling from their chimneys. Out on the river, they had encountered half a dozen sleighs bearing goods and passengers going both ways, as if the border were a negligible detail. No one paid them the slightest attention, even though Marc had decided to leave their own cutter at a livery stable in Windsor and rent a gentleman's fancy one-horse sleigh with leather seats and polished mahogany trim, locomoted by a charcoal filly with bobbed tail and beribboned mane.

Marc had to walk the filly up a winding path to Griswold Street above the wharf. The street itself was deserted, though the clanking of hammers on iron from the nearest building indicated that productive labour was going on behind its walls. Marc knew that Detroit had been a boomtown for the past five years, notwithstanding the currency crisis and banking disaster of 1837. Property here was selling for more than ten times its counterpart in Windsor; that is, until a few months ago when the economic bubble had burst. The scrambling and chaos that followed had left hundreds of men without employment and others desperate to hang on to what little they had—conditions conducive to easy recruitment by the Hunters. The streets and alleys had also become extremely dangerous, so much so that a group of vigilantes known as Brady's Hundred had been organized to patrol the town from dusk till dawn. It would not be prudent to move around Detroit and environs without due caution and a plausible excuse for doing so. But Marc felt that he and Cobb were well prepared.

With studied ostentation they drove their fancy rig up Griswold to Jefferson Avenue, where the way was suddenly alive with traffic, human and animal. The boardwalks on either side were crowded with shoppers, sliding in and out of small clots of loiterers, who could have been lounging thieves, lurking spies, or simply the forlorn flotsam of the economic collapse. Whoever they were, they were following the progress of Lord Briggs and his man with sullen, unwelcoming eyes.

"You sure ya want every dog and his fleas knowin' we're here?"

"That's the plan. Remember, the story here is that we've just arrived from Cleveland en route to Chicago."

"Well, then, I figure we better get a move on."

At Jefferson and Woodward, the main intersection, they drew

up in a lane beside the Michigander, the city's premier hotel. Marc was impressed by the abundance of trees and shrubs along the thoroughfares and around the sturdy brick and stone dwellings. Handsome retail shops vied for attention with smoke-belching factories. Though a third the size of Toronto, Detroit was in the process of catching up and quickly. While Bartlett went looking for the ostler, Lord Briggs checked in, letting his polysyllabic English ripple across the carpeted and discreetly lit lounge. A few minutes later, Bartlett joined his master in the presidential suite, replete with fresh fire, hot food, cold beer, and a bathroom sporting a copper tub.

"You go on down to the tavern, Cobb, and get yourself refreshed. I'm going to have a bath and a nap: I need to have all my wits about me before we set out. Please wake me at three-thirty."

"If I don't collapse with my chin on the bar."

Marc was dressed in the expensive, tailored garments he had brought with him from England three and a half years before and rarely worn since. His suit coat was plum-coloured and velvet-trimmed, with matching trousers and fashionable ankle-length boots. The overcoat was fur-collared and rakishly cut, and the beaver top hat was spanking new. Under it, his lordship boasted a powdered wig, borrowed from the Baldwin collection. The two days' growth of beard was shaved so close, his cheeks looked as pliant and pink as a sow's buttocks.

"Jesus, Major, I better stay upwind of ya!" was the valet's summary opinion.

They stepped out of the lobby onto Woodward Avenue, where the sleigh and filly were waiting. They drove slowly up towards Larned Street, looking for the Woodward Tavern, passing several posh hatters and haberdashers and two noisy pubs that were not the one they were seeking. They came up to the intersection and peered ahead towards the soaring steeples of three churches.

"It ain't likely to be in that block, Yer Gentleship," Cobb said. "Maybe young Tompkins was havin' us on."

"There was a dingy-looking house on the other side of the road," Marc said. "Let's check it out." They wheeled back down Woodward. The place spotted by Marc was a clapboard cottage, or had been at one time. A new rectangular window with expensive glass had been set into its low façade, but it was now nearly opaque with frost and grime. Marc got down from the rig and walked over to the window, pressing his face up close to the glass: "I can just make out a *W* and two *O*'s. I think this is it."

"Nice spot fer a run-day-view."

Marc pushed open the door, and in they went. It took thirty seconds for his eyes to adjust to the murky light inside, but eventually he could make out a plank bar along one side of a large room, and five or six tables along the other. As far as he could see, no one occupied them at the moment. A bald-headed fellow with side-whiskers and a filthy apron was swabbing the bar with a rag that could have been related to the apron. As Marc crossed over to him, signalling Cobb to remain at the door, he spotted a shadowy figure seated in a far corner nursing a glass of beer in one hand, while holding his chin with the other. His heavy-lidded eyes did not turn in Marc's direction.

"Tell me, my good fellow, is this the Woodward Tavern?" Lord Briggs said to the bartender.

"It was, the last time I looked at the letterin' on the window." This may have been a humorous sally, but it was delivered without obvious intonation. However, the bartender was scrutinizing the newcomer with undisguised interest.

"I'd like a glass of your finest ale, if I might."

"Well now, you might if we had such a thing."

Marc smiled amiably. "Then anything warm and frothy will do."

"I reckon you ain't from around these parts," the bartender said, going over to a tapped keg and drawing a quantity of beer into a battered pewter stein.

"I'm from London, England, actually. My name is Lord Athol Briggs. I am a journalist with the well-known weekly *Egalité*."

"Sounds Spanish to me." He plopped the stein on the bar.

"It's French for 'equality.' My editors and I are fascinated by the success of the American experiment. I have been sent out to America to gather stories and do interviews with republican enthusiasts and, in particular, with leaders of the underground movement known as the Hunters' Lodges. My man and I have just arrived from Cleveland."

"You won't haveta go interviewin' none of them lads, Athol ol' boy. Just stop anybody on the street here and ask them about freedom and democracy. Ya see, in this country everybody's born equal and everybody is free to choose what he wants to do with his life. I chose to be a barman, you see. But if I'd've had a mind to, I could've become the president or a senator or a banker. It's all a matter of choice, not where ya was born or how pretty yer palaver is."

"Sir, that is precisely the sort of sentiment I have come to record for the thousands back home who read *Egalité* and are starved for such stirring examples of individual human endeavour. I have been told that the Hunters' Lodges have been formed spontaneously by men who love liberty and find their own government unwilling or unable to assist in freeing the shackled citizens of Upper Canada."

"Well, I wish ya luck—"

"I've also been told that I might meet a Phineas Quincy in this tavern, a chap who may be able to put me in touch with those I seek to interview."

The bartender blinked. "Well, Athol, I reckon you was told wrong. I ain't seen Quincy in here in over a year."

The dozing figure in the far corner came awake at this point and struggled to its feet. "I might be able to help you."

Marc turned to the voice and said affably, "Oh, I do hope so. I've come a deuce of a ways in the foulest weather—"

"Lemme have a gander at yer newspaper."

Marc removed a copy of *Egalité* from under his arm and handed it to the stranger, who came up to the bar and began to peruse it in better light. "You the fella that wrote this?" he said, pointing to the front page.

"Guilty as charged," Marc said cheerfully. "Bartlett, see to the horse!" he snapped at Cobb, who scowled briefly, then clumped out to the street. "There. We can talk in private, gentleman to gentleman. Do you know where I can find Mr. Quincy?"

"I do. But if it's the Hunters you're interested in, I'll do as easy as him."

"And you are?"

The fellow grinned, exposing the gaps in his rodent-quick teeth. Above them a pair of tiny, protruding, metallic eyes looked bolted in place. In fact, his entire face appeared to have been pushed forward, as if some malcontent had punched him in the back of the head: nose, cheeks, lips, chin—all squeezed frontally, like a spooked weasel's. "I go by the Hunters' name of Uncas."

"Your members have pseudonyms?"

"Only them at the top of the heap."

"I've been given confidential information that there are meetings going on at the present moment a few miles south of here. I'd like to attend one of these, get the flavour of your group gatherings, as it were, and interview your chief."

"President, we call him. And you're in luck. The meetin' tonight is to select a new president fer the Michigan branch. It's at the Wayfarers Inn at eight o'clock. Be there early, yer bona fides'll haveta be checked out before you'll be let in. Come unarmed."

"Will I need a password?"

"You will. It's 'Paul Revere rides a donkey.' Think ya c'n remember that?"

"I'll write it down." Marc tossed a coin on the bar. "Tapster, give this gentleman a drink." Then, as if he had just thought of it, Marc said to Uncas, "Oh, by the way, sir, would you happen to know where I could find a Mrs. Gladys Dobbs?"

Uncas's eyes narrowed. "Now, what would you be after her for?"

"She is the sister of one of your distinguished military heroes, Major Caleb Coltrane, the Pelee Island Patriot."

"That she is. But her brother's rottin' in a British prison."

"I am hoping to get background information on him. My sources in Cleveland and Sandusky have given me a vivid account of the Pelee Island battle last winter. I intend to write its history for my periodical, and whenever possible I like to add personal, familial touches to such material."

The weasel's teeth nibbled at its lower lip. "Can't see no harm in it." He turned to the bar, where he seized the proffered whiskey glass, drained its contents, and intoned conspiratorially, "Corner of Larned and Shelby, a white cottage with a blue door."

"Thank you, sir. I trust we'll meet later this evening?"

"As I said, come unarmed."

Five minutes later Marc pulled the rig up in front of a white clapboard cottage with a pale blue door. Some children ran past, hurling snowballs like grenadiers. One of them paused long enough to wave a welcome to the anonymous visitors. Two little girls, scarved and bundled against the cold, stood on a neighbouring stoop and stared at the gleaming sleigh and its bewigged charioteer. Puffs of woodsmoke lazed above the cottage's chimney pot.

"Hard to believe Coltrane came from a peaceful place like this," Cobb said as they walked in single file up to the door with the fading blue paint.

Marc's knock was answered immediately. The woman who stood before them was clearly in mourning, clothed entirely in black, including the apron about her waist. She was wiping her hands on it as she stood before them, appraising and suspicious, before asking, "What can I do for you gentlemen today?"

"Please pardon this intrusion, ma'am." Marc smiled, then bowed and removed his top hat. "My name is Lord Athol Briggs. I'm a journalist with a British newspaper, *Egalité*, and my man Bartlett and I have just arrived from Cleveland, where I was privileged to learn many details about your brother's heroics at the Battle of Pelee Island and the raid on Windsor."

"You know who I am, then?"

"Mrs. Gladys Dobbs, sister of Major Caleb Coltrane?" Mark took his cue from her stricken expression at the mention of Coltrane's name. "The late Major Coltrane. We were very sorry to be told of his death."

Gladys Dobbs's defenses dropped slightly, and she gazed at them with new interest.

Marc pressed ahead. "I hope you will forgive our intrusion at this terrible time, but I have been following your brother's exploits and his fight for democratic ideals with great admiration. I'd like to tell my readers about his life; indeed, it is all the more important that the world know of his heroism now." Marc winced inwardly at having to float such lies before a woman who looked to be still in shock with her grief. He promised himself that he would write to her after the trial and tell her as much of the truth as he knew. She deserved nothing less.

"Then do come in, sir. In fact you've come at a very good time."

"How so?" Had someone preceded them?

"All Caleb's treasures arrived here last night from Toronto. The authorities say his body will follow shortly. Until I have him home again, I am comforted by his possessions. You may think me a sentimental old woman, but I've just been polishin' up some of his favourite snuff boxes."

"I would be honoured to see them, ma'am, and any other memorabilia you may care to show me."

Marc stepped into a tidy, pleasant room.

"You ain't gonna leave Mr. Bartlett out there in the cold, are you?" Gladys was peering around Marc at Cobb stamping his feet on the stoop and looking suitably hangdog.

"Bartlett generally keeps an eye on the horse," Marc said.

"Well, you just invite him on in, Mr. Briggs. I got hot tea and fresh biscuits just outta the oven. We don't let folks stand out in the snow by themselves—not in this country, we don't."

Marc accepted the gentle reprimand and waved Cobb in. There was a bit of the Coltrane spirit in Gladys Dobbs after all.

After tea and biscuits were served and further condolences expressed, Gladys Dobbs settled the two gentlemen on an afghan-covered divan, in front of which sat two opened crates of Coltrane's books and treasures. Gladys did not shrink from regaling the distinguished London journalist with stories about her illustrious brother and the future he had been denied. She did not speak of the circumstances of his death, perhaps too recent and too horrible to confront, Marc thought. Gladys loved and admired her brother but did not wholly embrace or understand his cause.

It took three pots of tea for the somewhat disjointed biography of the remarkable Major Coltrane to be played out: his boyhood feats, his bravery as a teenager at the Battle of New Orleans, where he first acquired a taste for shooting at redcoats, his stormy tenure as representative in the Ohio legislature, his half-dozen spectacular failures in business, his pivotal role in the rapid expansion of the liberation lodges, and so on. The closest she came to recent events provided Marc with a valuable tidbit.

"Caleb was to be the next president of the Michigan branch of the Hunters' Lodges, you know. They were holdin' up the vote till he came back to Detroit."

Marc listened, took notes with dutiful deference, and occasionally prompted when the multiple plot-lines got too entangled. During one judicious pause, Marc said, "You haven't mentioned any women in your account, Mrs. Dobbs. Did the major have time for romance?"

Gladys smiled indulgently. "Of course he did. He was a red-blooded American, after all. But his loves and losses don't have a lot to do with the more important things, now do they?"

"Ah, but they can make him seem fully human to my readers in England, who put much store, perhaps too much store, in such matters."

"Well, as a young man he did have a crush on our cousin, Almeda Rankin. She was a dear girlhood friend of mine, as well as a relative."

"So you haven't seen her for some time?"

"But I have. She came for a visit last May and stayed three days. We had a wonderful reunion, and as it happened, Caleb was here at the same time. He and Almeda went back over old times and chatted up a storm."

"And perhaps revived their relationship?"

Gladys's pause suggested to Marc that he had asked one question too many, but she continued willingly enough.

"Heavens, no. Almeda is a married woman in Toronto now. We had three happy days together, though, reliving lovely memories." Gladys Dobbs's eyes suddenly brimmed with tears.

Marc cleared his throat to break the spell. "Well, we've taken up so much of your time, Mrs. Dobbs, and you've been very kind. I have more in my notes than I can use. But before I leave, would you mind if Bartlett and I thumbed through your brother's collection of books here? I'd like to see what he'd been reading and browse through any correspondence he may have kept—to better understand his republican philosophy and perhaps discover some quotable passages in his own voice, as it were."

"Oh, please go right ahead. But I'm afraid you won't find any of his letters or articles in these boxes."

"No?"

"They sent back all my letters to him, but I couldn't find a scrap of anything important he'd been writin' up there in Toronto. I do have three personal letters he sent to me in December. You're welcome to see them."

Gladys opened a drawer in the nearby desk and came back with the letters. Cobb meanwhile had begun thumbing discreetly through Caleb's books, seeking another and more significant letter. Marc set Gladys's letters on the couch beside him, as if he were only casually interested.

"Well, then, I'll go and do up these dishes while you gentlemen admire Caleb's treasures. Are you interested in old snuff boxes by any chance?"

"I am indeed, ma'am. These appear to be antique masterpieces. I promise to handle them with great care. And I'll put these personal letters back in the drawer so they won't get mixed up with other items."

"Thank you. Caleb would be so proud to see gentlemen of your quality appreciatin' his collection."

Marc cringed inwardly but managed a grateful smile. Moments later he and Cobb were left alone to intensify their search for Almeda Stanhope's note. Every page of every book was flipped through. The boards or leather covers were scrutinized for hidden pouches or telltale bulges. Marc assumed that the colonel had destroyed all the papers with Caleb's handwriting on them after combing through the rest of his possessions, then shipped them off by express post before anyone else showed an interest. But neither Marc nor Cobb found a stray paper of any kind.

While Cobb, visibly frustrated, began thrashing through volumes he'd already scanned, Marc read through the three letters from Coltrane to Gladys. Finding nothing of significance, he went over to the desk and placed two of the letters back in the drawer. Before replacing the third, he withdrew the concluding page from it and put it in his pocket. They might need a sample of Coltrane's script with an attached signature. He would return the page later. Still, he could not hide from Cobb his own disappointment in not finding the very thing they had expended so much time and energy to uncover here at Mrs. Dobbs's. He felt acutely that he had callously exposed Cobb to danger and needless suffering.

"Would you like to see Caleb's room?" Gladys was standing in the kitchen doorway with a tea towel in her hand.

"I would be honoured," Lord Briggs said with aristocratic élan, and he followed Gladys through a narrow hall, which led to a bedroom on either side. Inside what was now clearly a shrine, she took Marc through the remaining artifacts of her brother's life, turning up for his approval every medal, framed citation, dismantled weaponry, militia regalia, and the half-dozen books that had not followed him to Toronto. There was no incriminating letter in this archive.

Meanwhile, Cobb began fiddling with the snuff boxes nearest him, holding them up to the light and rotating them in his right hand as a jeweller might an exotic gem. Setting them down at his feet, he poked and prodded and kneaded. Suddenly, one of them sprouted a drawer from its base, a slim cavity no roomier than a gentleman's cigarette case but capacious enough to secret a one-page billet-doux.

FIFTEEN

Back at the hotel, as they prepared for the ten-mile trip to the Way-farers Inn, Marc perused the discovered (and purloined) letter for the third time, and said to Cobb, "What made you think of a secret compartment in one of the snuff boxes?"

Cobb's reply was immediate and simple. "Well, them con-trap-shuns is all made by fellas from foreign places in Europe, eh? And I figure them countries are forever squabblin' amongst themselves, and so they'd be full of spies and secret agents, and they'd need hid-den drawers and such—more'n most of us would. And they tell me they all puff snuff like a hog sucks swill."

"Brilliant! So tell me what you make of the letter." Marc handed the note to Cobb.

November 1, 1838

> *My Dearest C:*
>
> *Come soon or I'll be driven to find my own route*
> *to your heart, with all the risks and fretful dangers to*
> *our secret. And when you do, tucked in your strong arms*
> *and safe in your embrace, I promise faithfully to supply*

you with enough kisses to keep you forever attached
to me and our mutual goal. And should our reward
be in Heaven only, I'll treasure those blessings received
already. But I must go—he's had me watched since Saturday!

Ever yours,
D

"Well, it's a bill-an'-coo all right," Cobb opined.

"It should be helpful in Dougherty's hands. He'll be able to prove that something was going on between Caleb and Duchess Almeda, enough to give Stanhope a motive for murder and weaken the case against Billy."

"But it could all've been in Coltrane's head, couldn't it?"

"I doubt it, Cobb, now that I see this letter."

"So Mrs. Dobbs was lyin' to us?"

"Fibbing a little, I suspect, to protect the reputations of those dearest to her. But it doesn't matter much how far the renewed relationship went, does it? It's the letters themselves that are damning. And we now have a complementary pair."

"Which ain't exactly signed," Cobb felt constrained to point out.

"Dougherty will deal with that, I'm sure."

"So why don't we just head fer home now? We got what we came for."

"We could, but beyond getting Billy acquitted, I am determined to find the real murderer as well. I feel I owe it to Billy to have him fully exonerated, and I now have a debt to Mrs. Dobbs that I must repay. Knowing who killed her brother, and why, might justify the subterfuge we had to enact there this afternoon and might also bring the bereft woman some peace of mind."

"That's quite a conscience you got, Major," Cobb said, reaching for his coat.

• • •

The journey down to the Wayfarers Inn was unexpectedly easy. With a bright moon in a starlit sky and a single passable road to the south, the Michigan Hunters were not likely to deceive themselves into thinking their meeting could be secret. A dozen riders thudded past Lord Briggs's cutter without a sideways glance, and they weren't on their way to Toledo at seven-thirty of a winter's evening with the temperature near zero. But three times before they reached the crossroads that justified the existence of the inn, they were stopped by a brace of well-armed men and asked where they were going. As soon as the Wayfarers was mentioned, the passwords were demanded and given. Such cloak-and-dagger business seemed slightly surreal to Marc, seeing that the U.S. Army could have staked out the place at any time during the day and hauled the lot of them off to jail. But they hadn't, despite the promises made by President Van Buren.

At the crossroads, Marc was surprised to find an unprepossessing one-storey hotel and tavern, set in a ragged clearing on the east side of the road. A single sleigh and two horses stood outside. Where were all the Hunters? The answer came soon enough. Two riders, cloaked and in a hurry, galloped in from the west crossroad, cantered across the clearing, and swung into the bush behind the inn. Marc guided the cutter after them and found at the back of the building a broad and well-used pathway, just wide enough to accommodate a sleigh. Following it as it wound through the woods, they came to a gate and four or five stout chaps with muskets in hand.

"Paul Revere rides a donkey!" Marc declaimed in his most orotund tones.

"Pass," came the muffled reply.

And they did, negotiating two more bends before coming out onto a huge clearing, at the end of which loomed a large, barn-like structure. In front of it a dozen sleighs of various sizes and types were parked, with their horses stamping their feet and emitting frosty breaths as big as sugar bags. Several youths were tending to the beasts, and one of them dashed up and took Marc's filly by the bridle. At the wide double door, Marc again gave the passwords, and he and Cobb found themselves guests of the Michigan chapter of the infamous, and dangerous, Hunters' Lodge.

They were standing at the rear of a rectangular hall with a high, vaulted ceiling and, at the far end, an unpainted plank stage beneath a Stars and Stripes bigger than most circus tents. Torches set in sconces on brick pillars along the side walls threw out both light and heat. In each of the four corners, iron stoves throbbed red-hot, like swollen, aggrieved hearts. The centre floor was occupied by a crowd of men sporting deerstalker caps and woollen plaid shirts of bluish hue. No one seemed to take any notice of the two unconventionally attired strangers. The meeting had already begun, and something spoken from the platform had stirred catcalls and other unhappy comment from the audience.

"Brother Hunters! I have come tonight to bring you definitive news of Hunter Bumppo." The speaker stood behind a lectern, tall and gesticulating above it, the wavering torchlight washing shadow in and out of his angular features.

This announcement was greeted not with respectful attention but with strident cries of "Bumppo fer President!" "We want Bumppo!" "Call the question, Deerslayer!" "Resign, ya limey-lover!"

Above the din, the embattled speaker—flanked by two portly Hunters whose posture suggested they were not bodyguards but very important persons attempting to remain above the undignified fray below them—shouted back at his detractors. "There will be no presidential vote tonight!"

At this, one of the naysayers bounded up onto the stage. The three platform figures froze just as four more active ones stepped out from behind the draped flag with muskets poised and live pistols quivering in their leather belts. But the interloper merely wanted to address his fellows on the floor. He turned to the assembly and hollered, "Our constitution says we can vote for a candidate in absentia! And in America, constitutions are sacred, are they not? Hunter Bumppo led our glorious liberation army against the tyrant not once but twice. He shed his blood for us upon the tyrant's soil. The oppressed peoples of Canada are counting on us!"

These sentiments inspired a wave of guttural cheering whose enthusiastic exhalation came close to extinguishing the pillared torches. Chairman Deerslayer allowed the righteous indignation to wear itself out, and something in the stillness of his demeanour prepared the Michigan Hunters for what he was about to say.

"Fellow Hunters, it is my sad but solemn duty to inform you that Hunter Bumppo is dead."

The silence was palpable and eerie, coming as it did after the raucous display of democratic fervour. It was followed by a feverish murmuring among the stunned Hunters. Deerslayer spoke quietly above it. "Our agent has just returned from Toronto. He was delayed when his cover was blown in London and he had to spend two days hiding out in the bush. He made his report a mere two hours ago."

The membership began to find its democratic voice once again: "Who killed him?" "You swore he'd be rescued!" "Down with the executive!" "Throw the bums out!"

"Hunter Bumppo was savagely and callously murdered in his jail cell by one or more of his captors, the cringing lackeys of the British Queen!"

Marc and Cobb began to edge back until they were touching the double door behind them, for the outrage that now seized the hall was monumental and seemingly unassuageable. The simple glimpse of an English periwig might push them into a frenzy in which murder and mutilation would be mere preliminaries.

"Order! Order!" All three dignitaries on the platform were screaming at once, to no avail. But the abrupt thunder of four muskets exploding and the curious shower of wood splinters and buckshot from the rafters above did what no appeal to parliamentary rules of order could.

"If you don't keep your gobs shut, I won't be able to give you Hunter Mohican's report!" Then into the sullen, shaky silence that ensued, Chairman Deerslayer said, "Mohican spent five days in the tyrant's capital, at great risk to his personal safety. As instructed, he met with our sympathizers in the region and scouted the dungeon where Hunter Bumppo was incarcerated. A master of disguise, he succeeded in getting an interview with Bumppo, during which he hoped to firm up the escape plan."

"What the hell happened, then?"

"I'll let Hunter Mohican tell you himself." Deerslayer reached down and pulled up beside him a slim figure. Beneath their mortician's smiles, the two flanking Hunters looked particularly pleased with the proceedings so far.

Mohican limped to the podium and stood beside it. In hopping up onto the stage, his cap had flown off, releasing a mane of yellow curls that bounced on his shoulders. In the torchlight, the burn scar on his face glistened grotesquely.

"Brother Hunters, I am here to testify, upon my sacred oath as a founding member of this Lodge, that during my half-hour interview with our great and irreplaceable field general, he ordered me to abort all plans fer his escape, sayin'—and I swear this on my mother's Bible and George Washington's grave—sayin' that he had his own plan fer breakin' free. We were not to worry, he had everythin' in hand. But they assassinated him before he could bring it off! He's dead! Poisoned like a rat in a trap!"

When the outrage at this tragic revelation subsided slightly and the calls for swift and savage revenge grew hoarse with repetition, the chairman drew a pistol from his pocket and banged on the podium with its embossed butt. "It is my sad but solemn duty to declare Hunter Pathfinder here the new president of the Michigan Lodge—by acclamation!"

During the ensuing furore and general dismay, Mohican retreated from the limelight, but as he was stepping down from the platform, his eyes met those of a fashionably dressed, bewigged gentleman staring at him from the back of the hall.

"It's Rungee!" Marc hissed. "And he's spotted us."

Cobb was already out the double door.

Fortunately for them, Mohican, or Rungec or whoever he was, could not move through the agitated throng with any speed, nor could he get the attention of anyone who might intercept the fleeing foreigners. Marc and Cobb were able to reach their sleigh unimpeded. Marc mumbled some excuse to the lad tending it and tossed him a shilling. Without looking back, they skidded off towards the high road to Detroit.

"If that bugger gets on his horse," Cobb said, as they raced northward under the bright moon and companion stars, "he'll catch us up in a wink."

"Maybe," Marc said, snapping the reins above the frightened filly. "But there's been so much traffic back there, he won't know whether we've gone north or south, or even west along the side road. Let's hope no one at the inn spotted us leaving."

A few minutes later they slowed for one of the checkpoints, but they were waved through without delay.

"There could be a whole posse after us, Major."

"If so, we'll hear them before they see us. There are farm roads and logging paths all along the route. We can turn off and hide out in the hinterland if we have to."

"You bring yer tinderbox?"

Marc nodded, but as it turned out, they did not need it. An anxious hour passed, but they approached the flat plain just below Detroit without incident. Marc let the filly slow to a trot. "We've run her as hard as we dare, Cobb; we won't get far with a dead beast between the poles."

After several minutes of sedate progress, Cobb said, "Well, what do you make of all that Yankee palaver and screechifyin'?" The tone was casual but the implication clear: why did we just risk our necks?

"I think we learned a great deal of importance to Billy's case."

"We did?"

"First, Mohican was the man I observed spying on Chepstow the day before the murder."

"And the fella that my snitch Nestor said he saw in the Cock and Bull talkin' to some Americans."

"Exactly. But if he got in to see Coltrane as he claimed back there, why was he still skulking about the place last Wednesday?"

"You think he was lyin'?"

"No. I remember seeing the name 'E. Mohican' in the sign-in book and thinking it was a joke."

"I didn't see much humour back there."

"It's conceivable," Marc went on, "from what we just saw and heard, that Hunter Pathfinder coveted the presidency of the Michigan Lodge so much that he preferred to see Coltrane—Hunter Bumppo as they so quaintly dubbed him—go to trial and be hanged."

"You think Rungee might've been there to stop him from gettin' away?"

"I do. And perhaps more."

"Ya mean that be-seein'-ya business about the election?"

"Right. If the membership, who obviously preferred Coltrane to Pathfinder, were prepared to force a vote for president during these mid-month meetings—while Coltrane was still alive—he could, under their constitution, be elected while in absentia."

"So you figure Pathfinder and his cronies wanted him dead before that could happen?"

"We have to consider that, yes."

"Then the mysterious Mrs. Jones you told me about could've been Rungee, with a vial of strychnine for his fellow Hunter to snuffle. Coltrane wouldn't likely be suspicious of one of his own, would he?"

"True, but I can't see Mohican with a limp and a burn scar posing as a lady from Streetsville, however much he's a master of disguise. He would have no idea whom he might have to deceive to get into the cell, even if he did spot Jailer Bostwick hightailing it the evening before the murder. After all, the usual protocol of visits included a close screening by Gideon Stanhope before the event, and Mohican, it seems, had already come there once and passed muster. I don't see any way you could disguise a facial scar that grotesque."

"He could've seen the colonel go out to his tailor's on Thursday mornin'."

"Right. But even Shad was likely to recall that scar and sound the alarm."

"Too bad, then." Cobb sighed. "Because he'd be a good bet fer the killer. Even King Arthur might prefer a Yankee cutthroat to a local hero."

"But don't forget that Mohican wasn't working alone. We have Nestor Peck's account of his rendezvous with known republican sympathizers in downtown Toronto."

"What're you drivin' at?"

"Mrs. Jones could have been any one of a dozen confederates willing to do Mohican's bidding—perhaps even a woman."

"Oh, I get it. This Jones person gets into the cell and—"

"Uses a password or code to identify herself as a Hunter or associate, and, with Coltrane's guard relaxed, plants the poison. I'll wager that even the request for a visit relayed to Coltrane by Shad itself contained a coded message that would have gained her instant access. You've just seen how obsessed these people are with pseudonyms and passwords and the like."

"But how does any of this help Billy?"

"What we've unearthed here is another plausible alternative to the story that the Crown will present to portray Billy as the killer. I'll suggest that Dougherty call me as a defense witness, and I'll then be able to recount my sighting of Rungee at Chepstow and how what I witnessed here tonight makes it conceivable that there was a Hunters' conspiracy to eliminate Coltrane—for crass political gain. And of course, I have you to corroborate the details."

Cobb gulped but did not otherwise respond.

"With the reciprocal love letters between Caleb and Almeda Stanhope—both of them now in our possession—Dougherty will be able to offer the jury two plausible alternative theories. It doesn't matter, for Billy, whether the colonel or his agent or Mrs. Jones actually did the deed. Any Toronto jury will be sympathetic to Sergeant McNair, so the presentation of credible alternatives should be enough to get him acquitted."

"Maybe so, but I don't see them anxious to hang their own Pelee Island Patriot either. I think we oughta push this Rungee business."

"Well, partner, we aren't lawyers yet. We'll leave those decisions to Robert and Doubtful Dick."

At this point the glow of lamplight from the houses on the outskirts of Detroit was happily visible.

"I think we made it, Major. And by the way, where do you suppose them Hunters came up with all those fancy names?"

"Pure fiction," Marc said.

At the hotel, Marc proposed they return to Windsor without delay. Cobb readily agreed to collect their belongings from the hotel, while Marc tended to the horse, which had already suffered a hard run in severe cold.

Marc led the filly to the barn behind the main building. All the stableboys were either asleep or AWOL, so Marc went inside, found a thick wool blanket, scooped some oats into a feedbag, and came back out. He put the blanket over the shivering horse and hung the feedbag on her. The snow on the ground had already provided her with drink, but Marc looked around for the water trough anyway.

He was just lifting a pailful when he felt a cold poke on the back of his head.

"That's a pistol agin yer skull, Mr. Edwards. One flicker and you're a dead Englishman."

Marc did not need to turn his head to know that the man behind him was Hunter Mohican. He recognized the voice that had delivered the details of Coltrane's fate an hour and a half earlier. Marc stiffened, set the pail down carefully, and waited.

"They told me some English pouf'd been seen sniffin' around Gladys's place. They reckoned you was some bigwig who'd do us a great favour. But I had my doubts, and now I see I was right. I seen you back in Toronto and spotted you in a second in the hall. It takes an awful lot to fool a Mohican."

"What is it you want of me, Mr. Rungee?" Marc said, staring towards the hotel, where he expected Cobb to emerge at any moment. "I have not come here to do any harm to the Hunters. In fact, I'm trying to discover who really did—"

"Shut yer gob or I'll send ya flyin' to Hades now instead of later."

Marc said nothing. There was no sign of Cobb, and Marc was actually glad that his friend was delayed. Rungee had surely brought other Hunters with him, and they could be lurking anywhere in the vicinity.

"That's better. Now I want ya to turn slowly and walk ahead of me back to the barn. If you try to look back at me, I'll blow yer eyes out."

Marc did exactly as he was told. He could hear Rungee padding three or four feet behind him, cunningly out of arm's reach. Any attempt by Marc to whirl about in an effort to disarm the man would be futile and likely fatal.

"Stop right there. Stand beside the horse and look towards the hotel. I'm goin' to sidle back to the corner of the barn where I can watch you and blow yer brains out with one shot. I got another pistol in my belt, just in case."

Marc heard Rungee shuffling back ten feet or so to the edge of the barn, where heavy shadow would keep him out of the bright moonlight.

"Now when that fat fella with the bum wing comes out, you just wait till he comes over here. If he calls out, you say somethin' real friendly—if ya wanta live a little longer."

"What are you planning to do with us?"

"I'm marchin' the two of you up to the Pathfinder's place. He'll wanta know everythin' you know, and when he does, I'll have the pleasure of shootin' ya and tossin' yer bodies inta the nearest ditch. We got a lot of bad people runnin' around our streets at night, so the vigilante brigade won't be surprised to find a rich bitch like yerself robbed and shot."

"You'll have to get me and my associate past Brady's Hundred first. Are you planning to march us up Woodward Avenue with your pistols drawn?"

Marc waited for a response, even as his eyes never left the side door of the hotel. But none came. In its stead was a sharp crack, as of wood splitting, followed by a soft thud. Then silence. Marc dared not turn around to investigate.

"You c'n take a peak now, Major. The fractious is all over."

Marc turned to find Cobb standing over the felled body of the yellow-tressed Mohican, with half a stout branch in his good hand. The other half, having served its purpose against Rungee's skull, lay at his feet. Cobb set his section of the club down and picked up the loaded pistol.

"One of these days, it'll be your turn to rescue me."

While Cobb kept a lookout, Marc disarmed the unconscious assailant and bound him hand and foot with his own scarves, then used one of his mittens for a gag. Next he detached a wallet from the fellow's belt and rummaged through it.

"Hurry up, Major. There's bound to be more of these villains hereabouts."

Marc held several papers up into the moonlight. "His name is Ephraim Runchey."

"Nestor Peck's hearin's about as sharp as his brain," Cobb said, throwing their bags up onto the sleigh.

"What's this?" Marc whistled.

"Whatchya got?"

Marc threw the horse blanket over Runchey and dragged him a little ways into the barn. He dropped the wallet on the body, just now beginning to groan and squirm, and came back to the cutter with the papers in his hand. "He'll keep there till the grooms hear his groans." He handed Cobb one of the sheets he had taken from Runchey.

Cobb scanned it in the imperfect light. "It's just a bunch of scrambled-up letters," he said. "Unless it's Greek or somethin'."

"Almost," Marc said, climbing up next to Cobb and urging the filly cautiously out onto the deserted street. "It's scrambled letters all right. Two columns of them on each page and two words in each item."

"A list of some kind?"

"Yes. And I'll fry my hat and eat it if, when I break this code, I don't find we have in our hands the nominal roll of the Michigan branch of the Hunters' Lodge."

"Now all we gotta do is make it safe back to Toronto with all this stuff and our skins still stickin' to our bones."

Marc urged the filly into a full trot, and they sped down towards the river that provided a border between the fledgling colony and the redoubtable republic of America. No one followed. Even the wind had died, so that they were able to make their way across the ice bridge in relative comfort.

As the welcoming lights of the village of Windsor came into view, Marc said to Cobb, "Well, what do you think of the great American experiment, now that you've seen it up close?"

Cobb gave the question a moment's reflection, then said, "I figure they could do with a tad less liberty."

SIXTEEN

It was sometime after one o'clock Friday afternoon when Marc and Cobb raced along King Street towards the heart of the capital city. Cobb had divested himself of his wrist splint and the valet's obsequious demeanour. The lord's wig was packed away in the great man's leather grip. The two men were exhausted but exhilarated. They had come back with the prize they had sought and more. Cobb drew the team up in the service lane behind Smallman's.

Beth was at the back door to greet them. She hugged Marc, then Cobb, who was too startled to resist or blush, then Marc again.

"We were so worried," she said to Marc, meaning herself, of course, as she fought back uncharacteristic tears.

"You're all right, though?" he said, meaning the baby.

"We're both fine. Really. Now come on in. There's still a bit of soup left from our lunch."

So, while Rose Halpenny and her girls fussed over Constable Cobb, plying him with food and drink and draping his coat over a rack by the stove, Marc and Beth sat nearby holding hands and reassuring each other that a five-and-a-half-day absence had not altered their universe in any material way.

"Is Patricia still here?" Marc asked, after they had quickly worked through the health and status of Charlene, Jasper Hogg, Briar cottage, and its environs.

"Oh, no. She went back home on Sunday afternoon. By the time I got to see Almeda, the colonel had relented. Of course, by then the ball was over and—" Beth stopped. "You're looking pretty antsy," she said. "You have to get going?"

"I hate to, I really do, but the information we found in Detroit is vital to Billy's defense, and I've got to get it to Robert."

"Billy's holding up well. Dolly sees him two or three times a day. They'll be happy to hear your news."

"If you don't mind, then, I'll head straight down to Baldwin House and —"

Beth interrupted. "He won't be there. He's at the Court House."

"What do you mean?"

"Well, the trial started today."

"I know, but they'll still be empanelling the jury."

"They did that this morning. Robert come by an hour ago, to see if you'd got back, and said the Crown was calling their first witness at one o'clock. They're at it now."

Marc pulled Cobb's coat off the rack and tossed it in his direction. "We've got to go, Constable. Pronto!"

While Cobb continued on to Frank's livery stable, Marc ran up the cleared path to the main Court House door and dashed into the foyer. The courtroom lay straight ahead, and Marc brushed by the sentry, jarring Wilkie awake, and slipped inside. The place was jammed with the curious, the prurient, and those who had come to see what justice there could be in trying a bona fide hero for exterminating a killer, a vandal, and an incorrigible republican. Marc spotted Clement Peachey, Robert's associate, sitting on a rear bench. Peachey nudged his neighbour farther along the pew and signalled for Marc to squeeze in beside him.

"You shouldn't really be here," Peachey whispered. "You're on the Crown's witness roster."

"Funny, but I haven't received a subpoena in that regard," Marc said with a wink. Then they both turned their attention to the trial of Billy McNair, which was in progress before them.

Cupping his hand over his mouth, Peachey said, "The coroner's evidence about the poison and the medicine packet's been completed."

The Crown's attorney was now questioning his second witness: Gideon Stanhope. Marc's heart skipped a beat. Acting for the Crown was Kingsley Thornton, with his tall, impeccably erect bearing, a white sheaf of hair under the barrister's wig, and the clear and theatrical voice capable of chilling ironies and subtle stratagems. Thornton's penetrating gaze alone could strip a witness of pretense, will, and dignity. He'd had twenty years of distinguished service at the Old Bailey on both sides of the aisle before emigrating to Upper Canada and retiring on an estate north of the city in order to be close to his son, daughter-in-law, and five grandchildren. He was a member of the Legislative Council and had been confidant to three governors. While inactive as a barrister, he maintained his membership in the Law Society, and Marc had encountered him at meetings of the law clubs for apprentice lawyers. His presence here was not merely intimidating to the defense, it bespoke the governor's intention to get a conviction in a case he considered vital to the political interests of the province—which just happened to coincide with his own.

"Colonel Stanhope, we come now to the strange business of the duel that took place three days before the murder. I want you to tell the gentlemen of the jury in your own words what happened that fateful morning, insofar as you were involved."

Marc turned his attention to Gideon Stanhope, standing upright in the witness-box and seemingly hanging upon each syllable uttered by the prosecutor. He was not in uniform, though his expensively tailored clothes and stiff posture still projected an image of affluence, authority, and self-possession.

"I had risen at dawn, as is my custom since I became a soldier and an example for the men I lead. I had completed my toilet, donned my tunic, and was heading for my study when my butler—"

"That would be Mr. Absalom Shad, from whom we shall hear testimony later on?"

"The same. He was half-dressed and extremely excited. He said there was a commotion in the garden and that pistols had been fired. We dashed for the stairs to the cellar and the door to the garden."

"Naturally. You were concerned, I take it, that the gunshots might presage an escape attempt by your prisoner?"

"Precisely."

As Thornton led his friendly witness through the damning details of Billy's duel with Coltrane, Marc looked about him. He had sat in here a dozen times this past fall to observe a variety of trials during the assizes and had often remained in the august chamber alone for a few minutes afterwards. The high court, though barely ten years old, never failed to impress the apprentice barrister. No expense had been spared in its creation. Oak, maple, and ash gleamed from every angle—wainscoting, shallow side galleries, vaulted window sashes, benches, lecterns, prisoner's dock, witness stand, and, of course, the raised, throne-like dais upon which the high-court justices sat in all their lordly glory. On this day, the presiding jurist was none other than John Beverley Robinson, the chief justice of Upper Canada, in his engulfing periwig and ermine-tipped robes, staring down at the assembly from under his aristocratic brow and intimidating Roman nose. And high and vulnerable and wee in the dock, Billy McNair peered out at his accusers and could not breathe a single word in his own defense.

Robert Baldwin and Richard Dougherty were seated on the

front bench to Marc's left, waiting their turn to go at the colonel. Marc had no idea of the particular strategy they might have planned for cross-examining Stanhope or how long it might take. But if they were to float the theory of the colonel's powerful motives for murder—infidelity and blackmail—then the corroborating love letter from Detroit must be shown to them and thoroughly discussed. Marc scribbled a note, folded it, and whispered to Clement Peachey, "Would you slip this into Robert's hand for me? It's urgent."

Peachey nodded and began sidling up the aisle under the baleful watch of the judge. The note was brief: "Stall Stanhope. Letter recovered. Much else." Marc did not witness its safe delivery, but Peachey returned smiling.

"As clearly as you can recall, Colonel, what were Mr. McNair's exact words?" *Colonel* Stanhope but *Mister* McNair, Marc noted.

"He said the two of them were duelling and 'I did my best to kill the—'" Stanhope looked at Thornton, then up at the judge.

"You must repeat the exact word, sir, repellent as it must be to this civilized audience," Thornton said with disingenuous solemnity.

"'To kill the bastard.'"

The spectators—most of whom had heard the word used once or twice and had even uttered it themselves when occasion demanded it—susurrated in shock.

"We will hear testimony a little later, sir, from one of our own police constables concerning these very events and utterances, during which it will be revealed that you initially attempted to suggest to the authorities, who had arrived just before you, that what they were seeing was perhaps a mere game or charade. Why would a man of your standing do such a thing?"

The colonel hung his head for a necessary millisecond, then looked up and said forcefully, "Young Billy McNair was the best sergeant in my regiment, a sort of protégé whom I looked upon almost as a son. My first instincts were those of a father, I suppose, trying to protect his offspring. But it was clear to all that what had happened in the garden was in earnest, and I made no effort to continue my initial and less than honourable behaviour."

"You hold honour to be among the highest of virtues?"

"As an officer in Her Majesty's militia, I cannot do otherwise."

My word, Marc thought, Thornton is setting the man up as a saint, and Stanhope has become the master of the quick mea culpa and recovery. Both men would be a challenge for Doubtful Dick, even if he had managed to haul himself upright, ambulatory, and alert sometime in the past five days.

"You've missed the earlier testimony about Billy and all that bother about the battle down there," Clement Peachey whispered to Marc.

With the valour and genius of the Pelee Island Patriot duly noted, Marc thought ruefully.

Thornton had now moved on to the most incriminating moment of the duel's aftermath. "Again, Colonel, the defendant's exact words, if you please." He smiled grimly, as if braced for syllables even a seasoned counsellor ought never to hear.

"He shouted out, 'I'm going to kill the bugger, hanging's too good for him'—meaning Major Coltrane."

Thornton rewarded Stanhope with a grateful grin, then turned to the jury and shrugged his shoulders in mock helplessness. All eyes swivelled up to scrutinize the young blasphemer.

"And even though this infamous duel and the threats it engendered took place in your own garden and involved a man you assumed to be safely locked in his cell in your basement, you are swearing here on your oath that you knew nothing about it until you and Mr. Shad arrived on the scene after the exchange of shots?"

"That is correct. I was shocked and dismayed."

"Did you subsequently learn from one of your household how

the prisoner, Mr. Coltrane, was able to come into possession of one of your own pistols?"

"Hearsay!" It was the first word that Marc, or any other in the chamber, had heard Dougherty utter. The defense had waived opening argument, not having as yet a coherent one to offer.

Chief Justice Robinson frowned at the interjection, as if he had been telling a particularly good story at a garden party and been rudely interrupted, but said with polite deference to the prosecutor, "Try getting there another way, Mr. Thornton."

"Did you subsequently recognize the pistols as your own?"

"I did."

"Did you publicly upbraid Lieutenant Lardner Bostwick that morning for allegedly facilitating the duel?"

"I did. I threatened to have him drummed out of the regiment for insubordination."

"And he left your service, I believe, two days later—that is, on Wednesday evening of last week?"

"Yes. And I was compelled to assign Mr. Shad the task of jailer until I could replace Lieutenant Bostwick."

"Thank you for your forthrightness, Colonel."

Stanhope beamed. A triumph at the Twelfth Night gala and now this. Whatever sympathy and support Billy might have among the ordinary citizens in attendance here, no blame for his undeserved fate would attach to the man who had treated him like a son.

Thornton now moved on to Thursday, the day of the murder. As background for the jury, and in the absence of Bostwick, who had not been flushed by either side, Stanhope was encouraged to describe the jailing arrangements, his reinforcement of the prison chamber, Bostwick's duties, and the strict protocol placed on the unusual number of visitors.

"Is it not unorthodox, Colonel, for a criminal to be incarcerated in an officer's home and then to be offered a variety of privileges such as you provided the victim?"

Stanhope seemed delighted with the question. "It is, sir, if one looks upon Major Coltrane as a common felon. I did not. He was to all intents and purposes the commander-in-chief of an invading army and distinguished himself in two separate engagements. In a more gentlemanly world he would have given me his parole and I would have offered him the keys to my estate. As it was, I considered the basement chamber I provided, the carefully screened visitors, and the proper food a compromise. It was to me a matter of honour to accept a military adversary as such and treat him as a gentleman. The courts are the place to judge his misdemeanours, not my home."

Despite the universal animosity to Coltrane, the murmuring among the side galleries was wholly approving.

"Thus it was that on that fateful Thursday, Mr. Coltrane received several visitors. Did you personally greet them?"

"Only Alderman Boynton Tierney, who had been there three or four times before. I met him briefly because Shad was new to the business of keeping jail, and I wished to walk him through the procedures."

"Like having Mr. Tierney sign the visitor's book, which is an exhibit in this trial?"

"Precisely. I happened to be in the hall when Mr. Tierney left at ten forty-five or so. We said our good-byes, and as no other visitors were scheduled till the afternoon, I left the house to keep an appointment at my tailor's."

"But the book—which milord has before you—shows that a Mrs. Jones from Streetsville did arrive at eleven o'clock that morning and sign in."

"I know nothing of the visit or the lady herself."

"Nor does anyone else!" Thornton cried, with a little pirouette behind his lectern, and received a few cautious titters for his remark. To the jury he said, "Mr. Shad, whom we shall call shortly, may shed more light on this mysterious incognita." He paused, like a bad tragedian before a soliloquy, then moved the jury towards the afternoon visit of Billy McNair.

"What occurred below the main floor of your home that Thursday after luncheon will be detailed by two witnesses to come, but your testimony in regard to what transpired only moments after those events—"

"Milord, there's been no testimony as to these putative events!" Dougherty again, rising almost imperceptibly.

The judge did not look his way but leaned over towards Thornton and said cordially, "Just take the witness through what *he* observed, if you please."

"My apologies, milord. Now Colonel, where were you when you heard a commotion about one-thirty on the day in question?"

"I was sitting with Chief Constable Sturges in my study while we waited for Billy McNair to finish his authorized visit to Major Coltrane."

Thornton winced at the word "authorized" but did not go in that dangerous direction, for the governor's eagle-eyed staff was seated two rows behind him on the VIP benches. Thornton then led the colonel through an account of Billy's escapade in the hallway—whom he saw and where and in what sequence. Marc braced for what he knew must come.

"Describe the defendant's actions when you first saw him in your vestibule."

"He was excited and shouting for a doctor, waving his arms frantically, and pushing his way towards the front door. He knocked Constable Cobb aside, and as the sentries came in to see what the ruckus was, Billy bumped into one of them, fell to one side, and nearly toppled the hall tree. He regained his balance and started pawing at the coats and hats. He seemed hysterical."

"Did you see him do anything else at that moment?"

"Yes. He had one of his hands stuck in a pocket."

Marc drew in his breath at this. The colonel's story had sharpened quite a bit from the initial rendering that Marc had elicited.

"We shall hear testimony that a packet containing granules of strychnine was subsequently found in one of those pockets. Think carefully now, did you see the defendant with such a packet in his hand at this time?"

"No, sir, I did not."

"But you did see one of his hands fumbling at the pocket of a coat?"

"I did. But that was all. There was noise and confusion, as I've said."

"Thank you, Colonel Stanhope. I have no more questions, milord."

He didn't need any more, Marc thought. He had established Gideon Stanhope as a credible witness and honourable man. The duel was pointed to as Billy's first, and failed, attempt at murder, followed by unequivocal death threats. Cobb and, if necessary, the rear-gate sentries would corroborate this testimony. Then, galling though it be, Marc and Cobb would be used to attest to Billy's statements about why he hated Coltrane and to give the damning details of the Thursday visit and its immediate aftermath. It would be Cobb, alas, who would tap in the final coffin nail: finding the poison packet in Billy's coat, where the lad's hand had been seen "fumbling." This was the story that the defense team had to break or diversify.

"You do have questions for this witness, I presume?" the judge said, squinting down at the defense bench.

"One or two, milord."

"But you mustn't ask them sitting down, Mr. Dougherty," the judge said, and did nothing to stint the giggles rippling through the chamber.

As the heads of the dignitaries bobbed and weaved in front of him in an effort to observe the rise of the seated counsellor, Marc was able to spot Celia and Broderick Langford sitting nearest their "uncle" in the front row of the side gallery. Broderick wore his formal business suit and Celia, a modest, muted frock in a style now current (if Beth's shop were an indicator of approved fashion). It took Dougherty all of two minutes to lift his mammoth bulk to an upright position, wobble up on his spindle legs until they adjusted to gravity, and take two flesh-jiggling steps to the lectern, which he then seized in both huge hands to steady himself. The wheezing, gasping effort at locomotion left the spectators spellbound and the defense counsellor pink and breathless. Somewhere a tailor had been found who could imagine a cut of cloth bizarre enough to encompass such girth, for his black barrister's suit coat was brand-new, his striped gray trousers uncreased, and his waistcoat free of debris. Upon his bald dome there slithered a scruffy wig, three sizes too small, like an abandoned bird's nest.

"Are you quite ready, Mr. Dougherty? We could bring in a block and tackle tomorrow if you would find it helpful." The chief justice turned to accept the laughter due him.

"Milord is most kind."

The cross-examination was about to begin. Dougherty conducted it as he was to conduct each interrogation during the course of the trial, with his eyes and voice only. The sloth's body was incapable of gesture. The only dramatic effects it was able to achieve— and these may well have been unintentional—occurred when, on rare occasions, he teetered an inch or so to the left or right or half an inch forward. At such moments, the onlooker was compelled to consider whether defense counsel would topple to the floor with a gargantuan thud or whether the lectern would explode under the additional weight, like a shrapnel bomb. Thus did Doubtful Dick Dougherty, late of the New York Bar and a fall from grace, make his debut in the Court of Queen's Bench, Upper Canada.

"Good afternoon, Mr. Stanhope. I was intrigued by your lofty description of the relationship that developed between you and the deceased Mr. Coltrane."

"I wouldn't characterize it as a relationship, sir. We practised the customary courtesies of the officer class."

"Indeed. However, beyond acceding to every whim and fancy of your prisoner, you claim to have visited him in person only during the initial week of his more than three-week sojourn under your roof."

"I did not 'claim,' as you put it, I stated the facts."

"Would you mind stating to the jury, then, your reason for neglecting to mention your private audience with the victim on Wednesday evening, mere hours before the poisoning occurred?"

Stanhope's Adam's apple bobbed twice, and he glanced over at Kingsley Thornton.

"The prosecutor, sir, is not permitted to prompt—alas. You must answer on your own tick, I'm afraid."

Stanhope gave Dougherty a malevolent look, smiled tightly, and said, "I was not asked that particular question, sir. If I had been, I would have said that I received a note from Major Coltrane indicating he wished to see me. As soon as I finished a short meeting in my study with Mr. Farquar MacPherson, my banker, I went down and let myself into the prison chamber."

"Lieutenant Bostwick was not on duty?"

"He left my house a little after six and hasn't been seen or heard from since."

"What did you and Mr. Coltrane discuss?"

This time Thornton did not need cueing: he was on his feet. "Milord, I don't see the relevance of these questions."

"Nor do I, Mr. Thornton. Mr. Dougherty?"

"I was ambling towards the snuff boxes."

"Then amble more expeditiously, please."

"Mr. Stanhope, did you and Coltrane discuss any matter that might remotely impinge on his subsequent murder?"

"Milord, I must—"

"Overruled."

"None that I can think of," Stanhope said forcefully, with a glance at the nearby jury.

"Did either you or Coltrane take snuff during your little tête-à-tête?"

"I do not indulge, sir. But the major may have. He was an inveterate snuff taker and invariably snorted when he had visitors."

"How many snuff boxes were on his desk that Wednesday evening?"

"Two. He always had at least two. And drew from them randomly, as far as I could make out."

"So, even if he did take snuff that evening, he may have used only one of the two boxes available?"

"It's possible, yes."

"Where is this going, Mr. Dougherty?" This time it was the judge who interrupted.

"Straight to the point, milord. Mr. Stanhope, it is conceivable, then, that you, or someone there before you—like Mr. Bostwick or one of Tuesday's or Wednesday's visitors—could have planted the strychnine and the victim not have sampled that particular box until one o'clock the next day!"

"That's preposterous!" Stanhope cried. "The major took snuff morning, noon, and night—from both boxes! And what about the medicine packet with—"

"Mr. Stanhope, please refrain from editorializing," Dougherty said evenly. "You're here to answer my questions."

"And he has, Mr. Dougherty," the judge said less evenly. "However, you do have a problem with that packet, don't you?"

"Thank you for pointing that out," Dougherty said from under his bristle brows. He cranked his head twenty degrees to face the witness. "Let us now move the clock back to Monday, the day of the duel."

Stanhope looked wary but still very much composed.

"You are, sir, a much-decorated militia officer and lieutenant-colonel of a Toronto regiment, I understand."

"I am."

"And so organized and successful that you were asked to help train a new regiment down in Essex last November?"

"I was."

"Milord . . ." Thornton was on his feet, pleading.

"Get to the point, Mr. Dougherty. Now."

"Yet you would have us believe that, despite your creating a prison chamber in your own home right down to the nth detail and supervising the sentries front and back and vetting every visitor, you were unaware that a duel had been planned to take place in your garden with two pistols taken from your premises, a duel to be fought between your prisoner and the defendant?"

"I have answered that question already, sir, and I find your tone impertinent."

"Did Mr. Bostwick have ready access to your pistols?"

"You've taken that line as far as it will reach," the judge said to Dougherty. "Move on."

Dougherty glanced down at the blank sheets on the lectern that comprised his notes, then said in a most pleasant tone, "You mentioned earlier in your casual chat with Mr. Thornton that you thought you saw Sergeant McNair stumble into the hall tree and get a hand improbably jammed in one of the coat pockets."

"Did see," Stanhope corrected.

"But according to the same testimony, that part of the hallway, no more than six feet across, I'm told, was crowded with screaming, jostling people: a police constable, two soldiers from outside, one maid descending in shock from the second floor, your wife and daughter from their sitting rooms, you and Chief Sturges and your butler, Absalom Shad—in addition to the man who occasioned the commotion."

"That's correct."

"So, even if you are able to swear to what you believe you saw, it is conceivable that almost anyone present during those critical, hectic minutes could have surreptitiously placed the incriminating poison packet in any coat lying or hanging about?"

Stanhope was unruffled. "I can only tell you what I saw, sir."

In Marc's estimation, Dougherty had picked some tiny holes in the prosecution's skein of events, but all in all, the colonel had held up well. So far.

"Let's go back even further now. At the very beginning of your testimony, you told the jury that Sergeant McNair had been extremely upset at the tragic death of his lifelong friend, Corporal Melvin Curry."

"Billy confided this to me shortly after the battle, as I said."

"He confessed to you that he harboured animosity towards Major Coltrane, an enemy officer he had tracked down and captured?"

"I told him this was normal, and that it would fade away when he got home and well away from the battlefield. But the last time we spoke, in mid-December here in Toronto, he admitted that that had not happened."

Why was Dougherty going back here? Marc wondered. You didn't let a witness repeat damaging testimony and embellish it.

"Still, at the actual scene of battle, near the redoubt where Corporal Curry died and Coltrane was captured, Sergeant McNair had a perfect opportunity to let the wounded captive die, did he not?"

Thornton started to rise, but the Colonel, warming quickly to military palaver, forestalled him by saying, "That's exactly what I told the lad at the time. He had already passed the crucial test. Alas, it turned out to be of little help."

Thornton sat back down, smiling.

Dougherty may also have been smiling, but the perpetual flutter of his lips made it impossible to be sure. "Was not the principal source of the defendant's continuing anger the fact that Major Coltrane arranged an ambush near the abandoned redoubt, during which his friend and several others died? An ambush he considered cowardly and unworthy of an enemy officer?"

At the word "continuing," Thornton turned to his junior with a shrug of incredulity.

"That is so. Again, I did my best to dissuade him of such a view."

"Was the ambush not aided and abetted by the enemy's suddenly and unexpectedly discovering a cache of rifles and bullets in the earthen walls of the redoubt, crates of ordnance that you were responsible for leaving there despite orders to clear all of it out of the place a week before?"

Thornton leapt up so precipitately that he nearly cracked his skull on the lectern. "This is irrelevant and unprofessional!"

The judge looked sympathetic but said, "Well, Mr. Thornton, you allowed the topic to be introduced earlier, and it does go to motive. Mr. Dougherty, are you trying to show that your client may have felt some personal guilt over the failure of his unit to remove those crates of ammunition?"

"Yes, milord. I meant to imply only that a militia detail involving Sergeant McNair and his commanding officer had been the very one to have inadvertently left those rifles where they were subsequently used to decimate the unit a week later, and—"

"I wish to answer your insidious question, sir!" The colonel had almost climbed out of the witness-box. "Lieutenant Muttlebury was accused, posthumously, of incompetence in the matter, but I accepted full responsibility for it. The lieutenant was cleared of any blame and I received a reprimand—along with a citation for courage under fire."

Both the side galleries and the dignified benches reacted to this declaration with a chorus of muted "Hear, hear's," and for the first time the chief justice had to wield his gavel, albeit gently. Into the silence following the gavel's appeal, Dougherty said to the witness, whose stamina and patience seemed inexhaustible, "Now, Mr. Stanhope, tell me about your daughter's romance with the dashing major."

Thornton was apoplectic and the witness stunned, along with most of the gallery. "This is an outrage, milord!"

"How dare you—"

"Please, restrain yourself, Colonel Stanhope," the judge said quickly, "and I would not go so far as to label the question an outrage, Mr. Thornton. However, Mr. Dougherty, you had better have an explanation for it. We do not tolerate cheap theatrics or the abuse of witnesses in the Queen's courtrooms, whatever the policy may be in your own republic."

The great advantage that Doubtful Dick had, despite his near immobility, was that his deep-set, piggish eyes were almost impossible to read and thus disconcerting to anyone trying to do so. "I wish to explore a possible motive that someone other than the defendant may have had for murdering Coltrane, someone who also had opportunity and means," he said serenely to the judge.

"Milord!"

"Are you referring to this witness, Mr. Dougherty?"

"I am. Mr. Stanhope has already provided testimony on how he arranged for the victim's incarceration and how he scheduled and vetted all visitors. A key part of that testimony has been omitted, and I wish to ask the witness about that—with a view to constructing a competing theory of the crime."

"You have every right to attempt such a tactic, sir, but I must caution you that Colonel Stanhope is not on trial here, and your questions must address facts already in evidence or questions directly relevant to those facts. If you digress one degree, I'll stop you and dismiss the witness without right of recall."

"I understand, milord." The huge head with the perilously perched wig eased back to Stanhope, who was still fuming and glowering. "Your daughter was a regular visitor to Mr. Coltrane, was she not?"

"She was. She took him his breakfast every morning." Stanhope bit off each word, and his scowl was venomous enough to poison a dozen defense counsel.

"At whose request?"

"Initially mine, when the maid took sick. Then Major Coltrane's."

"Did you at any time discuss with your wife or anyone else the growing possibility that Patricia, your daughter, might be romantically attracted to an officer in your enemy's army?"

Stanhope grimaced in an effort to maintain his composure.

"Well, sir? You are under oath."

"My wife mentioned it to me a few days before the major's death. I gave it no credence. I told her that even if it were true, the man would be hanged and forever out of our lives within the month. Why should I be foolhardy enough to poison a man already destined to die?"

It was the very question that seemed incapable of being answered, the one that reared up like a perpendicular cliff before the defense and all their efforts.

"I suppose, sir, the only possible motive would have to be one of such overweening passion that such a consideration would seem irrelevant. For example, the cuckolding of a proud, public figure, followed by a vicious blackmail scheme."

"I must protest, milord, in the strongest possible terms!" Thornton screamed into the excited and noisy response of the galleries.

The gavel came down and came down again. "I warned you, Mr. Dougherty. You have gone too far this time—"

"Milord, I have proof of the claim here in my hand." Dougherty was waving the letter they had recovered from Almeda's gown, the one in which Coltrane proclaimed his love and alluded to the blackmail "proposal." "I would like this letter entered into evidence, with permission to establish its authenticity through a handwriting comparison, and subsequently to recall this witness and question him on its contents."

"Let me see the letter, sir."

Dougherty handed it to Robert Baldwin. Chief Justice Robinson took the document and perused it, while Thornton shuffled nervously from side to side and the colonel looked simultaneously perplexed and enraged. And for the first time, fearful.

"This letter is not signed," the judge said, into the prurient buzzing of the assembled citizenry.

"May we go into chambers to discuss the matter?"

"No, sir. You will kindly provide the Crown with a copy. I'll take written submissions on the matter by seven o'clock this evening. I'll rule on the question of admissibility at ten o'clock tomorrow morning. Court is adjourned until then."

The chief justice rose. Day one of the trial was ended abruptly amid sensation and speculation throughout the courtroom. Only Doubtful Dick Dougherty appeared unperturbed.

SEVENTEEN

Since Doughtery had to be taken directly home and secured in his chair before his spindle legs gave way, Marc, Robert, and Clement Peachey found themselves seated in a semicircle facing the sprawled, exhausted form of their leader and waiting for any words of wisdom that might drift their way. It was five o'clock and growing dark. Everyone was tired and hungry, but the only refreshment was a pot of weak tea served to them by Broderick Langford. The room was chilly, the fire smoky, the atmosphere sepulchral: the ideal setting for a post-mortem.

Dougherty had his bare feet propped on his footstool, soles hearthward, and his new trousers rolled up to the knee to facilitate Celia's massage of his calves with some sort of pungent liniment. The three men watched her supple fingers play over the veined flesh and were rewarded with intermittent, shy smiles. The pouches around Dougherty's eyes intimated that he might be asleep.

It was Robert who broke the silence. "What are our chances of getting Coltrane's letter admitted?" he asked the figure in the wing chair. "It indicates both a blackmail attempt and a romantic liaison, either one of which provides Stanhope with a motive goading enough to override the issue of Coltrane's eventually being hanged. And it is just such an irrational rage that we have to demonstrate."

"And we now have Almeda's love letter to bolster the romance theory, found among Coltrane's possessions by Cobb and putatively used to continue the blackmail after his arrival in Chepstow," Marc added.

In the foyer outside the courtroom, the bailiff had served Marc his summons: the Crown wanted him as a prime witness. After which he had ridden with Robert and Dougherty in the lead sleigh over here. Thus he had had a chance to outline what he and Cobb had found in Detroit. Marc had been particularly keen to sketch out a second alternative theory of the murder: poisoning by an agent of the Michigan Hunters to ensure Pathfinder's election to the presidency. Dougherty, thoroughly fatigued, had said nothing.

"I suggest that in our submission to the chief justice we include Almeda's love letter in order to give Caleb's letter more legitimacy," Robert said.

"The initial 'C' at the bottom of Caleb's letter and the handwriting sample Marc brought back from Mrs. Dobbs should convince the judge that we have reasonable grounds to accept it as written by Coltrane," Peachey said. "But unless we can somehow get Thornton to put Almeda Stanhope on the stand, I don't know how we can get around the business of the nickname 'Duchess.'"

"And if we call her," Marc said, "she'll be a hostile witness and deny everything—or else claim husband-wife privilege. We don't even have an independent sample of her handwriting."

"The judge will give us only so much latitude in developing competing theories," Robert reminded them. "Thus far he's not been unreasonable. So what are our chances of getting Coltrane's letter admitted?" Robert again addressed Dougherty's comatose form.

The eye pouches did not move, but the lips did. "Not good, though I'll make as strong a case as we can. We won't throw in Almeda's love letter though, tempting as that might be." The voice was low and rumbling, as if the words were being forged somewhere below the throat and exhaled like oracular pearls at Delphi.

"But surely we need all the proof we can muster," Robert suggested. "Robinson's not likely to expose to needless embarrassment a regimental colonel whom Sir George decorated last Saturday before the town's elite at the Twelfth Night Ball."

"But if the judge throws out Coltrane's letter tomorrow, he would in effect be throwing out Mrs. Stanhope's billet-doux with it," breathed the oracle.

"And you want to use the latter, I take it?"

"I want to use both of them. But tomorrow I may not need either." The lips fell slack. One hand dropped from the chair's arm and dangled like a spent trout. Doubtful Dick was asleep.

Celia rose from her kneeling position, every movement unconsciously sensuous. "He'll only nap for half an hour," she said to the carpet.

Broderick came over with a portable writing desk in his arms. "He'll dictate the statement for Justice Robinson to me, and I'll run it over to the court," he said.

"Then we had better go back to Baldwin House," Robert said, with some reluctance but little choice. They had cast Billy's lot to Dougherty and that was that. "We'll get a bite to eat. Then we'll start sketching out our defense strategy, using the Hunters' conspiracy as a fallback position. And if Cobb can locate Bostwick before the weekend is out, we can add him to the mix. Also, Marc, we need to prep you for your own testimony. After all, you're likely the Crown's favorite witness."

Marc got home at nine o'clock. Beth was sitting up on the chesterfield, dozing, but she roused herself with his arrival. Marc insisted that she tell him all about her days with him away. He was growing weary of his own obsession with Billy McNair. Even an hour of casual talk and amiable gossip would be a sign that normal, everyday life was not only possible but inevitable.

The extra work entailed by Saturday's gala had kept Rose Halpenny and the girls happily engaged—a blessing for Dolly, whose flagging spirits had to be continually boosted, both for her sake and for the sake of Billy, whom she visited with evangelical determination. Colonel Stanhope and Almeda had paraded up to the podium of honour at the dance (their daughter, unfortunately, "felled by the grippe" and unable to accompany them). Sir George had gritted his patrician teeth and pinned a medal to the colonel's tunic, the latter feigning modesty with admirable aplomb. The petty aristocracy had thundered with applause. These details had come to Beth, in a variety of interpretations, on Monday and Tuesday, as soiled or torn gowns were brought in for rehabilitation. Patricia Stanhope had stayed secluded in Rose Halpenny's apartment above the shop until late Sunday afternoon, when Beth received a note from Chepstow, in which Almeda stated tersely that the prodigal daughter was now welcome in her own home.

"So the family's closing ranks?" Marc said.

"And that isn't good for Billy, is it?"

"No, it isn't."

At the reference to the trial, Marc sighed and, seeing Beth wide awake after her nap, launched into an account of his trip to Detroit and a sketch of the evidence they had uncovered and the alternative theories they were pursuing. He seasoned the forensic narrative with comic asides about Cobb's Bartlett and his own flamboyant lordship, and finished up with a faithful rendering of Cobb's reunion with his father.

"I've asked Dora to deliver our baby," Beth said.

"You don't want Dr. Withers?"

"He's a good coroner," she said.

After a bit, Marc said, "Did Patricia tell you anything more about what went on up at Chepstow?"

Beth hesitated. "She did. But if I tell you, you must promise not to use it in the trial."

"Even if it means Billy's life?"

Beth took that in.

"Please, believe me, darling, we would only use such information if we needed to, and even then with the utmost discretion." While he was thinking of himself and Robert in this regard, he knew he couldn't speak for Dougherty.

"Coltrane seduced her," Beth said.

"Jesus—"

"A few days before Christmas, she said. And it only happened once."

"Did she tell her mother or father?" Marc said, his hopes rising.

"I'm afraid not. She was wise enough to know how they'd react. Besides, her lover swore her to secrecy. And she was mad for him. Still is, poor thing."

Marc sighed. "Even so, Almeda had her suspicions, though she swore to me that she didn't pass them along to her husband."

"Would you?"

Marc yawned. He had been up since dawn and he was beyond fatigue, but his mind had not stopped racing with thought all day. "I'm sure to be called tomorrow. That means I'll have to sit in the witness room until I've given my testimony."

"You want me to go to court?"

"Do you have the time?"

"I'll take Dolly," Beth said. "She's too scared to go by herself."

Before the jury was brought in, Chief Justice Robinson summoned Robert Baldwin and Kingsley Thornton to him and rendered his decision on the letter found in Almeda Stanhope's ball gown.

"I am not going to allow the defense to use this letter at this time. It would be speculative and prejudicial without a proper foundation. First of all, the letter, according to the affidavit sworn by Rose Halpenny, was found sewn into a dress belonging to Mrs.

Stanhope, it is addressed only to 'D' and signed only as 'your demon lover, C.' So, while Mrs. Stanhope may be the possessor of the letter, it does not appear to have been meant for her. Without her corroboration of its provenance—a maid could have placed it there, as after all, such a gown is used only on rare occasions and, if out of style, never again—we have nothing usable. Moreover, while the handwriting sample you supplied, with an affidavit from Mr. Edwards as to its source, is similar to that of the letter in question, I am no expert, and a forgery is a distinct possibility, given its inflammatory contents. Hence, without a foundation, which can only be provided by direct testimony from Mrs. Stanhope, you cannot introduce the letter or allude to its contents or any implications thereof while cross-examining Colonel Stanhope. However, it is conceivable that you may be able to establish its legitimacy and relevance later on during the presentation of the defense's case."

With that, the judge set the offending letter beside him and called for the jury.

Beth was seated beside Dolly and Rose Halpenny in the front row of the side gallery nearest the defense bench, where she got her first and appalled glimpse of Richard Dougherty. He rose before her in a languid, agonized waddle towards the trembling lectern. Colonel Stanhope was back on the stand and reminded of his oath. To the surprise and delight of the crowded room, he stood proud in his regimental uniform, a near replica of the regular's redcoat. Only the sabre was missing.

"Good morning, sir," Dougherty began. "I wish to begin by asking you a question you may find offensive, but it is one I wish you to answer in the forthright manner you so ably displayed yesterday."

The colonel acknowledged the compliment with a single twitch of his moustache, but his cold eyes were narrow and wary.

Dougherty's pea-green eyes, however, had removed themselves from the witness to stare up at the letter lying harmlessly beside the judge. Stanhope, who had not been present for the ruling, blinked uncertainly. He followed Dougherty's gaze up to the letter, then he glanced sideways at Thornton, who shook his head almost imperceptibly. If the judge noticed, he did not react to the impropriety.

"You are a man of honour, sir," Dougherty said, "a military man to whom a sworn oath is sacred." He peered up at the letter again. "And you have sworn to tell the—"

"Please put your question, Counsellor."

"Did you at any time between May and the end of November of last year receive, directly or indirectly, a blackmail threat?"

The galleries drew in their collective breath.

Stanhope flinched and, as he was wont to do when discomfited, grew rigidly erect.

"Colonel?" Those tiny porcine eyes veered back up to the letter.

Beth realized what Dougherty was doing. If the colonel had been receiving blackmail threats about his wife's alleged infidelity, then he had to presume that there were possibly many letters with incriminating potential in existence, one or more of which may have found their way into the hands of the defense, in addition to the one beside the judge.

"Yes," Stanhope said in a hoarse whisper.

The onlookers stirred and craned to hear more.

"Tell me when they came and what they demanded, please."

He has omitted any reference to the source of the threat, Beth thought, and smiled.

"The first came in September, while I was still here in Toronto." The colonel's voice had regained its confidence. "It was from Caleb Coltrane and demanded money. If I refused to pay him five hundred dollars, he threatened to reveal information to the press which he assumed would cause a scandal in my family. When I ignored the letter—I burned it—I received another two weeks later."

"Now this may be painful, sir, but you must answer—"

"Milord!" Thornton was on his feet. "This has gone far enough. The witness has already denied any involvement in the murder and pointed out the incontestable fact that no one other than an enraged and aggrieved youth like the defendant would murder an already doomed man."

Beth saw the respectable burghers of the jury nodding in sympathy.

"Mr. Dougherty?"

"Milord, I cannot show sufficient cause for a plausible alternative theory of the crime if I am not permitted to probe for that cause."

Chief Justice Robinson, who had seen Caleb's letter, paused for a second only before saying, "Take it step by step, Counsellor. And when I say stop, you stop, even if you are in mid-sentence."

Dougherty's massive head swivelled back to the witness stand. "What was the precise nature of the threat?"

The colonel was fuming but also attempting to smile at the jury to convey his unshakeable confidence. Even his ears stiffened. "Major Coltrane claimed that when my wife paid a visit to his sister in Detroit last spring, she had become romantically involved with him."

The sensation in the room had to be gavelled down, while the colonel reddened to the colour of his tunic.

"The revelation of such a claim, if accompanied by sufficient detail, might well ruin you, is that not so, Colonel?"

"It would ruin any gentleman," Stanhope said vehemently. "But as it was a vicious lie and its source an enemy of the Queen, I had no real fear of its being made public."

"And how did you determine it was a lie?"

Stanhope looked over at Almeda, who, not being on the witness list, was sitting near Kingsley Thornton. He smiled with his teeth and said loudly, "I went to my wife and asked her."

Murmurs of approval here from many in the crowd.

"So, satisfied that the claims were groundless, you simply ignored the threat. Did you receive a third letter?"

Thinking the ordeal was over, the colonel blinked and sputtered, "I did, sir. The fellow was insufferably bold and offensive, but I maintained my silence in the face of his insidious provocation!"

"But this is the man, you have already testified, whom you deliberately volunteered to imprison in your home, whom you coddled like a visiting uncle, to whom you ordered your daughter to serve breakfast each morning—"

"Milord! I must—"

"I told you that I did so out of a sense of honour and duty, sir! The fellow was a true soldier, whatever his other failings might be. Besides, I had no money to pay any blackmailer—my business has not done so well lately—and my wife's behaviour in all this has been beyond reproach. If you don't believe me, ask her!"

Dougherty swung his head slowly towards Kingsley Thornton, who was quivering with rage behind his lectern, and gave him a gelatinous smile. They both knew that the defense had just got what it so desperately needed: Almeda Stanhope would have to take the stand.

"That's enough," the judge said to Dougherty, who was already in the process of leveraging his bulk down on the bench behind him. "The witness, who is not on trial here, has denied acquiescing to blackmail, and unless you have more tangible evidence in that regard, please move on."

"I have no more questions at this time, milord. But I would like to reserve the right to recall the witness later on."

Dismissed, the colonel looked as if he'd like to produce his sabre and do something felonious to Dougherty. He stumbled as he came down from the stand, righted himself, and marched out. Beth saw Almeda staring after him, terrified. But her attention was brought back to the front when she heard the clerk call out the name of the next witness: Mr. Marcus Edwards.

● ● ●

Marc, of course, had been unable to see what had been achieved so far this morning, though he heard a full account later in the day. While sitting in the witness room with the assistant bailiff, Absalom Shad, and Horatio Cobb—and forbidden to talk—Marc whiled away the time by working on the coded membership roster of the Michigan Hunters that he had taken from Ephraim Runchey in Detroit. He had been too tired to scrutinize it until now. Next to him Cobb flexed his sore wrist, hummed, and rattled a newspaper. Shad stared at the floor, visibly nervous. Just before his name was called, Marc cracked the code.

The approach Marc would take on the stand had been decided in Robert's office early the previous evening. If the two or three helpful things Marc wished to say in defense of Billy McNair were to be credible and persuasive, he would have to be seen as forthcoming and cooperative. Any attempt to evade Thornton's questions or consciously manipulate the facts would be sure to fail. Even so, Thornton made Marc boil inside. His evidence, alas, was mainly supportive of the Crown's case, and the prosecutor made it seem even more damning than it was. Marc was compelled to provide detailed accounts of his efforts to persuade the jailed Billy McNair to agree to the reconciliation proposal and visit to the prison chamber. The source and depth of Billy's anger were repeated and sharpened for the jury. Dougherty's hearsay objections were brushed aside by the judge as Thornton cunningly focused on Marc's role in these discussions and his description of Billy's attitude and demeanour. Finally, when Marc was able to say that in the end Billy had agreed to the visit and a written apology, he was cut off before he could emphasize the genuine change of heart he had observed and Dolly's part in it. Thornton then moved right to the fatal visit itself.

"You say you were able to hear the tone of the conversation between McNair and Coltrane through the partly open door of the cell?"

"I could."

"At any time during your watch in the anteroom, did you detect a tone that might be termed confrontational or angry?"

Marc blinked. His candid discussion of these events with Chief Sturges while they had examined the crime scene and waited for Dr. Withers to arrive had unfortunately been passed along to the Crown, as they should have been. He did his best: "For the most part it was—"

"Answer my question, sir, not your own."

"At one point, and one point only, I did hear their voices raised. But Coltrane—"

"What was the source of this angry exchange?"

"I could detect no words that I could put together coherently," Marc equivocated, pretty certain that Thornton could have no inkling of the version that Billy had provided—and was forbidden by law to repeat in open court.

"Given your knowledge of the defendant's violent history and penchant for duelling, did you consider getting up to intervene?"

Marc hesitated. "I considered it, but—"

"So you're saying that this flare-up was so contentious that you actually thought you would have to forcibly intervene? And all this during a meeting designed to be conciliatory?"

"Milord," Dougherty interjected, "the prosecutor is not a ventriloquist."

"Try not to speak for the witness, Mr. Thornton," the judge chided gently.

"Given this flare-up, this sudden, angry outburst on the part of the defendant, is it not possible, sir, that Mr. McNair was dissembling all the while, that he merely pretended to be regretful and compliant in order to get himself conveyed once more to face the man he hated and had threatened to kill?"

"At no time then did I think that, and I do not think it now," Marc said. But he knew what was coming next, and the budding barrister in him perversely admired Thornton for omitting it earlier and coming back to it now.

"Then tell me why the defendant asked to be driven to his home, where he was permitted to spend several minutes unattended in his bedroom?"

Again, Marc squirmed and silently fumed, but the facts came out, and the members of the jury, sympathetic as they must be with young, brave Billy McNair, looked distinctly uncomfortable. Several frowned and stole worried glances up at the dock opposite them. No doubt they were thinking about the poison packet found in Billy's coat.

What came next was not much better. Marc had to describe Billy's wild exit from the prison chamber and his blind rush for the stairs and the front door. Once more, Thornton stressed the possibility of Billy's dissembling and his need to find a way to dispose of the incriminating packet. Even Billy's calls for a doctor were characterized as the actions of a cunning man, devoured by rage.

Dougherty did his best to undo the damage. As Thornton had introduced the matter of Billy's demeanour and the negotiations that had preceded the fatal visit, Dougherty was able to elicit from Marc a more sustained and convincing description of Billy's general character, his reengagement to Dolly, and its effects on his contrition and compliance with regard to the apology and the conditions of any subsequent parole. Thornton interjected often to disrupt the continuity but made no inroads. Marc finished up with his key point: both before and after the "flare-up," the dialogue was congenial and, on Coltrane's desk, he had discovered the signed document indicating an amicable settlement.

"As for Mr. Thornton's unsubstantiated assertion that Sergeant McNair's pleading cries for a doctor were part of an ongoing charade, do you suppose a murderer would try to plant an incriminating piece of evidence in the pocket of his own coat?"

"Of course not. It would be foolhardy—"

"Milord! The witness is—"

"Sustained. The witness will refrain from giving an opinion on matters in which he has no expertise. And Mr. Dougherty, you know better."

In the redirect, Thornton went for the jugular. "If the defendant was able to deceive you into thinking he had given up his desire for revenge, did it not occur to you that it was in his own interest to appear conciliatory to Coltrane, to put him off his guard long enough to salt the snuff?"

"It did not," Marc said, but the jury might think so now.

"Colonel Stanhope testified that the coats on the hall tree were tumbled about when the defendant fell into them. Is it not likely that, in those circumstances, the accused merely stashed the poison packet in whatever crevice he found nearest to hand?"

"It was not possible, sir, because he did not have the packet."

Thornton flinched, frowned, then swung around to the jury box. "We should all have such loyal friends, eh?"

"Mister Thornton!"

"I apologize, milord. Now, one final question, Mr. Edwards. You have touchingly described the so-called reengagement of Mr. McNair and Miss Delores Putnam and its effect on the former's attitude. But do you not find it passing strange that the same young romantic, just three days prior to the murder, strode into the garden at Chepstow and took up arms against the victim with the express intention of shooting him dead, before a witness?"

"My point was that the lad had had a change of heart."

"Some heart!" Thornton spun around with his coattails flying and sat down with a theatrical flourish. "No more questions, milord."

Dismissed, Marc squeezed in beside Beth. He reached over and patted Dolly's hand. Robert turned towards them and mouthed, "You did what you could." Then they all looked towards the witness stand, where Horatio Cobb was being sworn in.

Poor Cobb did his best also to minimize the damage to Billy's defense. But he was no match for the wily, relentless Thornton. He forced Cobb to admit that the stopover at Billy's house had been unauthorized and had come as an unwelcome surprise to his chief. He was tricked into suggesting that Billy, having stashed the poison packet, was on his way out the door to freedom when he had crashed into the sentries. And of course, he confirmed finding the packet in one of the coats and reporting it to Sturges. Then, even more troublingly, he had to give the damning detail of the duel and its aftermath, confirming the colonel's account and adding to it. Billy's wild and seething words about killing Coltrane were repeated by Cobb and echoed several times by the gleeful prosecutor.

The only angle of reentry for Dougherty was to have Cobb re-iterate Marc's testimony about Billy's calm and serious demeanour before leaving the jail for the visit, and a vague reference to his good character and behaviour as Cobb knew it from casual contact with him over several years. Thornton made such short work of this effort that Dougherty regretted bringing it up. Stunned, Cobb stumbled out of the box.

"Don't worry," Beth whispered to Marc, "he's gotta put Almeda on the stand—soon."

At the moment, this seemed their best hope.

However, it was not Almeda Stanhope who was called at two o'clock, but Absalom Shad. Marc and the three lawyers had had luncheon in a comfortable chamber down the hall, where Marc was brought up to speed and where he handed Robert the Hunters' Lodge roster with the code explained and several examples laid out and flagged. Dougherty, who had to be assisted down the hall by his wards and fed like an invalid by Celia, seemed well pleased with Marc's effort.

Under Kingsley Thornton's gentle guidance—for Shad was

exceedingly nervous, not making eye contact with anything but his fingers on the railing in front of him—the butler of Chepstow denied any foreknowledge of the duel, corroborated his master's account of the scene in the garden, and confirmed that Lardner Bostwick, erstwhile jailer, had stomped out the front door on the Wednesday evening without explanation. Thereupon he, Shad, had been ordered to replace Bostwick and took up his duties in the anteroom at dawn on Thursday. Yes, Miss Stanhope brought Coltrane his breakfast as usual at eight o'clock and stayed until nine-thirty. No, he was not privy to their conversation, the cell door being shut and secured from the inside. At ten o'clock Alderman Tierney arrived, signed in, and spent nearly an hour shouting at the major. But he came out chuckling, and Coltrane appeared afterwards to be in high spirits. Yes, there was freshly spilled snuff on the desk, and Coltrane had remarked, "I love disputing with a man who ain't afraid of a pinch of snuff!"

Shortly after eleven, Shad was startled when the doorbell rang upstairs and he answered it to find a strange woman there demanding to see Coltrane. As the colonel was out of the house, Shad said he didn't know what to do except to check with Coltrane. The newcomer was a middle-aged woman who claimed to be a Mrs. Jones from Streetsville who was known to the prisoner. She gave Shad a note to take in. Being unarmed and nonviolent, Shad said he was afraid to open the cell door but eventually did so, delivering the note. Whatever was in it did the trick, for Mrs. Jones was welcomed in and spent a half-hour with Coltrane, though, as he neglected to have her sign out, he couldn't be sure of the time. After lunch, of course, Billy McNair and Marc Edwards arrived, but after letting the former into the prison chamber and settling the latter in the anteroom, he went straight to his own den, where he remained until the ruckus over the poisoning erupted. And alas, he could shed no further light on the business of the poison packet, as he had gone straight out to fetch Dr. Withers.

Dougherty began his cross-examination by motioning his associate, Robert Baldwin, towards the high bench. Robert handed up to Justice Robinson a single sheet of paper, then walked over and gave a similar one to Kingsley Thornton. Finally he placed a third before the nervous Mr. Shad.

"What you have before you, milord, is a partial mock-up of a document which was seized in Detroit last Tuesday evening by Mr. Edwards. Mr. Baldwin is now giving you this original document along with Mr. Edwards's sworn statement of its provenance."

The judge held up his hand for silence and then perused the material before him. With a puzzled glance at Thornton, he said, "Proceed, Mr. Dougherty."

"Mr. Shad, please tell the court how long you have been a member of the Michigan branch of the Hunters' Lodge."

This stunning remark caused a sensation in the chamber and a fearful trembling in the witness.

"I don't know what you mean," Shad stammered, with a weak attempt at truculence.

"I think you do, sir."

"Milord! Counsel is badgering the witness! Moreover, he's off on yet another of his fishing expeditions!"

"Where is this going, Mr. Dougherty? There's been no reference to the so-called Hunters' Lodges in Mr. Shad's testimony."

"My question goes directly to the credibility of this witness, milord. As the mysterious Mrs. Jones was the last person to see Coltrane before the defendant did, I need to explore fully Mr. Shad's account of her arrival and her actions thereafter. I do not wish the jury to accept at face value his claims thus far."

"I'll allow it," the judge said. "But go slowly."

Dougherty nodded and may even have smiled. His eyes moved to the witness's and locked on them. "Please look at the paper before you, sir. On it you will find a dozen coded names selected from the original document now in Mr. Justice Robinson's hands. Below this list is an explanation of how the code works. It is fairly straight-forward, based on a three-point, repeated sequence. That is, to de-cipher the first coded letter of a name, we count one letter ahead in the alphabet. Thus a *B* would be translated as a *C*. To get the second letter of the name, we count two letters ahead, and to get the third letter, three letters ahead. At the fourth letter, we start at one again. Using this formula, my associate has decoded the heading that ap-pears on the document. Please read it aloud for the jury."

Shad's voice shook, but he managed to say haltingly, "Member-ship List of Hunters' Lodge, Michigan Branch."

The crowd's excitement had turned now to expectant silence.

"Very good. Now, sir, read aloud the first decoded name on the list."

"Lucius Bierce."

"The so-called general of the Windsor raiding party, was he not?"

A ragged chorus of assent from the galleries supplied the answer.

"Now, read the one below it."

"Caleb Coltrane." Shad's voice was a mere whisper.

"And the second last name on this selected list?"

Shad started to tremble all over. "Absalom Shad."

The buzz in the room took an angry turn. The judge gavelled it down.

"Would you please answer my original question, then. When did you join the Hunters?"

"I have no idea how my name came to be on that list! I've been livin' here for years."

"Mr. Shad, I submit that not only are you a bona fide member of the heinous Hunters' Lodge, but you have been acting as a se-cret agent on their behalf, and that—as the defense will show when we present our side of the story—you were ordered by another high-ranking member of the Lodge, one Ephraim Runchey, to poison Caleb Coltrane so that he could not be elected in absentia president of the state branch of the Lodge." Dougherty delivered these accusations in a steady, rumbling basso, devoid of theatrical dudgeon.

"That's a lie!"

"Milord!"

"You, sir, had the readiest access to the victim, you—"

"I was never a member of the Lodge!" Shad shouted to the agitated spectators. "My brother Simon was; he got caught stealin' guns from the Detroit armoury and General Brady put him in jail. He had no money for a lawyer and my mother was desperate. Runchey come to me and said the Hunters would help him, but only if I cooperated with 'em."

"Mr. Shad," the judge said kindly, "there's no need to—"

"But it had nothin' to do with murder. I was to vouch for him so he could get in to visit Coltrane, and when the time come for him to escape, I was to help them. I didn't know they put my name on their list!"

"And so you helped Runchey, then?" Dougherty said.

"He come to visit the prisoner on the Saturday, five days before the murder. I told the colonel that he was a friend of mine I knew from Detroit. But that was all. I wasn't asked to help with any escape plan, and I wouldn't've done it anyways. I despised Coltrane and all he stood for—"

"Enough to poison him?"

"No!" Shad's eyes were wild with fear, outrage, hurt. "I wouldn't do a thing to harm the Stanhopes or bring shame on their house! Mrs. Stanhope took me in when I had nothin', when I was a hopeless drunk. She brung me here and give me a job in her own home. She saved my life!"

"Are you quite through, Mr. Dougherty?" the judge said sternly.

Thornton was on his feet, teetering with feigned rage. "Milord, is Mr. Dougherty going to prove that every witness for the Crown is independently guilty of murdering Caleb Coltrane?"

The simmering anger of the crowd was now turning slowly towards sympathy for the abused and loyal butler.

"The witness is dismissed, and this court is adjourned until ten o'clock Monday morning!" the judge said, with a fearsome rap of his gavel.

And none too soon, Marc thought. It was going to be an interesting interval.

EIGHTEEN

Robert ordered Marc to spend Saturday evening and all day Sunday at home. The two-hundred-mile trek from Detroit to Toronto, followed by an exhausting day and a half in and out of court, had left him visibly fatigued and mentally drained. "If we need you, we'll send for you, though you've already done yeoman's service. Now leave the lawyering to the lawyers."

So, that night Marc and Beth curled up in front of a blazing hearth and read to each other, while Jasper Hogg—putatively present to chop kindling and top up the cistern in the water closet—talked nonstop to Charlene in the kitchen. Early Sunday morning, Marc and Beth harnessed Dobbin and went for a leisurely drive into the countryside. Two hours later, with Charlene and Jasper, they strolled through a goose-feather snowfall to the new Congregational Church on Hospital Street at Bay. It was only on the way home that Marc began to wonder what tactic Richard Dougherty might work on poor Almeda Stanhope, who had been, as expected, added to the Crown's witness roster. Would he not be better off laying out the defense case, rather than badgering the Crown's witnesses to the point where the jury felt sorry for them and thus more likely to accept their version of events? Brilliant as he was,

Dougherty seemed to have forgotten that he was an outsider with a checkered past, and physically off-putting to boot.

It was just past suppertime on Sunday evening at the Cobb residence on Parliament Street, and Cobb was snoozing in his favourite chair. With a splint no longer needed, his sprained wrist was healing steadily. He could flex it without pain, but it still had little strength in it, certainly not enough to make a two-handed collar of some wriggling miscreant. The half-read newspaper, resting on the fulcrum of his nose, rose and fell with his contented breathing.

"Dad! Wake up!"

Cobb blinked awake, scattering all four pages of the *Constitution*. It was Fabian, looking more excited than usual. "Where's yer mother?"

"Out on a call. But come see! Somebody's prowling about the chicken coop!"

Cobb was up in a flash and, with one foot fast asleep, hobbled into the summer kitchen towards the back door. "Stay in here," he ordered, then stepped warily onto the stoop. The skies had cleared, and the partial moon on the fresh snow threw enough light for him to make out the silhouette of the coop thirty feet away. The chickens by the sound of it were in turmoil. A fox or coyote? No, Fabian had said some*body*. Cobb reached down and picked up a stout walking stick he kept beside the door. He quickly spotted the shoe prints. They seemed to indicate that a single person had been moving back and forth across the yard, perhaps casing the house for an attempted burglary.

Just then the rooster let out a fierce squawk, and Cobb trotted towards the sound. As he got to the henhouse door, he heard a yip, then a yelp, and a second later a dark male figure came staggering out into the moonlight. Cobb lashed at it, aiming for the bare head, but the cudgel smacked against one of its lurching shoulders.

"Ow, ow, ow, ow, ow!" The figure howled like Poor Tom on Lear's heath. "Ya've gone and busted my back!"

"Jesus Christ and a donkey!" Cobb shouted. "What in hell are you doin' rummagin' about in my henhouse?"

Nestor Peck ignored the question, vigorously rubbing his throbbing shoulder with one gloveless hand.

"You're damn lucky Shanty-clear didn't pluck yer pecker off! He don't appreciate competition."

"I was just comin' to see ya, and I thought I might borree an egg whilst I was here," Nestor said, and added, "I need a cup o' tea, Cobb. I'm frozen right through to the nub."

Ten minutes and two cups of tea later, Nestor got to the principal point of his house call, a risky move for a known snitch. "I had ta come here 'cause you're not out where you oughta be," he whined. "So what I've come ta tell ya oughta fetch double the usual."

"I'll let ya know after I hear it. Them's the rules."

Nestor smiled, exposing a mushy set of blackened gums. "I know where Lardner Bostwick is."

Cobb did his best not to look elated. "And where would that be?"

"He's been drinkin' up at the Tinker's Dam, drinkin' steady fer a week. Right now he's holed up in Tipsy Dan's shack."

"If he's still there when I get to it, Nestor, I'll give ya a dozen eggs and throw in the rooster!"

"The eggs'll do fine."

Cobb quick-marched the two and a half blocks to Briar Cottage to relay the news to Marc. Fifteen minutes later, they were whizzing along in the cutter, northwards to the end of Jarvis Street, with Jasper Hogg perched on the seat back and hanging on as if clutching Charlene. The plan was simply to burst into Tipsy Dan's shack—just off the lane that led into the shantytown of thieves, inebriates, and ne'er-do-wells—grab Bostwick, and haul him into the sleigh before anyone could ask why or raise an objection. It went off without a hitch, except for the fact that Bostwick was indeed comatose and a deadweight. Tipsy Dan didn't even bother to wake up. As there was no room in the cutter for the body and three pallbearers, Marc volunteered to walk down to Baldwin House and bring Robert to Cobb's place, where they had decided to take Bostwick for resuscitation. Robert came to the door himself, tossed his dinner bib to a startled Cummings, and raced after Marc with his overcoat dangling from one arm.

Cobb met them at his front door and directed them to sit in the parlour near the fire. It seemed that when he and Jasper had lugged Bostwick's stinking bulk into the kitchen, they had been greeted by Dora, just returned from a successful delivery. She had immediately banished the upright males to the next room, shut the door, and set to work upon the unknowing victim. They heard the scrape of the tin tub across the kitchen floor, followed by the swish and gurgle of hot water (always on the boil in a cask-size kettle), a sequence of thumping noises, a mammoth splash, and a wrenching, drawn-out moan.

"Missus Cobb'll sober the bugger up or else scare him to death," Cobb said reassuringly.

Moments later, Dora's head swung into view. She smiled at the visitors. "I got the stink washed off him and enough coal-tar on his noggin to kill a ridge-o-men of cooties. He ain't sayin' much, but he's awake."

The men went into the kitchen, where they found Lardner Bostwick wrapped in one of Dora's flowered flannel robes, glowing pink of cheek and chin. The eyelids sagged, but the dark orbs behind them were taking in the world again, and not liking much what they saw.

Unable to douse the fiery demons in him with drink, Bostwick had apparently decided he would try drowning them with talk.

No interrogation was needed: his story poured out so quickly that Marc's shorthand scribble could not keep up with it.

"I don't know what kinda hold that bugger Coltrane had over the colonel. All I know is every time he farted, I had to run and wipe his arse. We gave him wine and whiskey and snuff and brung his personal effects from Detroit. But the colonel's been like a big brother to me, so I put up with it for his sake. I worried about Patty bein' in there alone with him every mornin', but it was the colonel's call, though I did tell her mother about the visits.

"Then this Billy fella, one of our own sergeants, gets in a spat with Coltrane and agrees to a duel. Coltrane tells me to get the colonel's permission—or else. So I go to the colonel and he's furious. He says no. I wait a while and he comes to me and says it's okay as long as I don't tell him any of the details—he's coverin' his own rear end, eh?—but when he points to the pistols in the study, he says, 'It wouldn't be a bad idea if you put a paper ball in one of the pistols and make sure the Yankee shot chooses it.' Then he walks away and pretends he knows nothin' about what's gonna happen. So I load the pearl-handled one with the blank—'cause I know the major will take the best-lookin' weapon—and the other gets a regular ball. Then Monday mornin', Billy shows up, and I present the pistols. Wouldn't ya know it, but the Yankee picks the one with the bullet. I almost shit a brick."

"That's why I only found one bullet—in the wall behind Billy where Coltrane's shot ended up," Cobb said.

"I couldn't believe he coulda missed, 'cause of the way he was always braggin' he'd been a crack shot since the age of eight. But I was damn glad he did. Then the coppers come, and the colonel storms out there like he's outraged and pretends to chew me out."

"So he really didn't drum you out of the house or the regiment?" Marc asked.

"No. He give me fifty dollars and told me to go to ground fer a few weeks."

"You damn near went *under*ground," Cobb said.

But Lardner Bostwick did not hear the comment, for suddenly his eyes rolled back into their sockets, syllables spilled out of his mouth with gusts of spittle, and his whole body began to quake.

"Christ!" Cobb cried. "He's got the heebie-jeebies!"

Dora was summoned to minister to the stricken man. She managed to get a large dose of laudanum down his throat, and he was soon calm enough to enter a fitful sleep. Cobb carried him over to the stove and wrapped him in three blankets.

In the next room, with Jasper reluctantly dispatched home, Marc and Robert conferred on the significance of what they had just been told.

"Our biggest problem, Marc, will be to get him strong enough to testify. By the look of it, considering we'll have to start the defense tomorrow, that won't be possible. In the least, we need a signed affidavit. I'll take your notes and have Clement draw up a statement. If the fellow dies, it might be enough."

"Either way, this testimony is helpful, Robert. Stanhope was counting on Billy's killing or seriously wounding Coltrane—despite the possible loss of face attendant upon his not delivering Coltrane to the court. Still, no one could fault him for a duel he could claim he didn't condone, and who better to assassinate the meddlesome blackmailer than a young war hero? One way or another, what we know for sure, and what Dougherty can exploit, is that Gideon Stanhope made one indirect attempt upon the life of his blackmailing prisoner. Why not another?"

Robert nodded. "I suppose Cobb will have to report Bostwick's reappearance to his chief in the morning."

"They're welcome to him," Marc said, "whatever's left of the poor sod."

• • •

Everyone involved in Billy's defense was up at the crack of dawn. Clement Peachey arrived at Cobb's house at seven-thirty, where a somewhat recovered Bostwick was able to sign Robert's rendering of last night's statement with a trembling hand. The Cobbs acted as witnesses and Peachey notarized it. At about the same hour, Marc arrived at Baldwin House. He and Robert took the Baldwin's four-seater up to Dougherty's, and while young Broderick assisted his guardian in dressing behind an enormous screen near the fire, they related the events and consequences of the previous evening. As usual, Dougherty made no comment, not even a grunt to indicate he was paying attention. When Robert finished, Dougherty said, "I think you should go to the bank today, Brodie. They're expecting you."

"We're both coming to court," Broderick said.

"I think this statement of Bostwick's could be our best hope," Robert said. "It confirms intent, and along with motive and—"

"Our best hope," Dougherty said, "is Chief Justice Robinson. The fellow may be a wool-dyed Tory, but he *reveres* the law."

As you do, Marc thought.

Marc watched as Almeda Stanhope walked with grace and self-composure up to the stand to be sworn in as the Crown's first witness of the day. He was sitting between Dolly and Beth in the front row of the left-hand gallery. The Cobbs and Mrs. McNair were in the row behind them. Dolly peered up at Billy standing in the dock until he noticed her, then gave him an encouraging smile. He returned an abbreviated version of it, then looked over at the bench and the witness stand beyond it. Each day so far, he had clamped his gaze onto the proceedings and kept it there. What he was thinking as he did so, no one knew.

Kingsley Thornton seemed to realize that in the case of this witness, reluctantly called, less was more. He asked her in simple and straightforward words to corroborate her husband's testimony that he had received a blackmail threat from Coltrane regarding an alleged affair with the colonel's wife, and that she and Gideon had discussed it, knew that the claim was unfounded, and ignored the audacious attempt at extortion. He succeeded in doing so without ruffling a feather or disrupting the jury's sympathy.

Then it was Dougherty's turn.

"There is no reason to be apprehensive, Mrs. Stanhope," he began. "We are all in pursuit of the same goal here: to persuade the truth into light."

"I have never feared the truth," she replied, her face pale and drawn but nonetheless beautiful. This was a woman of character, who might well be a match for Dougherty's wit.

"Let's begin, then, with the letter—"

Thornton rose. "Milord, the letter has—"

"I sense this is another letter," said the judge. "Am I right, Mr. Dougherty?"

Doubtful Dick smiled. "You are, indeed, milord. The clerk will provide you, ma'am, with the original and then give copies to Mr. Thornton and the foreman of the jury to pass along. I have already submitted to the chief justice an affidavit explaining the provenance of the document."

Almeda picked up the copy handed to her. She drew in her breath quickly but gave no other sign of concern. She looked up slowly, waiting.

"My first question is this: do you recognize the handwriting?"

"I do. It resembles mine."

"Milord, I must protest. Here we have yet another letter with both salutation and complimentary closing in the form of a single letter only: 'C' and 'D.'"

"True, but I must allow Mr. Dougherty to ask the witness if she herself can clarify the identities. If not, then he will have to move on."

"But I fail to see the relevance here." Thornton had worked himself into a righteous quiver—at ten-fifteen of a Monday morning.

"Continue, Mr. Dougherty."

"Do you, in fact, recall writing this letter on or about November first, 1838, the date indicated on it, and just two days before your husband left for Essex?"

The members of the jury were scanning the contents of their copy of the letter Cobb had discovered in Detroit, as it was passed along to them. They were shaking their heads with a kind of sorrowful disbelief, but they all looked up at the critical question.

She did not hesitate to reply, "I do. I wrote this in the afternoon of November first, and my maid posted it later in the day."

The spectators, who did not yet know the tenor of the missive, leaned forward in anxious expectation. What could it be?

"Out of deference to you and your position in Toronto society, ma'am, I shall not ask you to read all or even part of the letter. But would it be fair to say that this is inarguably a love letter written by you to 'My Dearest C'?"

The galleries and benches gasped and wanted to buzz, but not so much as they needed to hear the lady's response.

"It is wholly a declaration of love, sir. And it was posted to Caleb Coltrane in Detroit."

Justice Robinson was swinging his gavel even before the onlookers got started. Marc was baffled. Surely this admission of authorship and Coltrane's later use of the letter were potent facts in establishing a motive for her husband to kill his wife's lover. Was she naive or merely addicted to truth telling?

"And according to the affidavit of Mr. Edwards, this billet-doux was recovered from a secret drawer in one of Mr. Coltrane's silver snuff boxes in Detroit, the letter and snuff box having been sent there by your husband the morning after the major's death."

Kingsley Thornton looked ready to spring, but something in Almeda's face and posture gave him pause.

"Caleb was a great one for secrets and codes," Almeda said.

"I shall return to those facts shortly, but right now I'm interested in obtaining your response to your husband's testimony on Saturday, which my learned colleague alluded to a few minutes ago. At that time he told the court that he had received at least three letters from Coltrane in September and October, in which Coltrane attempted to extort money from your husband—using an alleged adulterous affair between you and him. He also testified that he came to you immediately and was so reassured by your response that he ignored the threats and did not pay the blackmail. Did you, ma'am, deliberately deceive your husband?"

"Milord, this is outrageous!"

"I'm exploring motive for an alternative version of the crime, milord."

"Proceed."

"Well, Mrs. Stanhope?"

"I did no such thing, because I was not romantically involved with Caleb Coltrane."

This lie was uttered with amazing conviction, Marc thought. What was the woman up to?

"Do you wish me to read your own words into the record?" Dougherty said, raising his rumble a notch and glancing at the letter before her.

"I can explain, sir. When I stayed with my cousin and best friend, Gladys Dobbs, last May in Detroit, her brother Caleb joined us. He did make an attempt to renew a passion we had shared over twenty years ago. We went for a few walks to revisit the haunts of our childhood and told each other stories about our lives lived apart. When I got home, I wrote Gladys a long letter expressing the genuine joy I felt during my three-day visit. I waxed lyrical, overly lyrical as it turned out, about my feelings of friendship for her brother. It was this careless but entirely innocent paragraph that Caleb must have used to try and extort money from Gideon. My husband showed me a copy of my words taken from that letter, and the twisted interpretation put upon them. I was hurt, of course, but I also knew that Caleb was an idealist, obsessed with liberating the oppressed of the world."

"Your testimony, then, is that you and your husband together agreed to ignore the blackmail threat?"

"Yes. But Caleb kept it up, sending more letters and upsetting my husband at a time of great worry. His business was not doing well and he was preparing to go off to another battle. So, two days before departure for the west, he came to me with a bold plan to silence Caleb once and for all."

"Which was?"

"I would write an unambiguous and exaggerated love note to Caleb. But I would deliberately write it so that my script wobbled and slanted. It would look enough like my own hand to fool Caleb, but eccentric enough to suggest a poor forgery. Also, Gladys had given me a present of some beautiful vellum paper from New York. The ruse was that I would write an obvious forgery on paper that could be shown to be foreign—certainly not the usual paper we use. I signed it 'D' for my childhood nickname, Duchess. I thought it a risky scheme, but Gideon insisted on it, hoping Caleb would make the phony letter public so he could unmask his treachery. He even offered to compose the letter."

"Are you telling us that these romantic effusions were concocted by your husband?"

"He wrote them out, and I then copied them onto Gladys's paper word for word, while he watched me."

"Did the ruse work?"

"We never found out. Gideon left two days later, and within a month the two men were shooting at each other in Baby's orchard."

Whatever else the Stanhopes had fabricated in this amazing tale, Marc thought, the letter itself had been written on expensive vellum paper, possibly from New York.

"Yet Mr. Coltrane kept this letter on his person and managed to bring it with him to his prison chamber in Chepstow, where he hid it in the secret drawer of one of his many snuff boxes. Are you suggesting that Coltrane used a bogus document, composed by your own husband, to gain favourable treatment whilst incarcerated?"

"I am saying, sir, that such a letter was *not* used in that way. As a blackmail threat, it was useless. Caleb may have kept it, thinking he could produce it as a last desperate measure to save himself. If so, he was deluded. And in the event, he did not live long enough to deploy it."

Game, set, and match. Marc sighed.

Thornton, who knew when it was best to keep mum, did so. Almeda Stanhope was excused and walked past the jury with her head held high to sit beside her daughter in the gallery.

The rest of the morning was taken up with the Crown's final witnesses. Knowing the value of leaving the jury with critical facts and phrases ringing in their collective ear, Thornton called both sentries who had followed Cobb into the duelling scene, and of course each was seduced into repeating the exact phraseology of Billy's death threat. They were succeeded by Stanhope's upstairs maid, who, with a modest prompt or two, was led to confess that, just before fainting, she did see Billy McNair tumble into the coats and thrash about, after which he tried to sprint out the front door.

Dougherty declined to cross-examine. Had he given up?

"Is the defense prepared to present its case after luncheon?" the chief justice said to a hushed chamber.

"No, milord," Dougherty said quietly. "Before doing so, I would like to recall Gideon Stanhope."

Marc walked with Beth to Smallman's. He was deflated by the morning session, for which they had had such high hopes. It was inconceivable that Stanhope's favourable treatment of his prisoner was based solely on notions of courtesy. If Bostwick were telling the truth, the duel had first been acceded to and then utilized by the colonel in a vain attempt to have Billy kill off the blackmailer for him. But why would he do so before being lionized at the Twelfth Night Ball? And if cuckoldry were not the basis of extortion, what was? More immediately to the point, if Stanhope, who had not heard his wife's testimony and was ordered to keep away from her during the break, were to confirm his wife's story of the phony love letter (and who knew what pillow talk had surfaced at Chepstow on Sunday?), Dougherty would be left with only the Hunters' conspiracy as a defense strategy. Even if they could resuscitate Bostwick, whom would the jury believe, a desperate drunk or the Pelee Island Patriot?

Thus it was a glum luncheon at Smallman's. Marc knew that he had to be back at the Court House to confer with his colleagues by one o'clock, but it was with reluctance that he kissed Beth on the cheek and pulled on his coat. Beth, bless her, had suggested that she and Dolly remain there, as a mountain of stitchwork might succeed where false cheer had failed.

At the door, Beth said, "One thing's been puzzling me about Almeda this morning."

"Oh?"

"Why didn't the colonel just dictate the love letter or give her the gist of it? She's a very smart woman, perfectly capable with words. Why would he ask her to copy out what he'd written down for her?'

"Maybe he just thought it would be too embarrassing for her to compose such a declaration of false affection."

"A man's more likely to blush at using intimate words than a woman."

Marc pulled his copy of the letter out of his briefcase and read it again.

My Dearest C:

Come soon, my love, or I'll be driven to find my own route
to your heart, with all the risks and fretful dangers to
our secret. And when you do, tucked in your strong arms
and safe in your embrace, I promise faithfully to supply
you with enough kisses to keep you forever attached
to me and our mutual goal. And should our reward
be in Heaven only, I'll treasure those blessings received
already. But I must go—he's had me watched since Saturday!

Ever yours,
D

"My God!" he cried, "that's it!" And he dashed out into the street without saying good-bye or amen. His mind was racing. How could he have been so blind? Once you looked for it, it was clear as day. He now knew not only who the murderer was, but the motive as well. As he ran full out towards the Court House, he hoped that Clement Peachey had been able to get hold of the field reports Dougherty had requested and that Broderick Langford had not gone back to work at the bank. He might well possess the final piece to the puzzle.

Gideon Stanhope was not in uniform. Although he had sat in the witness room all morning to be available for recall, he had not really expected to have to take the stand again. As a result, bereft of his tunic, he seemed unexpectedly vulnerable. He was also edgy, not knowing what was to come.

"Since we last talked, sir," Dougherty began, "new information has come to light that requires a response from you. Your absconding adjutant, Lardner Bostwick, has turned up and provided us with a sworn statement concerning the infamous duel in your garden, a document now in possession of the court."

Dougherty paused to let that chilling fact do its work upon the witness. Stanhope licked his lips and kept his posture rigid. His expression did not change.

Dougherty continued. "You told us on Friday, sir, that you had no foreknowledge of the proposed duel between Sergeant McNair and Caleb Coltrane. Would you care to emend that statement before you are charged with perjury?"

Thornton made a gazelle-like leap to the balls of his feet, but the judge got in before him. "There will be no more of that, Mr. Dougherty, or it is you who may find yourself charged."

"My apologies, milord," Dougherty said, then moved his acid stare back to the witness. "Well, sir?"

"I was asked if I had advance knowledge of the duel. I did not, although I knew that the major had requested one. When Lieutenant Bostwick came to me about it, I told him I would not permit it."

"Did you not give him access to your pistols?"

"He had a master key that gave him access to most parts of the house. He was my most trusted officer."

"So you are saying that Bostwick went ahead on his own and arranged a duel that you, his commanding officer, had expressly forbidden?"

"He must have."

"And you did not suggest that one of the pistols be loaded with a paper ball?"

Thornton interjected forcefully. "Milord, the witness has already testified as to the extent of his foreknowledge of the duel and clarified his earlier statement. Let the defense bring in Mr. Bostwick if they wish to further dispute the matter."

"I agree. Mr. Dougherty, until you produce Mr. Bostwick, I must ask you to move along."

So, Marc mused, it will come down to Bostwick's word against the colonel's. Still, there was the letter.

"In her testimony this morning, Mrs. Stanhope told us about

how you and she responded to the blackmail threats from Caleb Coltrane. Again, she alluded to details that you in your testimony on Saturday failed to mention."

"I answered all questions precisely as they were put."

"Indeed. Now tell us, sir, about the letter you and she cooked up to try and thwart Mr. Coltrane's extortion scheme."

The colonel gave no indication of surprise. While neither he nor Almeda had known about its recovery in advance, perhaps they had discussed the possibility yesterday and prepared for it. But when a copy was handed to him, he gave it a wary glance, as if the words there were sheathed but lethal weapons.

"Did you ask your wife to write this as part of an elaborate ruse to deceive Coltrane and perhaps flush him out into the open?"

"Yes, I did."

"And did you yourself write it out first and then ask her to copy it exactly as written?"

Stanhope hesitated and for the first time looked uncertain as to how he should reply. "I don't recall doing so. My best recollection is that we discussed the contents together and she, of course, had to do the actual writing if the major was to be fooled."

"Now, sir, I want you to read aloud from your copy—which is an exact replica of the original—the last word of each line in the body of the letter."

Stanhope went white. The veins in his forehead bunched and stiffened.

Thornton was apoplectic. "Is this some sort of parlour game, Mr. Dougherty?"

"The witness must answer," the judge said sternly. "Please, sit down, Mr. Thornton."

Stanhope, trembling, barely breathed out the words. But they were nonetheless catastrophic. "Route—to—arms—supply—attached—reward—received—Saturday."

The crowded chamber went into momentary shock. Nothing

had prepared the jury or the spectators for this revelation. Before the room could erupt in reaction, Judge Robinson declared loudly, "There will be no hubbub in my courtroom. I will clear the chamber at any outburst." But none came. The news itself had silenced them.

Stanhope glared defiantly at his tormentor, his frame still rigid, but it was all show. Something inside him could be heard crumbling.

"Did you, sir, visit the Commercial Bank on the morning of November the first and deliver five hundred dollars to Mr. Farquar MacPherson in order to forestall the bank's foreclosing the mortgages on two of your four warehouses?"

A denial was on his lips, but the colonel seemed to recognize its futility. "I did," he said.

"And was this the 'reward' referred to in your letter to Coltrane?"

"The source of the witness's income is not relevant!" Thornton cried.

"Leave that for the moment," the judge said to Dougherty, but his avid attention had been gained, and he gazed down at the witness with some of the same incredulity as the ordinary, hero-worshipping citizens in the room.

"Colonel Stanhope, I submit that, given the evidence already before this court, the meaning of the coded sentence you just read aloud is unequivocal. We have been told that Sergeant McNair's rage against Coltrane was rooted in the ambush at the redoubt near Windsor. Two crates of ordnance were left buried there by a detail you were in charge of. I subpoened the field reports of the Battle of Windsor from Fort York, one of which includes a close description of the pursuit of Coltrane's escaping squad and his eventual capture. It is signed and verified by you. In that report, it is stated that no more than ten minutes elapsed between the time Coltrane reached the redoubt and the militia's arrival on the scene. As Coltrane's men were already hiding in the nearby bush with fresh ammunition, we must assume that the major, in the space of ten minutes, chanced upon the useless, crumbling fort, flailed through the mounds of earth there, happened by a stroke of good luck to stumble upon just what he needed to save his troop, and instantly improvised a deadly ambush. Do you expect anyone in this room to believe that you did not mail Major Coltrane a map showing him the whereabouts of the arms cache, for which the Hunters' Lodge paid you the five hundred dollars you needed to forestall bankruptcy and continue to command your regiment? And that this coded letter was not your confirmation of the deal?"

Kingsley Thornton knew he ought to intervene on several counts, but he seemed as mesmerized by the sudden turn in the proceedings as everyone else.

All the stuffing abruptly went out of the colonel's pomposity. His gaunt body collapsed into his suit.

Merciless, Dougherty moved in for the kill. "Now, what has all this got to do with the poisoning of Caleb Coltrane? Well, sir, I submit that it was this letter that so terrified you, that was secreted by Major Coltrane and used to blackmail you into treating him more like a minor potentate than a captured criminal. And that, weary of his demands, you initially used the duel to try and have your sergeant do away with him and take the blame. And when that failed, you yourself poisoned him!"

Thornton had finally found his feet. "May I remind Mr. Dougherty that the witness has not admitted to actually composing the letter. We have only his wife's testimony to that effect."

"Mr. Thornton is right," the judge said.

"Well, then, let me ask the question again," Dougherty said. "Did you write out this letter as we now see it, and then ask your wife to copy it exactly as written? Because, if you didn't, then we must assume that your wife did it on her own and that, in conjunction with the letter we found hidden in her dress, she could very well be charged with aiding and abetting treason."

Stanhope raised his head with agonizing slowness, but it was not to stare down his accuser. He peered past Kingsley Thornton until his eyes found those of his wife. In his face was a look of infinite regret.

"Did you compose the letter, sir?"

"I did," Stanhope said with surprising force.

"And did you decide to murder Caleb Coltrane to end the torment of his increasingly outrageous demands?"

Some of the old regimental fire leapt back into Stanhope's eyes. "He deserved to die. He was evil incarnate. For the first week or so he behaved as if he were a gentleman and an officer. Then, as soon as his books and snuff boxes arrived, he announced that he had the coded letter somewhere nearby, that his agents would know where to find it in the event of his death. He was then confident of rescue by the Hunters, but in the meantime he expected me to supply everything he asked for. I had no choice but to give in. He was insufferable, a braggart and a liar. He alienated the affections of my beloved daughter and drove a wedge between her and her mother."

Dougherty spoke over the growing murmurs of the astonished onlookers. "So when the idea of the duel surfaced, you tried to turn it to your advantage, hoping Billy, with a live bullet in his pistol, would do Coltrane in?"

"Of course not. I didn't want either of them hurt at that time."

"Not until after the Twelfth Night Ball anyway."

"Coltrane told Bostwick he wouldn't harm the boy, just give him a proper scare. And Billy had never fired a pistol in his life. The odds were he couldn't pot Coltrane if he'd been given five free shots. But I took no chances. Bostwick was supposed to supply two blank pistols, but the drunken fool got my instructions confused."

"So when did you decide to resort to poison? And why, after suffering his demands for so long?"

Stanhope's voice was now eerily calm, as if a decision long delayed had been taken at last. "It was Wednesday evening. Bostwick was nervous about being arrested for his part in the duel, so I gave him his back wages and he left. Farquar MacPherson came to complete the financial rearrangements that would save my business. Just before Lardner left, however, he slipped me a note from Coltrane. It demanded my immediate presence below. I went down and let myself in with the master key. What he wanted was for me to let him escape. He seemed to suspect that his mates in Detroit had forsaken him, and my help was now essential if he were to avoid the noose. I stalled by saying I might be able to rig up something by the next Monday."

"That is, after your triumph at the gala on Saturday?"

"More or less."

"During which escape attempt you might be given the opportunity to shoot him with impunity?"

Stanhope's expression confirmed that such a serendipitous notion had entered his mind. "But he insisted that it be arranged for the next day or Friday at the latest. I demanded the letter. He said he would tell me where it was when he was free and clear. I did not trust him. I could not release him and have him retain that damning letter. Bostwick and I had searched his chamber three times while he was asleep: he was a heavy sleeper. But the next day he would laugh at our futile efforts. I came to believe it was in the hands of a Hunters' agent in the city. I also knew he was too wily to let me shoot him in the back. He was more likely to shoot me with the pistols he demanded."

"So he had to die, even if it meant tarnishing the honours expected Saturday."

"Yes. I felt then that I would be doing my fellow citizens a favour. I would say he committed suicide. It was all I could think of. I was distracted and desperate."

"How did you get the poison in the snuff box?"

"As I said, he was a heavy sleeper. Bostwick, who often slept in the anteroom, was gone. I got strychnine from the gardener's supply in the summer kitchen and put it in an empty packet that had contained my sleeping draft. He usually didn't take snuff until an hour or so after his breakfast. He snorted it like a horse, not a gentleman. I figured he would be dead by ten o'clock, before Alderman Tierney arrived. But he wasn't."

"So putting the blame on Billy McNair was just a chance opportunity?"

"I didn't think he would be convicted, he was a popular—"

"But you did slip the packet into his coat?"

"I—I had it in my tunic, I really just forgot about it, and—"

"Mr. Dougherty," the chief justice broke in finally, "I don't really think we need to go on. This is not Mr. Stanhope's trial." He looked pointedly at Kingsley Thornton.

Thornton shook his head, like a man in shock or one appalled at the news he would be taking to his governor. "In view of what we have just heard, milord, the Crown is prepared to withdraw the charges against William McNair."

The courtroom burst into applause, and the judge made no move to quiet the demonstration. Gideon Stanhope let his head drop to the railing in front of him. Then he raised it slightly, searching for his loved ones.

Doubtful Dick's record remained intact.

NINETEEN

Later that afternoon, all those concerned with the triumphant defense of Billy McNair gathered in the comfortable and spacious drawing-room of Baldwin House to celebrate the defendant's release from prison and partake of a high tea in the traditional English manner. Young Billy, bathed and suitably reattired, arrived with his mother, his fiancée Dolly, and her parents. Rose Halpenny donned a dress she thought she would never have occasion to wear again, and showed up with Beth in tow fifteen minutes before everyone else. Robert Baldwin was joined in his hosting duties by his sister-in-law, and Clement Peachey and the legal staff walked across the hall for a rare visit to the domestic quarter of the premises. A cutter with two horses at its head was dispatched to pick up Horatio and Dora Cobb, who gave only nominal resistance to the unexpected invitation. The commandant of the defense corps, however, was too exhausted to attend, though the prospect of fine food and chilled champagne made his eyes water. He was driven home and tucked into his wing chair by his wards, who surprised and delighted the assembly by joining the festivities a few minutes later. Among the notables, only Marc was missing.

He had just put Rose and Beth into their sleigh in the lane behind Smallman's when Annie Brush, the apprentice seamstress, poked her head out the door and called out that an urgent message had come for him. Marc took the note and read it with some disappointment and much puzzlement. It was from Magistrate Thorpe, informing Marc that Gideon Stanhope had made a full confession and had been formally charged. And, for reasons not given, wished to see the lieutenant right away.

"I've got to go to the Court House for a minute," he said to Beth. "You and Mrs. Halpenny go on ahead. I'll join you as soon as I can."

And so, while the champagne flowed and the hors d'oeuvres were nibbled at Baldwin House, Marc found himself in the magistrate's study in the presence of James Thorpe and the newly charged felon. Stanhope's confession seemed to have lifted some burden from his shoulders, for he had regained his upright posture, and in his face there lay a resigned and calm sort of dignity. He nodded politely to Marc but swung his attention immediately back to Thorpe, whom he gazed at with a fixed stare. Something had been exchanged between the two men besides courtesies.

Thorpe did not keep Marc in suspense long. "Thank you for coming, Marc. I know you are expected elsewhere."

"That's perfectly all right, sir. Is there a service I can perform for you now that I'm here?" He suspected that his summons must be connected to the charges or some anomaly in the confession. But the note had said it was Stanhope who wished to see him.

"Yes, there is. Colonel Stanhope has requested of me that he be allowed to return briefly to Chepstow to retrieve his uniform and say farewell to his wife and daughter in familiar surroundings. I have acceded to this wholly reasonable request and have cleared it with Chief Sturges. He has kindly provided a sleigh for transportation, and Wilkie and Brown will act as driver and guard. The colonel also wishes you to accompany him in the sleigh and inside his home. He feels that as a former soldier and wounded veteran, you would be the most appropriate person to do so, and, moreover you are a man he can give his parole to with all his heart."

Stanhope looked to Marc, but there was no pleading in his face, merely hope. Thorpe's demeanour intimated to Marc that the magistrate thought the favour was the least they could do for a man who had, despite the obvious shortcomings of his actions, fought at Pelee Island and Baby's orchard with consummate courage and dedication. It was the putative treason, of course, that weighed most heavily upon the magistrate and the public, not the poisoning of a creature no better than a rat or a wolf.

"You would like us to leave right away?" Marc said.

"Good man," Thorpe said, getting up. "The constables are waiting outside."

They drove through the darkening streets at a sedate pace and without attracting much attention. Those on the sidewalks or trampled paths who did remark their passing seemed more intrigued by the sight of two constables perched like liveried postilions on the bench of the cutter than by the nondescript pair of gentlemen in the plush seat behind them.

"You must believe me, Lieutenant, when I tell you that I did not deliberately leave those two crates of ordnance at the fort near Windsor."

They were moving west along Hospital Street towards Chepstow. The odour of woodsmoke from Walmsley's clay works, a blacksmith's stuttering hammer, and a donkey treading a creaking mill outside the tannery suggested that life in the city had found its customary groove once again. Snowflakes fluttering out of the early-evening darkness brushed their cheeks and melted there, like tears.

"I must admit, Colonel, that I did wonder about your endangering the lives of your own men and even risking the mission you had dedicated yourself to achieving in Essex."

"I trusted it would not come to that. We knew from our intelligence that General Bierce intended attacking near Windsor or Sandwich, though we weren't sure when. We knew that Caleb Coltrane was one of his officers. I planned to kill Coltrane in battle long before he got inland or near the fort I assumed we had emptied, or else die in the effort. Either way, the business of the weapons was moot."

"But it turned out that it was your protégé who brought him in—alive."

"Yes. At first I was delighted because Sergeant McNair was well trained and knew enough to strip Coltrane of his papers and bring them straight to me. The map to the fort showing the positions of the buried crates was among them, and I promptly destroyed it. But I suspected that Coltrane was cunning enough to keep back the coded letter."

"Even though you tried to lessen its potential danger to you by having your wife write it in the guise of an adulterous confession."

The colonel continued looking straight ahead. This near monologue was not about expiation but explanation, about setting the record straight.

"Yes. Coltrane began his ugly scheme by threatening to brand me a cuckold. Then he offered money to forestall my becoming a bankrupt. I had the map of the weapons cache to trade for cash. The letter was intended to deal with both. And the silly bugger was addicted to codes."

He tried to smile at this but failed. "After his capture, I went to the infirmary and searched the major's kit and his person but did not find it."

"It was placed in his Bible by the medic."

"Ah. Even so, I began to hope either that he would die of his wounds or that he no longer possessed the letter. But he recovered. We did not meet again until I heard he would be taken not to London but to Toronto, for a criminal prosecution. I volunteered to escort him, and when we got here, I suggested that I house the prisoner because both the military and civilian jails were full."

Marc had picked up on something. "Wait: you say you assumed the cache at the fort had been emptied?"

"Exactly. When I heard what happened and had to enter it into my field report, I was devastated. You see, when we were ordered to remove the ordnance from the fort, I went around with my sketch and marked the spots with my sword in the earth. Poor Muttlebury missed the last two, and paid for it with his life. But it was I who was responsible for checking his work and counting the crates, and my only excuse is that I was distracted and anxious. I had supplied Coltrane with the map expecting him to find nothing at the fort. I was certain he and I were meant to settle matters on the battlefield."

"Did you, then, plan to imprison him at Chepstow in order to do there what you weren't able to do in Baby's orchard?"

"Oh, no. I had only two thoughts. First I wanted to demonstrate, to all those who doubted, that a forty-seven-year-old drygoods merchant was worthy of donning the tunic of a British officer by giving a despised enemy commander all the courtesies due him without prejudice. And I wanted to keep him where I could see him: he was as conniving and heartless as a starved pack rat."

"You extended simple courtesies; he made insatiable demands."

"Correct. He didn't have to say a word about the fort or the arms cache or the alleged affair with Almeda, but he let me know that he had the coded letter in his possession and was poised to destroy me. I didn't believe him at first, but he wrote out an exact copy in his own hand, right in front of me."

Marc felt strangely reassured by Stanhope's revelations but also disquieted that he may have seriously misread the man. His head swam with fresh questions: Had he realized how far his daughter had been involved with Coltrane? Did he know that Almeda had very likely slept with Coltrane in Detroit? Did he order Bostwick to leave one pistol blank or two? Would he have allowed Billy McNair to be condemned in his place? But the cutter had reached Chepstow. On the way back, Marc intended to press for answers.

The colonel opened the front door himself. No butler or maid greeted them in the dark vestibule.

"Almeda and Patricia will be in the sewing room," he said to Marc, and hesitated.

"Please, go right ahead. I'll wait for you here on the bench." So the women had been forewarned, it seemed.

The colonel nodded, took a deep breath, and eased the door partly open. He stepped inside and shut it behind him. Marc waited and listened. Above the colonel's masculine tones, the higher voice of Almeda could be heard, then the softer, more callow sound of Patricia. There were no cries, no weeping, not a word that could be described as raised in anger or sorrow or recrimination. It seemed to Marc to be the sort of hushed murmuring of long acquaintances in the far pews of a church or the back rows of a burial service, not wanting their intimacy to obtrude or offend. Ten minutes passed. Still, no maid bustled about upstairs or in the kitchens beyond the hall. No light showed beneath the door to the butler's den.

Finally, the sewing room door opened and the colonel came out, again closing the door firmly behind him. He was resplendent in his uniform. The red jacket with the green-and-gold militia facing had been freshly pressed. The leather belting gleamed, even in the gloom of the hallway. Someone had lovingly polished the battle-stiffened boots. Possessed now of a quiet dignity and devoid of the vanity that had contributed so much to his downfall, the colonel walked up to Marc and said simply, "My cap is in the study." His gaze locked onto Marc's, but the thoughts behind it were unreadable.

Marc nodded, the colonel's lips twitched as if anticipating a smile, and then he spun about and marched into his study at the far end of the hall. Marc sat bolt upright on the bench. Not ten seconds elapsed before he heard the plosive snap of a pistol shot. What surprised him was not that it had happened, but that he had done nothing to stop it.

"They're not going blame you for it, I hope?" Beth asked anxiously.

"No, darling, there's no chance of that. The whole sad business was prearranged between Thorpe and the colonel at the Court House. A message was sent to Chepstow to alert the women. I was merely the facilitator."

"But the magistrate used you—"

"He knew, alas, that I still had more of the soldier left in me than I myself realized," Marc replied. "Anyway, no one, including the magistrate and the governor, wanted to see our Pelee Island Patriot dangling from a gibbet in the Court House square."

They were snuggled deep into the goose-feather duvet, relying upon it, the fading ripple of the warming pan, and their own shared body heat to keep out the chill of the room. It was after eleven, but neither was in the mood for sleep.

Hoping to banish that ghastly image, Marc said, "Tell me about the celebration at the Baldwins'."

Beth gave him the highlights, then added, "I got a chance to talk with Celia Langford too."

"Oh, good. I'm just surprised the great man let her out of his sight."

"It's more than that now. She told me her uncle's decided to send her to Miss Tyson's Academy to continue the schooling that was interrupted when they had to leave New York."

"Splendid. I was, frankly, very concerned about her being stuck in that house day and night with a man like Dougherty."

"You don't have to dance around it for my sake, love. I'm not a schoolgirl."

"Well, then, let's say I'm glad she's going to get out into the world and have the opportunity to meet some of the young men and women her so-called uncle seems to be keeping her from."

"Sometimes an uncle can be as good as a father," Beth said softly.

Marc leaned over and kissed her forehead. "Thank you, I deserved that." How easily he had forgotten that his own late Uncle Jabez had served lovingly as his adoptive father for all the years he could remember. And that outward appearances can be misleading.

"And you don't have to worry about Mr. Dougherty pestering her."

"How would you know about that?" Marc said quickly, startled at his own prudery.

"Celia told me, in so many words, that her uncle preferred the other sex."

Marc tried to take this in, astonished that Beth would have the least inkling of such sordid social taboos and even more that Celia Langford would confide them to a perfect stranger. However, he had more than once underestimated Beth's uncanny ability to gain the trust of others and more than once sworn never to repeat the error.

He recovered sufficiently to reply, "Well, then, that may explain his being drummed out of New York society and the legal fraternity. The sin was too horrible to air in public, so instead of disbarring him, they just put him and his belongings on a donkey cart and pushed it towards the border."

"And the way Brodie Langford was ogling the Baldwins' maid, I don't think you need worry there either."

The moonlight, playing with a set of fickle clouds, shimmered and shied on the coverlet. Though sufficiently warm by now, Marc and Beth made no move to separate.

After a while, Beth asked, "So the murder of Coltrane had nothing to do with adultery?"

Marc's thoughts had likewise returned to the courtroom drama and its enigmatic central players. "Not directly. The truth turned out to be a lot less romantic. Stanhope had spent most of his sparse capital outfitting himself with uniforms and expensive horses and subsidizing the regiment he had created in order to feed his vanity. The Commercial Bank was threatening to call his loans, so that not only his four warehouses but Chepstow itself was at risk. Broderick Langford gave us the gist of this over the noon hour. Together with the decoded 'love letter,' it pointed straight to Stanhope's desperate need of cash to stave off bankruptcy and carry on soldiering."

"But how did he actually convince Almeda to write to Coltrane saying she loved him?"

"I'm guessing here, but when Coltrane's offer of money was agreed to by the colonel, he needed a safe way to confirm the transaction. The map itself was vague enough unless you knew the context. Billy, for example, thought it was a battle plan when he saw it. But I suspect that while the colonel was pondering this problem, Almeda received Coltrane's letter to her."

"And she had problems of her own."

"Four to be exact. One, her three-day fling back in May had apparently prompted Caleb into declaring his lifelong commitment. Two, he was drawing her into his treasonous conspiracies. Three, he had already approached her husband with a scheme that sounded like extortion. And four, Caleb claimed her husband already knew of their affair. I'm sure she went straight to him, partly because she knew Caleb had a letter or two from her that could be interpreted as confirming her adultery, and partly because she is a strong and intelligent woman who realized her best bet was to try to limit any damage already done."

"Confess to a little indiscretion before it starts to grow hairs?"

"Precisely. Now when the colonel sees that letter, he realizes he must explain the nature of the 'proposal' mentioned by Caleb. He can't confess to his having agreed to treason and doesn't want to admit his desperate need for money. But he knows that if he agrees with his wife that nothing more than a flirtation has taken place in May, then he can play the hero—his favourite role—by pretending to reject what he tells her was a blackmail threat, not a treasonous deal for arms."

Beth said, "And she was happy enough to copy that code letter and go along with his plan to supposedly expose Caleb."

"I don't know how much each of them knew or guessed about the other's dissembling, but they carried it off just the same."

"But then she goes and tucks Caleb's letter away as a keepsake."

"And Caleb hangs on to the coded letter and the map, for later use."

"The message hidden in it is the one thing in the whole wide world the colonel had to keep secret."

"At any cost," Marc agreed. "Alas, Stanhope was no match for his adversary, even though later he was the jailer and Coltrane the prisoner. The threat of his treason's being exposed must have left Stanhope in a panic. At the same time, he was compelled by his own boasting about protocol and courtesy to appear totally in control and regimentally dignified at all times.

"What about the duel? Do you think the colonel hoped Billy would kill Coltrane?"

"I don't think so, but Bostwick is such a hopeless drunk he could have set up those pistols either way. We'll never know. It's even conceivable that Stanhope hoped Billy would be killed."

"Why?"

"I think he was so paranoid by that time that he might have misread Billy's melancholy as having to do with Billy's possible perusal of the letter or sudden insight into the meaning of the sketch he found in Coltrane's kit near the fort. I don't want to believe that, but I do think that Stanhope's behaviour in the days before the murder can only be understood by focusing on his obsession—bordering on madness—with his appearance at the Twelfth Night Ball. Despite the increasing demands of his cunning captive and the people marching on Hospital Street to protest the colonel's molly-coddling, he wanted Coltrane alive at least until his honours were bestowed that Saturday night."

"But in spite of all that, he poisoned him anyway. Do you think he was telling the truth about the escape business on Wednesday evening?"

"I'm certain of only two serious lies he told on the witness stand. One was his seeing Billy put his hand in one of those coat pockets on the hall tree, as we know Billy did no such thing and Stanhope had given me a different version when I first interviewed him."

"I guess he figured now that Coltrane was dead and the coded letter hadn't shown up, he needed to make sure Billy was convicted instead of himself. That's what I can't forgive in the man." Beth sighed.

"There's a good reason for that, my dear, because the other lie he told was a whopper. He did not poison Caleb Coltrane."

Beth sat up, allowing the chilly air back into the bed. "What do you mean?"

"He did not kill Coltrane, and he was pretty certain for a long while that Billy did do it. By lying about the packet, perhaps he assumed that he was merely helping to expedite matters."

"But Billy didn't do it!"

"No, no, of course he didn't. It was—"

"Mrs. Jones!"

"Yes. Though I can't prove it, and I doubt if anyone but God gives a damn."

"But we don't know who she is."

"Hell hath no fury . . ." Marc prompted quietly.

"Almeda," Beth breathed, scarcely countenancing the word she had just uttered. "Jilted for her own daughter."

"Something like that. It was, in the end, a crime of passion and love rejected. I think she had fallen deeply in love with Caleb a second time. But it was more than physical desire. Consider her situation. She was over forty and married to a vain, shallow, and controlling man who had suddenly entered a crisis of his own. His obsession with the militia must have come close to destroying any intimacy they had left, and he was risking bankruptcy and even their home for his own selfish ends. Then along comes a swashbuckling freebooter in the guise of her girlhood lover. She is still a beautiful woman, and he appears happy to rekindle their former passion."

"Aren't you laying this on a bit thick?"

"I think not. Remember, she kept that letter in her ball gown, a letter that, however indirectly, alluded to treason and openly to their renewed love, going so far as to suggest that she shared her lover's republican ideals. She kept it, even though it was a bomb waiting to explode. And then, when he is fortuitously imprisoned in the same house with her, one floor below her sitting room, he spurns her and seduces her daughter—laughing at them both as he does so."

"How awful. But do you really think she would have run off with him?"

"No. I think she was committed to her home and her daughter. She knew what Coltrane was. But there was a hidden part of her—like the letter she prized—that believed she was still worthy of being loved with his kind of passion. It was this illusion that he shattered by seducing Patricia."

"So she knew."

"There is no doubt she did. And given Patricia's age and Coltrane's predatory zeal, she must have considered it an act of rape."

Beth's breathing had quickened. "But wait," she said. "Almeda couldn't have done it without the butler's help."

"Right. Shad had to be involved. It might even have been he who administered the poison. Remember that impassioned speech he made in the courtroom? He owes his life to Almeda. I'm sure he would die for her. Their opportunity came on Thursday morning.

Bostwick had left Wednesday evening and the colonel was off to his tailor. It was then or never. A disguise would allow for an unscheduled visit from a stranger, a meeting that would provide cover for any voices the other servants might hear. If Coltrane had died earlier, Shad could tell the police that a mysterious woman from Streetsville had been the last person in there. Unfortunately for Billy, the poison took effect while he was with Coltrane and there were two policemen in the house. Shad knew which coat was Billy's—he'd taken our coats at the door—and used the confusion in the vestibule to slip the seeded packet into Billy's pocket, possibly as he left to fetch the doctor."

"I see all that, love, but it doesn't make any more sense, really, than the colonel's confession. Why would the colonel confess when it was Billy who was likely to be convicted?"

"I need to tell you more about the colonel and why I began to doubt what I and everyone else in the court believed at the time to be true. When Gideon Stanhope walked into his study to kill himself, the pistol went off no later than ten seconds after he entered that room."

"He must've had it loaded and ready to go off."

"Exactly. The police confiscated his duelling pistols, but this one was a Derringer, a small lady's pistol, easily hidden. That's what got me to thinking. I'm convinced that Stanhope was prepared to commit suicide at a moment's notice, ever since Coltrane threatened him with the coded letter. He realized that Coltrane was unmanageable, a viper in his own nest, but he couldn't kill him before the ball, as everything he had done for the past ten months pointed to a single night of triumph.

"But on the Wednesday, Coltrane says he needs to escape before that."

"Yes, and we'll never know whether Stanhope would have tried to kill his tormentor during an arranged escape or kill himself instead. He certainly knew that Coltrane was wilier and more ruthless than he, and might easily foil any attempt to shoot him in the back. And besides, the poor devil still did not know where the letter was or who might be prepared to use it against him."

"So you're saying he was still dithering when Almeda and Shad did Coltrane in?"

"Yes. I could never accept the notion that Stanhope would plant the poison the night before, risking the involvement of his daughter. It was one thing to have her infatuated with the monster but another to have her implicated in his murder. And even though he confessed to planting the empty packet, would he really have kept it in his tunic while sitting with the chief constable waiting for the poison to take effect downstairs? And if he did, he had little chance to plant it with the women screaming all about him and Cobb beside the hall tree."

"But I still don't see why he confessed in open court to a murder he didn't commit."

"It happened like this. On the stand this afternoon Stanhope learned that we had dug up the very coded letter he has spent five weeks trying to find and destroy. He also learned from Dougherty that Almeda's involvement in its composition has been put on the record earlier that day when she admitted it was her handwriting. Suddenly the nightmare was real. He was compelled to read aloud what is tantamount to a confession and his own death warrant. His treason had been exposed in the most horrific way imaginable: before the very people who have bestowed upon him the honours he so relentlessly coveted. His life was effectively over. Taking it himself—before the state could—was the only route left to him, if he could just get to the Derringer in his study.

"But suddenly there was an even more overriding concern. Dougherty was accusing his wife of treason or complicity in treason. Stanhope knew that Dougherty and the judge had seen Caleb's letter alluding to the proposal put to her husband, as if she already knew what it was, and to her putative sympathy with the Hunters' cause. Therefore, Dougherty was not necessarily bluffing. Almeda Stanhope might well be in serious trouble, even mortal danger."

"But you told me earlier that he seemed completely crushed when his own treason came out like that."

"True, but then I watched Stanhope pause, stiffen his resolve, raise his head, and look about for someone in the courtroom. He found Almeda. I felt at the time that in that mutual gaze, something critical was exchanged between them. Perhaps, after hearing the testimony against Billy challenged by Dougherty on Friday and Saturday, he had begun to suspect that if it wasn't Billy, that it had to be Almeda. Even if he didn't, I believe he decided then and there that the only way to keep his wife from being part of a treason trial or herself charged after his suicide, was to confess to the more immediate crime. Even if he never got to the Derringer, he knew he would be convicted and hanged within a month—hence the quick and detailed confession—after which no one would care to pursue the treason charge with its principal malefactor dead. In addition, there was the matter of his protégé's wrongful conviction, for he had certainly perjured himself and sealed Billy's fate with his definitive statement about the lad's hand in that coat pocket."

Beth sighed against her husband. "All those people dead because of one man's vanity: Lieutenant Muttlebury, Melvin Curry, three soldiers at the fort, Caleb Coltrane, and the colonel himself."

"True. But he tried to make up for some of it in the end, didn't he? In taking the blame for the murder, he performed a truly selfless and noble act."

Beth smiled. "There's still love in the world, isn't there?"

EPILOGUE

The matched pair of Belgians from Frank's livery stable stood patiently in the snow a few yards from Cobb's residence, while Delia and Fabian reached down from the four-seater to help their mother hoist her considerable avoirdupois up onto the sleigh. Three suitcases and a small steamer trunk were already safely stowed in the luggage compartment under the driver's bench. Dora landed with a sigh beside Delia, the sleigh rocked amiably, and the horses sensed it was almost time to go. Dora was as excited as the children, though her eight years as a midwife had led her to temper any extreme emotions, joyous or otherwise. Babies often came out kicking and squalling for their rights, only to expire an hour later of indeterminable causes.

"Are we really going to stay in an inn?" Fabian asked for the fourth time.

"It's too far away fer us to get there in one day, luv."

"I do hope they got my letter," Delia said. "It'd be awful if we got there and they didn't know we were coming."

"I don't suppose they'd mind either way, dear."

At last the front door opened and closed, and Cobb trundled down the path towards the sleigh. Without saying a word, he put one boot on the footboard and pulled himself up onto the driver's bench with his good right hand.

"Ya took yer time," Dora said.

Cobb stared straight ahead, as Fabian clambered up beside him. "Time's what I seem to have plenty of," he complained. "But I'm here, ain't I?"

"Can I drive the horses?" Fabian asked.

Cobb handed the reins to his son.

"Giddyup, you fiery-footed steeds!" the boy cried with unsuppressed delight.

And off they sped towards Woodstock, to see a dying man who loved Shakespeare.